THE NEW ANGELS
EARTHS

I0564293

L FERGUS

EARTHS

Copyright © 2021 by L. Fergus

@FallenAngelKita

http://FallenAngelKita.com

5x8 paperback ISBN: 978-1-949789-16-4

Cover art by Mark Gardner and Mrinmoy Kar

ALSO BY L. FERGUS

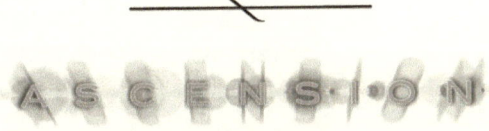

Angel of Yorq
(Available in print versions of *Birthright*)

Birthright

Razor's Pass

Project Omega
(Available in print versions of *Razor's Pass*)

Fall and Rise

Return

Sarin's Heart
(Available in print versions of *Breakout*)

Breakout

Her Glory
(Coming 2022)

The Price of Glory
(Coming Soon)

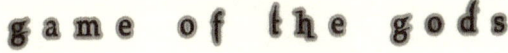

Rebirth

Clouds

Sarin's War

Li've

THE NEW ANGELS

Earth 168

(Available in print versions of *Breakout*)

BykeChic

Earth 832

Earths

Earth Y4K

(Coming Soon)

———————×———————

NON-KITA BOOKS

Warmache

RETURN OF THE FALLEN ANGEL

Return of the Fallen Angel: Book 1

Return of the Fallen Angel: Book 2

Return of the Fallen Angel: Book 3

Return of the Fallen Angel: Book 4

CHILDREN OF THE EMPEROR

Rescue

Children of the Fallen Angel

Sacrifice

IRRUPTION

(Coming soon)

Unbalanced

Fusion

Retreat

Sins

Reformation

Metamorphosis

For my #1 fan,
Here's your bedtime story.

I SWEAR THEY MAKE IT EXCRUCIATING ON PURPOSE. LIKE IT'S A great cosmic joke. Kita lifted her head off the floor and sat up on her legs. She spread her wings and fluffed her black and pink feathers. Taking in the world around her, she wasn't in a good position. Lion-like creatures in heavy armor had guns pointed at her. A tall, slender rabbit-looking creature with white fur and black spots wearing a sarong with a color scheme only a three-year-old could appreciate stood before her with arms crossed. A chain holding something disappeared under her sarong.

A loading bar from the computer in Kita's head appeared in her mind. *That should answer some questions.*

"Where is the Axiom? What happened?" demanded the rabbit.

Kita looked into the rabbit's giant red eyes at her own reflection. She had her wings, which meant she had her abilities. She must have wanted something badly if her Axiom had transformed her. *It would be nice to know what I wanted.*

She rotated her head, stretching her neck while debating if killing everything in the room would hinder her from getting what she wanted. Deciding the best course of action was to stall for time and wait for her computer to finish processing her last lifetime's worth of memories, she indulged the rabbit.

"My name is Kita. The Axiom did what it was supposed to —find me, protect me, and in case of great need or danger, it transforms me into my true form—an Angel. I will graciously let you take your leave and let me find what I'm searching for—"

"Shoot her," ordered the rabbit. "We'll carve up the body to get answers."

What?

The lion standing behind Kita flicked his rifle up and fired two rounds in the back of her head.

A brief red error message flashed in Kita's mind before she collapsed unconscious.

———————✕———————

KITA SNARLED AS SHE AWOKE TO AN ELECTRIC *ZAP* AND A shock behind her right ear. A screen appeared in her mind with the word, "Booting..." *Oh, great. Now I'm completely offline.* She tried to move, but she was stuck. Looking down, she found herself buried up to her neck in sand.

"My surprise, you're still alive," said the rabbit from above, "but I have more...entertaining ways to kill thieves. I wouldn't move if I were you. The diako in your tank are drawn to movement and sound. I suggest you keep your answers straightforward and short."

Kita looked at the rabbit and her surroundings. She was in some kind of industrial warehouse. Rows of tanks connected by walkways filled the space. The rabbit and the lions stood around Kita on a walkway. Identifying the lion with the shock rod in his hand, Kita would remember to kill him last and slowly.

"Well," said Kita, "since I don't know what's going on or why I'm here, that should be easy."

"Don't play dumb. Bring out the Aurorian."

And what is an Aurorian? And why would I care about one? A message appeared in Kita's head. *System files corrupted? Everything offline? Do I want to run repair? Of course I do. I've got to get out of here.* Her computer opened a tool and executed it. The progress wheel said it would take over an hour to fix her corrupted files. *Oh, great. I doubt this bunny is going to sit around and wait for me to kick her ass.*

A pair of lions escorted a beautiful creature down the central walkway. *So, that is an Aurorian. She's gorgeous eye candy. I wonder why I was interested in her?* The Aurorian's short, silky halter-top dress didn't cover much of her golden skin. Four-inch silver heels matched the dress, and her shapely, spindle-like legs glided effortlessly over the walkway. Her perfectly symmetrical face was accented by the colorful scales that would have been hair on a Human. Her piercing eyes had a burning intensity, and her movements were brimming with confidence and grace.

The trio stopped next to the rabbit, who had squatted down and was tapping her long foot rapidly. When the rabbit stood up, she walked on her toes, making her slightly taller than the Aurorian. *Unless you count the two-foot ears.* Both looked small in comparison to the lions. The broad-chested brutes' manes stuck out of the collar of their armor.

"What is the meaning of this, Turnip?" snapped the Aurorian at the rabbit.

"I thought you'd like to say goodbye to your savior."

The Aurorian looked down her slender nose at Kita. "I don't know this Human."

No need for insults.

"She was a Human...then she touched the Axiom, and both vanished. This winged Human was in their place."

The scales on the Aurorian's head stood up and rippled in a colorful display. "That doesn't help. One Human looks the same as any other Human."

Sigh.

"Where is the Axiom, Mai'la? What did it do? And why is this Human here?"

Kita cleared her throat. "I can't answer most of your questions, but I can tell you I'm not a Human, but an Angel."

Turnip and Mai'la looked down at Kita as if she had just appeared.

"Where is Katrina?" said Mai'la.

She must mean me. Interesting I'd choose to go by Katrina. Only my parents called me that and only when I was in trouble...which was often enough. "I'm right here."

Mai'la's lip curled, and she glared at Kita. "You don't look like Katrina. You might be her birther."

Do I look that old? I tell you, having kids ages you in a hurry.

"I want the Axiom," demanded Turnip.

Kita shrugged with her eyebrows. "It did its job. It turned me into an Angel."

"What good is an Angel?"

"Well, if I wasn't up to my neck in sand, I'd show you."

"Tell us. Why would the Axiom give a useless Human wings?"

"It does it to protect me and to help me get what I want," said Kita with the smile she used when she wanted something.

"And what do you want?" Mai'la demanded.

"Ah...not sure. I'm trying to remember. It'll come to me." *If you don't mind waiting an hour.*

"For a creature about to be diako dinner, you're not special," said Turnip as she chattered her big buck teeth. "The Axiom granted Frich'itit great power. The power will be mine. Where did the Axiom go?"

"I'm it."

Mai'la looked at Turnip, "Give her some pepinal. She'll tell you all you need to know."

And who's side are you on? I thought I was helping you. "You can't get blood from a stone."

Turnip ignored Kita and waved to a guard, "Go get it."

The guard trotted to a table on the main walkway, retrieved a case, and brought it to Turnip. He opened the case, and she took out an injector and vial. Loading the vial, she knelt at the lip of Kita's tank, leaned over, and pressed the injector against Kita's neck.

"Ow!" yelped Kita.

"That is only the beginning," said Turnip harshly.

"Not that," scoffed Kita. "Something bit me."

"In minutes, you will be unable to resist, and you will tell me what I want to know."

I doubt that. The computer in my head may not be working, but that doesn't stop the sympathetic nervous system. Kita gritted her teeth as something bit her again.

"You can't fight it," Turnip said with a smile that showed off her two large front teeth.

Kita rolled her eyes. Turnip was in for a surprise in less than an hour. Until then, Kita had to figure out a way to kill time. The first thing she did was turn up the heat she generated to discourage anything else from biting her. Without her computer, she couldn't go as hot as usual, but it should be enough to dissuade critters from trying to make her a meal.

The drug would only be effective for a short while. Long enough for her to see how it made her feel. *Maybe I can use the drug to my advantage. It'll make me super talkative. But what can I talk about? I don't remember much about my life. That's all stored away on the computer...But they're so curious about the Axiom and Angels, maybe I should give them an education.*

Kita could feel her muscles weakening and her eyes rolling around. Her mind went blank as her head lulled back, and she smiled.

"Excellent," chattered Turnip. "Now, you're going to tell me everything I want to know. Do not leave out any details."

Any suggestion sounded good to Kita. "Yes," she slurred.

"Where is the Axiom?"

Kita blinked stupidly. "Gone."

"Where did it go?"

"It became me."

"Do not play games with me," Turnip snapped harshly. "Where did it go?"

Kita's head rolled around and came to rest on the sand. "It's technically right here. It became me."

"Where is Katrina?" said Mai'la.

"Her files are currently being scanned and repaired."

"What does that mean?"

"When I tried to integrate her memory files into my computer, two bullets to the back of the head interrupted the processes and corrupted the files."

"She's babbling nonsense," Mai'la huffed at Turnip. "How much pepinal did you give her?"

Not enough. Kita felt her head clear, and her eyes focus. She kept the stupid smile on her face while her head lay in the sand.

Turnip stamped her foot. "How did the most powerful artifact in the galaxy produce such a useless winged Human?"

Kita giggled. "Angels aren't useless. We're the most powerful race in the galaxy."

"Says the one neck-deep in sand being eaten by diakos."

Kita rolled her head, so she was looking up. Her biological memory didn't contain much, just fuzzy memories from her last couple of lifetimes. Still, there were some interesting Angel stories in them. "Let me tell you..."

"KITA, WHERE ARE WE GOING?" SAID APOCALYPSE AS KITA pulled her by the hand through the crowded skyway around a knot of Verisom princesses.

Their daughter, Jynx, flittered behind them. The pre-teen was going through a phase where she refused to touch the ground.

"I've got someone I want you to meet," said Kita as she smiled back at her partner navigating around a large Djinn male with his harem.

"Why are we in such a hurry?" called Jynx.

"The matches start in..." Kita looked at the time crawling by on a lighted billboard. "...twelve minutes. And I have to stop and get money—if I have any left."

Jynx looked confused. "Didn't you just die? Who'd take your money?"

"What were you doing in this lifetime?" said Apocalypse cautiously.

"I was an artifact procurement dealer," said Kita with a grin.

"Can't you ever be anything other than a thief or assassin?" said Jynx rolling her eyes.

"But this time I had an office."

"So, what killed you? Do we need to be careful?" said Apocalypse.

Kita sighed. Ever since Apocalypse wanted to be mother of the year, she'd grown more cautious and reserved. Kita didn't think Jynx needed such attention or protection. The kid was doing fine on her own.

"No. I was never an Angel in this lifetime, just a Human. I didn't even find my Axiom."

"What about the other Angels? Weren't they here with you?"

"I might know where some of them are."

"I thought you were staying together?" Apocalypse said with an unhappy sigh.

"We decided to go our different ways."

"Don't you keep tabs on them?"

"I do...but that's been lost since I died."

"What if they get into trouble?"

"They're big girls. They can figure it out." Kita stopped in front of an Automated Banking Machine and pressed a button to select her form of identification. With so many races, there were lots to choose from—some general, others race specific. Humans had been part of the galactic society for three hundred years and were well established. Angels were not. Still, Kita could pass a thumbprint scan, as her Angel DNA was built off her Human DNA.

Kita grumbled at the cost of purchasing a replacement credit chit. Grall had most likely helped himself to her old one —if he could crack the encryption. As a procurer, she didn't use the bank's standard encryption and used a third party instead. Kita transferred all her available funds to the chit. *Might as well. Not like they're going to do me any good staying in the bank.*

"Is that a lot of money, Momma?" asked Jynx looking at the numbers on the screen.

It was, but Kita wasn't going to tell her daughter that. "I had enough to eat and afford a place to live. Why? Did you see something you wanted in one of the stores?"

"No. I don't know what any of it is."

Kita frowned. She disagreed with Apocalypse that Jynx wasn't allowed to enter a universe on her own. When Apocalypse did take her in, it was always for school. *How is the girl ever going to learn?* It had taken Kita pleading with Apocalypse to let her take Jynx back into universe 876. Apocalypse agreed, but only if she could come. Kita was overjoyed to have her partner along. She just wished Jynx could have more freedom. Jynx was twelve and needed to get out and see the universe and learn to handle everything that came with it.

"Well, I'll have to take you shopping. The Aurorians are big into fashion—so are the Verisom." Kita added quickly. *She'll probably like the bright colors and warm-weather fashions of the*

Verisom. The Aurorians were much more glamorous and probably wouldn't interest the pre-teen.

Kita hit a button to transfer her funds to the credit chit. The ABM warned her about moving such a vast sum of money and that they were not responsible if something happened to the chit. Kita shrugged. *And what's it going to do otherwise? Collect half a percent of interest every month?*

"Kita, I thought we were here to meet a friend of yours," said Apocalypse pushing in next to Kita. "How long are you planning on staying? Chelsea shouldn't be away from Roost for too long."

"She needs a chance to see the universe. I just want to meet my friend and finish a little business."

Apocalypse folded her arms and scowled. "With you, a *little business* sounds dangerous."

Kita smiled warmly at her partner. *I should have brought Velositi.* Kita's Morphicon girlfriend was nearly done raising their three daughters and was ready to explore the universes. "There's nothing that dangerous here. If there is, just look at it and melt it." Kita hoped reminding her partner that she was an Angel with incredible powers would ease her mind.

Apocalypse and Jynx hadn't lived in a universe since leaving 832. Kita had tried, but Apocalypse was sure something would happen to Jynx. Since the incident in universe 832, Apocalypse had insisted that Jynx master her education and forbade her from practicing her sword and abilities. Kita countered that she had trained their daughter to use various weapons and given her an arsenal of abilities. Though through child stubbornness, Jynx still carried the sword Kita gave her.

"Hey Mom, check this place out," called Jynx from over the railing of the skyway.

Kita and Apocalypse turned to see Jynx gliding into the sky lane full of float cars.

"Chelsea!" screamed Apocalypse.

Kita put a hand on her partner's shoulder to calm her. Kita looked at her daughter and called, "Make sure you look behind you. I don't want to have to pay for a float car."

Jynx giggled. "I'm watching, Momma."

Kita smiled. She and Jynx both had photoreceptors in their skin that let them have panoramic vision.

"What do you think of the Tetrahedron?" Kita asked her daughter.

"It's incredible. I can't believe people built this in space!"

Kita looked at Apocalypse. "See? She's fine. Let her explore and see the universe."

Apocalypse frowned. "You don't worry something will happen to her?"

"We made her damn near indestructible, and she's got more abilities than I have. We better hope she doesn't go on a destructive rampage—we may not be able to stop her."

Apocalypse gasped. "Are—are you saying she could be a monster?"

Kita chuckled and hugged her partner. "I'm saying she's going to be fine. You've taught her well. She now needs to spread her wings and apply what she's learned."

"What about Leaf?" said Apocalypse with a gulp.

Kita sighed. She missed the little Angel and knew Apocalypse blamed herself for her death. "Leaf was not your fault. Her death was my fault. I underestimated Unixilite when I told him Angels were indestructible. He called my bluff. It happens. The best we can do is be prepared, and Chelsea is almost as prepared as she needs to be."

"What do you mean *almost?*" Apocalypse said with a frown.

"We've given her the best education—now she needs experience. She won't get that on Roost. She needs to get out and explore. Better she gets it while she's young than at nineteen as a doe-eyed cadet." Kita winked at Apocalypse, reminding her partner of her experience going through Officer Candidate School and the shock it had been after growing up secluded in the White House.

Apocalypse wrinkled her nose. "I still say she's too young."

"Believe me, kids can take care of themselves—if you let them. If they need you, they'll come and find you. All my other girls did fine navigating the world at a young age—Kami was six, Kylee was eight, Quill and Spike were nine, Lina was twelve and had been on her own before I took her in—kids are resilient problem-solvers. Just give her a chance."

"But what if I miss something?"

"Love, there's nothing more magical and special than when your kid comes up to you and says, 'Mom, come check out what I found,' or 'Mom, I have something to show you.' When you see the pride and confidence in their faces, you know they're going to be ok. You just have to give them that little bit of freedom. I'm not saying let them run wild—that was my mistake with Kylee—boundaries are good. But they need some freedom. It's time to let Chelsea have hers."

Apocalypse sighed as she leaned against Kita. "I just worry something will happen to her, and I won't be there to save her or...what if she doesn't need me anymore?"

"She's got the tools; experience will teach her how to use them. I admit there is a period when they grow up where they think they don't need you, and you have to let them learn. On the other hand, we have to learn to be patient, let her make her mistakes, and be there to catch her. Failing is part of the learning process. She'll learn she needs us, not as a parent, like when she was little, but as a friend. No matter what, we'll always be *mom* to her." Kita put her arm around Apocalypse and stuck her head in her partner's hood to kiss her.

"What are you girls talking about?" said Jynx as she flittered over.

"You," said Kita.

"Oh," said Jynx with a downtrodden sigh. "What did I do wrong?"

"Nothing," replied Kita. "I'm just telling your mom how impressed I am with you and how much you've grown."

"Does this mean I get to go into a universe?" said Jynx excitedly.

Kita smiled from under her hood. "Let's see how you handle this one. Getting hit by a float car is not a good start."

Jynx tossed her head back and forth, causing her two short pink pigtails to bounce. "I know, I know, situational awareness. I was watching, and I wasn't anywhere near the float-thingy."

"Just stay out of the sky-lanes. They're not used to Angels or other races flying into them."

"Ok. Can I still fly on the skyway?"

"Just remember how much space your wings take up. Again, the other races aren't used to Angels. The Tet is not the same as Roost."

"The other races do look cool."

"I'll tell you about them on the way." Kita took Apocalypse's hand. "Ready, love?"

"Yeah. The crowds are overwhelming."

Kita chuckled. "You've been on Roost too long. Half a billion people live on the ten petals of the Tet—Tetrahedron." Kita led her family from the overlook back into the flow of the crowd made up of a dozen or more races who called the Tet petal home. "There are six major races—Aurorian, the golden goddesses looking like they're going to the club, Verisom, they're the bunnies, Zentonians are the giant squirrels, Diamocks are the armored dog-goats, you won't see many of them outside their compounds, the Djinn are the misogynistic lions that hide their females, and you know about Humans."

Kita crossed a sky-bridge to another building complex.

"How high are we?" said Apocalypse after looking through the glass that made up the bridge's deck. Below, other sky-bridges and sky-lanes filled with traffic going between towering gleaming buildings with vegetation and water features covering entire sections. Above them were more.

"We're in the MidCity," said Kita. "About a hundred or so levels above the ground. The HighCity is over two hundred. Only the wealthy and political elite live there."

"Have you ever been there, Momma?"

"Sure. It's where I conducted most of my business."

"Where you stole from," said Apocalypse with a teasing wink.

Kita shrugged. "I lived in Twilight. Just above The Dark, where the light of the petals never reaches. It's where the lower classes live—mostly Zentonians, unitless Diamocks, and warrenless Verisom. Some Djinn males, mostly older ones, have lost their prides and are waiting to die. It's also filled with the minor races."

"What are the minor races?" said Jynx.

"Anyone who isn't a major race. You'll see some in MidCity. Just be polite and smile. No one means you any harm and are just trying to get where they're going—like us."

Kita walked past a line of shops—all with holographic ads and signs hawking their wares. Most stores were race specific, but there were some general stores for the adventurous. Mixed in with the shops where various restaurants, cafes, and eateries serving the various races' favorite delicacies, generic meals, or fusion foods.

Pulling her family into a wide storefront, they passed signs that flipped between several languages—one in Common read ALGINON'S TOURNEY. The sliding glass doors pulled open, revealing a wide breezeway filled with groups of people —mostly Prii males, gray Humanoids with three sets of big horns on their bald heads—clustered around holoscreens. The breezeway sloped down to another set of sliding glass doors. Directional signs on the doors read TOURNEY PITS and WAGERS.

Kita moved between groups, looking over shoulders scanning the matches. Halfway down the hallway, she stopped behind a small crowd. She floated upward to see. Across the bottom of the holoscreen were the names Al'ice and Fri'x.

"Found it," Kita announced to her family. She waved them up to join her. Kita pushed back her sleeve to reveal her Arcom. She tapped on the screen and connected to the tourney's bookie. She placed a five hundred credit bet on Al'ice —the max amount she could without a secure account.

"What is this?" said Apocalypse as she frowned at the colorful furry creatures doing battle on the screen.

"This is a Prii tourney. The Prii are a minor race from Verisom space. The females have a unique ability that lets them control certain creatures with their minds. In a tourney, they fight using genetically engineered critters."

"Who do you want to win, Momma?" said Jynx.

"We're rooting for Al'ice." Kita put a hand on her

daughter's shoulder. "Don't jinx the fight. That's unsportsmanlike—plus, Al'ice should have no problem."

"I wasn't," huffed Jynx.

"Eh-hem," said Apocalypse.

"You know your mom knows when you're lying," said Kita.

"So not fair—Whoa! That thing just breathed fire like mom."

"Chelsea," Apocalypse scolded. "No one needs to know about that."

"Why not?" said Kita. "I think it's sexy."

"You have to be home long enough to do that," Apocalypse replied tartly.

Kita smiled and turned her attention back to the fight. Apocalypse had wanted to be a mother; Kita had been there, done that, and knew how to balance motherhood and career. Apocalypse was caught in that first kid trap. Kita didn't blame her, but at the same time, it wasn't going to stop her from understanding how to create a universe and explore them.

They watched the match taking place on a platform surrounded by water and cheered Al'ice's little pink and blue spotted fire-breathing fuzzball—to Kita, they looked like descendants of armadillos. The other creature in the match was squat and covered in scales. It had long claws and would roll up into a ball and fling itself at its opponent. Al'ice's creature's fur was long and dense, absorbing the attacks, often bouncing the opponent back the way it came. The furry creature reared and blew fire, causing its opponent to curl up in a ball.

"So, is this to the death?" said Apocalypse turning up her nose.

"In underground matches it is, but in sanctioned matches, the object is to drive your opponent out of the ring and into the water or have the most points when time runs out. Sometimes you can score a knockout. Notice how their backs are curved? If you get a pip—that's what the critters are called—on their back, they can't get up."

"Is it a knockout in the underground matches?" said Jynx.

"Ah, no. There it's a setup for a kill shot."

"And how many underground matches have you been to?" asked Apocalypse with a disapproving look from under her hood.

Definitely should have brought Velositi. "They're a good place to meet clients for exchanges, payments, or contracts."

On the holoscreen, the opponent's pip flew at Al'ice's pip, causing it to roll into a ball. When they collided, the opponent stuck in Al'ice's pip's fur. It unrolled and carried the stuck opponent toward the edge of the ring. The opponent did its best to unroll, but its neck and head were stuck. It still attacked, kicking and clawing at Al'ice's pip, but the attacks were lost in the dense fur. The opponent still scored points and had more than Al'ice, but the determined trainer was going for the win. Al'ice's pip carried its opponent to the edge of the ring, stood on its front feet, and dumped the other pip into the water.

Only a handful of people in the crowd cheered—including Kita.

"Why is no one cheering for Al'ice?" said Jynx.

"Al'ice isn't sponsored. So, she doesn't have a big following or anyone to pay for her matches. She has to wait and go through the pairing pool—which is a random selection. Fri'x is sponsored, and they rarely enter the pool—unless they're trying a new pip, testing new techniques, or gearing up for a sponsored match. Those matches can draw big crowds."

"If she's so good and caught your eye, why isn't she sponsored?" said Apocalypse.

"Why do you think we're here?" said Kita with a grin.

"How much money do you have?"

"Enough to sponsor Al'ice and exact my revenge."

"Revenge?" Apocalypse raised a disapproving eyebrow.

"Grall double-crossed me."

"Something you don't do to Momma," said Jynx.

"You know it."

"I thought this was a family outing?" huffed Apocalypse.

"It is...trust me. It'll be a good bonding experience and educational for Chelsea."

"Do I have to write a paper?"

"Consider this a practical exercise. Come on, let's go find Al'ice."

Kita led her family away from the holoscreen down the breezeway to the sliding glass doors. Following the sign to the tourney pits, Kita stopped at a doorway guarded by a large lion-like Djinn—young male Djinn were popular bouncers and guards for their size and biological need to protect a pride. In modern times when only older males had prides, they substituted pride with anything people paid them to. In this case, this one was paid to guard and collect the entrance fee to get into the pit's viewing area.

The bouncer gave Kita and her family a suspicious stare. "Three Humans will be a hundred credits."

"We're not Humans," Kita said as she opened her wings and flapped them.

"Humans with wings are still Humans."

"You ever see a Human do this?" glared Kita as she grew a fireball in her hand.

"Aurorians are three hundred each," the bouncer growled.

"We're Angels," said Apocalypse. "We're new to the Tet."

"This isn't a place for sightseers. Get lost."

"I'm Al'ice Sie'nna's sponsor," Kita snarled, crossing her arms.

"I thought you were new here?" the bouncer snarled.

Kita sensed he was losing his patience. His only problem, she was out of hers. "They're new here. I've been around since you were a kitten." Kita hoped the insult would enrage the Djinn.

"*Why are you antagonizing him? Just pay him,*" said Apocalypse over the Angel's internal communicator.

"*Because sponsors get in free,*" replied Kita.

"*How did you get in before?*"

"*I snuck in when I could.*"

"*Isn't that one of Momma's rules? Why pay when you can steal.*"

Kita chuckled at her daughter.

"*Don't encourage her,*" huffed Apocalypse.

"*You know, there was a time when you'd sneak in with me.*"

"*Now, we have to set the example.*"

"Leave!" roared the Djinn getting everyone in the lobby's attention.

Within seconds, a crowd had gathered in anticipation of watching a Djinn tear into a Human.

Kita hoped they could live with disappointment. "Make me, pussycat."

The Djinn let out a long snarl that turned into a roar displaying their legendary quick temper. His elongated paw with long, curved claws on the ends of his short, stubby fingers took a swipe at Kita's face.

Kita threw up an arm and stopped the Djinn's attack cold. Grabbing his wrist, Kita spun and threw the young Djinn over her shoulder, slamming him hard against the friction carpet. She stood over the winded Djinn and put her boot on his neck. She held a flaming finger in front of his nose.

"Should I make my partner a Djinn mane shawl? She doesn't have one yet."

"Ok, Kita, that's enough," exclaimed Apocalypse.

Kita put her finger out as she looked into the Djinn's eyes. "So, how much for Angels?"

"Get out," said a terrified Prii wearing an Alginon's Tourney yellow sash across his bare gray chest, "before I call Tet-Sec."

"I'm a sponsor, and all I want is a fair price for my family and me to see the tourney."

"Who do you sponsor?"

"Al'ice Sie'nna."

"Never heard of her. Please leave, or I will call Tet-Sec."

"Follow me," said Kita as she walked past the employee. She walked around the line to the betting cages to the first window. "Excuse me," she said, giving a Zentonian a determined look as she pushed him away from the window with her wing.

The angry Zentonian chattered his big squirrel-like teeth. "Hey! Thief!"

Kita looked at the screen. The Zentonian was logged into the micro-wagers. *For those who don't have the stomach for actual risk.* "Like I'd steal ten credits."

The employee took a communicator off his belt.

"Wait. I can prove I'm legitimate." Kita cleared the screen of the Zentonian's transaction and looked into the retinal scanner. A list of bets appeared. The topmost had a claim button for twenty-five thousand credits flashing. Kita tapped the transaction and brought up the details. It showed her bet from fifteen minutes ago and Al'ice's picture. Tapping Al'ice's picture brought up a list of all the wagers she'd placed on the Prii.

"There," said Kita pointing to the list of winning wagers. "I've been unofficially sponsoring Al'ice since she started. I would like to make that official. I just need to tell her and pay my sponsor's fee." Kita held up her credit chit.

The Prii employee looked doubtful. "That's half a million credits."

"You don't think I'm good for it? Maybe you should look at my list of wagers."

"I, ah..."

The Zentonian Kita had pushed aside returned with another Prii with a red Alginon's Tourney manager's sash across his chest.

"Oh, good. Just the person I was about to send this fine employee to find," said Kita wielding her favorite I-want-something smile. "I'd like to sponsor Al'ice Sie'nna. I have my fee right here." She held up her credit chit.

The manager gave Kita a dubious look as he frowned momentarily before resuming his professional demeanor. "This patron says you're trying to rob him."

Kita looked aghast. "I would never do such a thing. I just needed to show—" Kita pointed to the Prii in the yellow sash.

"Mal'ak."

"—Mal'ak, that I was a serious supporter of Al'ice Sie'nna and that I had the money to be her sponsor."

"Human—"

"Angel, actually."

"What is an Angel?"

"You're looking at one." Kita fluffed her feathers and wiggled her wings. She floated off the floor to prove the wings weren't for show.

Those in the wager line who had gathered to watch took a step back and gasped. Flying wasn't something any other sentient race did.

Kita touched the tall ceiling, glided around the wager line, and landed back in front of the manager. Around them, people had different devices out recording and taking pictures of Kita.

"You heard it here first!" Kita yelled to the crowd. "Angel Kita Roosevelt is sponsoring Al'ice Sie'nna! And I guarantee she'll win her first fight!"

The manager's eyes shifted back and forth while he looked uncomfortable. "Perhaps we should talk about this in my office."

Kita ignored him and addressed the crowd. "I'd like to tell her now. It's a surprise."

The waves of excitement and suspense from the growing crowd told Kita she had them. The ability to sense emotions was an ability Kita inherited from her A'ahegre—a dark energy alien residing inside her. To her satisfaction, the manager was overwhelmed and uncertain. Kita decided to give him a task.

She leaned into the Prii and handed him her credit chit. "Why don't you go run my sponsor's fee?"

He nodded and stood aside as Kita addressed the crowd, "Come along, everyone. Let's go meet our newest elite trainer, Al'ice Sie'nna!" As she led the mass toward the tourney pits, Jynx and Apocalypse fell in next to her.

"I forgot how good you are at getting out of trouble and getting what you want," said Apocalypse.

Kita chuckled. "It's even easier when I'm an Angel."

"Being Human has limitations?" said Jynx.

"Yes. And someday, you'll experience it."

Apocalypse made a disapproving sound.

"What?" said Kita. "She's got to learn, and there's no better way to learn to master your god-given natural talents than when you can't rely on your Angel abilities."

"Yeah, but I thought I was born with all my abilities," said Jynx.

Kita put her arm around her daughter. "You are special, but

you've got to learn to make it without them. Believe me, you're just as charismatic as your moms."

"How do you know?"

"I'm god, remember?"

Jynx giggled. "You're just Momma."

"To a child, there is no difference," said Kit with a smile.

"Not like I get to brag about it on the playground."

Kita looked at Apocalypse. "Why not?"

"You didn't create a playground on Roost...or other kids for her," hissed Apocalypse.

"That's why she needs to come into the universes. Learning to socialize is as important as anything else."

"Don't fight," whispered Jynx. "I had lots of fun playing with Bernoot."

"Sorry, Jynxie," said Kita. "I just want what's best for you."

"You think there's something wrong with me?"

"No. You're perfect. Your mom has done a good job educating and raising you. I just feel you're ready to expand your education."

"Do I ever get to stop learning?"

"When you're dead."

"So, never."

"To rule Reality, you can never stop learning."

"Can I have a pony instead?"

Kita cocked her head and touched her tongue to her upper lip as she pondered the answer. "I think I can make a stable on Roost...or we can visit a time when horseback was the main means of transportation."

"Like when you grew up?"

"Sure."

Kita led the crowd through the glass doors, down a tunnel, and onto the balcony of the tourney pits. Ten rows of seats surrounded the pit. Screens above the pit gave close-ups of the action. In the pit were ten rings, each surrounded by water held in a tank. The matches were over, and the referees and trainers were busy cleaning up or preparing for the next round.

Gliding to the rail, Kita spotted Al'ice at table five. She was busy with her pip, rubbing its tummy and giving it a treat. The Prii didn't seem to notice the gallery filling up.

"There she is," said Kita pointing Al'ice out.

"You're going to tell her by yelling across the room?" Chided Apocalypse.

"Of course not."

Vaulting the glass railing, Kita glided over the pit, leading the other Angels to land next to table five. On the balcony, the manager pushed his way through the crowd with a pair of Djinn. *Looks like someone found his moxie. Oh well, too late.*

"Al'ice!" Kita called in a friendly tone.

"Oh! Hi, Ki—," Al'ice looked up from her pip, and her dark lips frowned. "Do I know you?"

Kita swept off her hood. She looked similar to her Human form, but her angelic beauty did away with the need for most makeup. But the black makeup she did wear accented her features and highlighted her blue eyes. Her floor-length braid tumbled down her back, and the throwing star braided into the end swung menacingly.

"You're right, Al'ice. It's me, Kita."

"You're not the Kita I know."

Kita opened her hand, and a hologram of her as a Human appeared. She was dressed in one of her favorite thieving outfits, and half her head was shaved. She zoomed in on the hologram head and put hers next to it. She batted her lashes and smiled.

"See? It's me. I, ah, died, and I'm back for a visit in my true form. This is Kimmy, my partner, and Chelsea, my daughter."

Al'ice's blue tongue traced her dark blue lips. "You almost got me, but the Kita I know would never have offspring or have a partner...at least, that's what you told me."

Kita chuckled as she fended off a dark look from Apocalypse. "True...but I can explain. I'll tell you everything, but right now, you need to look happy for the crowd."

Al'ice looked around the gallery. "What's going on?"

"I have officially sponsored you. You're now an elite trainer. These people are here for the announcement."

"All these people for me? No one knows who I am...except you."

"What Kita is failing to mention is she also guaranteed your first win," said Apocalypse.

Kita scratched the back of her neck as Al'ice's eyes—one blue, one purple, each with two connected pupils—shifted back and forth as her mouth fell open, conveying the shock and dismay she felt.

"It's nothing I know you can't do."

"Kita! Or whoever you are, I don't have the pips for that. I can't fight an elite! I don't have the training or the facilities for training the pips—if I can even get them. And you don't have that kind of money!"

"Actually, she does," said the manager as he approached with his Djinn bodyguards. In his hand, he held a tablet.

"You said you were a poor commodities dealer," cried Al'ice.

"Commodity acquisition and sales..."

"Is that what you put on your resume to hide you're a thief?" said Apocalypse.

"Not helping," muttered Kita.

"I don't consort with thieves," huffed Al'ice, shaking her head making the tassels attached to the horns curling around her long-pointed ears dance. She had two other sets of straight horns—a small set protruding from her forehead and a large set from the side of her head—poking through her shoulder-length two-toned blue and purple hair.

"I promise there's more to it," said Kita. "Just hear me out. And please accept the sponsorship. Whatever you need, I'll get. I have the credits. I promise I'm the Kita you know...just with feathers."

Al'ice looked at Kita, confused.

Kita raised a wing straight up and waved it around. From the look on Al'ice's face and the shock and awe she let off, she hadn't noticed the Angels' wings yet.

"What in the Void are you?" gasped Al'ice.

"Long story short, I was murdered in my Human form. I've

come back in my Angel form to get revenge. I want you to help me get it."

"Do all Humans do this?"

Kita and Jynx giggled. "They wish. We disguise ourselves as Human to fit in—usually. Angels do come from Humans—"

"Eh-hem," said Jynx.

"Ok, most Angels come from Humans. Will you please come with me? I'll explain everything. If you don't want to help, I'll kill Grall myself."

"If they can kill you, how are you going to stop them from killing me?" said Al'ice, gulping and taking a step back.

"I promise no one will hurt you," said Apocalypse. "Angels are the most powerful creatures in the universe."

Al'ice looked around Kita at the Djinn and back at Kita.

Jynx opened her hand and displayed a hologram replaying Kita throwing the Djinn bouncer.

"Please?" pleaded Kita. "I'll buy you dinner."

Al'ice raised a purple eyebrow. "My choice?"

"Anything you want. Just look happy. You made it to the elite league."

Al'ice smiled for the first time. Her face brightened, highlighting the purple and blue freckles on her cheeks.

Kita seized Al'ice's hand and raised it into the air. "The next elite champion!" she yelled to the crowded gallery.

People applauded and cheered as others took photos. Kita and Al'ice appeared on the pit's holographic display.

Kita dropped Al'ice's hand and gave her a hug.

"You do hug like her," said Al'ice.

Apocalypse tapped on Kita's shoulder. "Something I should know?"

Kita grinned. "Nothing to worry about. Just friends, that's all."

"Angel Roosevelt?" said the manager as he approached.

"Yes?" said Apocalypse.

"What?" huffed Kita.

"Me?" Jynx replied.

The manager looked perplexed as he looked between the Angels. "I have your sponsorship kit ready."

"Excellent!" Kita snatched the tablet from the manager and looked into the tablet's camera. The tablet verified her identity. She showed to it Al'ice. "See? It's me, Kita."

Al'ice wiggled her leathery deer-like nose. "I believe you... not because of the tablet, but I know only you are so persistent."

Kita shrugged. "When I want something, I'm going to get it no matter what."

"Yeah, that's you alright."

"Come, let's go find dinner." Kita tossed the tablet back to the manager.

"The competition committee will contact you about your first fight," said the manager. "I hope you're ready," he added snidely.

"Don't worry. We will be."

———————✕———————

Kita pulled a low-backed chair out for Apocalypse and yanked another out of the way with her foot so Jynx could float and eat. They were at Buttercup's, a local eatery that served Verisom cuisine—A mix of vegetables, fruits, grains, and plants native to the tropical world. Kita, experienced with the Verisom diet, pointed out what to try and avoid to her daughter and partner.

Kita set her plate down and took a seat. She'd picked her favorites as she wasn't hungry. Neither were the other Angels, but they were excited to try the food.

Al'ice sat next to Kita with a plate full of multicolored leafy plants. Kita noticed she'd grabbed some brown and orange leaves—native to Diamock. They were a costly delicacy for the various vegetarian races. *She must be testing to see if my credits are good.* The Prii unslung a leather satchel from across her body, flipped the flap up, allowing two pips out, and set them on the table. She took a large purple leaf off her plate, tore it in two, and gave it to the little creatures.

"Those are really cool...and cute," said Jynx.

Al'ice smiled. "Thanks. The fluffy furry one is Vi'ne, and the spike-covered one is Cu'lu."

"What's Cu'lu do? We saw Vi'ne fight earlier."

"Other than eat?" Al'ice chuckled. "He can shoot his spikes, jump high and far, and whips his tail."

"Are these traits they've evolved?" asked Apocalypse.

Al'ice shook her head. "No. These are bioengineered in a lab."

"Momma says you control them with your mind," said Jynx.

"I do. I have a special sensory organ in my small fore horns that send signals to an organ in the pip's hindbrain. Ancestors on my homeworld used them to harvest nuts and fruit in the tall ti'ti trees."

"Is it like our comm?" Jynx asked Kita.

"Similar, ours is more advanced. I haven't studied Prii anatomy or physiology to know the difference."

"Bet that's going to change," said Apocalypse. "Still have a bunch of empty rooms on Roost."

Kita smiled to herself.

"Is Roost your homeworld?" asked Al'ice.

"It's home," said Kita. "But it's not a world. It's a space station but much smaller than the Tet."

"Explain to me this metamorphosis. I've never seen or heard of a Human dying and resurrecting with wings."

"That's not something Humans do. You kill a Human, and they stay dead. Angels...are a little different. Except for Chelsea, we're not an organic race. We come from other races —Aurorian, Human, Diamock—I modify and add to their DNA to give them wings, and abilities like the Aurori have— just a thousand times more powerful. But this is where I have to stop and ask you a question. What I have to tell you will transform how you see the universe."

"I've never studied the universe. I'm just a poor trainer trying to make a living."

"Do you want to know the truth?"

"What—"

"Once I tell you, it can't be undone. Everything as you know it will change. Your life will change. You'll still be you, but everything else will be different. The Verisom hole you'll enter is stranger than you can imagine. You don't have to say *yes*. You can decline, we'll finish lunch, I'll transfer you my nine hundred million credits, and you can live your life comfortably and happy. We Angels will disappear, and you'll never see us again."

Al'ice gasped. "You have that much money?"

Kita smiled wickedly. "I'm very good at procuring—stealing —things."

"If I say yes, what do I get?"

Jynx giggled. "I bet Momma is mastering Prii DNA right now."

"You'll at least get to come live on Roost," said Apocalypse.

"I get to come to your home?"

"It's more like a plane of existence. There's nothing in this universe like it."

Al'ice gave off waves of confusion, curiosity, and uncertainty as she looked at her food. "How do I know you're for real?"

"Besides the wings? It's a leap of faith. Think of everything you've seen over the last two hours. Have I lied about anything?"

"No...What would I do on Roost?"

Kita shrugged. "Anything you want. You go anywhere, do anything, be anyone...whatever."

"I feel like I'm being tempted by a god...in the stories, there was always a catch."

Jynx grew a fireball in her hand. "The only catch is you have to be Momma's friend."

Al'ice gave the young Angel a questioning look, "I thought I was."

"But now that you've experienced Kita the Angel, not just Kita the Human," said Apocalypse, "the question is: do you still want to be her friend?"

"I don't see much difference, other than there's just more... and what I knew about you was a lie."

"Not a lie," said Kita. "I was protecting you from bad people who would have harmed you to get to me. I protect my friends, and I'll do whatever is necessary to keep them safe—even if it means lying. I know it was wrong, but I had the best of intentions. I would rather die than see you harmed."

"It's true," said Apocalypse. "I can sense when people are lying, and I've heard Kita's stories and the lengths she'll go to protect those she cares about."

"I care about you a lot, Al'ice," said Kita. "You were a good friend during my time here. I want to thank you and show you how much I appreciate what you've done for me. And I want to return the favor."

Al'ice looked at the fireball in Jynx's hand. "I've heard stories of Aurori who can do such things—"

"Yeah, but they can't do this," said Jynx as she grew an iceball in her other hand. "If you can't make up your mind, you can always flip a coin. I have one if you want." She absorbed her balls and dug her large coin out of her belt. "Here. heads you say no and take the money, tails—marked by the X—you say yes and come home with us."

Al'ice blinked hard. "I...I.."

Jynx flipped the coin, caught it, and slapped it down on the back of her hand. "Last chance to back out."

"What does it say?"

Jynx removed her hand to reveal the X side of the coin. "Looks like you're coming home with us."

"*She's as bad as you!*" exclaimed Apocalypse to Kita.

"*Did she lie?*"

"*No. But I can't detect if she manipulated the coin, either.*"

Jynx had many abilities, but her special power was the ability to control the random number generator that controlled Reality, allowing her to change the numbers and control Luck.

"*You don't like Al'ice?*"

"*I think she's fine.*"

"*Then what's the matter?*"

"*Our daughter thinks like you.*"

"*You would've done the same if you wanted her.*"

"*I didn't say I disapproved. But Al'ice is going to learn eventually that Chelsea can control luck and that coin flip wasn't random.*"

"We'll deal with that if we get to it." Kita looked at Al'ice. "Do you accept?"

Al'ice stared at the coin until Jynx flicked her wrist, caught the coin, and put it back in her belt. "I guess so...but if this is a joke..."

Kita chuckled. "I'm a master manipulator, but jokes aren't my thing. I'm serious. I wouldn't do that to you."

"Then...can we go to my apartment and get my stuff?"

Kita chuckled. "Right, don't worry, everything will be taken care of. Anything you want, I can get. Now, what if I were to tell you that everything around you—your pips, you, the Tet, space, the universe—is nothing more than a giant computer. And we," Kita motioned to her and Apocalypse, "are its masters."

"Are—are you saying I'm not real?"

Kita shook her head. "Oh, you're very real—inside this computer sim. There are three levels of reality. The reality you're in now is level one; a computer simulation runs in level two. Kimmy and I occupy level three, the computer that generates level two. What I'm going to do is, copy you from level one to level two."

"So, what are you?"

Kita shrugged. "I don't know. I'm still working on who built my computer."

"Does this mean you're like a god?"

"When I'm inside level one universes, I can't snap my fingers and alter them—that was a loophole I fixed after I took over."

Al'ice scratched her lower horn. "So, you didn't come from level three? I'm a bit confused."

"It's a long story that would take more than lunch. But I came from a level one universe. This universe—known as universe eight-seventy-six—was based on the universe I came from. Kimmy and Chelsea come from eight-thirty-two."

"What happened to the original universe, and why so many?"

"These universes are trial runs as I—and some people you'll meet later—learn how to create, control, and maintain them. We've come a long way. Early attempts imploded quickly or were unstable with numerous glitches. It's one of the reasons I enter the universes, to make sure they're working correctly. I also do it to find friends. I found early on existence by yourself is lonely. Once upon a time, I used to have a flock of almost forty Angels. I miss their friendship, loyalty, generosity, laughter, compassion, and honesty—"

"Speaking of honesty, Momma, maybe you should tell her why you want her help," said Jynx. "Cause I already know everything you're going to say, and I'm getting bored."

Kita smiled at her daughter. "One day, I'm going to subject you to the etiquette classes like your mom, and I suffered through growing up."

"Rich bitches," scoffed Jynx.

"Chelsea!" Apocalypse scolded.

"What? That's what Lizzy calls you."

"And you're the daughter of two," reminded Kita. "Don't make us dive into what our mothers used to make us do."

"What are you going to do?"

"One of my favorites." Kita opened her hand and encapsulated Jynx in an opaque gray sphere.

Jynx scoffed and opened her hands, but nothing happened.

Kita gave her daughter a wry smile. "Don't forget who Momma is. You'll never be as powerful as me."

Jynx huffed, folded her arms, and pouted.

Kita smiled at Al'ice. "Sorry, kids. But she is right, you do need to know my plan. I told you I was double-crossed by the Djinn named Grall. He runs a respectable freight business moving goods around Tet space. He also runs a not-so-respectable business smuggling weapons and contraband to quarantined planets, pirates, and other Tet's threat list groups.

"He hired me to steal him a special jacksaur—I assume you know what that is?"

Al'ice stroked her lower horn with a worried look. "They're one of the most feared predators on my homeworld."

Kita looked at Apocalypse. "They're big, nasty, have lots of teeth, claws, scales, and one of the few large creatures a Prii can control. The particular jacksaur Grall wanted was kept in the Verisom Royal Zoological Gardens."

Al'ice let out an, "Eep! That's an ancient jacksaur. How'd you get it off Verisom?"

"Bribes, mostly. I disguised my crew as keepers. We hid the crate in the manure truck. After lacing the jacksaur's favorite snack with a tranquilizer, we used him to lure the beast in the crate—"

"Prii are a jacksaur's favorite!" exclaimed Al'ice.

Kita held up a hand. "Don't worry. He was hornless."

"What's that mean?" said Apocalypse.

"Verisom enslaved the Prii. Those that went willingly had their horns removed," said Al'ice as she turned up her dark, leathery nose. "Those that resisted were taken in by the Aurori and brought to the Tet. That was generations ago. The Verisom still enslave the Prii, but it's not allowed on the Tet. The two groups have grown quite different. Horned Prii still fight for our homeworld's independence, but the hornless have submitted and accepted their enslavement and refuse to fight. The Aurori have been trying, but the Verisom are backed by the Djinn and the Zentonians. They're slavers in their own right."

"Tet politics must be fascinating," said Apocalypse. "Go on, angel. I'm interested to hear how you got this creature off-planet."

"The crate and manure were loaded into a shipping container. I used the manure to hide the crate and life support systems to get through inspections. You should have seen Grall's face when I opened the container's doors, and a mountain of animal dung fell on his nicely manicured sand."

"Is that why he killed you?" said Al'ice.

Kita knew she was only partially kidding. Djinn were very particular about their sand. "Might have been part of it. But I refused to take only half my payment. So, he kept his payment and fed me to the jacksaur. It was a little hungry after its journey."

"Angel!" exclaimed Apocalypse.

"Tell me about it. Al'ice, I've died a thousand different

ways, and being eaten alive is my least favorite." A chill ran down Kita's spine as the memory flooded her mind.

Al'ice pushed her half-eaten plate away. "I don't even want to imagine that."

Kita opened her mouth, but Apocalypse cut her off. "I don't even want to hear about it. I'm with her. What I can imagine is bad enough. Is this why you want revenge?"

"Yep."

"Are you going to feed him to the jacksaur?" said Al'ice.

"As poetic as that would be, no. That's too good for him and too quick. I want lasting punishment. Grall wanted the ancient jacksaur because he's big into the underground Prii tourneys and wanted his personal trainer to use the jacksaur to rule the ring. Al'ice is going to kill it for me."

Al'ice's mouth fell open as she nervously stroked a horn with both hands. "I—There's no way. I don't have the skills or the experience. My horns aren't that powerful. I'm just a...a nobody who barely gets by. You want a grandmaster!"

Kita looked at Jynx, sulking in the gravity sphere. "You ready to come out?"

"Yeah," came the muffled reply.

Kita dropped her hand, and the sphere vanished.

"How come I couldn't break out of it?" demanded Jynx.

Kita chuckled. "You'll have to figure that one out on your own."

Jynx rolled her eyes. "Being the daughter of gods sucks."

Kita raised an eyebrow. "Why don't you tell Al'ice why I picked her to kill the jacksaur."

"I don't know," replied Jynx in a surly attitude.

"Ah, she's becoming a teenager," quipped Kita.

"If she's going to be this way, she's all yours," said Apocalypse.

"How do people become Angels, Jynxie?"

Jynx let out a big sigh. "Need, reward, potential, or friend."

"Or a combination thereof. Why do I like Al'ice?"

"From the list of bets she's won for you, I'd say potential, and she likes you—why I don't know."

"Also need. She's the only one that can fight in the Prii

tourneys." Kita looked at Al'ice. "If you don't think you can do it, we'll go home. I won't renege my offer."

"Al'ice," said Apocalypse, "there's no harm in trying. From this point forward, nothing bad can happen to you or any of us. I will tell you that Angels are the best at what they do. I conquered my homeworld. Kita saw the potential in me and helped me achieve my goal. She sees similar potential in you. If she thinks you can be the best, I believe you will be the best. It means work, sacrifice, and dedication, but you will have friends to help and support you. You only need the desire. I believe you have it. You wouldn't be as good as you are without it. Due to circumstances, you probably have gotten as far as you can go alone. With Kita, there is no limit to what you can achieve. You just have to want it."

"Where—where are you...we—"

"—We going to find you an ancient pip?" Kita said with a twinkle in her eye.

"We can't go to Prii! The Verisom will dehorn me."

Kita held up a hand. "Don't worry. We're not going to Prii. There is a Verisom lab, Chokecherry Industries, on Petal One that researches and supplies genetically engineered pips."

A wave of disgust came off Al'ice as her freckles darkened. The Verisom were the only suppliers of pips in Tet space, and they sold them to the horned Prii for exorbitant prices. The two pips Al'ice had were probably still under loan. Kita made a note to make sure she paid the balance.

"Those are no match for an ancient. They're too small. They'd be eaten in one gulp."

Kita traced her tongue around a sharpened canine tooth. "This lab makes pips for more than entertainment. They have a military division with some unique specimens that we can liberate."

Al'ice tapped the side of her horn. "I'd say it's impossible...but..."

"I'm sure Kita has a plan or is working on one," said Apocalypse raising an eyebrow at Kita.

"I looked into it when I was stealing the jacksaur. I don't know if I can do it with the four of us. Wrong skillsets. But I know some people. While I work on that, Al'ice, we'll get you a coach and set up your first sponsored match."

"A coach?" Al'ice freckles went white. "I've never—"

"You've got raw talent," interrupted Kita. "We need someone who can shape it and turn you into a champion."

"Where are you going to find a coach on such short notice?" said Apocalypse.

"I'm going to poach one. I've already sent out offers to two."

"I...I might know of someone," said Al'ice.

"Oh?"

"There's an ancient Prii that takes in old pips. The stories say she was a grandmaster trainer decades ago, then her favorite pip died mysteriously during a match. She refused to fight after that. Legend says she lives in The Dark."

"Interesting..." muttered Kita as she stroked her braid. "I'll look into finding her."

"Where are we going to live?" said Jynx. "And what am I going to do?"

"I think you'll spend some time with your mom and me as we figure this out. I think you're old enough to explore the Tet on your own." Kita looked at Apocalypse for approval.

Kita's partner scowled under her hood. Kita had laid a blatant trap for her. "If you feel it's safe. She and I will go out the first couple of days and limit her boundaries to around wherever we're staying. If she can handle that, we'll look at letting her roam further. She still has schoolwork to do if we're going to be here any length of time. You did say this was going to be a short visit."

"Did I? Maybe I did. But things change. And what's the first rule, Chels?"

Jynx tossed her head back and forth as she recited the mantra, "Adapt and overcome."

"Good girl."

Kita looked around her daughter to the crowd passing on the skyway. She checked her Arcom for the time and then scanned the crowd again. On a sky-bridge close to the restaurant, she spotted a pair of Aurori in sparkly dresses and sashes escorted by Diamock and Djinn Tet-Sec officers clad in yellow uniforms and body armor.

"It seems," said Kita, "That our housing solution will be coming to us."

Apocalypse rolled her eyes. "You better not mean some little apartment that's too small for the three of us."

Kita shook her head. "No, but I should collect my things before looters break-in. Our official welcoming committee is coming. And this time, they brought the boys. If anything, the Aurori are predictable." She pointed to the group led by the Aurori, skirting a crowd gathered to watch a pair of Human street performers.

"Why would they come for you?" said Al'ice.

"I made a bit of a scene before I found you. But don't worry. The Grand Ambassador isn't here for that."

Kita finished the last few bites of food as Apocalypse said, "Do you know the Grand Ambassador?"

"Not this one," said Kita with her mouthful.

"What happened to etiquette?" chided Jynx.

Kita swallowed her food. "I've forgotten more etiquette than you'll ever know, Miss Smarty-pants."

Apocalypse shook her head while laughing. "She is definitely your daughter."

"I know she's fearless, tenacious, and brilliant. But can she be the greatest? See if her sword lives up to her mouth. Love you, Chels."

Jynx playfully rubbed her cheek. "Always gotta jump from the top rope. I'll be great before you were."

"I don't doubt it. I'll be disappointed if you wait until you're twenty-three."

"Oh! That's so old. I've already battled monsters before you did."

Apocalypse let out an unhappy sigh. "I thought we were trying to give her a normal childhood."

"Yeah...growing up the daughter of gods is normal."

"I swear, she doesn't have this attitude with me."

Kita smiled at her daughter fondly as the grand ambassador and her entourage stopped in front of the table. Cocking her head and smiling at the arrivals, Kita said, "Grand Ambassador, it's good to meet you. I'm Angel Kita, my partner Angel Apocalypse, and our daughter, Angel Jynx. This is our friend, Al'ice Sie'nna. I've been awaiting your arrival. I accept our embassy on Embassy Row. We don't have a homeworld, but I've been on the Tet for a while. However, Apocalypse and Jynx are new and would like a tour. We are employed as the tourney sponsors for Al'ice and have enough credits to support ourselves. We currently are not under threat from any race or group and do not need protection—we are capable of protecting ourselves. I'm sure once I talk it over with Apocalypse, we will gladly sign the non-aggression treaty and submit to the rules and regulations of the Tet."

Kita's remark unbalanced the senior diplomat, though her perfectly symmetrical face didn't waver. "Which of you is Roosevelt?"

"I am," the three Angels answered together.

The Grand Ambassador pressed her lips together. "I'm impressed with your knowledge of the Tet government. Excuse my ignorance, but Angels closely resemble Humans. Are you a sub-race they have not told us about?"

Kita steepled her fingers and leaned her elbows on the table. "Humans are Angels, but not all Angels are Human. Angels are not a product of evolution but of engineering. One in ten thousand Aurori can control an element. Every Angel has multiple abilities." Fire erupted from Kita's elbows and marched up to her hands. From under her hood, Apocalypse fired ruby-red beams from her eyes, causing a glass of water to boil. Jynx became translucent as balls of ice, lightning, and metal floated around her.

Kita stood up and offered a fiery hand to Al'ice. "Don't worry. It won't hurt you."

Al'ice took Kita's hand and stood.

"Sorry," said Kita, "but this is going to hurt."

A wave of panic escaped Al'ice. "What—what are you going to do?"

"Welcome to the flock." Kita's flaming finger touched Al'ice's leathery nose. "Boop!"

Al'ice screamed and fell forward, reaching out for the table. Her weight caused the table to tip, and she fell to the floor, pressing her face against the dull metal.

The other restaurant patrons looked over in alarm. The Grand Ambassador covered her mouth in shock. Her escort went for their pistols. Apocalypse jumped up and raised her arms. "It's ok, folks. Just an Angel hatching. She'll be fine in a minute."

Kita stepped around the table and with a burning finger, burned slits for wings through the white synthetic crop-top the Prii was wearing.

Al'ice cried in pain as she banged her purple and red painted split-hoofs against the floor. From between her shoulder blades, gray limbs grew and formed joints. Buds appeared on the long spindly limbs. They grew until bursting with purple and blue feathers. Feathers sprouted, some short, others over six feet long. When the long flight feathers finished growing, Al'ice looked up, sniffling as tears streamed down her face.

Jynx and Apocalypse knelt next to Al'ice.

"Rise, Dominica," announced Kita.

The other Angels helped Dominica to her hooves.

"Keep the weight forward," said Apocalypse. "It takes a bit to get used to."

"What happened?" said Dominica.

"These," said Jynx as she pulled one of Dominica's wings around while Apocalypse kept the new Angel steady.

"Me?" Dominica exclaimed.

"Welcome to the flock, sweetie," said Apocalypse as she hugged her.

Everyone turned to look at Kita.

She shrugged. "I figured an object lesson would better make my point."

"So, you are just a sub-race," said the Grand Ambassador.

Kita held up her hand. Several strands of DNA appeared. "These are Prii, Human, Aurorian, and Djinn DNA—all pretty much the same." The strands vanished, replaced by a much more complex and longer stand. "This is Angel DNA. It holds sixteen times the information of your DNA and is a hundred times as long. We keep the form we came from because it's easier. But some Angels have multiple forms. Love?"

Apocalypse stepped away from Dominica and glided up above the skyway. She transformed into a hundred-foot silver and red dragon. Her long spike-lined neck swung around to bring her head above the Grand Ambassador. She opened her mouth and roared while breathing a cloud of fire.

The Tet-Sec guards aimed at Apocalypse as people on the crowded skyway ran for cover.

"You shoot her, and I will skin you alive," yelled Kita.

Apocalypse dropped her head to be eye level with the Grand Ambassador. With a dragon sneer, she blew smoke out her nose, enveloping the Aurorian.

Jynx nudged Dominica. "I love it when Mom goes all dragony."

Kita crossed her arms. "I don't think Empress Apocalypse likes that you insinuate that we're just Humans or Prii."

"W—what are you?" said the Grand Ambassador as she took a few shaky steps backward, causing her to trip and fall out of one of her crystal high heel shoes.

Kita fluffed her black and pink feathers. "Angels. We're few in number, but we're the mightiest race in the universe. We mean you no harm, as long as you treat us with respect, dignity, and friendship."

"I—I'm going to have to ask that you come to Tet-Sec Headquarters. We have a report of a winged Human—an Angel—assaulting a Tet citizen."

"They don't send you out for that," reminded Kita.

"New races are always welcome on the Tet, and we have no record of your arrival or coming through security."

Kita tapped on her Arcom and brought up her Tet identification. It listed her as Human, but that was just a minor inconvenience. Opening her hand, Kita displayed her ID. "It says Human, but we can hide our wings." To prove her point, Kita made hers disappear.

"Will you submit to a DNA test to prove you are what you say you are?"

"If, after the analysis, the sample is destroyed. Once we're established as a minor race, can we have our embassy? We don't have any other place to stay."

The Grand Ambassador gave off a wave of relief. "Once it is established, we will help you to the best of our ability."

"And if not?" said Apocalypse as she transformed back.

"Then we will hand you over to your respective embassy, and they will help you."

"And how much is my fine for assault?" asked Kita.

"That will be determined at a separate court hearing."

Kita rolled her eyes. Knowing how fast the Tet administration moved, she'd be long gone by the time her court date arrived. "Well, since we're done with lunch, I guess we can go with you. I hope you don't mind if we give the newest member of our flock her introduction?"

The Grand Ambassador looked at Dominica. "You aren't being held against your will, or they aren't coercing you in any way, are they?"

"No. I'm a pip trainer, and Kita is my sponsor. The wings are part of my sponsorship."

"*I like her,*" said Apocalypse to Kita. "*She thinks fast on her...hooves.*"

"Alright then," said the Grand Ambassador with a sigh. "Let's settle this."

"To be fair," replied Apocalypse, "most people have that reaction when dealing with Kita. I will tell you from experience, she's going to be right. Angel, why don't you and Chelsea explain being an Angel to Al'ice. I'll talk with the Grand Ambassador."

———————✕———————

"And this is your embassy," said the Grand Ambassador as the glass door slid open to the tiny office space. Kita, Dominica, and Jynx trailed Apocalypse and the Grand Ambassador inside.

Behind the counter was an empty desk. Computers and other supplies would be arriving over the next few days.

Behind the desk led to a short hallway of doors and an elevator at the end.

"Thank you, Illia," said Apocalypse. She and the Grand Ambassador had become fast friends, and Apocalypse had helped her navigate Kita.

"Upstairs contains a living space for six. If more Angels do arrive, we can arrange for a space where you can live together. Techs will be by to convert the amenities to your needs. Administrator Kele can arrange for food and any other needs you may have. She will be assigned to your embassy to help in any way you need." Illia gave Apocalypse an apologetic look. "I'm sorry it's so small. Once you become established and more Angels arrive, we can move you into a larger space."

Apocalypse smiled as she pulled back her hood. "It's perfect for our needs, Illia. Thank you for all your help and for making the process as easy as possible. Administrator Kele will be most helpful, I'm sure. We look forward to becoming members of Tet society and helping any way we can."

"It's been my pleasure, Kimmy. If you need anything, please don't hesitate to call me."

"I won't. I hope the rest of your day goes well."

Kita let the pair exchange pleasantries as she sized up Administrator Kele. The Aurorian was an unwelcome surprise. Kita doubted Kele was just a lowly administrator. The Aurori were diplomats by nature, but they still had soldiers and spies —and Kita didn't need a spy in the middle of her operation.

Apocalypse showed the Grand Ambassador out. When she returned, she pointed at Kita and motioned for her to follow.

Kita raised an eyebrow but still smiled and followed her partner down the hallway into an empty office. Apocalypse closed the door behind Kita and swept back her hood, revealing her dark hair. Seeing no place to sit—or retreat if she needed it—Kita leaned against the bare white far wall. From the look on Apocalypse's face and the unhappy emotions she gave off, she was upset. Kita pulled her hood back and pulled her large braid around, and stroked it nervously.

"Yes, love? Something the matter?"

"Yes. I'm just not sure where to start."

Kita lowered her head. She could guess at what Apocalypse was mad about, and she probably had a right to be. Still, she couldn't be all that mad. Apocalypse had backed her up and did what was needed to get them into an embassy.

"Sorry."

"You don't even know what I'm mad about. You're not getting off that easy."

"I'm sorry about the way I behaved with the Aurori and made you clean up the mess."

Apocalypse crossed her arms and glared. "I'm not mad about that. You always act that way around people with authority. At one time, you could guess at what I'm mad about, but you haven't been around, and you've forgotten."

Kita winced at the verbal slap. She had arguments but knew they would only make it worse. "What are you mad about, love?" she whispered.

"You're undermining my parenting of Chelsea. I let you do you for years, and you left Chelsea with me. You're not allowed to suddenly come in and throw away all the work I've done because you feel like acting like a parent for a few minutes."

Kita bit her lip, drawing blood. Her rage erupted and filled her with vile hate. "How dare you!" she screamed. "While you were running your empire, I was training and teaching her."

"You spent more time with Velositi and the triplets than you did with her and me!" Apocalypse screamed back.

"I came and saw her every day like you demanded. The triplets needed attention and training, but I didn't let that take away from my time with Chelsea. I did more to prepare her for life than you did. And when we got to Roost, you took her from me and suddenly became mother of the year, shutting me out. I invited you both multiple times to come inside a universe, so I could spend time with you and Chelsea, and she could grow and gain experience."

"She's a child!" cried Apocalypse. "Where you want to take her isn't safe. All you care about are your universes, not your family! If you cared, you would stay home. Let the others explore and make sure the universes are stable."

Kita ground her teeth. "I know she's your first kid, and you want to protect her, but keeping her locked in an ivory tower only harms her. She needs to see the dangers of the world and learn to defeat them."

"She's seen them, and that was your fault! An eight-year-old fighting giant Morphicons is not what she needed. She needs education, protection, and to feel safe."

"In your own words, she did outstanding. Her confidence, self-esteem, and attitude soared. She was proud she helped take them down and talked about it for months. She felt like she was part of the flock. Then you shut her away and wouldn't let me train her. Now, she's mopey, unhappy, and bored."

"I've been a good mother!" screamed Apocalypse. "You're the one with six dead kids. Don't lecture me on what it means to be a good mother. You're the failure, not me. I won't let Chelsea be number seven."

Kita's mouth slowly opened as tears flooded her eyes. She transformed into her dimensionless black cloud given to her by the A'ahegre and drifted upward.

"Wait!" Apocalypse pleaded in a gentle tone. "Angel..."

Kita drifted through the upstairs apartment to the roof. Benches and planters lined a half wall, and palm vegetation grew upward while vines grew down the side of the building. She settled in a front corner and transformed back, sitting with her head buried in her arms resting on her knees. A breath turned into a loud sob.

She cried for her long-dead children—Nina, Spike, Quill, Kamikaze, Lina, and even Kylee—she also cried for their mothers Sarin and Snowy. Even her ability to compartmentalize had limits. Her perfect memory kept the emotions from fading. To her, they might as well have died minutes ago. Her inability as a god to bring them back made it worse. To have all her power and still be unable to protect the ones she loved broke her heart.

Kita threw back her head hard against the metal wall as another loud sob escaped her. The physical pain didn't register, overwhelmed by her sadness and loneliness. Apocalypse and Jynx had filled the hole the others had left, and now they were gone. It was more than her heart could bear. And there was no end. Not even death would be an escape.

Opening her hand, holographic images of her dead children and partners cycled. "I'm so sorry," Kita wailed to each one. When Sarin appeared, Kita blubbered through her tears, "Jane, why did you sacrifice yourself for me? I didn't deserve your love. They're all dead because of me. I should have been the one deleted, not you. I deserve it." She slumped to one side against a planter, pressing her face against the large orange terracotta pot, her tears leaving a trail down the side.

Kita felt herself rise into the air as a familiar set of arms picked her up. She opened her drenched eyes, and through the blurriness, a pair of blue eyes glowed brightly.

"For someone who does not feel grief, you do substitute well for it," chirped Velositi with a smile. "This is the first time I have seen Jane. She is a striking beauty, and I assume if she was partnered to you, a deadly one."

Kita wiped her eyes and then threw her arms around Velositi's black metal midsection in a possessive hug.

"Oof," exclaimed Velositi. "You have not hugged me like that since you were little Kita."

"Don't die," Kita whispered.

"I heard what this was about. I am sorry some of your past children and partners are dead. But it is not your fault."

"If only I had been—"

"Do not play that game, Kita. You did everything in your power to keep them safe. I am sure of it. The same you do now for your family and friends. If it was not for you, none of us would be alive. For those that have died, we will remember them. You are not alone—always remember that."

"Death used to always follow in my wake."

"What was it you told me...from destruction's end, comes life's new beginning. You are no longer just a destroyer. You are a creator of life. You should celebrate it."

"I don't feel much like celebrating."

"If you want, you can tell me about your past family. You have only ever mentioned them in passing."

"You've only told me their names. You've never mentioned

Jane before," said Apocalypse, appearing in front of them. "I hope you don't mind. I asked Velositi to help me apologize. I hope you'll talk to me."

"Why? You're right. I'm an awful mother," Kita whispered.

"You are not!"

"No," Kita shook her head violently. "You're right. I've been running away—hiding—in the different universes trying to escape them. All of them—my daughters, my partners, my Angels. They're all dead because of me. I traded them all to be a god. Leaf was the last one…and I traded her for you. I'm an evil person. There is no forgiveness, no absolution…just endless suffering."

"Whatever you did in the past doesn't matter. It's what you do next that matters. You have me, Chelsea, Velositi, Knockout, Bombshell, and Stunner all here for you. And you've been here for us. You said yourself there is no evil, just decisions that help the right people. Right now, that's your family. That's Velositi and me."

"Yes," said Velositi. "And your past family may be gone now, but Ryan, Sprokkit, and Stunner are working on ways to bring them back. Someday your families will be united. There is hope."

Kita looked up, blinking her tears away. "There is?"

"There is?" echoed Apocalypse with a questioning look at Velositi. A quiet moment passed, then she said, "All we need is time, and we have plenty of that."

Kita didn't doubt that. She didn't believe the others were working on saving the other Angels. Otherwise, they would have told her. But hope was all she needed—just a sliver, enough to chase away the dark thoughts. Her goal was to restore her universe, but saving those who had been deleted had been deemed impossible. But that was before she had Ryan, Sprokkit, and Stunner working on the universe computer. They already understood it better than she did. And that sparked her hope.

"I can wait," said Kita. "I just need a little hope." Kita looked down at Apocalypse. "I'm sorry, Kimmy. I don't mean to override your authority as mom. Chelsea's done well with your guidance and care. I should be more concerned about her than me."

Apocalypse stepped up to Kita and took her hand. "You don't have anything to be sorry for. I put all my energy into Chelsea and ignored you. I didn't realize you hurt so much over losing your previous family. And it was a mean, bitch move on my part. You're a wonderful mother for Chelsea when you're with her. I wish you were around more often, but that's partially my fault, too. I refused to meet you halfway. I'm sorry—for everything. I know this is our first time seeing your world, and I haven't been very open-minded. I know Chelsea is growing up and...and I don't know what to do. I was raised in the White House until I was eighteen, and then I was thrust out into the world. I was scared, alone, and had no one for support—other than Dan. I don't want to do that to Chelsea. I'm scared I will scar her for life if I let her out of my sight. I don't see how you did it, and I don't trust she won't come home injured or worse... because I don't want to have to go through what you've been through."

Apocalypse wiped away tears with her free hand.

"I know that's not fair, and it's mean, but I'm not ready to lose my baby. I don't know how you do it. I'll never be as strong as you are. I'm sorry for being greedy, but...she's my baby."

Kita slid out of Velositi's arm and wrapped her arms and wings around Apocalypse. "I understand. I've been there. But part of being mom is knowing when to let her go. Not all at once, but step-by-step until she no longer needs to hold your hand. You go from being protector and nurturer to friend and mentor. It's a learning process for her and for us. She has to learn to do it on her own, and we have to learn not to rush in and save her—right away. The hardest part is waiting to be asked for help. She's going to think she can do it without us, and she's going to try. She'll have successes and failures. The failures should teach her we know what we're talking about, and she'll come back...not as a child but as an adult. It takes a few years, and the waiting is hard, but I have no doubt she'll persevere and be a great adult. She'll always be our baby in our eyes. A...little potato with wings."

Apocalypse laughed. "I remember that. She was so tiny, and her wings were so little."

"And then she started to fly."

"Oh god. She was into everything."

Kita opened her hand and displayed a picture of Apocalypse sitting at the Resolute Desk in the Oval Office with Jynx in a harness flying circles above her mom while tethered to a leg of the desk.

"She was so cute," sighed Apocalypse. "She used to fly in circles, then she'd suddenly get tired and sink into her blanket. I didn't know you had these."

"I've got all sorts." Kita changed the image to Spike and Quill in matching pink and white school outfits. "It was their first day of school aboard the UEE Emperor's Wrath. They were ten. I haven't looked at this picture for eons."

"I'm sorry, angel."

"They're cute kids," said Velositi looking over Kita's shoulder.

"Yeah. They grew up into impressive Angels."

The elevator door opened, and Jynx, Dominica, and Kele stepped out.

"There you are," said Jynx. "We've been looking all over for you. Hey, Velositi. When did you get here?"

"Hi, Chelsea. Kimmy needed help with Kita and asked me to come."

"What are you?" exclaimed Kele.

"I could ask the same of you," replied Velositi, her eyes dimming—how Morphicons show emotion.

"Kele, this is Velositi. She is a Morphicon Angel and my girlfriend. Velositi, meet Administrator Kele. She's an Aurorian from the planet Aurora and here to assist in the running of our embassy. If you need anything around the Tet—that's the space station we're on—she's the one to ask."

"Nice to meet you, Administrator Kele. I am sure I will have questions."

"How did she get here?" demanded Kele.

"How rude," quipped Velositi as she stood up straight and extended her wings.

"Let's just say she flew in from the skyway," muttered Kita. She motioned for Dominica to come over. Jynx followed as well. "Velositi, I'd like you to meet Al'ice, our newest Angel."

Velositi waved. "Hi, Al'ice. Welcome to the flock. My, you're beautiful. I like your coloring. How do you do it?"

Al'ice freckles lightened. "It's, ah, natural."

"Don't mind her," said Kita. "Velositi likes beautiful people and is unabashed. You don't have to answer her questions if you don't want to."

"Kita likes beautiful girls as well," Velositi retorted, her eyes glowing brightly.

Kita shrugged. "Wait until you see what Al'ice can do. Kele, I need to talk to Kimmy. Why don't you take the other Angels for a tour of Embassy Row?"

"What am I going to do with Angel Velositi? She could start a panic."

"We didn't when we were walking around," said Apocalypse.

"You've already planned to announce us to the Tet. Instead of burying us in the news cycle, Velositi will make us the lead. And don't worry. She has experience dealing with the media and can keep them busy for hours."

Velositi chirped laughter. "Before I go, are you two going to be alright, or do I need to stay and mediate?"

Kita exchanged a look with Apocalypse, who said, "I think we're ok. We still have some stuff to talk about. Thank you for coming. I know you're busy."

Velositi's eyes brightened. "I am never too busy to help you and Kita. It's good to get out, and I look forward to traveling with you. Kids take up so much time."

Apocalypse smiled grimly. "Yes, they do."

"Right here," interjected Jynx.

"I know you are. I haven't forgotten."

"Come along, Chelsea," said Velositi. "Let us give your parents some time to sort out what they need to. I am excited to see this space station. Administrator Kele, the Angels will meet you out front. Ladies, let's get an aerial view while the Administrator makes her way downstairs."

"You mean fly?" said Dominica. "I've never flown before."

"We will teach you. It is not hard, just takes some concentration. Can you spread your wings?"

"Wait!" cried Kele. "No one is going anywhere until I call the Grand Ambassador. We can't have an eight-foot-tall winged robot running loose. And none of you are cleared to fly. There are privacy concerns and the flyways. You can't just go wherever you want. Everyone is to go downstairs until I get this resolved."

Velositi's eyes dimmed. "No. We will not. You can call your Grand Ambassador, or you can take it up to god herself," she motioned at Kita, "but we do not answer to your authority. Angels are free. We do not need your protection. Your guidance would be preferable, but I believe Al'ice knows her way around the Tet. She can show us around. I will give you twenty minutes. That should give Chelsea and me enough time to teach Al'ice how to fly. We will meet you at the front door." Velositi dismissed the Aurorian with a wave of her hand. "Come, Al'ice, Chelsea. Let us give Kita and Kimmy some privacy."

"Thanks, Velositi," said Apocalypse. "Call us if you get into trouble."

Velositi's right arm transformed into a double-barrel cannon. "I do not think we will run into any trouble I cannot handle."

Kele's eyes went wide as she fainted.

"They're a little gun shy around here," quipped Kita.

Apocalypse knelt next to the Aurorian and checked her over with the medical scanner in her hand. "I don't know anything about them, but I don't detect any injury."

"I know some," said Kita as she knelt next to Apocalypse. She extended the barb from the heel of her hand and injected Kele with a stimulant to wake her.

Kele's eyes opened, and she rubbed her head. "Can—can you all do that?"

"We're all armed in some way," said Kita as she and

Apocalypse helped the Aurorian to her feet. "Why don't you go contact the Grand Ambassador. The other Angels will meet you downstairs when they're ready."

Kele made a face that said the situation was out of her league. "Just stay around the building." She turned and hurried toward the elevator.

Kita was impressed she could move so fast in her heels. Kita took Apocalypse's hand and guided her to a bench between two palm trees. After pulling it out away from the wall, they sat.

Apocalypse put her arm around Kita. "I'm so sorry, angel. I know your family means everything to you, and it was a real bitch move to use them against you. I hope someday you'll forgive me."

Kita rested her head on Apocalypse's shoulder. "It's not you that needs to be forgiven. It's me. I sacrificed them to destroy everything...to get the power I craved. I—"

"I don't believe that," countered Apocalypse. "I know you... I don't know the you of then...but I don't believe you would sacrifice your family and friends. I don't know what happened, but I know it wasn't that. I think you just tell yourself that to punish yourself for their deaths, and you don't need to do it. Leaf said most of the Angels were deleted by Kylee and Ht'ead. That's not your fault. I know she said others weren't deleted; that died fighting. She thought it was possible to bring them back. I'll sacrifice Eight-Thirty-two to bring her back if that's what it takes to bring you peace."

Kita closed her eyes as the faces of past Angels danced in her mind. So many lost...could so many be found? She was touched Apocalypse was willing to sacrifice her home universe to bring Angels she didn't know back. But she didn't want Apocalypse to sacrifice her past for her. It was true most of the Angels were dead when Kita decided Infinity—the home of the gods—had to fall, and the multiverse and reality needed to be destroyed. Two Angels had remained at the end—Babydoll, her best friend, and Tina, her sister. Both had been loyal to Infinity and tried to stop her, and she defeated both. At the time, their deaths didn't register; she was so driven. And now, for the first time in eons, she thought about them and how much she missed them. *Their deaths are my fault...but I didn't delete them. Babydoll was cast into the White—the basis from which a universe was built—and Tina I just truncated her equation. They're not dead, just their code is not executing. Trapped in a computer purgatory. They can be found.*

She raised her head and kissed Apocalypse on the cheek. "Thank you. You gave me that spark of hope."

Apocalypse stroked Kita's hair. "A little bit of hope is all you need to chase the bad thoughts away."

"I'm sorry for undermining your mothering of Chelsea. You've done a good job, and I haven't earned the right to—"

"You're her mother, too. I'm sorry for being so possessive of her, and you're right...I've been wrapped up in being mother that I've ignored you, our friends, and Reality. I haven't been the partner I think you hoped for. After Europe, I was upset because I thought I'd been a good parent to Chelsea, and I discovered I hadn't been. You'd been doing all the important things. I was upset you didn't include me, but I know now it was your experience and my lack thereof. I wanted to prove I could be a good mother...and I've gone too far. I'm sorry. I think it's time I rejoined the rest of you, and it's time for you to take a more active role with Chelsea. She needs to be ready for the real world, and I can't teach her that. That's my shortcoming—I blame my parents, and I've let my own powers wane. Working with Grand Ambassador—Illia—reminded me how much I miss adulting. I'm sorry it took such an ugly fight to make me realize my mistakes."

"I'm sorry I retreated into the Triplets and Velositi. I should have been more vocal about what was bothering me."

Apocalypse took Kita's hand. "I have to admit I was upset that you decided to have kids with her. It did feel like you were abandoning us. I should have said something. We could have had one big happy family."

"It's never too late to start. I mean, we have the big family, and everyone gets along. It's just us who aren't happy."

"Well, let's start. We'll parent Chelsea together, relying on your experience. And I will rejoin the flock."

Kita smiled. "I promise not to dwell on the past so much."

"Someday, the past will join with the present. I can't imagine how big a family we'll have then—but I am a little intimidated by Jane. She's gorgeous."

Chuckling, Kita raised her head and kissed Apocalypse. "But you're the only one I want."

"BY THE VOID! SHUT UP!" SCREAMED TURNIP.

Kita did stop, but only after Turnip had been yelling for most of the story.

"Maybe it's a side effect of the pepinal," said Mai'la. "I've never tried it in a Human before."

"I'm an Angel," said Kita. *Didn't I make that clear?*

"I've never heard of an Angel or Prii or Morphicon before—"

"I don't give a rex's foot about her wild story," snarled Turnip as she thumped her foot on the deck. "I want the Axiom! Tell me where it is!"

Kita ignored her to check her computer. It was still in recovery, trying to piece together the damaged files. She asked it how long, and it responded with a computer version of a shrug. *Looks like I haven't gotten rid of all of Omega's code.*

"Where is it?" Turnip screamed as she hopped down into the sand-filled container and kicked Kita across the face.

"I told you. It turned Katrina into me."

"That's not what it does," shrieked Turnip. She bent down and struck Kita on the cheek with the short claws growing from her fingertips, leaving three bloody lines. Turnip yelped and jumped back onto the walkway. "Frost and fire! Why aren't you being eaten? The diakos should have eaten you alive be now."

Kita raised an eyebrow. *Didn't I tell you how much I dislike being eaten alive?*

"Maybe they don't like the taste of her," suggested Mai'la.

The Verisom princess gave the Aurorian a dirty look. "Maybe I should feed her to the Djinn."

"Then you'll never get the Axiom," said Kita.

"You *do* know where it is," huffed Turnip. She bounced over to the table and picked up the injector with the pepinal. "Maybe you just need a stronger dose. I've heard Humans are stubborn."

"Turnip," said Mai'la putting her hand on the injector, "are you sure that's a good idea? It could kill her. And she's no good to us dead."

Who are you, Aurorian? And whose side are you on? You knew my Human name and are sympathetic to me...I can't decide if you're helping this deranged bunny or trying to hinder her. You're not in a position to fight your way out...are you biding your time? For what?

"And what do you suggest?" hissed Turnip as she yanked the injector from the Aurorian's hand.

Mai'la turned and looked down at Kita. "You say the Axiom became you. How? And why? The last owner of the Axiom wore it around his neck. He rarely slept or ate. Was stronger than ten Djinn and could heal in seconds. He could see things only a computer could, and no one could sneak up on him. I don't see it around your neck."

"The Axiom is a vessel for my Angel DNA and contains a gene splicer to join my Human DNA with my Angel DNA. When worn by others or embedded in my person, it gives me what's known as the basic Angel package—a series of basic abilities that every Angel has. When I'm under great duress or need, the Axiom transforms me into my Angel form. Obviously, when you captured me, it transformed me. You just interrupted the process, and I'm waiting for my memories to coalesce. I can't be any more help until they do."

"What garbage, you pathetic lying Human," roared Turnip. "Draga! Add more diakos and get the big ones." She twisted a knob on the injector. "There. That should be a dose big enough to overcome your worthless, pathetic Human stubbornness."

Mai'la didn't look so sure.

Does she believe me? I can feel her emotional turmoil. She's worried for me. That's a good sign.

A Djinn trotted over with a container and stood over Kita. He pulled back the lid and dumped the diakos onto Kita's head. A few took exploratory bites before disappearing into the sand. *I hope I burned your teeth off.* It turned out diakos were large leech-like creatures with round mouths full of needle-like teeth. When they bit you, they sunk their outer row of teeth into their victims' flesh to hold on, while the smaller inner rows ripped the flesh away. Once they were attached, the only way to get them loose was to cut off the head and pull the teeth out individually.

Mai'la held out a hand. "I'll give it to her. The diakos can't bite through my shoes."

Turnip, favoring her bitten foot, handed the injector over. Mai'la jumped down into the sand, landing on her toes and keeping her stiletto heels from sinking in. She knelt and, using her body to block Turnip's view, turned the dosage knob on the injector down.

"Continue your story as long as you need to remember who I am," she whispered to Kita as she bent over and pressed the injector against Kita's neck.

Kita, remembering the last time, let her jaw go slack, and her eyes roll up in her head as it fell to one side. This time, she barely felt the effects of the drug, just momentary lightheadedness.

Mai'la jumped back onto the walkway. She handed the injector to Turnip. "She should be ready."

Kita could see her reflection in the Verisom's big red eyes as Turnip demanded, "Where is the Axiom?"

Kita pretended to be incoherent. "Axiom? I have a story about the Angels."

"No," screamed Turnip. "No stories. Answer the question."

Mai'la put a hand on Turnip's arm. "She might need to work through a memory to get to the answer. Give her time and let her talk. I think Angels and the Axiom are connected."

"Speak fast," growled Turnip.

"I EXPECTED IT TO BE DARKER," SAID VELOSITI AS THE Angels stepped out of the elevator into a dimly lit alcove of rusted bare metal and cracked plastic walls. Trash was piled in the corners, and the smell was wretched.

"It's called *The Dark* because sunlight never reaches here," said Kita as she led the others from the alcove into a passageway. "This is the Tet's dirty little secret. Most of the population of the Tet—Zentonians, Humans, and other minor races—live down here in single and double room flats."

"What do they do?" said Apocalypse as she looked up and down the passageway.

"Some work the docks and other maintenance or support jobs—"

"—Most don't have work," said Dominica. "They live off food credits and spend the day scavenging the recycler piles and other rubbish collection points."

"How awful," said Apocalypse. "What of the other races?"

Kita took a left and followed the pools of light, stepping around puddles of liquid dripping from pipes above. "Humans are everywhere—like usual. Rich or poor, they dominate the classes. The only Djinn and Verisom you'll see are wealthy ones up above, and they do everything in their power to keep the others down. They tried hard with Humans, but there were too many Humans with too much wealth. There are some rich Zentonians, but there are so many of them their homeworld can't support the population, so the government sends them here. The Aurorians are also rich but believe in sharing the wealth as much as possible—without losing their status. The Diamocks don't care as long as it doesn't interfere with their military machine."

"What about the unitless Diamocks?" said Dominica.

"Diamock Command doesn't care about them. We might run into some down here. If we do, stand your ground and don't show any fear."

"Sounds like a dog," said Apocalypse.

Kita chuckled. "They look like armored dogs with goat feet." She led the others around a corner down another passageway, passing doors every twenty feet on both sides. "These are the flats."

Some doors were open, and the people inside were sleeping, eating, or watching TV on flat panels mounted to the back wall. A few people sat in chairs in their doorway, watching people pass.

"*Ok, ladies,*" Kita said to the others over the Angels' internal communicator. "*Watch those sitting in their doorways. Sometimes they can be scouts for gangs or bandits.*"

"*Will I ever get used to voices in my head?*" said Dominica.

"*At least you can talk back to these voices,*" said Velositi.

As they passed an open door, a gremlin-like creature jumped out and grabbed Jynx. It pressed the long claws on its hand against her throat. Its big orange eyes with dark lizard-like pupils darted back and forth, taking in the Angels.

"No move!" it yelled in a high, gnarled voice around a mouthful of razor-sharp triangular teeth. "Credits!"

"Chelsea!" cried Apocalypse as she brought her fist up.

Kita blocked her partner's arm. "*Let Chelsea handle this.*" She turned to the Grocha and crossed her arms. "And what are you going to do, snagglepuss?"

"Blood! Little one die! Credits!" The Grocha talked fast while stumbling around its lengthy tongue.

"*Chels, you ok?*" Kita asked.

"*His breath stinks. He's stronger than he looks.*"

The Grocha was short, thin, and covered in scales with a network of scar tissue on his exposed skin. This one wore black and red rags with a yellow fist painted on the chest.

"*You're free to do whatever you want to get loose.*"

"*Really?*"

"*Bonus points if you kill him.*"

Kita pointed behind the Grocha to Velositi with her arms morphed into cannons. "She might say otherwise."

"Bluff!" cried the Grocha, but his eyes and head shifted trying to see behind him.

"*Velositi, give Chelsea a chance.*"

Jynx grabbed the arm pressed against her throat. She pulled it away, twisted it, and threw the Grocha over her shoulder, spiking him into the deck. Drawing her sword, she spun it to reverse her grip and plunged it between the Grocha's eyes. Yellow blood leaked down its face after Jynx removed the blade.

"Chelsea, are you ok?" said Apocalypse as she rushed toward her daughter.

Kita reached out and grabbed Apocalypse's arm, and pulled her back. "*It's not dead yet.*"

Jynx leaned down to use the rags the Grocha wore to wipe the blood off her sword when its hand grabbed the young Angel's left arm.

Surprised, Jynx dropped her sword and tried to yank her arm back. The Grocha swiped Jynx across the thigh with its free claws. Blood darkened the young Angel's jeans. She looked at Kita and Apocalypse for help.

"Fire!" Kita said with a wink.

Jynx burst into flame, setting the Grocha's hand on fire. Howling, it released her arm and yelled in gibberish, waving its burning hand around in the air. A lance of flame erupted from Jynx's hands, hitting the Grocha in the chest. She held the flame on it until it burned like an inferno. The Grocha ran around screaming until it smashed into a wall and fell to the ground. Its whimpers and cries died away until there were just bones and ash left.

Apocalypse rushed to Jynx and knelt in front of her. "Let me see your leg," she ordered.

"It doesn't hurt, Mom."

"We don't know what kind of venom or disease that thing could carry." Apocalypse waved the medical scanner in her hand over the wound.

"As far as I know, they're just teeth and claws," said Kita. "She'll be fine."

Kita's assurances didn't stop Apocalypse from extending her barb and taking a blood sample.

"Chels, you ok?" said Kita.

"I'm ok, I guess. I froze, didn't I?"

"It's a learning experience. I believe it's also your first kill."

"I helped kill some Morphicons."

"True, but this is your first solo kill."

Apocalypse stood up after healing the wounds in Jynx's leg. "I don't detect anything in her system." She hugged Jynx possessively.

"She did good," said Kita as she joined the hug.

"I didn't do good," Jynx said in a small voice. "I froze, and I needed your help."

"You're just out of practice," said Kita. "We'll work on it. Your mom has agreed to let me train you again."

"Really?" Jynx looked at Apocalypse.

"Yes. You need to be prepared for the dangers of the world."

"Ah, thanks, Mom." Jynx gave Apocalypse a warm hug. The young Angel looked up at her parents. "So, this was a test, huh?"

"Yes," said Kita. "And you passed."

Jynx frowned. "I didn't pass. I needed help from you."

"Yes, but you performed the actions," said Velositi. "Sometimes, we just need to be pointed in the right direction."

"You ok, Al'ice?" said Kita. The Angel was standing to one side, looking nervous.

"I've, ah, never seen anyone kill someone before or smelled a burnt body. Sorry. My stomach is a little upset."

Apocalypse broke from her family and gave the new Angel a comforting hug. "It's alright. The feeling is normal. It takes a little getting used to. But being around Kita, you'll get used to it in a hurry."

The other Angels laughed as Kita rolled her eyes. Dominica didn't look happy.

"You kill a lot?"

Kita shrugged. "Not as much as I used to. But I'm no stranger to it."

"You don't expect me to kill people, do you? I don't think I could do that."

"You can do what you're comfortable with—like winning

matches in the tourney. You can leave the killing to the rest of us."

"It's easy," said Jynx as she wrinkled her nose. The smell of the burning Grocha was becoming potent. The young Angel's eyes bulged as her cheeks puffed up. She ran away from Kita and behind Velositi. A retching sound followed.

Velositi stepped to one side, revealing Jynx on her hands and knees with an arm against the wall.

"You ok, Chels?" said Kita as she and Apocalypse went and put their arms around their daughter. Dominica ducked into the Grocha's flat.

"I'm fine," the young Angel moaned.

"It's ok," said Kita. "Everybody goes through it."

"Here," said Dominica—holding her nose—while holding a bottle of water out for Jynx.

"Take it. It'll get the taste out of your mouth."

"It's not my mouth," whined Jynx. "It's the smell—" She bent over, and dry heaved a few times. When she finished, Apocalypse held her.

Kita stuck her head into the Grocha's flat and wrinkled her nose. The smell was ghastly. Cooked Grocha smelled better. Seeing the tap, she turned it on and, using her ability to control liquids, guided the water into a stream. She directed the flow out the door and doused the dead Grocha causing the burnt flesh smell to dissipate.

"Better, kiddo?" asked Kita.

Jynx nodded, her head against Apocalypse's chest.

"I'm glad I don't have a sense of smell," said Velositi.

"I thought they smelled awful when they were alive," commented Dominica.

"Are we ready to go?" said Kita. "We're attracting attention."

"Do we have to explain this to Tet-Sec?" asked Apocalypse.

Kita shook her head. "They don't care. One less darkling they have to worry about. It's his clan that'll be after us. Better get moving before we're neck-deep in them." Kita put her arm around Jynx. "Come on, Chels. Moving will ease the stomach."

"I AM BEGINNING TO THINK YOU DO NOT KNOW WHERE YOU are going," said Velositi as the group wound through the underground labyrinth of passageways.

They passed hundreds of flats with thousands of people moving around. Mixed in were eateries—walk-up kitchens that served preportioned universal meals in exchange for food credits—and shops that sold whatever they could. One of the more profitable professions for those in The Dark was scavenger and procurer. Kita started in The Dark and proved she was dependable and ruthlessly efficient at getting what her customers wanted.

"I'm following the directions my contact gave me. There wasn't a closer elevator."

"And how much do you trust this contact?" asked Velositi, her eyes alight.

"Right now, a hundred thousand credits worth. If we don't find this Prii, I'm going to rip my credits out of his squirrelly hide and mount his tail on the wall."

"Please don't," said Apocalypse sounding disgusted.

"You paid a hundred thousand credits to find her—for me?" exclaimed Dominica.

"If we find her, it'll be worth it," replied Kita. "He was adamant that he knew where an ancient Prii with lots of pips lived. He said he'd seen her and been to the subterranean forest."

"I've never been to a forest before."

"Where did you grow up?" asked Apocalypse.

"On the Tet in Twilight. My mother was a trainer. I never met my father. Mother said he was a degenerate gambler that never did anything for us."

"Why would your mom hook up with a guy like that?" said Jynx.

Apocalypse turned and shook her head at her daughter. "Chelsea, that's not appropriate."

"It's ok," said Dominica. "That's how most of the male Prii are. No one will hire them, except for the tourneys, and those that don't have jobs gamble what little money they do make. It's sad, but it pays us trainers. My father must have been a fan of my mother. She never had a big following—I guess I'm following in her footsteps. Just no males have taken an interest in me."

"Count yourself lucky," scoffed Kita.

"You may have a small following," said Velositi, "but you did impress the right person."

"I do owe you a thank you, Kita. Your bets kept me and my pips fed."

"They should have done more than that," said Kita. "I bet hundreds of thousands on you. I thought the trainers got a percentage of the take."

"We're supposed to get ten percent."

Kita scowled. "I might have to go have a talk with the manager of Alginon's. You should have been living well. By the way, I need your creditor information for your pips."

Dominica frowned as her freckles reddened. She whispered, "You don't have to pay for them. I...I can manage."

"How much do you owe?" asked Apocalypse gently.

Tears filled Dominica's eyes. "I don't know. I'm way behind. I was paying them what I could, but the Verisom kept demanding more. Now, I delete the collection notices. I know they're going to take them from me. Every time I see a Verisom, I hide. I don't know what I would do if they took them."

Kita knew the bond between a Prii and her pips was strong. When they joined, they shared memories and consciousness. Kita had heard that when a female Prii dies, so do her pips. She didn't think that was true. Otherwise, there wouldn't be legends of an ancient Prii female taking in old pips. Kita did think the loss of a pip was equivalent to losing a child.

"You let me worry about it," said Kita. "Any long-ear varmints come sniffing around for you, yell for one of us, or rip the metal off the walls and beat them to death with it."

"How would I do that?" Dominica laughed glumly through her tears.

"If you don't want to physically rip the wall apart, you can control plants."

"Like you do?"

Kita chuckled. "When I was younger, I did have the ability to shape metal for a time, until it made me sick—my bionanites attacked the nanites I absorbed from the metal shaper. But we'll show you. Remember to pick up some seeds in the forest."

Dominica's freckles turned pink. "I don't know what you're talking about."

"Here comes the bionanite lecture," whined Jynx.

"You haven't heard it in years," retorted Kita. "Anyway, you may want to pay attention. Someday you might make Angels."

Jynx's head snapped towards Kita, causing the young Angel's pigtails to wobble. "Are you serious?"

"I gave Kamikaze the ability. Why not you?"

"What do I have to do?"

"Listen and learn."

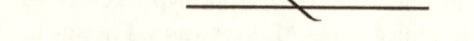

"How big is this place?" said Jynx. "We've been down here for hours."

Kita opened her hand and displayed a holographic map of the bowels of Petal Three. She zoomed in deep into the interior—they were nearly in the center of the petal—onto a blinking dot that represented their position, following a line through the holographic corridors and to a large cavern.

"Almost there," said Kita as they rounded the last corner.

As the group took a few steps down the corridor, a set of shimmers in the air caught Kita's attention. She kept walking but opened her vision so she could see behind them.

"*Everyone, switch to thermal vision. We're not alone.*" Kita changed her vision spectrum, and four yellow, red, and green figures appeared against the dark blue of the corridor. Behind them, three more figures were at the intersection they'd just come through.

"*Grocha?*" asked Velositi.

"*Kind of...I think these are Grochar—molted Grocha,*" said Kita. "*Our friend came from a better clan than I thought.*"

"*They're going to need a lot more than seven,*" said Jynx.

"*I've never fought them before—only rumors of what they're capable of. I've heard their scales are tougher than composite armor, and they regenerate quickly.*"

"*Have you heard of any weaknesses?*" asked Apocalypse.

"*No,*" said Kita. "*But they think their invisibility gives them an edge. Jynxie, I don't feel like messing around. Use your gravity sphere to take out as many as you can from the group behind us. See them?*"

"*I'm watching them, Momma. I've got two close together.*"

"*I've got a pair on the left. Kimmy, see if you can get the two on the right. Velositi, take down whatever Jynxie can't get. Al'ice, stay between us and yell if you get in trouble. On my mark...*" Kita raised her arm to point down the passageway. "*Go!*" She rotated her hand, and an opaque gray sphere appeared ten yards away. Inside, sections of two Grochar appeared. Kita clenched her fist, and the sphere collapsed, removing the sections of the trapped Grochar from the rest of their bodies. What was left of their yellow and silver scale-covered bodies appeared and crumpled to the deck. They wore black and red armor with yellow fists painted on the front.

Well, damn. How'd that idiot Grocha get into a mercenary pack?

"Yeah! Got two!" cried Jynx.

Next to Kita, Apocalypse's ruby-red beams appeared brilliant white in Kita's thermal vision as they hit the two remaining Grochars in the chest and head. The beams that hit the Grochar in the chest reflected off, one burning a big hole in the wall, the other putting a hole in a water pipe above them. The beam that hit the Grochar in the face moved across its narrow cheekbone up into its eye, causing the shiny black organ to explode. The injured Grochar reared and screamed, clutching its face.

"How do we stop the other one?" yelled Apocalypse to Kita.

Kita drew her swords. Powered weapons were illegal to carry on the Tet, but swords and similar weapons were considered ornamental. Many races had claws or other natural armaments and were considered nonthreatening. Kita had demonstrated why they were wrong on multiple occasions.

The uninjured Grochar lunged at Apocalypse, slicing through her coat. It spun and landed a kick in her midsection, tearing its toe claws across her bare midriff. She flew backward and hit the wall head first. Sliding to the ground, she lingered there, disoriented.

"Kimmy!" Kita cried as the injured Grochar slammed into her unprotected side with its claws. Disoriented by the creature's swift attacks and gnashing teeth, Kita missed her block as the creature sliced open her breast. The Grochar pushed her down and pounced on top of her snapping its teeth and swiping its claws in a frightful frenzy.

"Get off!" yelled Dominica. She slammed her horns into the injured Grochar's side, sending the creature flying into the wall next to Apocalypse.

Kita rolled toward the stricken Angel. "Kimmy! Get your shield up!" Kita screamed.

The frantic tone must have penetrated Apocalypse's haze because a pearly-white translucent bubble encapsulated the Angel.

Kita sprang to her feet and spread her wings to protect Dominica. She flourished her swords at the pair of advancing Grochar. The frenzied, injured Grochar ignored the warning and attacked in a flash of claws and teeth. Kita parried the strikes. Driving the claws to one side, she spun and brought her sword, Dead, down on the creature's extended arm. The blade hit an arm scale and slid under the overlapping upper arm scale. There, the weapon stuck. Kita yanked and twisted, causing the upper arm scale to tear away, leaving it hanging by a few strings of flesh and exposing the muscle underneath. Kita shot her other hand forward, extending her barb and jabbing it into the exposed flesh. Flexing the muscles in her hand, she injected the Grochar with a potent venom from the cone snail—a creature found in the oceans of Earth. The Grochar spasmed and collapsed face down, the venom paralyzing the creature as respiratory failure took hold.

The remaining Grochar had turned and attacked

Apocalypse's impenetrable bubble while Kita fought his frenzied counterpart. The Grochar's back was covered in scales and had a pair of large shards on its back. Kita guessed these uncouth creatures could fly. But she saw no weak spot in the back. *There has to be a way of killing them quickly.* She and Jynx couldn't wait for their gravity spheres to recharge. The Grochar was wet from the water spraying out of the pipe, so was the floor.

"Everyone, get in the air!" Kita yelled. "Jynxie! Velositi! Hit the water with lightning bolts."

"We tried that! It didn't work," retorted Jynx as she swung at the sole remaining Grochar she and Velositi faced, her strike bouncing off its scales. Velositi grabbed it and held it at arm's length.

Kita thought furiously, looking for something. Maybe if she couldn't zap it, she could drown it. Gathering up a large ball of water, she plunged it down over the Grochar's head attacking Apocalypse. The submerged creature stopped attacking and jumped to one side. Kita followed him. The angry Grochar turned and rushed Kita, ignoring the water.

"Chelsea!" Kita yelled. "I need you to freeze this one."

Chelsea looked around Velositi and pointed her hand at the water collecting on the deck. The water near her froze and radiated toward Kita.

"Al'ice get out of the water," Kita yelled as she floated into the air while reshaping the water encapsulating the Grochar, so it mixed with the water on the floor.

The ice moved rapidly, freezing the water solid. When it reached the submerged Grochar, it froze the creature in a column of ice.

Kita turned and flew toward Velositi. She slashed at the water pipe above the Morphicon, flooding the passageway.

"Velositi, get him in the water. Jynxie, freeze it," Kita ordered.

Velositi turned, her front covered in deep red gouges from the Grochar's claws. She held the creature under the water.

Jynx raised her hand to the gushing waterfall, and it froze

from the pipe to the floor. Velositi pulled her hands and arms free before she was frozen with the Grochar she was holding.

"Does...does that mean they're dead?" asked Jynx. She sounded upset and nervous.

"I don't know," said Kita, "but I do know of one way to make sure." She went to the first frozen Grochar, heated her finger, and pushed it deep into the ice. She formed a small red ball in her hand and pushed it down the hole. "Take cover," Kita instructed as she pulled Dominica behind her and raised her heat shield. She snapped her fingers, and a large hole blew out of the ice-encased Grochar. "Chels, your turn."

Jynx glided over to the frozen waterfall with her trapped Grochar. She repeated what Kita had done, but instead of a red ball, hers was purplish-black. She put up her own pearly-white bubble around her and Velositi as Kita and Dominica remained in Kita's heat shield. The young Angel snapped her fingers and blew the frozen waterfall with the trapped Grochar apart.

"I...I...do not think that one is coming back," said Velositi weakly. She sat down hard and leaned against the wall.

"Velositi, are you ok?" cried Jynx as she lowered her shield.

"I...It just hurts. I need a few minutes."

Kita, ignoring the excruciating pain and blood flowing down her front and side, rushed over to her girlfriend. Velositi's front was crisscrossed with deep, gnarled gashes that pulsed red.

"Chels, look around and see if you can find a power conduit so Velositi can get some plasma."

"It's acid," said Apocalypse weakly as she limped over with the help of Dominica. Kita's partner's middle was blistered and red as blood seeped from the gashes in her stomach. Dominica helped Apocalypse sit next to Velositi.

"Bloody moons, love!" exclaimed Kita.

"Mom!" cried Jynx as she flew over and hugged Apocalypse while tears tumbled down her face.

"It's ok, Chels," whispered Apocalypse as she pressed her blood-covered hand against the gashes in her stomach. "I can heal the damage. Gather me some water so we can flush the acid out."

"What about Kita?" said Dominica, motioning to the Angel's bloody and shredded side and breast.

"I'll be fine," said Kita. Acidity explained the overt burning sensation above and beyond the damage done by the Grochar's claws. She walked over to the water still spilling out of the pipe. Jynx's explosion had knocked the frozen plug out of it. Gathering up a ball of water, she went back to Velositi and Apocalypse. "Show me where to squirt."

"Do Kimmy first," said Velositi. "I can wait."

Kita looked at Apocalypse.

"Across my stomach."

Kita aimed a jet of water and washed out the gashes as Apocalypse clenched her teeth. The bloody water ran down Apocalypse's silver and red pants and streamed over the icy floor.

"That's good," said Apocalypse. "I can heal the rest. Do Velositi and then yourself. By that time, I'll be ready to heal you."

Kita turned to Velositi. The gashes on her chest were widening. "Ready, love?"

"Yes." Velositi stood, exposing her black and pink chest.

Kita squirted her with water, flushing out as much acid as she could.

"That feels better," sighed Velositi when Kita finished.

"Jynxie," called Kita, "find that power conduit for Velositi."

The young Angel looked up from watching Apocalypse heal herself. She looked between her moms, unsure.

"It's ok, Chelsea," said Apocalypse. "I'll be fine. Go help the others."

"Come on, Chels," ordered Kita. "You're the only one of us who can."

Jynx looked worriedly at Apocalypse as she floated towards the pipes and conduits running along the ceiling.

Kita used the remaining water to wash off the staggering amount of blood covering her. The water revealed long gashes in her side running from her left breast down to her hip bone.

Blisters and burnt flesh-covered what skin remained. She looked at it and rolled her eyes. It was apparent that Jynx wasn't the only one who needed to train.

"Ah, come on. Come loose, you stupid piece of junk," huffed Jynx as she pulled and struggled against a conduit.

"Here, let me," said Velositi as she stood up. "Which one?"

"The orange one," replied Jynx.

"Hand me your sword."

Jynx handed over her katana. Velositi used it to cut through the plastic conduit and strip away the insulation. When the bare wire was exposed, she grabbed it, dimming the few barely functioning lights in the area.

"Is that better?" Kita asked Velositi.

"Yes. The pain is subsiding, and the injuries are healing. Go attend to yourself. There is no need to be a tough girl now."

"Come on, Momma," said Jynx with a worried look on her face as she pulled Kita toward Apocalypse.

"I'll be fine," muttered Kita as she followed her daughter to her partner.

Apocalypse scowled worriedly when she inspected Kita's wounds. "Lie down. This is going to take a bit."

Kita did as instructed and pulled up her top, exposing both her breasts so Apocalypse could work.

"Angel, you need to be more careful," scolded Apocalypse.

Kita raised an eyebrow but didn't say anything. *I saw your stomach. It was as bloody a mess as mine.* "I think we're all a little out of practice," she said at last. "I've been Human for far too long."

"Not much work for assassins?" said Velositi.

"Not here or at home. Chels and I will be training each other. I've been ignoring my skills now that Leaf is gone." When the little Angel wasn't working in the universe room, she was dragging Kita to the practice mat. It had kept Kita's skills sharp. But since Aspen's passing, Kita had avoided that room.

Apocalypse frowned. Kita felt her guilt. In response, Kita lifted her hand and touched her partner's face. Apocalypse nuzzled Kita's hand as she healed Kita's injuries.

"Not your fault," said Kita.

"Why don't you bring her back?" said Jynx.

Kita blinked a tear away. "Because she's the last of her generation of Angels and the last of the old gods. Their time is over...It's your mother's and my time. We must learn like they did."

"Can't you bring them back without the gods? Leaf told me there was a time before she was a god. She was just an Angel assassin."

"I don't know how..."

"It would be worth looking into," said Apocalypse. "If you want to return to your original universe, there can be no other gods than us."

Kita pressed her lips together in thought. "Yeah. One more thing for Ryan's plate." Kita had met Ryan Callaghan, Velositi, and Apocalypse in the same universe. He was a Cali boy attending CTech University. After their adventures on Earth 832, Kita invited him and his fiancée to live on Roost and study universe construction. He led a research team consisting of Sprokkit—a Morphicon who arrived with Velositi—and Stunner—one of the lauded triplets and daughter of Velositi and Kita.

She wasn't sure how Ryan was going to strip the god parts out. Aspen had retained her god part, though it gave her no special powers in Kita's universes. But Aspen wasn't mad at Kita. Some of the other Angel gods had left upset with her over banishing her daughter Kylee. Kita didn't want them to find a way to establish a connection with her universes and run amuck. She wanted to avoid the chaos that had plagued her original universe when the gods could change the universe's equation when it suited them. And maybe, removing the god parts from those Angels would remove what they were angry about.

"All done, angel," said Apocalypse as she squeezed a ticklish spot on the inside of Kita's hip bone.

Kita let out an "Eep!" and twisted around, coming face to face with Apocalypse. She looked into her partner's brown eyes and felt her heart flutter. "Hey," Kita whispered before leaning in to kiss her love.

"I haven't seen you girls do that in forever," muttered Jynx.

"It has—" Kita kissed Apocalypse again. "—been a long time. I think your mother missed me."

"Little bit."

"Well, now you have to take me with you wherever you go. I need to get back into shape, too."

"Yes, we all seem out of practice," said Velositi. "I blame the children."

Kita and Apocalypse laughed while Jynx rolled her eyes.

"While Al'ice is training, so are we," said Kita. "I'll have Kele rent us a gym."

"We can start on the roof," said Apocalypse. "It will be a good warning to the rest of the Tet."

Kita went to get up, but Apocalypse put her arms around her neck and kissed her again. When Kita went for air, Apocalypse sucked on her lower lip, sending a spine-tingling shock down her spine and making all her feathers stand up. When Apocalypse let go, Kita blushed deeply, trying to get her feathers to lay flat.

"I forgot how good you taste," purred Apocalypse.

"Is—is this a mating ritual?" said Dominica to those not involved.

"Yes," said Velositi. "And if we let it continue, they will have sex here and now."

"Ew," huffed Jynx.

"This passageway is way too gross," said Apocalypse, "but sex does sound good. I think I'm a little pent up."

"You and me both," said Kita. "Velositi, you want to come?"

"I was hoping you would ask. It has been a long time since I have seen either of you naked. You are so beautiful to look at and make the best faces."

"Ok," said Apocalypse. "Let's leave the details out. We still have a minor present."

Jynx had a look on her face like she was trying to wrap her head around something.

"What's on your mind, Jynxie?" said Kita, seeing her daughter's perplexing look.

"Did...did you just invite Velositi to have sex with you?"

"Not the first time," said Kita with a grin. "Why?"

"I...I..."

"I think her mind has just been broadened," Velositi chirped.

Kita and Apocalypse hugged their daughter.

"It's ok, Jynxie," assured Kita. "Nothing to worry about. Someday it'll be your turn."

"I'll never look at the three of you the same," whispered Jynx.

Apocalypse squeezed Jynx. "Someday, you'll find a nice boy—"

"Ew, no, Mom!" Jynx exclaimed, twisting out of her parents' embrace.

"Sorry, sweetie. I didn't know sex still made you uncomfortable. I'm sorry we brought it up. Your mother and I are—"

"It's not sex, Mom," Jynx yelled. "I've already explored like Momma told me. I get why you like it. It's boys I don't like."

"Oh," said Apocalypse and Kita to each other.

"But you have not been around many boys or girls your age," said Velositi.

"I didn't say I liked girls either."

Kita and Apocalypse traded a look.

"Who are you attracted to?" asked Velositi.

"Jynxie, you don't have to answer that," interjected Kita. "Who you like is up to you, and you've plenty of time to figure it out. It took me a long time, and I've been with Humans, whatever you want to classify Snowy as, Angels, and Verisom. What you find attractive changes over time. I have to admit I lucked out finding your mom. I just want you to find someone that makes you happy."

Jynx sighed. "It's like...I don't know...Humans don't interest me. Al'ice is cute." Her cheeks reddened as she looked at the ground.

Kita raised an eyebrow. *Is this a phase, lack of choice, or the beginnings of something else?*

Dominica stroked her horn, trying to look invisible, and then she disappeared.

"Never has someone learned so fast," chuckled Kita.

"What?" said Dominica.

"Invisibility. Look at your hand."

Kita changed to her thermal sight so she could see the Angel waving her hand around.

"Where'd it go? Am I missing it? Will it come back?"

Dominica reappeared.

"I'll explain," said Apocalypse. "Kita's notorious for not explaining the Basic Angel Package to new Angels."

"I get around to it."

"Yes, when you need them to do it right now."

"Come on, Jynxie. You can talk to me about your future love life."

"Do we have to?"

"We can talk about mine."

"Considering you've had one, I bet it's more interesting."

Kita shrugged. "I am interested in hearing your thoughts on what you're interested in."

"I would like to hear about the Verisom," said Velositi.

"We'll start with Cotton, the royal Verisom princess. If Chels feels like talking afterward, she can go. Love, we're moving out."

Apocalypse waved Kita to go as she and Dominica brought up the rear.

--------×--------

"Here we go," said Kita looking at the holographic map floating above her hand. There was a door to the left. "Jynxie, I don't care who you bring home as long as they're good for you. And I know who your mom and I think is good for you and who you think is good for you will differ sometimes. My adoptive parents were right about Snowy. She wasn't good for me—though they got it right for the wrong reasons. Jane was good for me; Galina wasn't. I wasn't with Casey long enough to know which...though she reminds me a lot of your mom. I think that's because both were princesses and empresses."

"Momma," said Jynx in a judgmental tone, "I think you have a thing for princesses. Jane is four. She's the industrialist princess."

"Would you believe there's a fifth?"

"Bloody moons, Momma, you need help."

Kita laughed as she inspected the door, pointing out what she was looking for to Jynx. The door had an OFF-LIMITS sign on it. Kita didn't think much of it. It wasn't an official Tet-Sec sign, nor did the lock look standard. With Jynx looking over her shoulder, Kita heated a finger, melted around the lock panel, and pried it off. Inspecting the circuitry, she found the microchip that controlled the door and lock.

"Here, Jynxie, you do it," said Kita.

"Ok," she said uneasily. Placing her finger on the silicon chip, short, conductive fibers extended and connected to the chip's pins. "What do I do now? My cracking software won't recognize the chip."

Kita connected the computer in her head to her daughter's and copied over the adaptive cracking software she used. It was up-to-date with this universe's Tet hardware.

"Try that," instructed Kita.

"Running..."

The door made a *clunk* sound as the bolt retracted.

Jynx removed her finger, and the door slid aside.

"Good job," said Kita.

"Does this new software work at home?" asked Jynx mischievously of Kita.

Kita smiled. "Yes. Use it wisely." She led her group down a narrow passage with multicolored conduits and pipes on the wall. A handful of flickering, dim lights led the way to an opening.

Exiting the passage, they found tall, purplish-green grass that disappeared into a forest. As they walked, the grass glowed ultraviolet. A breeze blew through the tree leaves, causing them to glow as well. Ultraviolet insects flew around the tree's green and ultraviolet trunks. They seemed to be attracted to the large dark purple glowing flowers on the trunks. High above, lights gave off the ultraviolet glow. Kita changed the viewable spectrum in her eyes and saw the lights gave off lots of ultraviolet energy.

"It's an ultraviolet forest," said Kita as she marveled at the spectacle. She turned to Dominica. "Welcome home!"

"This...This is my homeworld?" the Prii gasped.

"At least part of it. It looks like the Prii weren't the only things the Aurori saved from your homeworld."

"It's amazing," said Dominica as she ran her hands through the grass and looked at the forest with awe.

"This seems like a magical place," said Apocalypse.

The Angels followed the path through the grass into the forest. Glowing vines swayed in the breeze, lighting the dark forest full of different kinds of purplish-green bushes with glowing flowers.

"Look at Al'ice's horns!" said Jynx from the rear.

Everyone stopped and looked at Dominica's purplish glowing horns.

"What's wrong with my horns?" said Dominica worriedly as she reached up and touched one. The freckles on her face were glowing.

"You're glowing," said Kita. "A good sign that you belong here. Do you feel any different?"

"I...I..." She leaned out and touched a tree. "What the!" She jumped back, shaking her hand.

"What's wrong?"

"I...heard a voice. Not like you...slower, calmer, older..."

"Did you speak to the tree?" said Jynx.

"I don't know."

"Let's not touch anything else until we find this ancient Prii," suggested Kita. "She might be able to explain what's happening to Al'ice."

The group wandered through the forest, leaving a trail of glowing leaves and grass. Coming to a clearing full of grass and flowers, Kita stopped everyone and scanned the area for threats. To her right, something streaked by in the shadows. When she opened her vision to get a better look, she saw a similar streak to her left.

"Ok, girls, something is out there. Be ready."

"What is it?" asked Apocalypse.

"I don't know," said Kita. "It's moving too fast to see." She led them into the grassy clearing, following the trail while watching the woods for more of the fast-moving creatures.

As she took a step, her foot came down on something soft that gave like it was organic. A bleat cut through the silent air as whatever Kita stepped on sprang to its feet. Out of the grass appeared six small deer-like creatures with pointy antlers and tusks jutting from their lower jaw. Their coats glowed purple as they bounded away from Kita's group.

"More locals," said Kita.

"They gave me a heart attack," muttered Apocalypse.

Kita continued through the grass to the far wood line. The trail was more evident here as she found scat and fur attached to a thorny bush. *More locals must be in the area.*

They followed the game trail through the forest while dodging glowing hanging vines and thorns. The sound of falling water came through the trees, and moments later, the forest gave way to a large pond with a waterfall on the far side. In the water, fish and other creatures swam and moved about, their ultraviolet glow refracting off the water's surface.

"Did my ancestors really live in a place like this?" gasped Dominica as she looked around at the beauty of the glowing trees, grass, and water.

"Get out of my forest, rootless," said a voice from atop the waterfall.

Kita's hand went for her swords but stopped when she saw the ancient-looking Prii—missing her left small horn and had a hand on a tree—its branches and leaves draped over the stream and waterfall. She wore large leaves fashioned in a skirt and a triangular piece of yellow cloth across her chest. Her hair and horns were two-toned like Dominica, but yellow and orange, instead of purple and blue.

"Your forest?" said Apocalypse.

"You see anybody else living here? Get out before you remind the long-ears it's down here."

"Who are you?" asked Kita crossing her arms. She really disliked dealing with cantankerous old people.

The ancient Prii glared at Kita as dozens of animals, mostly pips, sprang from the trees, grass, and bushes. The deer appeared out of the gloom and a spotted black cat with two purplish glowing tails. "The trees say you don't have mi and aren't connected to the flow of the universe."

"And what if I were to tell you they're not wrong?"

"The trees want to know what you've done to the rootless," the ancient Prii demanded.

"She's an Angel Prii. We're here for your help."

"The trees say there are no Angels in the universe."

"Who am I talking to, you or the trees?"

"The trees and I are one, as it should be for her," the ancient Prii pointed at Dominica. "But you fools were swayed by the golden ones to abandon your roots and live without mi."

"Would you believe we made this universe?" said Apocalypse. "And that we're gods exploring it and looking for help to right a wrong?"

"The long-ears came as gods and destroyed us. No one has righted that wrong. If you were true gods, you would avenge your chosen people."

Kita opened her hand and grew a fireball. "I'm ready to burn it to the ground." Flame spread down her arm and across her body. She spread her wings wide as flame dripped from her feathers to the ground. Kita kept the foliage from burning—for the moment. "There are no chosen people—just individuals I care about. Al'ice is one and my friend. We're here so she can be trained and, if she wants, to reconnect with her people's history. I have a score to settle with Grall, and I won't be denied. If you can help us, you'll be rewarded. If not, we will leave. Annoy me further, and this cavern will be bare metal when I leave."

The ancient Prii pointed at the pond, and a fountain of water arced over the bank at Kita. Raising her arms, Kita halted the water. A struggle ensued as the two shapers fought for control of the element. Kita toyed with the ancient Prii, giving some, then taking it back. The water shrank and expanded as they fought. When Kita had enough, she flicked her wrist, and the water turned and collapsed back in the pond.

"Nice try," said Kita as she doused her flame. "But I am god."

"Then why don't you kill Grall yourself?" the ancient Prii chided.

"Because that would be too easy, and he deserves to die a slow death. I want to take what he loves from him—a jacksaur I stole for him that he fights in the underground tourneys—and for that, I need Al'ice to be the best Prii trainer on the Tet."

"Bah!" the ancient Prii huffed as she waved Kita away. "You won't be fighting the best on the Tet. You'll be facing a mi master, and there are only two left. Me and Ma'rie...and she controls your jacksaur."

"Then train Al'ice. Whatever the cost, I can pay."

"Credits are worthless. But maybe there is something you can help me with—bird-god."

"I can't return your homeworld to you."

The ancient Prii waved her hand dismissively. "There's nothing left. The long-ears have eaten their way across it, leaving only desolation and destruction—even the trees couldn't recover. They withered and died and these—" she waved her hand at the forest, "—are all that remain. But they remember, and they too want revenge. You seem to be a god of revenge, and so my payment for training the rootless one is: A long-eared princess named Okra has been sniffing around looking for this place. I need you to make her forget and wipe all knowledge from her computers. If you make her restaurants go out of business, all the better."

"I'm not going to open an eatery next door," chided Kita.

"I don't care what you do, but I want the long-ears out." The ancient Prii jumped onto the water and rode the waterfall to the pond. With a confident stride, she walked across the water to the Angels. "What do you say, bird-god?"

"Train Al'ice, and I'll get rid of the Verisom."

"Good, that's what I wanted to hear." The ancient Prii pointed at Dominica. "Come here, rootless."

Dominica looked at Kita worriedly. Kita nodded and waved her to the ancient. Trembling, Dominica staggered over and stood before the older and wizened Prii with yellow and orange horns.

"Come on, rootless. I'm not going to bite. Call me To'va."

"Al'ice Sie'nna."

"Prii don't use surnames. That's a yoke of the golden ones. From now on, you're—"

"Dominica."

"I was going to say Al'ice, but—"

"It's her angelic name," said Kita.

"What in the mi is an angelic?"

"Angelic—Angel. Dominica is an Angel Prii. She lives in three worlds now—Prii, Angel, and Tet."

"If that's what she wants to be called. The trees are interested to know about Angels."

"Dominica can tell you the basics," said Kita rolling her eyes.

"The trees just need a chance to read her mi, and they'll know all they need to know. Come, Dominica, our first task is to get you rooted."

"You keep calling her rootless. What's that?" said Jynx.

To'va looked at the young Angel. "It means she isn't connected to the mi of the universe. To be a master trainer, she must be rooted. It will strengthen her horns and allow her mi to mix with the other creatures. The stronger her mi, the bigger and more powerful the creatures she can mix with. I assume, bird-god, you're going to get her a creature beyond the two pips she has?"

"My name is Kita. This is my partner Apocalypse, daughter Jynx, and girlfriend Velositi. I do have a place in mind to get her a special one the Verisom labs have hidden away."

"Be wary of what lies in the unnatural. Their mi isn't right. The pips are bad enough but small. A large creature with bad mi can taint the mixing and destroy the trainer's mind."

"I'll bring you with to make sure it's good."

To'va chuckled. "It's not me you have to worry about. Now, get out and let me go about my business. You have plenty to do."

Kita made a disapproving face as To'va escorted Dominica around the pond. "Well, let's go see about putting a princess out of business."

"First, we need to train," said Apocalypse. "We're no good in our current condition."

"A week or ten days should be adequate," said Velositi.

Kita nodded. "They're going to need at least that much time. Love, can you get To'va's attention?"

Apocalypse put her fingers in her mouth and whistled. Kita waved to the Prii as they turned around.

"We'll be back in two weeks," yelled Kita.

To'va waved Kita off, turned Dominica around, and led her into the forest.

"I hate her already," muttered Kita. "She reminds me of Megan."

"Who's Megan?" said Jynx.

"Your great, great grandmother."

"Why do you hate her?"

"Because of what she did to your sister Lina."

"What she do?"

"Chopped her up trying to discover the source of her electrical power."

"What could she do?"

"She could generate electricity and store it like a battery. Then take that charge and increase the voltage like a transformer, generating massive electrical storms and thunderbolts. When she was working in her office, she used to plug herself into the building to provide it power to cut costs."

"Wow," said Jynx. "I thought lightning bolts were cool."

"You can do it, too," said Kita with a smile.

"She can?" said Apocalypse sounding unsure.

"How?" said Jynx excitedly.

"I'll unlock it when you master your other abilities."

"Ah," Jynx exclaimed, looking dejected.

"You have to master the basics before you get the advanced."

"But I'm so far behind," whined Jynx.

"You've got two weeks to catch up."

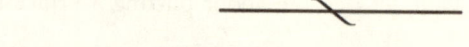

"Come on, Chels, you can do it!" yelled Apocalypse as the young Angel bounced on her feet with her fists up.

She punched, firing a lightning bolt at a water orb circling her a few yards away. The bolt hit the water, causing it to evaporate. Jynx dipped and dodged as more water balls on different orbits came at her. She let one go over the top of her before striking it with a fireball. The other balls increased in speed as they came at her. Jynx backflipped into a handspring and tumbled across the floor. As she went, she fired lightning bolts and fireballs, reducing her pursuers to puffs of steam. When she landed, she pulled up the sheet metal floor into a shield around her. She drew her sword and heated it white-hot as the water balls flew in over the shield. With a deadly flourish, she cut through the balls in rapid succession. What she didn't see was the fireball sneaking in from behind.

Kita shaped the ball into a pointed finger and playfully tussled Jynx's pigtail. The young Angel spun around and looked up. The fiery hand waved playfully. Jynx frowned.

"The enemy always comes where and when you least expect them," said Kita. "You closed your vision trying to concentrate. You need to keep it open and react on instinct. But that's an advanced lesson. Good job, kiddo. You've improved a lot over the last week."

They all had, including Kita. She felt she was in good enough shape after practicing with Jynx and Velositi that she wouldn't have any more poor showings like against the Grochar. Jynx had rebounded quickly. Kita didn't think she was up to the level she was before, but her muscle memory came back quickly. She just needed practice to bring up her reaction time.

"Excellent performance," said Velositi. "Soon, you will rival Kita."

Jynx sighed, frustrated. "I'll never be as good as Momma."

Apocalypse patted the bench next to her inviting her daughter to sit. When she did, Apocalypse put her arm around her. "Momma has eons of experience. You're only twelve. Do you think you were this good at twelve, angel?"

Kita chuckled. "No. I didn't start doing tumbling and advanced techniques until after Sarah."

"Who was she?" Jynx asked, lifting her head from Apocalypse's bear shoulder.

Kita fidgeted with her sports bra strap. The three Human Angels were all wearing color-coordinating sports bras and leggings. "Sarah...was my first broken heart. She taught me the basics of being an assassin. Then when I became a Legion commander, she took a contract for my head, and I took hers instead. Turns out I loved her, but she never loved me. I was just a game to her."

"Oh, Momma," said Jynx sympathetically as she slid off the bench and gave Kita a hug.

Kita hugged her daughter. "The lesson is, love is a dangerous game."

"But a few years of joy is worth a lifetime of pain," said Apocalypse.

Is it? Maybe that's why I always have a lover. I never have to feel the pain of those who have gone.

"Who was your first, Mom?" Jynx asked.

Apocalypse blushed. "Your momma. I had been with several other people, but your momma was my first love."

"Are you looking for your first love?" Velositi asked Jynx.

"No. But I am hungry. Can we eat now, Mom?"

Apocalypse looked at Kita.

"Sure. I have a list of Verisom restaurants for us to visit."

Apocalypse raised an eyebrow. "They wouldn't be owned by a certain Verisom princess, would they?"

"I've been working on a way to put her out of business. Let's go get changed, and I'll explain."

"Wait!" said Jynx.

"What?" said Apocalypse, surprised and worried.

"I want to ride the dragon."

Apocalypse rolled her eyes. "I thought you were hungry?"

"I am, but I want to ride the mom dragon."

"There's not enough room in here, Jynxie," said Kita coming to Apocalypse's rescue.

"But if we do it outside, Kele will get mad."

Kita stroked her hair. "How about we fly to the restaurant. If your mom feels like it, she'll give you a ride."

"Please, Mom? Please?"

"Let's see how traffic from the embassy to the restaurant is."

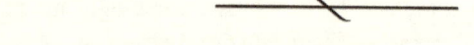

"Momma, is this food?" asked Jynx as she looked over the menu lacking pictures and descriptions.

Kita looked at the names of the dishes and shrugged. "I don't know." She could read Verisom, but it didn't help much when the dish names were made up. As a vegan, Kita didn't mind the vegetable and leafy green diet of the Verisom, but this was a next level she wasn't prepared for. The menu lacked prices, which also made her suspicious.

Looking around at what the other patrons were eating didn't make her feel better. Small servings of plants she didn't recognize wasn't helping her appetite. They could eat at all five of Princess Okra's restaurants and still be hungry. Which was the plan, but now she was rethinking that. She didn't want to deal with a hungry teenager all afternoon.

Kita put the menu down and stood.

"Where are you going?" said Velositi, tearing herself away from watching a glittering Verisom princess walk by. She seemed to be taken by the long ears, fluffy tails, and big feet of the Verisom princesses sitting around. Most were dressed in brightly-colored gaudy sarongs and more jewelry than Kita had ever owned.

"The lady's room."

"What?" exclaimed Apocalypse.

"Don't worry. I'll be back. Keep trying to figure out the menu."

Apocalypse thumped the piece of thick, stiff-backed electronic paper down. "Their writing looks worse than Chelsea's five-year-old scribbles. Whatever you're doing, I'm coming with you."

"What do I do?" exclaimed Jynx.

"Both of you extend your barbs," said Kita.

Apocalypse and Jynx held out their hands and extended the hypodermic needle-like organ from the heels of their hands.

Kita extended hers and touched the tip to theirs. "I'll tell you what this is later. Right now, manufacture this and do your best to deposit it on the other tables. Your mom and I are going to the kitchen. Velositi, keep an eye on her."

"Huh? Oh, of course. 'Tis a shame what you're about to do all these beautiful people."

Kita rolled her eyes. "Remind me to tell you about how bad a Verisom princess can be."

"I am sure you were a gorgeous couple."

"That's one word for it. Come on, love. Let's go see how the food is prepared."

Kita and Apocalypse weaved around the tables with bright, tie-dye table cloths and wicker chairs with matching brightly-colored cushions. The walls were decorated with murals and moving pictures of the beaches of Verisom. Plants from the planet were arranged neatly in pots, and terrariums held multi-winged birds. Kita followed the male Verisom waiters as they made their way to and from the kitchen.

Pushing through the stainless-steel door, the Angels entered the controlled chaos of the kitchen. Verisom males worked at tables chopping, cutting, and slicing up different vegetables and passing them onto more males to be dressed, arranged, and plated.

"*You go right, I'll go left,*" Kita instructed Apocalypse. "*Try and get that virus onto as many surfaces as you can.*"

Apocalypse turned and maneuvered through the kitchen staff toward the prep tables. She dragged her barbs on all the surfaces she could touch.

Kita went around to the stoves where different pots of various soups simmered. She touched her barb to the stove tops, prep surfaces, and bent down to deposit some on the hard yellow tile floor. As Kita stood up, she was face to face with a black and white Verisom male chef. His narrow red eyes and twitching nose told Kita he was upset.

"Sorry," said Kita. "I slipped looking for the little girl bunny's room."

"Hey! Quit shoving. I'm leaving," cried Apocalypse.

"Touch me, and you'll be leaving feet first," warned Kita.

The chef either didn't understand her warning or care as he reached out and tried to push Kita. She grabbed the small, fuzzy white hand with claws on the fingertips and flipped the seven-foot bunny over her, landing him on his fluffy white tail. Kita punched the chef in the back of the neck, and he collapsed.

"I warned you," Kita said as she stepped over him to go catch up with Apocalypse.

Kita pushed through the kitchen door to find an angry restaurant manager chastising Apocalypse. *She must be way down on the Verisom princess list if she's working in a restaurant.* As Kita approached the pair, a Verisom male pushed her aside and hopped up to the manager. She tried to ignore him, but he said something in male Verisomese that made her abandon Apocalypse and rush past Kita to the kitchen.

With a smile, Kita went to Apocalypse and pulled her away by her arm. "Time to go," she cooed.

As Kita and Apocalypse entered the dining room, Jynx was busy agitating a trio of Verisom princesses.

"Jynxie," Kita called, "time to go!"

The young Angel said something to the Verisom as she waved her hand over their food. She flew over several tables, her hands spread, as she caught up to her parents.

"Good job, Chels," said Kita. "In an hour, everyone in this place will be sick."

"Angel, we have a problem," said Apocalypse as she pointed toward the exit.

A pair of Tet-Sec officers with their weapons drawn were

coming through the door. The manager ran past the Angels, yelling for the officers to follow her to the kitchen.

Kita stepped aside and let them go. When they were gone, she waved to Velositi, and the Angels left. Out on the promenade, an ambulance landed, and a trio of paramedics rushed past into the restaurant.

"What did you do?" said Velositi.

"I told the chef not to touch me," replied Kita. "He did, and I planted him for it."

"And that requires an ambulance?"

"I might have knocked him out."

"Where now?" said Apocalypse as another Tet-Sec cruiser came into land.

"On to restaurant two," said Kita.

"So, what have I been spraying in people's food?" said Jynx.

"Just a stomach virus I made. Most chemical cleaners won't kill it, so it'll linger in these restaurants for months. I plan to call Tet-Health and the media when we get back."

"Devious," said Velositi. "I thought you were going to bomb them all."

Kita chuckled. "I thought about it, but that wouldn't put them out of business for long. After this virus is done, no one will want to eat at Princess Okra's restaurants."

"How are you planning on making her forget about the ultraviolet forest?" said Apocalypse.

Kita flicked her tongue. "Still working on that. She makes enough to live in HighCity. We just have to figure out how to get at her."

———————⟨———————

KITA AND THE ANGELS LANDED IN FRONT OF THEIR EMBASSY after sickening the other restaurants. A pair of Tet-Sec cruisers sat blocking the promenade and the flagstone stairs to the embassy door.

"I wonder what's up," said Apocalypse.

"Could it be the bunny chef?" said Velositi.

"I guess we'll have to go in and find out," said Kita as she bounded up the stone steps to the glass doors.

The Angels entered the embassy and found Administrator Kele talking to four Tet-Sec officers.

"Angel Kita," snapped Kele. "I've been calling you for two hours. Why haven't you answered?"

Kita made a show of revealing her Arcom. She'd been ignoring the dings and vibrations while they were at the other restaurants. "Huh, I must have forgotten to turn notifications back on. Sorry. Is there a problem?"

"Witnesses say you assaulted and killed a Verisom in his workplace—Harvest Moon. His warren princess is pressing charges and is suing for damages, lost earning potential, and the cost of replacement."

"Did I kill a citizen of the Tet, or did I break a piece of furniture? Anyway, I protest. He assaulted me first. I gave him fair warning that if he touched me, I'd send him out feet first. I considered his act aggressive and threatening—he is a seven-foot-tall Verisom male, and they're aggressive by nature. Any Angel, by law, has the right to defend herself and take whatever action is required to assure her safety. I will not have any of my Angels bullied, assaulted, raped, or killed. We wandered into the kitchen by mistake. All they had to do was ask us to leave. Instead, they laid hands on Apocalypse and me first. I have proof."

Kita opened her hand, and her holographic display replayed the scene in the kitchen.

"The tap in the back of the head was to stun only. It was not strong enough to kill."

Kele frowned. "Verisom males have weak necks."

Kita shrugged. She'd only fought Verisom males in space armor, which made them walking tanks.

Kele turned to the Tet-Sec officers. "We haven't had time to discuss Angel law and how it fits with Tet rules and regulations."

"The Tet rules and regulations trump homeworld laws," said a Tec-Sec Zentonian officer.

"We don't have a homeworld and what I say is law," replied Kita. "My Angels are only subject to it."

"You can argue it to the magistrate," said another Tec-Sec Aurorian officer. "For now, you're coming with us to detention."

Kita snarled as she threw open her wings; her fury made them burst into a raging inferno. "I answer to no one," she thundered.

Behind her, the other Angels reacted by extending their wings and charging their weapons and abilities.

"You don't have an army big enough to hold us," snarled Kita.

"Ok, that's enough," yelled Kele as she jumped between the two sides. The Tet-Sec officers didn't look like they knew what to do with the Angels' naked show of aggression. Only militaries, Tet-Sec, and crime syndicates had powered weapons on the station. The most Tet-Sec saw from the general population were personal weapons—claws, horns, hoofs, and teeth. They were illegal to use, but that didn't stop the inebriated, desperate, or stupid.

"It's obvious this is a sensitive issue for the Angels, and a misunderstanding has occurred. Before you take Angel Kita to detention, let me contact the Grand Ambassador to see if an arrangement can be brokered. Until then, Angel Kita will remain in the embassy under house arrest. The other Angels can go as they please."

From the quartet of Tet-Sec officers, Kita could feel the anger and unhappiness coming from the Verisom and Djinn males. The Zentonian was disgusted, but the Aurorian was agreeable.

The Verisom male's translator erupted in a shrill as he protested, "The creature has broken the law by killing a warrened male and must answer for its crimes. His princess has lost face, and her reputation and honor must be restored. The creature should lose one of its own."

"You touch them, and I will destroy every Verisom on the Tet," retorted Kita in a low hiss.

The rainbow of scales on Kele's head, shoulders, and back

rippled in alarm. Kita felt her doubt mixed with dreaded certainty.

"Officer, stand down," ordered Kele. "That is not your place to decide. Officer Nu'lu," she waved the Aurorian officer to her. They put their heads together and spoke softly in Aurori.

Kita bet Kele thought the Angel didn't know their language. Instead, she eavesdropped casually, curious to hear what Kele's plan was.

"Abr'na, I need you to control the Verisom. Send him away if you have to. I will contact Grand Ambassador Li'eam and tell her what has happened. The Grand Ambassador and I believe The Angels are very important, and I will broker a solution with Angel Kita. I need you to observe and protect the Angels. Angel Kita is to remain here, but do not try and stop her if she wishes to leave. The Angels are powerful and scared. We cannot let them leave the Tet. I believe they are a valuable friend to Aurori, but they will lash out like caged animals if confronted. If Angel Kita does leave, follow her and call me. They are a level eleven diplomatic situation, so I can provide immediate help from the diplomatic corp. If Angel Kita is involved in another incident and you are the only one available, talk to her, calm her, bargain with her if you must, then escort her clear until a diplomat of level ten arrives to take charge of her. Whatever the incident, we will bury it. Understood?"

"Yes, Master Ambassador. I will make sure she is protected. Instructions if she terminates anyone?"

"Escort her to safety and bring her to our embassy. I will deal with the fallout."

The younger Aurorian nodded, and Kele dismissed her.

I wonder what Kele sees in me that's worth so much effort and protection? We are powerful, but there are only four of us, not a significant threat to Aurori or any other race...unless they worry we're just the beginning. I do want my empire of Angels again, but not here. Well, I won't be one to turn down a 'get out of jail free' card.

The Aurorian officer returned to the Tet-Sec officers and issued her orders, including sending the Djinn and Verisom officers to the roof to ensure the Angels didn't fly away.

Kele turned to Kita. "I request that you stay in the embassy until I can contact the Grand Ambassador. She will want to talk to you. You are safe here, and these officers will make sure of it. If you have a problem, come get me in the communications office."

"Is there a comm panel I can use? I have a few calls I need to make."

"Your office has been furnished and the computer and communications installed. I can show you how to use it."

Kita waved her away. "I know how. Thank you. Send my best to Illia."

Kele gave her a hesitant smile.

Kita chuckled at making Kele uneasy. Illia wasn't the first Grand Ambassador Kita had known on a first-name basis. *I wonder what she'd think if I told her the last one had become an Angel assassin?*

"The others are free to go?" Kita asked Kele.

"Yes, but the Grand Ambassador may wish to speak with all of you about the incident. So please, if you leave, don't go far, bring a communicator, and answer it."

Kita shrugged at the pointed remark. "I'll be in the embassy." Kita turned to the other Angels, "Looks like we're in for a wait, but you're free to wonder Embassy Row, the market, or the gardens."

"Can we go to the gym?" said Jynx.

Kita looked at Kele. The Aurorian nodded.

"Sure, if your mom wants to go."

"I think I should stay and talk to Illia," said Apocalypse.

"I will take her," said Velositi.

Kita nodded and smiled, then looked at Kele. "Looks like we're all set. You can go call Illia. Kimmy and I will be in my office."

Kita took Apocalypse's hand and led her around the counter and down the back hallway.

Velositi looked at Jynx. "Go get changed, and I will meet you out front."

The young Angel nodded and flew after her parents, passing them as they reached Kita's office. "Bye, moms! Have fun. I'll see you in a couple hours!" She glided into the elevator, touched the screen, and the door closed.

Kita opened the door to her office as the breeze of Jynx passed them. "At least she's excited," chuckled Kita.

"I'm excited to," replied Apocalypse with a wink.

Kita wasn't sure what that was about, but she felt that her partner was excited, optimistic, and loving. The room didn't offer much, a few chairs, a desk with a computer and comm panel, and a panel on the wall that showed rotating images of the Tet. Kita sighed at the black chair behind the desk. It was a low-backed ergonomic design suited for many races.

As the door closed, Kita walked toward the desk until Apocalypse hugged her warmly from behind. The other Angel squeezed Kita tight as she brushed back Kita's hood, exposing her neck, ears, and cheeks.

Apocalypse kissed Kita's cheeks and left a soft trail to her ear. There, she nibbled on the lobe and caressed it with her tongue. Moving to the spot behind Kita's ear, just in the hairline, she kissed and massaged it with her tongue.

A shiver went up Kita's spine and wings, making her hair and feathers stand up. It had been a long time since she'd gotten this kind of attention and her pussy tingled as she became wet.

"Ah...Wow..." said Kita feeling out of breath. "What brings this on?" She felt stupid for asking, knowing she should just run with it and ask questions later.

Apocalypse purred, "We have no kid...time alone...I thought we could use some quality time together. And I really missed how you taste."

Kita's mouth salivated at the idea of Apocalypse's pussy under her tongue. "Mmm, I like the idea, but can I make my calls real quick?"

Apocalypse cocked her head as she dropped her hands down around Kita's waist and tugged her bottoms down a few inches. "Fine, but I get to torture you while you make them."

Kita gulped, knowing that was a bad idea. "I don't think they want to listen to me scream."

"I do," Apocalypse whispered.

"Give me ten minutes, and I'll scream all you want."

Apocalypse let out a frustrated grunt as she released Kita and stomped to the far side of the room. "How come I have to wait? I've been waiting four years while you've been out whoring around your galaxies. I've let it slide because I know it's not really you...but I know you remember all those other girls!" she yelled.

Kita's eyebrows and hands shot up. "There hasn't been anybody but you. I haven't had a relationship with anybody while Human or Angel. Only Velositi, but I haven't had sex with her either. I've been waiting for you."

Apocalypse's frown receded. "You're not lying."

"All I want is you," whispered Kita. "And I'll wait forever if I have to."

"Then why haven't you jumped me the first chance you had?"

Kita looked sideways. "I thought you were just playing with Velositi and me, and you just want me to be a better parent to Chelsea."

"Is that what you think? Is that what I give off?"

Kita could only answer with a shrug.

"I love you, Kita. You're the only one I want to be with. I'm sorry for the last four years—"

Kita held up a hand. "I know you do. Don't be sorry. Chelsea needed a mom, and you were a great one—"

"And a terrible partner to you."

"I was no better. I didn't fight for us. I just let go and hid with Velositi."

Tears trickled from Apocalypse's eyes. "What are we going to do?"

"Chelsea's old enough. She doesn't need us always. That gives us more time for us. If that's what you want."

"Of course that's what I want!" yelled Apocalypse through her tears. "I want you. That's why I agreed to become god, so I could be with you. Then, now, and forever."

Kita glided across the room and put her arms around Apocalypse. "I just want you. I love you, and that will never change."

"How do we make us right?" said Apocalypse.

"Doing this together is a good start. I miss working with you. I'm sure we can find time to go on a few dates. The Tet has some beautiful spots. Embassy Row at night is spectacular."

"So was the ultraviolet forest."

"We're going back. I'll take some holograms."

"Are there any better places to eat? I could use some fries and a burger."

Kita chuckled. "There are some Human restaurants that have a wide selection. I know of some good ones. Anything else?"

"My sleep cycle is coming up, and I expect you to be there."

"No problem. Can you wear those cute little shorts that show off your butt?"

"I haven't had those since Eight-Thirty-two. We'll have to go shopping."

"Sounds like a date."

"Let's start our date now and make those calls. Who are we calling?"

"Tet-Health and TMG media, to report the viral outbreak, and MNN. They're an anti-Verisom outlet that will want to know about the assault and virus."

Apocalypse smiled devilishly. "I still want to lick your pussy while you do it."

"Maybe we should get that out of the way first."

"You expect me to be able to think afterward? Remember, it's been four years. I've been waiting forever to feel you inside me," purred Apocalypse as she guided Kita's hand between her legs.

"Ten minutes," Kita replied weakly.

"Fine, but you better hope these walls are soundproof."

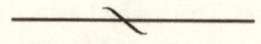

KITA SAT LEANING IN THE CORNER OF HER OFFICE, NAKED, cuddling Apocalypse. She thought about getting up, but her legs were numb and her head spinning. She didn't think she could get Apocalypse to move anyway. The Angel's head was pressed against her breast and an arm firmly around her. She seemed to be somewhere between bliss and sleep, and Kita didn't want to interrupt that.

Instead, Kita sent a trojan horse message to Princess Okra, offering to sell the Verisom a large quantity of comet ice preserved in stasis. It was a luxury item, with no commercial value, beyond what was turned into jewelry. Verisom and Djinn looking to climb in society took immediate interest, but the ice was not so rare as to be monitored by Tet-Sec. Kita used the ruse before and had verified lot numbers of the stasis machines, the name of the ship that collected the samples, and the date. It all came from her personal collection.

When the princess opened the message, it would deposit a virus on her home network, letting Kita override the system. So far, no anti-virus software had detected Kita's virus disguised as an addition to the home security system. All Kita had to do was wait for it to notify her of its installation.

When she did receive the notification, she had a worm virus ready to eat its way through Princess Okra's data and remove all traces of the ultraviolet forest. The worm would check the operating system for off-site backups and other data redundancies. Kita doubted Okra would be that trusting. People like her didn't want their secrets discovered and were paranoid about sharing their data with outsiders—even private data security firms that encrypted the information.

One person's paranoia is another's opportunity—so says the professional paranoid. Kita chuckled to herself as there was a knock on the door. She ignored it, even after it became persistent, not wanting to wake Apocalypse.

The door slid open, and Kele stepped in. She saw the Angels and gasped, dropping the pad she was carrying.

"I'm—"

Kita put a finger to her lips and made a shushing sound. "She's sleeping. What do you want?" Kita hissed in a whisper.

Kele bent down and collected her pad. "Grand Ambassador Li'eam wants to talk to you," she replied in a whisper.

"I'll talk to her later. I'm busy."

"I can't keep the Grand Ambassador waiting. She's taken time out of her busy schedule to help you."

Kita glanced at her clothes draped over the computer on the desk, then at the top of Apocalypse's head. She shrugged about the clothes and kissed the Angel's dark hair. Her mind temporarily drifted to the day she had to walk across her parent's castle in a towel. *Mother said there would be days when I would have to carry on naked. I wonder what she would think of me now?*

Kita waved the Aurorian to her. Kele knelt next to Kita, looking unsure as she handed the pad over. The Aurorian kept glancing at Kita's naked body.

"What?" Kita snapped. "My boobs aren't as big as yours, so what?" Kita winked at her. She knew the Aurorians were almost as promiscuous as the Verisom.

"You're going to talk to the Grand Ambassador like this?"

"Why not? I may not be as perfect as you, but I'm damn close."

From the look on her face and feelings Kele gave off, she disagreed. And Kita agreed with her. She was perfect, better than any Aurorian.

"Hit the button," whispered Kita.

Kele reached around and pushed the button to take the call off hold.

Kita held the pad up, trying to just get her face in the preview box. A second later, Grand Ambassador Li'eam appeared. Kita smiled warmly, "Illia, how nice of you to call. I hope I haven't kept you waiting."

"Angel Kita, always a pleasure. I understand you've had a bit of a cultural misunderstanding. The Verisom Princess Mulberry is distraught at the loss of her male—"

"The Verisom males in the kitchen were already assaulting Angel Apocalypse. She is more forgiving than I am. I warned him, and he ignored me. The blow to the back of the head wasn't intended to kill, just stun. It's not my fault they're evolutionarily inferior."

The Grand Ambassador kept a smile on her face. "If you wish to be a member of Tet society, we must work out compromises. The Tet has many people on it, and being inadvertently touched is common—"

"This was not inadvertently," hissed Kita. "It was deliberate, intentional, and threatening. We entered the kitchen by mistake. All they had to do was ask us to leave, and we would have. They are the ones at fault, not us. The Verisom male's death is on their hands, not ours."

"I understand your position, Angel Kita. But that doesn't excuse the death of a Tet citizen, even if it was a mistake. Now, Princess Mulberry, the male's warren leader, is demanding punitive damages, compensation for the male and the lost productivity. She is also requesting that you appear before a magistrate and be punished for your crime."

Kita rolled her eyes. "Sounds like it's already been decided. Well, you're welcome to try and bring me in, but you'll just be adding more bodies to the count."

Next to Kita, Kele flinched. *That's right. I'm not afraid to cut my way out of here.*

"Illia," said Apocalypse.

Kita looked down at her chest as Apocalypse lifted her head.

"Kimberly, I didn't know you were listening in."

"Sleeping, actually. My sleep cycle is about to start. I want to avoid making this incident worse, but it seems Princess Mulberry does not wish to resolve this matter amicably or see it as a mistake. If she wishes to pursue this course, I demand charges be pressed against the Verisom males who assaulted Angel Kita and me. I will sue for emotional distress, personal violation of my private person, and the cost to preen and clean my feathers. I will also demand an apology for both Angel Kita and myself for their treatment of us. On Kita's behalf, I demand an apology for the Verisom's assault on her and that she be compensated for the personal violation and emotional distress. The Verisom are in the wrong, not us."

The smile didn't disappear from Illia's face, but the ripple of scales around her head said her job just became harder. "Tet rules and regulations do not permit these kinds of suits to be brought forward, even if they are permitted by Angel Law—"

"So, what," snarled Kita. "We are to be held subject to your law, but you not to ours? If Princess Mulberry wants me, tell her to bring all her males, and I will meet her at Embassy Row Park. We'll settle this the old-fashioned way."

Illia's eyes flicked to Apocalypse. "I will help her, and so will the other Angels. Princess Mulberry had a chance to accept our apology and even our offer to pay, but no more. If she wants it, she's going to have to fight—and not in a court of law. She has now tarnished the honor of the Angels, and only blood can remove the stain."

Kita looked between Kele and Illia. The younger Aurorian's golden luster in her face was gone. Illia was tightlipped as all her scales lay flat against her head. Kita tossed the pad back to Kele and helped Apocalypse to her feet. The Angels collected their clothes and kit and walked to the door.

"Where—where are you going?" stammered Kele.

Kita looked at her and cocked her head. "To prepare for battle." Kita pulled her sword, Buried, from its sheath. "You're about to find out how big a mistake it is letting me keep this."

Kele looked at Apocalypse holding one of her tomahawks. "You're—you're serious. You'll fight an entire Verisom warren?"

"We will kill an entire Verisom warren," she replied as she juggled the throwing ax.

Kita opened the door and, with Apocalypse, walked to the elevator to their room.

"I can't believe they think we're serious," cooed Apocalypse after the door closed.

"We're not?"

"We're only serious as long as it keeps them off balance and worried what we'll do. If this Mulberry is dumb enough to march her males on us, then we'll prove our resolve and slaughter them all."

Kita nodded. It had been a while since she'd killed on that scale—and she missed it. *I must be getting soft in my old age.*

As the Angels entered their room to shower and dress, Kita received a message from her virus. Okra had opened the comet ice invitation message, and the virus installed itself. It had mapped Okra's home network and was ready for the worm.

Kita sent it and jumped when Apocalypse touched her bare shoulder.

"Hey, angel, I'm going to crash. Suddenly I'm exhausted. Cuddle me for a bit?"

"Sure. I just got word from my invitation. Okra's taken the bait."

"You don't need me for that, do you?"

"No, but I'll take Chelsea. She could use a real-world mission."

"You're not going to train her to be an assassin, are you?"

Kita shrugged. She hadn't thought about it. Most of her daughters she had not—only Kamikaze had shown interest. Quill and Spike had gotten some. "It'll be her choice if she wants to. Until then, I'm going to teach her life skills, abilities, and weapons training."

Apocalypse dumped her clothes in the cleaner. "That's good. Let her find her own way." She pushed back the comforter and slipped into bed.

Kita put her clothes on the table, climbed in next to Apocalypse, and put her arm around her.

"Lock the door when you leave," said Apocalypse. "Love you, angel."

Kita nuzzled Apocalypse's dark, wavy hair and hugged her tight, enjoying her partner's cool skin against hers.

TWO DIMENSIONLESS CLOUDS DRIFTED THROUGH THE panoramic glass of the high-rise apartment in HighCity. They floated through the living area, passed the wicker furnishings with oversized cushions, and the various statues and art from around the galaxy that Verisom princesses loved to collect. The large black cloud dissolved, swirling into Kita wearing her assassin kit and mask. The other cloud was Angel shaped and a mix of white and black. The hybrid cloud collapsed into Jynx wearing a black sneak suit.

"Check the camera feed and make sure they're still on loop," Kita instructed Jynx.

"*Shouldn't I have done that before we came?*" she asked.

Kita's smile was hidden by her mask. "*I did. I wanted to make sure you were thinking stealthily.*"

"*They're good. Okra is still in her bed. The active security measures are off. The automatic alarm has been rerouted to you.*"

"*Good. You're learning fast.*"

Kita led her daughter through the apartment, down a bright yellow and blue hallway toward the master bedroom.

"*Momma?*" Jynx said, sounding uneasy.

"*What is it, Jynxie?*" Kita replied, trying to be upbeat and positive.

"*Are—are you and mom ok?*"

Kita chuckled—one, that kids were so perceptive, and two, her daughter had the Angelic trait of bringing up issues during stressful and dangerous situations. Some non-Angels said the Angels did it because they were indestructible, and Angels didn't care about what danger it put them in. Kita liked to think stressful and dangerous situations lowered walls and brought things that could affect the mission into sharp relief.

"*We're doing good, sweetheart. It's been a rough couple of years. Your mom and I have had different priorities, but we've recognized this and are working to rectify it.*"

"*It was me, wasn't it?*"

"*No,*" said Kita firmly. "*It was a difference in opinion on how to raise you. Neither of us was wrong, but you're my seventh daughter and mom's first.*"

"*She wasn't happy with you after Europe. That's why she stopped my training.*"

"*Your mom felt you needed more attention and direction besides what I was teaching you. And she was right. You needed a chance to just have fun and be a kid. She taught you well, and I'm proud of her. You're a brilliant kid.*"

"*But I liked training with you. I want to be an Angel like the others and be part of the team. I feel like I'm so far behind. That I could be so much better.*"

"*You're doing superb, Jynxie. I wouldn't have brought you tonight if I didn't think you couldn't handle it. Don't worry, you're not behind. Education is more important than the sword. When I was younger, I*" *mastered the sword, but I was nothing until I mastered knowledge and learned to apply it. You're well on your way to mastering knowledge, and that is true power. The rest will come."*

"Mom kept telling me knowledge is power."

"She's right. Your brain will get you out of more situations than your sword will."

"So, you and mom are going to be ok? I was afraid you were going to break up over me."

"Never. We love you and—"

"I don't want to be the reason you stay together, either."

"Chelsea, your mom and I did go through a rough patch, but that happens to all couples. Your mom and I had different priorities that we didn't communicate well to each other. It was a mistake, but we've recognized it, talked about it, and are fixing it. Your mom and I are going to spend more time together, which will give you more independence to grow and explore."

"What if I want to spend more time with both of you? Mom spent a lot of time with me, and so did you, but this is the first time we've done anything as a family. I'm always with one of you, but not both."

That caught Kita off-guard. She thought she'd been there enough for Jynx. The lack of family cohesion never crossed Kita's mind.

"That's my fault. I was busy training the triplets with Velositi and trying to get the universe computer stabilized. I didn't realize my absence had such an effect on you. I'm sorry, but I promise we'll do more as a family."

"Can we explore more Earths? This place is cool, and I like being here with you and mom. I just want you girls to be ok and happy."

Kita's cheeks flushed. *"Your mom makes me happy. She always has and always will. But I promise we've talked and worked out a solution. We've got some healing to do, and that includes you. She and I need to reconnect, and we as a family have to as well. I'm glad you told me and didn't bottle it up and try and act like everything was fine."*

"It wasn't fine, Momma. I was lonely, and I thought you didn't want me anymore. Sprokkit said once I reached a certain age, you'd take interest in me. Am I old enough now?"

Kita's stomach knotted so hard she wished Sprokkit had

punched her. She couldn't blame the Morphicon; she had told him that—in jest.

"*Jynxie, it's not like that. I told Sprokkit that because that's how noble kids in Yorq were raised. Nannies took care of us all day, and we only saw our parents at dinner and special events. When we turned twelve, we became tiny adults and joined our parents. Boys learned to be knights and govern. Girls learned to run a house, sew, cook, art, boring stuff like that. I was lucky that my mother wanted me to learn to tumble and swing a sword. She came to my practices and encouraged me. I told Sprokkit I wouldn't raise you that way. I'm sorry I left, it was a mistake and a misunderstanding between your mom and me. You deserve better. And I promise to be better and be the mother you need. Your mom agrees with me. She said what she did was a mistake. We're going to fix it and be a family again. Does that sound good?*"

Jynx wrinkled her nose and forehead. "*Promise you won't leave me?*"

"*I promise. I've got a lot to make up for, and we'll do anything you want.*"

"*Teach me to be an assassin?*"

Kita stuck her tongue in her cheek as she thought how best to answer that. "*Let's work on the fundamentals first—your sword, bow, and abilities. Once you've mastered those and you still want to learn, I'll teach you, but I promise it won't be easy.*"

"*But Leaf said she learned when she was a kid.*"

"*Different philosophies. I'm old school.*"

"*So, how old do I have to be?*"

"*Age has nothing to do with it. When you're ready, you will show me.*"

"*So, if I do good on this mission that'll be enough?*"

"*That'll be enough for me to teach you something cool. Don't rush. You have plenty of time. Now, how are you feeling?*" Kita could feel her daughter's trepidation, hope, and guilt. She hoped she'd said enough to ease the girl's fears, but they as a family needed to sit down and talk it out before Jynx would be totally satisfied.

"*I'm ok. Let's go. I want to kick some bunny butt.*"

Kita chuckled. "*We're here to erase her memory.*"

"*That's too good for her. Especially after what her goons did to you.*"

"*We'll get revenge. Don't worry. Come on.*"

Kita walked to the end of the hallway and touched the pad to open the door, but it flashed LOCKED in big red letters. *Paranoid.*

Kita knelt and looked at the panel. Getting it open without damaging it would take a while.

"*I'll get it,*" said Jynx. The young Angel ghosted—an ability Kita had only ever given to one other Angel, her eldest daughter Nina—and passed through the door. Kita had given it to Jynx in case something went wrong, and she had to escape. Instead, the young Angel ran around the embassy scaring Kele for hours.

The door opened, revealing Jynx looking triumphant.

"*Good girl. Saves us a lot of time.*"

They moved to the large bed and looked down at the sleeping Verisom. She was tucked under a thick comforter that matched the brightly colored pillows and sheets. On the headboard was a collection of stones and crystals.

Kita shook her head. The Humans could sell anything—including age-old Human beliefs that rocks carried magical properties. The other races—many with their own superstitions—bought into it. Somewhere there were some wealthy rock collectors. *I wonder what she believes these rocks do for her?*

"*Ok, Chels, pull back the covers slightly and inject her with the stimulant and the hypno-suggestive drug I gave you.*"

Jynx leaned forward and tugged at the Verisom's comforter, pulling it down enough to expose Okra's neck and shoulder. Placing the heel of her hand on the sleeping Verisom's neck, Jynx extended her barb under Okra's skin.

Okra jerked and tried to sit up. Kita flashed forward to pin her down, but Jynx pushed hard with her hand, forcing Okra down as she finished the ejection.

"*Hold her until her ears go slack,*" instructed Kita. "*Good job catching her.*"

Jynx sent Kita a picture of a smiley face. When the Verisom's white and black two-foot-ears drooped, Jynx let go.

"Stand up," the young Angel commanded.

The Angels stepped back and let the Verisom climb out of bed. She stood before them naked; her soft, dense white fur with big black spots on her thighs and stomach were matted from sleeping. The black ruff on her chest was larger than any Kita had ever seen. *I see some of us won the endowment lottery...not that I want bigger boobs.*

"*Ok, Chels, I'll take it from here.*" Kita stood up and waved a hand in front of Okra's face. Her big red eyes followed Kita's hand as she chattered her big buck teeth. "Princess Okra, this is a dream, but what I say you will remember when you wake. What I say is the truth. Anyone who says differently is wrong. No matter what anyone else says or proof they show, you are right, and they are wrong. Do you understand?"

Okra nodded slowly. "Y—yes."

"You will forget any knowledge of the ultraviolet forests under the Tet. They do not exist. The last of these forests were destroyed by the Verisom. If you find evidence of these forests' existence on a Verisom computer or database, you will destroy the evidence. Anyone who has knowledge or evidence of the ultraviolet forests is wrong. If they have evidence, you will acquire it and destroy it. You have never been to the ultraviolet forests and never tasted the food that grows there. If any Verisom try to go to an ultraviolet forest, you will stop them. The ultraviolet forests do not exist, and you will stop any Verisom who tries to find them. Do you understand?"

Okra looked at Kita blankly, her eyes glazed over. "Yes. The ultraviolet forests do not exist. I will stop any Verisom who tries to find them. I will destroy all Verisom knowledge of the ultraviolet forests. Anyone who has knowledge of the forests is wrong."

"Good," said Kita. "You can—"

"Wait," hissed Jynx.

Kita looked down at her daughter, surprised.

Jynx pushed Kita's wing aside and stood in front of Okra. "Come here," she ordered, waving the Verisom to her.

Okra bent over, lowering her big round head to be level with Jynx.

"You're to leave my moms alone," she said forcefully.

"*You have to mention us by name,*" interjected Kita, impressed with her daughter's initiative. Kita hadn't thought of it.

"You're to leave Angel Kita, Angel Apocalypse, Angel Jynx, and Angel Velositi alone. What happened in your restaurant's kitchen was an accident caused by your male. It's his fault, and you will pay the Angels for the embarrassment and for picking on them. You will drop all charges against Angel Kita and Angel Apocalypse. They did nothing wrong. Do you understand?"

Okra cocked her head. Her eyes blinked several times, revealing black eyelids. She chattered her teeth angrily as her ears stood up. "Who...What..."

Kita shoved Jynx out of the way and punched the woozy Verisom between the eyes, causing them to roll up in her head. Kita caught Okra as she collapsed.

"Jynxie, get the covers. I'll get her in bed," said Kita as she picked up Okra and waited for Jynx.

Once the comforter was pulled back, Kita laid Okra on the silk sheets and tucked her in.

"*What happened?*" cried Jynx as she looked up at Kita, fear in her eyes.

"*It's ok,*" assured Kita. "*The dose you gave her wore off. But she'll be asleep for a while and will wake up with a massive headache.*"

Jynx's eyes frowned. "*I didn't give her enough?*"

"*Don't worry. Dosing is a tricky thing...body weight, race. You're still learning, and Verisom have fast heart rates. What you think is proper can wear off fast.*"

"*If I hadn't told her—Do we have to do it again?*"

"*No. What I told her held, not sure if what you said will last, but thanks for trying. It's sweet of you.*"

"*I don't want you and Mom to get in trouble.*"

Kita hugged Jynx. "*Don't worry. We're not in any trouble we can't get out of.*"

"*You did kill a seven-foot-tall rabbit.*"

Kita rolled her eyes. *"I've killed way more than one...Come on. Let's get out of here."*

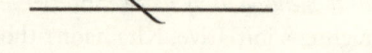

"HEY, MOM! HOW'D YOU SLEEP?" CALLED JYNX AS SHE FLEW from the elevator to the small kitchenette and dining area on the second floor of the Angel's embassy.

Kita followed her daughter in time to see her hug Apocalypse sitting at the breakfast bar. Her partner was dressed with her hood down, drinking a cup of something.

"Hi, Chels. I slept well. That bed's not as comfy as the one at home. If we stay here a while, we might have to invest in some better furniture." She looked over Jynx at Kita.

"I don't plan on being here that long."

Apocalypse nodded. "How was your mission, successful?"

Jynx scowled. "I think I screwed it up."

"Oh no, what happened?"

"Okra woke up when I was trying to tell her to leave you and Momma alone."

Apocalypse raised an eyebrow at Kita.

"The bit about the ultraviolet forest stuck. I'm not sure about what Jynx told her. It's my mistake. I didn't tell her how much of a dose to give a Verisom. I'm not worried about it."

"But I don't want you and Mom in trouble," protested Jynx.

"Your mom is not in trouble," assured Kita. "It's just me, and they can't do anything other than pester me."

"What if they throw you in jail?"

Kita chuckled. "And how long do you think they'll keep you from me? You'll have me out in no time."

Jynx giggled and shook her head, making her pink pigtails bob. "I couldn't get you out, but Mom and Velositi will turn into dragons and bust you out."

Apocalypse smiled. "She is excited. I'm pretty sure Momma will be out before I can file a formal protest. I've heard stories from Leaf that Momma is quite the jailbreaker."

"They've tried a few times and never succeeded," clucked Kita. "Where's Velositi?"

"She is out looking at people. If you need her, she said to call."

Kita shook her head. "No. I thought we should go do something fun since we have a few days before we're supposed to meet Dominica and To'va."

"Oh, that sounds good. We could have a regular family day."

"That's what I was thinking, but first, we need to explain to Chelsea what happened, why, and our plans for the future as a family, for her, and for us."

Apocalypse put her drink down on the bar. Kita could feel her hesitation and guilt and knew Jynx could too.

"It's ok, Mom. I'm not mad or nothing. I mean, I was, but Sprokkit told me when I was older it would be better."

Kita sighed. *Obviously, I didn't explain that well enough.*

"Oh, Chels," said Apocalypse with a worried smile, "That's not it at all. Your momma and I made several mistakes. After Europe, I realized I was not a good mother to you. Your momma had done all the hard lessons preparing you for a life and world I didn't want you to be part of. I wanted to keep you safe, and I became overprotective. I told your momma she wasn't allowed to train you or parent you. I drove her away, thinking I was protecting you. It wasn't until we got here that your momma and I talked, and we realized our mistakes. I don't know where Sprokkit got the age idea from, but that's not why we've been estranged for the last few years. But your momma and I have talked about it, and things are going to change. You can train, you can go on easy missions, you can go to approved areas by yourself, you can explore the universes with us—but your school work has to be maintained. Does that sound better?"

Jynx looked between her parents. "You and Momma aren't going to break up, are you? 'Cause you don't have to take me, or I won't go...I—I—"

Kita put an arm around Jynx as Apocalypse slid off her stool. They knelt before the young Angel.

"Chelsea," Apocalypse said in a gentle tone. "I love your momma. That never changed. We had a difference of opinion that led to a rough time between us. Those happen between long-term relationships. Neither of us was sure how to confront the other until we were forced to. We did have a fight, and I made your momma cry, and for that, I'm terribly sorry, but the argument made us realize our mistakes and that we needed to change. That change is not us splitting up but made us realize how much we missed each other. It brought us closer together and made us a family again.

"I realize you're old enough that I don't need to hold your hand and watch your every move. It's time for you to explore the world and learn to be part of it. I don't want you to be thrown into the deep end when you're eighteen like I was. Your momma has worked hard to ensure you have all the tools, skills, and abilities to handle whatever we encounter. I've worked hard to ensure you have the knowledge and wisdom to go with what your momma gave you. Now, it's time for you to go out and get the experience to become whatever you want.

"But I promise you, your momma and I are not splitting up. In fact, you'll probably see less of us around as we want to spend more time with each other. We're still a family, but I've missed your momma, and I know she's missed me. Do you understand?"

Jynx put her arms around her parents' necks, nodding and crying.

Kita rubbed her daughter's back. "It's ok, Jynxie. Everything is going to be fine. You've got nothing to worry about now."

Jynx nuzzled Apocalypse's neck. "Can we go flying some more? We never get to fly at home."

Apocalypse looked over at Kita.

"Of course. We can fly down Embassy Row and across the petal to The Edge."

"What's that?" said Jynx, looking up from Apocalypse.

"It's an amusement park by the edge of the petal. They have a roller coaster that goes out over the edge into space."

"That sounds cool."

"And later, I'll take you out into actual space."

"Really?"

"Anything you want."

———————————✕———————————

Kita closed and locked the door to the ultraviolet forest after examining it for tampering. From her examination, it didn't look like anyone had disturbed it or the forest.

"*Al'ice, we're here. How'd it go?*"

"*Oh, Hi, Kita. The animals said you were here. We're on the far side of the grove. We'll meet you at the waterfall.*"

Kita glanced around but didn't see any animals. Switching to her thermal sight, several warm lumps appeared in the grass and trees. *I thought she could only connect to one animal at a time, and they had to be close. I wonder what she's learned.*

Kita led the other Angels through the glowing ultraviolet forest to the waterfall. Around the pond were all kinds of pips and other animals among the glowing grass and flowers. Dominica and To'va stood atop the cliff next to the top of the waterfall. Dominica's overalls and cut-off shirt were gone, replaced by a purple triangular top and a skirt made of large palm-like leaves from a bush Kita had seen in the forest.

A creature with long legs and two tails ran up and pawed at Kita's leg. The Angel looked down, and it grinned at her, revealing long canines and sharp teeth. The ultraviolet spots on its black back and legs glowed.

"Hi, Kita," it said, coming out with a growl.

Kita looked up at Dominica. "Is that you, or can this thing talk?"

Dominica giggled as she glided down and landed next to the other Angels. "That's me. This is Spot. She's an ancestor of the wild carva from my homeworld."

"I thought you could only command pips."

To'va jumped off the cliff and landed on the water. She sauntered over, giving Kita an amused look. "How quick you are to think you know everything—I take it you're not that kind of god."

Kita raised an eyebrow. "I don't profess to know how the universe works, just what goes into creating one. What it does with it is why I'm here. I want to know what I've created."

"A female Prii can talk and control all manner of creatures. Without mi, they've been limited to mindless pips. Now that Dominica has connected with mi, she can connect to the creatures and forest of Uvra—our homeworld."

"What do male Prii do?" asked Jynx.

To'va rolled her eyes. "Carry things."

"Well, it appears Dominica has learned a lot," said Apocalypse.

To'va snorted. "She's learned more than a lot, but she's still only a tap root. But I've taught her all I can here. She needs to get out and apply what she's learned."

"That's what Momma's been telling me too," said Jynx.

To'va looked down her nose at Jynx. "For a youngling, you talk a lot."

"I might send them out together," mused Kita.

"You've been quiet. What have you been thinking about?" said To'va suspiciously.

"Looking over the Prii genetic code and seeing if I can expand who Dominica can control."

"Only creatures with mi."

"I'm not sure what mi is. I haven't detected anything special in the animals, plants, or Dominica. I have detected an unusual protein production in her small horns that other species are receptive to. I might be able to replicate this so she can talk to any creature or plant."

"She's not a plaything of the gods," huffed To'va.

Kita chuckled. "It's called science. But thank you for training her. I've sent out offers to other sponsored trainers for her first bout."

"Not so fast, bird-god. Her training's not done yet. She's barely scratched the surface."

"I thought you said she needed to apply what she's learned."

"I did, but that doesn't mean she's going it alone—unless you want to coach her."

Kita raised an eyebrow and crossed her arms. "So, you're coming with?"

"You got it, bird-god. Without a good coach, you might as well forget Grall."

Kita stroked her braid. "And what do I have to do to gain your services?"

"Kill Grall."

"What do you have against him?" asked Velositi.

To'va looked up at the Morphicon. "It speaks."

"She, actually. I am a Morphicon Angel. Your forest is beautiful. I have been admiring it and hope to get to explore it further."

"Sure, I give out tours to anyone who wanders in. Just don't touch anything." To'va looked at Kita. "Never seen a metal creature, neither have the trees. Where'd you find her?"

Kita chuckled. "Long story. But we've been together for a while. So why do you want Grall dead?"

"Besides being a worthless flea-infested sand-kicker? Once upon a time, I fought pips in the underground—pretty good at it, too. Grall was just a cub then—he was as much the arrogant boaster then as he is now—he made a whopping boast that I would lose to his favorite pip. He put the credits where his mouth was—and lost. Grall sent his goons after me—they killed my pips and took my left horn. Before they could get the other, something killed two of them and ran the others off. I never met my savior, but I never went back to the tourneys. I found the forest and have been rescuing pips ever since."

Apocalypse and Jynx looked at Kita.

"I may or may not have...I do remember the boast. Grall bet a hundred Djinn females and reneged on it."

"Let me guess...the bet was with you," said Velositi.

"Not directly. Through a mutual acquaintance."

"And what did you offer?"

Kita shrugged. "Several pallets of comet ice."

"How long have you had this ice?" said Jynx.

With a wry smile, Kita said. "It's one of the first things I stole. It's a valuable tool to con Djinn and Verisom."

"I think I'd remember if my rescuer had wings," said To'va.

"That's because I was Human then, and I might have had help."

"Guess I owe it to you then."

"We both want revenge on the same kitty cat. I say we work together."

To'va stroked her lower horn. "Deal. Let's go."

"Do you need to bring anything?"

An ultraviolet glowing fuzzy pip with a long nose and big ears ran up To'va's leg and skirt. It climbed up the light blue triangular top to the Prii's shoulder. To'va reached into a bag on her hip, pulled out a nut, and fed it to the pip.

"I'm all set. I assume you'll feed me?"

"You can munch on the plants growing on top of the embassy," replied Jynx.

To'va's leathery nose wiggled as her dark lips frowned. "You want to try that again, youngling? How about I tell you to go sit on an egg?"

"Angels don't come from eggs."

"Actually, you did," said Velositi. "Kita combined her and Kimmy's DNA and put it into one of Kimmy's eggs."

"Wrong kind of egg," said Jynx exasperatedly as she looked a little green.

"There's plenty of room and food at the embassy," interjected Kita.

———————✕———————

KITA LED HER GROUP THROUGH THE DARK, FOLLOWING THE dim mazelike passages filled with homes, shops, and workplaces. She would be happy to leave the dank, claustrophobic area behind as something dripped onto her feathers from a pipe above. *I hope it's not corrosive.*

They entered a wide area containing an open-air market with dozens of tables full of scrounged, repaired, and forged items along with various types of food—primarily funguses that grew in the dark. Kita knew some were tasty, but it depended on the growing conditions. She'd eaten some that tasted like waste oil and were probably grown in the stuff.

"Farillica Market," said To'va as the group moved along the edge path lined with doors to apartments. "If it was lost above, it'll be found here."

"Momma, what is this stuff?" said Jynx as she hovered over a table full of parts to hovercars, machinery, and who knows what else.

"You should get some and examine it," suggested Velositi. "I am sure Sprokkit can show you how to make something out of it."

The vendor, a skinny Zentonian with matted and oil-stained fur, looked over at Velositi. "How much for the robot?"

Velositi's blue eyes glowed brightly. "I am not a robot. I am a Morphicon Angel. Would you prefer I call you a squirrel, Zentonian? Or just a scrawny nut-chewer?"

The Zentonian pulled a screw gun from his belt. "I'll turn you into scrap, metal can."

Velositi morphed her right arm into her cannons and pointed it at the Zentonian's head. "Try it, squirrel, and I will mount your tail on my wall."

The Zentonian's oil drop eyes went wide as he lowered his makeshift weapon. His fur stood on end as his big front teeth chattered in fear.

"That is what I thought," cooed Velositi as her arm morphed back.

Above her, Jynx giggled. "Come on, let's catch up to my parents."

Kita and the others waited a few booths away, looking at locally grown funguses, mosses, and foliage.

"Where was this grown?" Kita asked the Human vendor.

"What's it matter? And where'd you get wings?" he demanded.

"What's it matter?" Kita shot back.

The deck under Kita's feet vibrated, causing her to turn to look around the market. The rest of the market reacted at once, closing down shop, trying to gather their merchandise, while shoppers ran for cover. The Human vendor scraped his food off the table into buckets, ran down the path, and pounded on a door until it opened.

"Something wicked this way comes," mused Kita as the vibrations under her feet grew.

"What is it, angel?" said Apocalypse.

"I can guess—Graniites."

"What are they? And why is everyone spooked?"

"Graniites are large rock golems with bad attitudes and mean tempers. They have a molten core, and their rock hide makes them damn near impossible to kill...only upside is, they're kind of stupid and love to fight—or squish, as they put it."

"What are they doing down here?" said Apocalypse as the vibrations grew.

"No idea. I would think they would be too big to fit down here."

"Have you ever killed one, Momma?" asked Jynx.

"I have. It made my reputation in the original Tet space."

"You might get to do it again," chirped Velositi.

Kita wasn't so sure she wanted to fight another one. The first time she'd been on top of her game. *Now...I think being a god has made me soft...or maybe too much time as a Human not being me.*

On the far side of the market, a black Graniite with glowing orange joints exited a passage. It wasn't as big as the Graniites Kita had seen in the past. That was probably due to a variation in the universe. Still, it looked formidable. When it was followed by two more—a gray one and a red one—Kita gulped.

The three Graniites tore into the market, smashing tables and ripping up awnings. They tossed the debris aside, making room for a large pack of Grocha, Grochar, Djinn, and Diamock thugs, all wearing red and black armor with yellow fists painted on the fronts.

As the three Graniites smashed a path to the Angels, Kita stood firm as the mercenaries approached, weapons drawn. They formed a semicircle; a Grochar with a missing eye was flanked by two Djinn in full power armor. They leveled their two-handed rotating repeaters at the Angels. The Graniites—

only eight feet tall but still rock—stood around the Angels looking menacing.

Kita flipped her braid around and stroked it as she glared at the Grochar with the missing eye. "Can I help you? Maybe help you find an eye?"

"Winged Humans," the Grochar snarled, "Die for killing brother Griss and Yellow Fist Pack members."

"And what makes you think all of you can kill us?" Kita cooed. "If the Grocha my daughter killed was your brother, then you should know he was an idiot for attacking her. You're an even bigger idiot for attacking me."

"You will die! Stone men smash them! Honor for Yellow Fist Pack!"

"*Kimmy, Jynxie, get the others out of here. I'll handle this.*"

"*Momma, no! I can help. Let me fight!*"

"*Jynx, go!*" Kita ordered. "*This is a fight beyond your level.*"

"*No! I can do it.*" The young Angel phased away and didn't appear anywhere in the market.

Kita swore. "*Kimmy, protect the others.*"

"*Can't we just run?*"

"*They'll hound us forever or until we kill them. I'm going with the latter.*"

Behind Kita, Apocalypse went to put up her pearly-white bubble around the other Angels and To'va, but Velositi stepped toward Kita.

"I can help."

She might be a good distraction. Kita knew Velositi's lightning ability would be no good, but her cannons might be able to scratch a Graniite's rocky hide. "Do your best to stay ranged. Don't get into a fist fight with them. You leave that to me."

"What are you going to do?"

"Prove why I *am* the greatest." Kita drew her swords—Dead and Buried—and flourished them, causing the mercenaries to laugh.

"Knife worthless!" yelled the Grochar leader.

Kita spun her ebony blades, and fire burst forth. The flame engulfed her arms and body. She increased the heat until she melted the metal deck. Slamming the hilts together, she formed the legendary great sword: Crypt. On the lava rock handle, the word *REAP* was inlaid in blood rubies. Kita twirled the flaming blade around her.

"Velositi, go!" Kita ordered as she leaped sideways at the red Graniite standing closest to her.

The red Graniite brought its arm up to block, Kita's blade slicing halfway through it. Leaning on the sword, Kita forced the super-heated edge through the rest of the arm. The stone appendage hit the deck with a dull *thud* causing the rest of the mercenaries to quit laughing and cajoling. Kita spun under the howling Graniite's other arm and slammed a blade into the stone golem's back. She twisted Crypt, using the obsidian shards inlaid in the blade to shred the Graniite's inside. Kita yanked her sword out, freeing a gush of lava from the wound.

Velositi took on the gray and black Graniites, her cannons blasting away rapidly as she flipped and jumped around them. The black Graniite ignored her and attacked Apocalypse's shield, banging on it with its fists. Velositi shot it in the back, but it still ignored her.

Turning her attention to the gray Graniite, Velositi fired. Pieces of the Graniite's gray rock hide chipped away after each series of cannon blasts, but it wasn't slowing the creature down, just making it mad. It thumped its fists against its chest like a gorilla, lowered its head, and charged Velositi, slamming into her narrow waist and driving her into the deck. The Graniite raised both fists and brought them down on her chest, splitting it like a coconut. Angry red lines created a spiderweb around the deep crack on Velositi's chest.

The gray Graniite roared in triumph while punching Velositi in the head. Her face shield bent as one of her blue eyes went out. The Graniite jumped, bringing its short, squat legs down on her armored pelvis. The weight of the golem squished her right hip and left leg.

With a distorted moan, Velositi raised her right arm and fired a lightning bolt into the gray Graniite. The loud boom echoed in the chamber as white light cast harsh shadows. The bolt hit the Graniite square in the chest, blasting chunks of gray rock in all directions and making the Graniite retreat.

Without a word, she morphed into her Kawasaki H2R hyperbike. Squealing the tires, she roared out of the market down a side passage.

"Velositi?" Kita whispered, perplexed. She'd never known her girlfriend to run from a fight, but she couldn't worry about that right now.

Kita slashed the wounded red Graniite across the back, leaving a long, deep orange line. Lava flowed down the creature's back and dripped on the floor, burning holes in the metal. Kita spun, split her swords, and plunged both into the opening. With a yell, she pulled her swords in opposite directions, cutting through the Graniite's barrel chest. Lava gushed from the wounds spilling across the deck, melting through the grating and causing a section to collapse, taking the Graniite with it.

I wonder what's down there? Besides a dead Graniite.

As Kita turned her attention to the other Graniites, the gray Graniite punched Kita in the head, sending her flying. Using her wings, Kita turned her uncontrolled flight into a roll and landed on her feet, gracefully reforming Crypt in her hand.

"Come on!" Kita taunted. "If you're going to hit me, HIT ME!" She grew a red ball—a thermobaric bomb—in her hand and threw it at the black Graniite still trying to penetrate Apocalypse's shield. The ball stuck to the creature's rocky, porous hide. Kita detonated the bomb with a snap of her fingers, blowing chunks out of the black Graniite's back and bouncing it off Apocalypse's shield toward Kita.

Kita flourished Crypt and brought the sword up, catching the flying black Graniite by the back of the head. She twisted, flinging the creature over her and slamming it into the deck, leaving a Graniite-sized dent.

The gray Graniite charged, slamming Kita in the back. She rolled into a ball, somersaulted, and stuck her hands out while kicking her feet up and around the Graniite's neck. Flapping her wings hard, she flipped the gray Graniite over her and drove him into the back of the struggling black Graniite.

The two tangled Graniites struggled to get up. Kita floated above them, twirling Crypt. With a mighty battle cry, she drove the blade into the back of the gray Graniite. Twisting Crypt, Kita ripped a large gash across its back. Twirling the sword with one hand, she grew a series of red balls and dropped them into the lava-leaking cut. She backflipped away from the pair while snapping her fingers three times.

The explosions ripped through the gray Graniite. Kita put up her heat shield as globs of molten rock were flung across the market—several hitting the stunned mercenaries. The black Graniite struggled to get to its feet from under the pieces left of its comrade. Orange lava clung to the black Graniite, melting its rock-hard exterior. It tried to take a few steps, but its legs sagged, and an arm fell off, then it twisted and crumpled to the ground, its lava core mixing with the lava on the outside. At last, the rocky exterior cracked and broke, oozing lava across the deck with pieces of the rocky shell floating on top slowly melting through the deck.

Kita collapsed her shield, raised Crypt parallel to the ground, and whispered, "Re—"

"Nobody move!" yelled Jynx as she appeared behind the mercenary leader with her sword across his throat.

"Jynx!" Kita cried in alarm. "Let him go and phase back to your mother!"

"I've got him!"

"You don't have them!" Kita screamed as some of the other mercenaries stopped pointing their weapons at her and moved to Jynx. "Cutting off his head won't kill him...even if you could get through the scales!"

Jynx pressed her blade against the Grochar's scale-covered neck and tried to draw it across. The sword was sharp and bit into the scales, but not enough to do any damage. The Grochar seemed to sense the young Angel's problem. He drew up his arms and thrust them back, hitting Jynx in the gut, causing her to drop her sword and send her crashing into a heap on the ground.

The pair of Djinn mercenary guards in heavy space armor leveled their guns at Jynx and fired. Tiny two-millimeter projectiles from the rotary railguns tore into Jynx's legs, body, and wings. From out of the passage Velositi had earlier escaped into came the high-pitched whine of a hyperbike. Velositi screamed into the market; using a broken table as a ramp, she jumped, twisted sideways to hit both Djinn in the back, knocking them to the ground. Landing, Velositi power slid around Jynx, her tires screeching. Velositi's arms extended from the bike, picked the wounded Angel up, and draped her across the seat. Bullets bounced off the H2R hyperbike as she gunned her throttle and took off around the formation of mercenaries.

Seeing the area clear, Kita raised Crypt parallel to the ground and yelled, "REAP!"

A blue cone of light erupted from the great sword, illuminating the mercenaries. There was a flash of blue light as ghosts made of white electrons were pulled from all living things inside the cone. The ghosts lasted a second before dissipating into the ether. The bodies left behind collapsed to the ground, dead.

Breaking Crypt back into Dead and Buried, Kita sheathed the swords on her back and rushed over to the other Angels, ignoring the people peeking out of their doors. Velositi sat against a wall not far from where Apocalypse kneeled over Jynx, moving her hands over the teenager's body. Dominica and To'va stood to one side, looking unsure of what to do.

Kita knelt next to Apocalypse. "How is she, love?" even Kita couldn't keep the worry and heartsickness she felt from her voice.

"I'm mapping the damage now. She's got a bunch of pellets throughout her. It's going to take time, but I can get them out and heal the damage. She'll most likely push most of them out and heal before I get to her."

Apocalypse's voice was clinical with an unnerving calmness. Kita guessed she'd escaped into her medical training as a doctor to avoid dealing with the emotions of being a distressed mother. That would come later but would be tempered by Jynx being healed.

Kita stroked Apocalypse's back before moving to Jynx's head. Tears streamed down the young Angel's face as her breath came in jagged gasps.

"Momma! Momma...It...it hurts...so bad...Am I...going to die? ...Momma...make it stop...please..." Jynx coughed and blubbered through her tears.

Kita stroked her daughter's hair. She couldn't remember the first time she'd been shot. It happened so often she'd forgotten the pain. But pain taught a valuable lesson.

"Chelsea, listen to me," Kita said firmly, trying to show some sympathy. She waited until Jynx's eyes focused on her. "Pain reminds us of our mistakes. When I tell you to do something, I have my reasons."

"Momma...please...It hurts...I'm sorry. Please, make...stop...I'm so sorry..."

Kita's eyes narrowed as she debated how much this lesson should continue. "How's it going, love?" Kita asked Apocalypse.

"I've got a long way to go. Chelsea, I need you to keep still."

"But...Mom...it hurts..."

"It's going to hurt a lot worse if you keep moving."

Kita pressed the heel of her hand against Jynx's neck and injected her with a painkiller. That should be enough to keep her quiet and still...and long enough for the lesson to be one Jynx wouldn't forget. Kita stroked Jynx's hair and kissed her forehead as the teenager's eyes unfocused.

Kita got to her feet and went to confront Velositi. She didn't know what happened during the fight to make Velositi run, but she owed her girlfriend for coming back and saving Jynx. Kita sat down beside the Angel Morphicon, pulled her biomechanical arm from under Velositi's head, and put it around her shoulders. Kita snuggled against Velositi feeling the warmth she gave off.

"Velositi?" Kita whispered. "Thank you for saving Chelsea."

Velositi rolled her head back and forth on the other arm across her knees like she was disagreeing.

"Velositi, it's ok. We won. I owe you for Chelsea. There was no way I could have gotten to her in time."

Velositi raised her head. Thin blue plasma streamed from her good eye. The eye was so dim, Kita could barely tell it was on. For Morphicons, the eyes were the window to the soul, and Kita had never seen her girlfriend so distraught.

"Kita, I am a coward. I saw death coming, and I ran. I am sorry. I have died before...and...I could not do it again. I am supposed to be a brave, fearless warrior, and in the moment...I ran. The pain of injury is only a fraction of the pain in my soul. I do not deserve to be an Angel. I have failed you, the Angels, and myself. I am sorry. Please do not forgive me. I do not deserve it. I should have been brave and faced my death." She put her head back down and withdrew her arm from around Kita.

Kita scooted around and knelt in front of Velositi. She lifted the Morphicon's arm and head to look into Velositi's eyes.

"Velositi, we all get scared, and death is a scary thing...even for us. But you're not a coward. You retreated—sometimes that's the wisest thing you can do, especially when you're overwhelmed—you regrouped, and you came back. I couldn't have saved Chelsea, but you could, and you did. You charged into the hail of gunfire and pulled her out. That's more than bravery; that's heroism and valor. I couldn't have done it without you. Today, you're my hero. You brought my daughter back to me, and I can't thank you enough."

Velositi's eye brightened some. "But I left you to fight them on your own. That is not what a good friend or warrior is supposed to do."

"What if you had stayed and died, then what? Sure, I can kill three Graniites, but even I'm not fast enough to save a teenager from herself."

Velositi chirped laughter. "They do find trouble fast. I do not want to disappoint you. You fight so fearlessly and let nothing stand in your way."

"You know what made my heart stop? When Chelsea appeared behind that Grochar. I was half a syllable from ripping my own daughter's soul from her body."

"Is that what happened?"

Kita chuckled. "No, but it's a good legend. The sword pulls the electrical energy from living creatures."

"I have never heard you talk about your sword or its power."

"It's a reminder of my past and the lengths I would go to achieve my goals. I prefer no one know of its power because, in the wrong hands, it could be dangerous."

"Even without that power, you felled three of those creatures like they were targets on the practice range."

"I have killed one before—"

"SHUT UP!" TURNIP SNARLED, HER BIG TEETH CHATTERING angrily. "No one can kill a Graniite—especially not three! You liar!" she looked at Mai'la. "Why isn't the pepinal working?"

"I don't know. From what she said, Angels have unique physiology."

"We must get the Axiom. With it, I will be Queen of Verisom and rule all of Tet space."

Kita raised an eyebrow. That was a lofty goal, even for someone with her powers. Which led Kita to a question. "You and what army?"

"With the Axiom, I won't need an army. I will crush all who oppose me!" Turnip cried as she thumped her giant foot.

"Yeah, but...even with all my power, I couldn't conquer a planet without friends and an army."

"Yes," said Mai'la, "but with the sword you mentioned, she could kill an army singlehandedly. Where is that?"

The pair looked down at Kita. She ran her tongue around her sharpened canine as she thought about what to tell them. It was on her back, buried in sand, but she wasn't going to tell them that. "It only works with the Axiom, and last I checked, the sword was part of some Djinn's personal artifact collection."

"What Djinn?" demanded Turnip.

Kita tried to shrug under the sand. "I think he went by Collector. I do know he doesn't know the power he possesses. If he did, a Djinn would be ruling Tet space."

Turnip chattered her teeth. "Fraj!" she yelled.

A Djinn in an impeccably tailored suit with his mane slicked back appeared next to Turnip. "Yes, Your Highness?"

Kita cleared her throat. "You mind telling me who you are, Princess? I'm bad with names and faces."

Turnip looked down at Kita and sneered. "Shut up, thief. You only answer questions and speak when spoken to." The Verisom turned her attention to the well-dressed Djinn. "Search the blacknet for a Djinn named Collector who collects rare ancient artifacts." She looked down at Kita. "Describe the sword."

Kita gave her a placating smile. "Sure. How do you know I'm not going to lie?"

Turnip's nose wrinkled as it turned red. "Insolent Human. If you lie, I will pluck out your feathers and make you eat them."

Kita raised an eyebrow. *That's an unusual threat.* Kita remembered the one time she'd been plucked, and it hurt to the Crushing Depths and back. She wasn't sure even her tough digestive system could break down feathers.

"Well, since you put it that way...It's a double-bladed sword named Crypt. It has ebony-colored blades with pieces of obsidian inlaid in the flat of the blades. The handles are lava rock with blood-red rubies inlaid to spell out *Death*. The sword can be broken in half to form the swords Hammer and Anvil. The names are etched into the silver quillons. It should be easy to spot."

Turnip looked at Fraj. "Did you get that?"

The Djinn's lip curled as he growled, "Yes, Your Highness. I will start the search immediately. Is there a price cap?"

Turnip's ears flicked and rotated to imply that was a dumb question. "No, moron. This sword is priceless. If you have to, take money from the Verisom Crown Fund. Tell Her Majesty it's my birthday present. When you find it, do not take *no* for an answer. I *want* that sword. If they refuse to sell, find its location." She looked down at Kita. "Our thief might still save his feathers."

"Her, actually," corrected Kita with a smile that hid Kita's hatred for being called a male. "We're all girls here...well, except the kitty cat. No need for insults."

Mai'la's scales rippled. "It's impossible to tell one Human from another. You look the same."

"Well, I *am* an Angel, and we're like Aurori. We only have one sex. So, maybe you should pay attention. Like how the sword is useless without the Axiom." Which was a fabrication on Kita's part. Anyone could command the sword. The weapon's only saving grace was its lengthy cooldown period, as it collected the required subatomic particles to power the electromagnetic coils that interacted with the electrons.

The mention of the Axiom got Turnip's attention. "Where is it, thief?" she demanded, her big red eyes looking at the Angel intently.

"I don't know. Maybe I dropped it, or maybe I used it."

"Liar!" screamed Turnip. "If you used it, you would have killed us all!"

Kita smiled whimsically. *Wishing I could because I'm growing tired of you.* "Maybe I'm just biding my time trying to figure out what's going on." Which was the truth. Kita checked her computer. It was only sixty percent done repairing the damaged files and still had the operating system to do. *Great. I need to keep talking.* "The truth is, I can't remember. I'd tell you if I could."

"What do you mean *you can't remember?*" shrieked Turnip.

Kita raised an eyebrow. "If you're not careful, you're going to give yourself a heart attack. I know Verisoms' hearts are susceptible to too much excitement." *Maybe that's how I should kill her.* Kita had a vision of Turnip in a cage as jacksaurs stuck their long teeth-filled snouts through the bars snapping at the Verisom, making her run in circles until her heart gave out.

"I will rip *your* heart out and feed it to Fraj, you insolent, despicable waste of a Human. Now, no more stories. You will tell me what I want to know, or the diakos will be the least of your worries."

I didn't know I was worried about them. I haven't received a nip in a while. I'm too hot a tamale. "If you don't like this story, I have others."

"I want the Axiom, you furless featherhead!"

"I told you—"

"You've told me nothing! Mai'la, give this Human the rest of the vial."

Mai'la went to the table and picked up the injector. She turned the dosage selector as she walked toward Kita. Hopping down into the sand-filled tank, she knelt in front of Kita, adjusting her silver sequined dress.

Kita raised an eyebrow at the Aurorian's shapely golden

legs and what lay between them. "Is this the last meal for the condemned?"

"To block her view of me readjusting the injector. How much longer do you need to stall?"

"How do you know I'm stalling?"

"I believe your story of your power. If you could save yourself, you would have done so. Whatever your reason, I will stall Turnip as long as possible."

Mai'la bent down and pressed the injector into Kita's neck.

Kita's head lulled back as she felt the drug pass through her system. *Is she trying for a set of wings? I wish I could remember who she was...*

Kita directed Jynx into her office. Holding Apocalypse's hand, she led her partner in and shut the door. Jynx, looking dejected in her hoodie and jeans covered in blood, took a seat in the farthest chair from the desk.

"You will stand, young lady," Kita ordered and pointed in front of her desk. She guided Apocalypse around to Kita's chair and set her partner in it.

Apocalypse flipped off her hood, revealing her exhausted and tear-streaked face. Jynx's blood covered her coat, shirt, and pants. Kita stood next to her and put a hand on her shoulder. Slinking to the spot her mother pointed to, Jynx stared at the desk, her own face streaked from tears and blood.

"Well?" Kita demanded.

Jynx gulped, and tears leaked from her eyes.

"Why are you crying?" Kita yelled. "Your mother sweated blood and tears putting you back together. You owe her an apology and a thank you for caring so much. So, let's hear it."

Jynx's mouth quivered as the tears fell off her chin. "Momma...Mommy...I'm sorry. SO sorry. I just wanted to help. I wanted to prove—"

"Did you see what happened to Velositi?" Kita barked. "Did you see what happened to me? If I hadn't been an Angel, they'd be kicking my head around like a ball. When I tell you to do something, you do it. Do you understand?"

Jynx was bawling when she answered, "I'm sorry, Momma. I just wanted to be like you. I wanted to prove myself. Please don't be mad. I'll train harder...please don't take my sword away. Please...please...Mommy, I'm sorry. Don't be mad. I didn't mean to scare you. I—I..."

"You were selfish and were not a team player," said Apocalypse in a tired voice. "Your momma sent you to me so she could concentrate on the fight and not have to worry about your safety. Instead, you blocked her kill shot and were shot up in the process, complicating the situation further. If it wasn't for Velositi, we would be burying you, Chelsea. Think about that. Do you want to be dead at twelve?"

Jynx's face fell as she couldn't keep her eyes open from the tears.

"Chelsea, I'm not mad, but I'm deeply disappointed. I hope you've learned your lesson."

"I have Mommy. I'm sorry. So sorry. I was just trying to make you proud."

"Do I look proud?" Kita yelled as she slapped the desk. "Do you want to know what assassin recruits do for the first three years at Leaf's dojo? They clean and maintain the dojo, learning respect, discipline, honor, loyalty, duty, and integrity. And do you know what the most important lesson is?"

Jynx shook her head slightly.

"When the Grandmaster tells you to do something—you do it!" Kita screamed. "Without question. But you're not even to that level yet. You're just an undisciplined winged punk with a sword and abilities you can barely control—and that's my fault."

"NO, MOMMA! Please don't take my abilities. I promise I'll do better. I can. I will. No, no, no...please, Momma." Jynx collapsed to the floor sobbing.

Apocalypse went to stand, but Kita pushed her back down, shaking her head. From her belt, Kita took out a blank credit chit and pressed hers to it. Using her Arcom, she transferred ten thousand credits to it in Jynx's name.

"Chelsea, get up," Kita ordered.

Jynx's loud sobs continued as she used the desk to stand. She stood trembling, her face full of fear.

Kita set the credit chit on the desk. "Take this and get yourself some new clothes and get cleaned up. There's enough money to buy you a new wardrobe if you want it—as long as you stay out of HighCity. I don't care how you do it, how long it takes you, just do it. I don't want to see those blood-stained clothes again, and neither does your mom. If you run into trouble, call me. Now, go." Kita waved her daughter out of the room.

Jynx's sobs died in her throat as her trembling hands

fumbled to pick up the credit chit. She looked at it, then at Kita.

"Your name. Get going."

Jynx wiped her eyes, pulled her hood over her head, and glided out the door.

Kita looked down at Apocalypse and let out a long sigh.

"Were we too hard on her?" Apocalypse said with a tired sigh of her own.

"No. She'll never do it again. You sure you've never done this before?"

Apocalypse laughed unhappily. "I channeled my mother and what she used to say to me. She'd never get mad, and I'd wished she had. Disappointing her was a fate worse than death. Is she going to be safe going out alone?"

"I'm sure Tet-Sec won't take their eyes off her. But I'll ask Velositi to keep an eye on her."

"She's never picked out clothes before. Is that really a punishment?"

Kita raised an eyebrow. "It wasn't supposed to be a punishment—maybe if I sent her with Jane and have to try on a thousand outfits. But that comes with chocolate-covered strawberries and champagne."

"So, what are we going to do?"

"We should go check on the others and make sure they got settled in ok. Then I have work to do."

"Do you need help?"

"Maybe. I need to talk to To'va about getting Al'ice in a tourney."

Apocalypse stood, but she was wobbly. "Maybe I should take a nap."

Kita took her hand and escorted her upstairs to the living area. There, Dominica and To'va sat with Kele at the breakfast bar. Dominica had her pips out and was feeding them nuts from a bag around her waist. Velositi was on the far side of the living area, looking out the window. Kita could feel she was depressed. To'va and Kele were discussing what happened in the market. When Kita and Apocalypse appeared, Kele broke off the conversation. Seeing the two unhappy Angels, her scales rippled in sympathy.

"Are you alright?" said Kele. "Do you need medical attention or counseling? Where is Jynx? She should be seen by a psychologist. I apologize. This kind of brazen attack doesn't happen on the Tet."

Kita raised an eyebrow. "You don't go into The Dark often, do you? Jynx will be fine. She's out getting new clothes and getting cleaned up. If you'll excuse me, I need to talk to my girlfriend." She sat Apocalypse on a stool, kissed her cheek, then glided across the living area and landed next to Velositi.

"Hey, Velositi. How's my hero?"

"Hi, Kita." Velositi shook her head. "I do not feel like much of a hero."

Kita hugged her. "You're dwelling on the negative instead of the positive. I don't see it as a mistake or cowardice—you took time to regroup after receiving a stunning blow. It happens to all of us. I'm proud you came back. If—if you're not busy, I have a favor to ask."

Velositi turned to look at Kita, her eyes glowing. "You still trust me?"

"Of course. I sent Chelsea out to get new clothes and get cleaned up. I'm sure Tet-Sec is watching her, but I was wondering if you could follow her and keep her out of trouble. You don't have to engage her; just watch."

"I—I—are you sure?" Velositi's eyes dimmed a fraction.

"There's no one I trust more. If you want to join her, go ahead. She's never picked out clothes before."

Velositi's eyes brightened. "That is great trust you put in me—to protect and dress your child."

Kita chuckled. "I was hard on her, but I gave her some freedom to think about her mistake. She could probably use a friendly face. I think both of you could."

"Yes. Shopping sounds fun."

"I don't think she's left yet. I'll leave it to you whether you follow or join her."

Velositi hugged Kita. "Thank you, Kita. Your trust makes me feel better."

"When you get back, I have a surprise for you."

"A surprise? I do not deserve a surprise."

"It's a surprise for everyone. I think we all need a pick me up."

"Yes. That would be good. Thank you, Kita. I will go find Chelsea."

Kita accompanied Velositi as far as the breakfast bar and joined the conversation in progress, which seemed to be Kele trying to get details out of Apocalypse, but Kita's partner wasn't offering much.

"We took care of it," said Apocalypse. "Nothing more needs to be done."

"We can't have mercenary groups attacking citizens of the Tet," argued Kele. "This is a matter for Tet-Sec."

"It's taken care of. I've contacted Tet-Sec," said Kita.

"You?" gasped Kele.

"Yes. I'm supposed to meet with them shortly. Now, if you'll excuse us, I need to talk to Al'ice and To'va about their first tourney and what they need. I can't have them going into the pit looking like they just crawled out of the wilderness."

"We did," said To'va.

"I will join you to talk to Tet-Sec," said Kele firmly. "You will need a liaison."

"I doubt that. But we will leave in a few minutes. So, go grab what you need." With a dismissive wave of the hand, Kita sent the Aurorian on her way.

"Something tells me you've been around, Angel," To'va said to Kita.

"I have begged for coins and made more money than I could spend in a thousand lifetimes. I've suffered oppression and conquered worlds. The things I've learned from those experiences have made me who I am. When I met Kimmy, I was a persecuted junkyard lesbian trying to keep my dad's dream alive."

"I bet you didn't order people to leave you alone like that."

"No. I learned that from my mother, the Duchess. Now, I've sent out offers for our first sponsored bout. I'm offering generous terms, but what matters is us winning and building a reputation. I don't know what you need to practice, but we need uniforms, preferably something hooded and attention-getting." Kita reached into her belt and pulled out a credit chit with Dominica's name on it, and handed it to the Angel. "That should cover everything."

Dominica activated the screen and gasped. She showed it to To'va.

The ancient Prii stroked her horn and said, "By the mi. Do you want these uniforms to be made out of Isopian kalmac silk? Where'd you get this kind of credit?"

"From your protégée," said Kita with a smile.

"Long-eared crap. This would let you live in HighCity."

"Well, you're in luck. You get to meet my crew."

"Crew?"

"They're coming to help us secure the pip you need to beat Grall."

"With your credits, you should be able to buy it."

Kita chuckled. "Why buy it when you can steal it? Come on, everyone. We have a lunch date."

Kita, the Angels, and To'va sat in the patio area of Chett's, a Human eatery in MidCity overlooking the sky-lanes. Seated overlooking the pedestrian skyway, Kita waited for her crew to appear. As she opened the menu to one of her favorite restaurants, Kele came hurrying up with her tablet.

Kita checked her Arcom. Kita lived up to her promise to answer Kele's messages. The Aurorian had made good time from the embassy.

"You look flustered, Kele," said Kita as she put down her menu and turned to Apocalypse. "Find something, love?"

"Yes. The *GroundRound* sounds like a burger. I could use some comfort food."

"They do make good shakes—so I'm told. They don't have soy milk for me. Kele, what do you need?"

"Princess Okra has filed a complaint that you broke into her apartment and assaulted her."

Kita was glad Jynx wasn't around to hear that. "Don't worry. I've already contacted Tet-Sec. They should be here any minute."

"What—are you turning yourself in?"

Kita raised an eyebrow as a Tet-Sec cruiser landed in the emergency landing area. The doors opened, and two Humans got out. "I'm hoping they'll get me off." Kita pulled back Apocalypse's hood to get her attention from To'va.

"Yes, angel?"

Kita guided her head toward the two Tet-Sec Humans. The others at the table followed the gaze.

Apocalypse gasped. "Holy shit! Karen! Zhi!" The Angel jumped to her feet and glided over to the two Tec-Sec Angels in Human form. She surprised Karen with a hug.

Kita and the others followed the excited Angel. Karen McKnight was the Angel Poison and a general in Tet-Sec. Zhi Shen was the Angel Venom and commanded Tet-Sec's air assets. Both were part of Kita's crew and helped her not only steal but cover up the crimes.

"Karen! Kita didn't tell me you were on the Tet!" exclaimed Apocalypse.

"Would have been nice if she'd told us she was back," said Zhi. "We thought we were on our own after Grall killed her."

"I couldn't let that go unpunished. Karen, Zhi, meet Al'ice. She just got her wings and is a trainer who's going to help us bury Grall. The old Prii is To'va, Al'ice's coach."

"Old? Compared to who? You said yourself you're as old as god."

Everyone laughed, except Kele.

"I'm older than that. General Karen McKnight, Fleet Commander Zhi Shen, meet Master Ambassador Kele. She's been helping us settle in and deal with some of the locals... specifically some annoying Verisom princesses who believe the new race is a pushover."

"So far, all I've seen is pretty feathers. I'm sure they'd make a lovely shawl," said a white Verisom princess with black spots sitting with a female Diamock at the next table over, glancing up from a tablet. The Verisom's red eyes narrowed, exposing black eyelids. She wore a tie-dye sarong, and her black ears tilted forward in a threatening manner.

"And I'll cut you up and feed Catnip to the kitties," replied Kita looking at the Verisom.

"You can't fight to save your life," said the Diamock as she pulled a pistol off her belt and put it on the table.

"You better move along," said To'va to the pair. "This feathered Human took down three Graniites and a company of mercs by herself."

"No one's ever killed a Graniite in single combat," scoffed the Verisom.

"You've got plates of steel for pulling that illegal pistol on Tet officers," said Karen firmly.

Kita moved To'va aside and looked at the Diamock. "You think you're that fast, unitless?" Before the others could blink, she had Dead out, pressing down on the pistol and the Diamock's hand.

"Void, Kita!" exclaimed the Diamock. "Where'd you get that?"

"You said to look for wings. I thought you'd gotten into some weird cosplay," said the Verisom. "Or you reincarnated as a bird." She stood, her fur rippled, and the black spots vanished. Her sarong changed to a black and white tube top with a matching pleated skirt. Large hoop earrings appeared in her ears as she laid them down her back. A black tuff of hair appeared on her head. Her tail wiggled back and forth, and a black bow appeared around it.

Kita put Dead away with a flourish. "How about a hug instead?"

The pair stood up. "So, did you get taller? I mean, it kind of looks like you. Sounds like you. But you know how hard it is to tell one Human from another," said the Diamock. She was a few inches shorter than Kita. "I used to tower over you."

"Human me has some limitations. Angel me, the real me, is god. Angels, this is Princess Catnip. She can hack anything and disguise herself to look, act, and sound like any Verisom. This cute Diamock pup is Flexi. She can shoot any weapon and build a starship out of the junk in Farillica Market."

Flexi chuckled. "I haven't been there in a while. See anything cool?"

"Three dead Graniites and a bunch of mercs."

"You've always had a god complex," replied Catnip, getting a hug.

"Well, it's true. I am, and I'm here to recruit."

The Verisom's ears wiggled in uncertainty. "You need a bigger crew?"

Kita looked at Kele. "I may have something, but *the Grand Ambassador has eyes and ears. Right, Master Ambassador?*" Kita said the last bit in Aurori instead of Common.

Kele's scales rippled in surprise and shock.

"*I mastered Aurori many lifetimes ago,*" said Kita. "The question is, do you want to stay trapped at the embassy, or do you want to see how far down the Verisom hole I go?" Kita looked at her friends, "That goes for both of you as well..."

"Is that a joke?" said Catnip as she chattered her teeth. "Because I'll take you to Verisom, and you can see how deep a real rabbit hole goes."

"Would I lie?"

Flexi slapped the table with her leathery hand covered in boney plates. "I'm in. What are we after?"

Catnip eyed Kita with a red eye. "What are we stealing?"

Kita looked at Kele. "When I want something, I rarely ask. I just take. You've been on my side since I appeared. I reward loyalty. So, believe me when I say this is going to hurt."

Kele's golden eyes widened as she threw her hands up. "Don't—"

Kita's hand darted around the Aurorian's arms to touch her nose. "Boop!"

Kele threw her head back and screamed, attracting the attention of the restaurant patrons and passersby on the promenade. She fell to her elbows and knees, pressing her head against the metal deck. From her back, between her shoulder blades, a pair of golden limbs grew out of her erect scales. The appendages grew upward, forming joints and limbs. Buds formed on the golden skin, growing until they burst into brilliant emerald green feathers with gold edges. When the last of the six-foot flight feathers finished, Kele's scream turned into a gasp. She pushed herself to her knees, tears streaming down her face.

Kita stepped forward and offered Kele her hand. "Rise, Alliance."

Alliance took Kita's hand and struggled to stand, getting her feet back in her heels and compensating for the additional ten pounds on her back.

"By the Void!" exclaimed Catnip. "Do me next!"

Kita chuckled as she raised a finger to her friend while putting an arm around Alliance. "You ok?" she asked the new Angel.

"What did you do to me?"

Apocalypse came over and pulled Alliance's wing around. "Welcome to the flock. I'll explain," she looked at Catnip and Flexi, "to all of you. Kita's really bad at it. She just expects you to figure it out on your own."

"I don't care how long it takes me to figure it out," said Catnip, excited. "Touch my nose!"

Kita passed Alliance to Apocalypse and looked at her friends. "You in?"

"Oh, Void, yeah!" said Catnip.

The quills on Flexi's face rippled, showing her concern and curiosity. "I'm in."

Kita stepped in front of them and touched each on the nose. "Boop!"

"Oh, by the Void, that—" Catnip changed to the Verisom female language and let out a long series of curses as she curled up in a ball flat on her feet. Her right foot thumped rapidly as she howled.

Flexi bared her dog-like teeth as she let out a long snarl. Unable to take the pain, she grabbed the table, causing it to tip. Landing on the ground, she slammed her fist against the deck as her wings grew.

Kita looked at Karen and Zhi. "You girls want your wings?"

"We have no idea where our Axioms are," said Karen.

Kita smiled. "Don't worry. I remember."

"Oh, hell, yeah!" said Zhi. "Pretties, Momma's coming."

"Give me a second," said Karen. "I don't want to ruin my jacket."

She and Zhi stripped off their formal Tet-Sec uniform jackets and undershirts, leaving them in their bras. Folding their clothes and placing them on the table, they nodded to Kita.

Kita laughed at Zhi's lace bra.

"What? I like to feel sexy chasing after bad guys."

Kita reached out and touched both on the nose. "Boop!"

"Oh shit," cried Zhi. "I forgot how much this hurts."

Kita stepped back to find Dominica and Apocalypse helping the other new Angels. She pointed to Catnip. "Rise, Mimic." Then to Flexi. "Rise Rivet."

"Oh, Void," groaned Rivet as she stood up, spreading her brown and orange wings.

"I got feathers!" cried Mimic as she waved her black and white striped feathers around wildly. "I got feathers! I got feathers! This means I can fly, right?"

"After some lessons," said Apocalypse.

"I will jump into the sky lane right now and—"

Apocalypse caught the Verisom Angel's arm. "Calm down. You've got more than wings. There's a lot to learn."

"My head does feel funny."

"I'm installing a computer in it, so, yeah," said Kita.

"You're doing what?"

"I'll explain over lunch."

"We've attracted a crowd," said Alliance. "My head feels funny, too."

"Angels are more than wings," said Kita. "You'll each get a unique suite of abilities, tools, and powers. Zhi, why don't you show them?"

Venom grinned as she fluffed her bright green feathers with blue interiors. She held out her hands, and holes opened in her palms. Lines of black widow spiders crawled out of the holes and marched up her arms and neck. She opened her mouth, and the spiders disappeared inside.

"By the Void," whispered Mimic.

"Onca uncia pardus!" chanted Poison as she drew a symbol

in the air with her glowing fingertips. A firework raced into the air and exploded.

"That's a cool party trick," said Mimic, the twitching and wiggling of her ears indicating she wasn't impressed.

"She's a witch," said Venom defensively. "You don't want to see her other tricks."

The crowd around the Angels was becoming large, and a reporter with a drone camera was reporting while trying to push his way to the front.

"We'll save the big tricks for later," said Kita. "For now, let's eat. Kimmy's dying for a burger."

"And you brought her here?" said Venom.

"Chuck's is way better," said Poison. "Don't worry, Kimmy, we'll take you for some real food. The vegan has no idea what good food is. She's only happy eating rabbit food."

"Hey! What's wrong with rabbit food?" yelled Mimic.

"Nothing, if you're a six-foot-tall bunny."

"And Chuck's is on Petal Nine," sighed Kita. "When we get back to the embassy, I'll explain what it means to be an Angel...or someone will."

"Hey, what about me?" said To'va. "You said to get uniforms, and I'm the only one out of uniform."

Kita raised an eyebrow. "I didn't think you were interested."

"It's one thing when it's just you, bird-god. It's another when you're giving it out to everybody."

Kita laughed. "Ok, but you have to do me a favor."

"I'm not doing enough for you already?"

"I want an ultraviolet forest on Roost. Think you can grow me one?"

"And what is Roost?"

"Home."

"I think I can raid my seed collection. I've only been tending that forest for decades."

"Deal." Kita reached out and touched the ancient Prii's deer-like nose. "Boop!"

To'va gasped and knelt, touching her hand to the deck. She cringed as ultraviolet wings grew out of her gray skin. When it was over, she pushed herself back to her hooves. "Not so bad. Not sure what you others were crying about."

Kita smiled. "Rise, Sage."

"Angel," said Apocalypse, "maybe we should get our food to go."

Around the restaurant, the crowd was twenty people deep, all trying to see or get pictures. Several reporters with their drones were broadcasting live, their images visible on the large displays lining the promenade.

Kita nodded. "Back to the embassy. Who's ready for their first flying lesson?"

"ME!" yelled Mimic, bouncing up and down excitedly.

"Kita, do you think this is wise?" said Alliance. "We'll draw attention to whatever it is your planning."

Kita smiled at the Aurori. "How'd you like to give a press conference to promote our very own Prii trainer? My offers to the other sponsored trainers aren't being received as well as I'd hoped."

"I've never done much promoting...is this why you made me an Angel?"

"You don't have to if you don't want to. I made you an Angel because you protect and help us. I wanted to return the favor. If you want to go back to the Aurori Diplomatic Corps, I won't stop you. What I gave you is yours to keep and do whatever you wish."

"I've seen you in action, and I know some of what you are capable of. I will remain in the Diplomatic Corps, but to further Angel interests and gain Aurori friendship—if the Corps will keep me."

"You're always welcome among the Angels."

Alliance waved to Dominica and Sage. "Come, let's introduce you to the Tet."

———————✕———————

THE ANGELS FILED INTO THE LIVING AREA OF THE EMBASSY. They had flown from the restaurant with a Tet-Sec escort. Along the way, Apocalypse gave the new Angels a primer on the Basic Angel Package. By the time they landed, everyone was comfortable with the basics. Though, Kita was sure the lessons on invisibility would be quite the show for the news drones that had followed them. Upon their arrival outside, Alliance and Poison chased the news crews away.

"Hi, Mom, Momma," said Jynx. She was sitting by the window, a fireball in one hand and water in the other. She was doing a drill Kita had taught her when she was six. The young Angel wore a black and electric pink plaid skirt that matched her wings, a white shirt with a black cartoon Verisom, and heavy black boots with electric pink sides. Her hair was in her usual short pigtails coming off the top of her head.

Velositi was next to the young Angel, encouraging her.

"Chelsea!" said Apocalypse excitedly. "Did you have fun? What did you find? Let me see!"

Jynx doused her fireball and put the water back in a cup, then glided to her parents. She twirled, flaring her skirt. "Velositi helped me pick stuff out. There's a bunch more upstairs."

"Very nice," said Kita. "It looks good."

"Velositi said you liked your kids in skirts," said Jynx sheepishly.

Kita laughed. "The twins definitely rocked them, and Lina liked her dresses. You can wear whatever you want."

"Who's the little Angel? And the big one?" said Mimic.

"Who's the bunny?" replied Jynx. "Why are we letting one in here? And why'd you give her wings?"

Kita raised her eyebrows in amusement, especially over seeing Mimic huff. "Everyone who doesn't know, this is Kimmy and my daughter, Chelsea. Affectionately known as Jynx."

"You have a kid?" exclaimed Mimic.

"I've had lots," said Kita. "And be careful; she's just like her mothers. The tall Angel is Velositi, my girlfriend. She's a Morphicon—a race of metallic beings that can morph into objects. I met her on Earth Eight-Thirty-two."

"Hey," whispered Mimic loudly. "Do they know about each other?" she pointed to Apocalypse and Velositi.

"It's a little late now, big mouth," said Rivet.

"Kimmy and I get along very well," said Velositi. "Are you trying to get a laugh or start a fight?" Her arm morphed into her cannon.

Mimic's ears stood up straight. "Yo! Just trying to get Kita to blush. I'm no fighter. I'm a lover. I've been with Kita since she dangled me out a window for trying to hack her credit chit."

"If you're not careful, I'll hang you out the window," said Apocalypse, "and drop you."

"I've got wings, you know."

Apocalypse made a fist and burned a hole in the ceiling with her beam. "They come off."

"Oi! Ok, ok..." Mimic put up her hands. "You girls play for keeps."

"Why don't we all grab a seat, and Kita can tell us what we're after?" said Alliance.

"Thanks, Kele. I prefer we all work together."

Alliance blinked and looked at Kita. *"Is this what you Angels were doing during those awkward silences?"*

"We take whatever advantage we can get. Welcome to the club."

Kita waved Apocalypse to Jynx and Velositi back to the window. The other Angels took seats around the room.

"Ok," said Kita moving to the middle of the room. "Everyone is allowed to make fun of my love life—to me. If the others want to discuss it, ask them politely. No one is going to pry into yours. Unless we see them leaving one morning—"

"Kita," said Alliance, "We don't have enough space for everyone. We'll have to requisition a bigger embassy or a nearby apartment building."

Poison spoke up, "It would be better if Zhi and I maintained our apartment separately to show we're not biased."

Mimic thumped her foot on the ground to get attention. "Hey, I'll behave—I'll do whatever you want if it gets me out of Verisom Manor."

Mimic wasn't a poor Verisom princess—quite the opposite —she'd made a fortune hacking and stealing others' assets by impersonation. But she was often in trouble with the other princesses and royal line because of her antics. One of the few punishments they had for wayward princesses was making them live at Verisom Manor.

"Living with a unit would be awesome," said Rivet.

The Diamock was unitless, meaning she had left the Diamock Military—persuaded as a young pup that a life of action and adventure awaited her in the greater universe. Kita had found her toiling in a private dock repairing junk ships and freighters for next to nothing.

"Where do you want to stay, Kele?" asked Kita.

"I have been so busy with you I've been staying here, but I do have an apartment in the Aurorian diplomatic zone."

Kita stroked her braid. "I think I'd prefer if we had a place where everyone had a room, just in case. I've found—in the past—this works well; even if people wish to stay elsewhere, they have a place to go in case of emergency."

"I will—hello? Is that you speaking in my head?"

"That's the Virtual Intelligence connected to the computer in your head. It's controlled by your thoughts, but I set it up to work like a Tet machine. You can change it if you wish. I'll give you and Catnip a lesson later."

Alliance put her hand to her temple. "I think I'm getting it. There. I sent the requisition to the Corps."

"By the Void!" squealed Mimic. "This is awesome! Wait...Why'd my display change to me being eaten by a laughing Djinn?"

Jynx giggled. "Noob."

"Kita, what kind of security did you give me if a kid can hack it? Ugh, I'm going to have to write my own."

"Ok," said Kita. "This is the last chance to back out before I get into the details. We are stealing something from Verisom's Chokecherry Industries. So, if you want to avoid trouble with them, back out now. No hard feelings."

"We are going home after this, right?" said Venom. "I mean, if I gotta blow up my commission in Tet-Sec, I want to go home afterward."

"This plan has multiple phases and moving parts, not just Chokecherry."

"They need to be burned to the ground," said Sage. "They're part of long-ear's subjugation of the Prii. And the golden ones help them."

"Hey!" squawked Mimic. "I had nothing to do with it, hornhead."

"Just being a long-ear makes you complicit."

"Enough," snapped Kita. "You're Angels—whatever you were before no longer matters. If you want, I can change you into something else. I just left you in your current form, guessing that's what you'd be most comfortable with."

"I'm a team player," said Mimic. "I'm not the one throwing around insults."

Jynx opened her hand and a holographic video played of Mimic calling Sage a hornhead.

"Damn. Can I do that?"

Kita opened her hand and projected a hologram of the Djinn Grall.

"Like mother, like daughter," said Alliance. "Jynx has as many tricks as Kita."

"You're an Angel; call me Chelsea."

Alliance smiled. Kita felt pride, trust, and acceptance in the new Angel. "As you wish."

"Someone wants revenge for being eaten," said Poison, looking at the turning hologram.

"Oh, Void, yeah!" cried Mimic. "I was sure our cash garden was gone after that."

"I still have scuffed plates from his goons," muttered Rivet. "Do we get to beat them down, too?"

"Ok, but you don't need all of us to get revenge as Angel Kita," said Poison. "If you wanted, you'd have destroyed the Tet to get to him."

The assertion startled the new Angels.

"There are stories of me ripping apart space stations, but I don't have that kind of power in a universe—at least, not anymore. I fixed that problem. Killing Grall is too easy. I want him to suffer like I did. The first step is to kill the jacksaur we stole in front of him. The second step is to feed him to whatever we steal from Chokecherry."

"What are we stealing?" said Venom.

Kita shrugged. "I don't know—"

Sage grunted. "Chokecherry is the only supplier of pips for the Prii. Their engineering is based on what they stole from Uvra. And they hold the female Prii in indentured servitude to pay for them."

"Ok, we get it," said Mimic with a big sigh. "You don't like them or us. You could just not buy them."

"And maybe you'd like to live without your ears and heart. The pips are the closest the female Prii can get to mi. Without mi, a female Prii is a useless suffering shell."

"Why haven't the female Prii filed a protest?" said Alliance.

"Because you golden ones don't talk to the females. The long-ears threaten any female Prii with the loss of her pips. Instead, you talk to the males, and those mi-less gold-diggers aren't about to let their only revenue source go."

Alliance frowned. "I'm sorry. I can file a petition to stop this practice."

"We're not here to solve social injustices," said Venom. "And I doubt we're going after Chokecherry to steal cute little creatures."

"It's not right," said Alliance.

"If you're objecting to us stealing, there's the door." Venom pointed to the elevator.

"No, it's not that. No one should be subjugated, by force, economically, emotionally, or spiritually. We need to know if the Grand Panel or the Diplomatic Corps are talking to the wrong people. No one should be profiting off your need to spiritually connect. You were brought here so you could live fulfilling lives as a member of galactic civilization. If we have failed, it must be corrected."

"The long-ears are going to fight you," replied Sage.

"Verisom will answer for these transgressions. It's bad enough they devastated your planet. They do not need to punish you economically and spiritually as well. And Kita, why does all this information pop into my head?"

"That would be the computer. It's a powerful VI that can automatically connect to networks and search them for information. It can then aggregate the data for your use. You just need to think of a topic, and it will search and give you what it finds. It can also help you run your office—scheduling, drafting paperwork, communications, propaganda, whatever you need. I learned a long time ago I need administrative warriors as much as I need actual warriors. Dev was my first, and she kept the Office of the Vicereine in shape to handle any emergency and kept our operations and propaganda moving smoothly."

"I hope to be as effective as she was."

"Do your best. That's all I ask." Kita looked around the room. "That is all I ask of any of you. We're a team, and we're only as strong as our weakest link—and nobody here is weak. Otherwise, you wouldn't be here. You've all proven yourselves to me.

"Now, Chokecherry does more than grow furry little creatures. They have a military arm where they grow big, mean, nasty creatures. Since they conquered the Prii, the Verisom have been trying to weaponize them. They have a collection of creatures, and I want to get the biggest, nastiest one we can steal, use it in a Prii tourney to kill the jacksaur we stole for Grall, and then I will feed Grall to the flies."

"You don't mean scaphism, do you?" said Apocalypse.

"I'll feed him the milk and honey myself."

"Whoa, Momma, that's brutal and disgusting."

"I skipped the course on torture and punishment," said Poison. "Milk and honey don't sound bad."

"It is when you're sandwiched between two boats and force-fed the stuff," said Jynx. "The most documented case is Mithridates who survived seventeen days of being fed and slathered in milk and honey—attracting all manner of insects and vermin who ate the milk and honey, his enriched feces, and then laid their eggs in him, the larva ate him from the inside."

"Lovely," said Poison, her chocolate skin looking a little green.

"Just when I think Kita's not that bad, she wants to do something like this," said Venom.

"I don't think she got the title God of Evil for being kind to her enemies," said Apocalypse.

"Wait. Back up," said Mimic. "God of Evil? Kita? Maybe God of Diabolic Schemes."

"She did hang you out a window," reminded Rivet.

"It wouldn't have killed me."

Kita smiled. "That was the point. I'd drop you, go down, pick you up, drag you by your ears to the next floor, and drop you again. Once you gave me back my money, I'd keep doing it until I'd broken every bone in your body—Then pluck your fur out, skin you alive, and let you hang around by your ears, singing."

Mimic's ears rotated back and forth, showing her confusion. "Singing?"

"I make my enemies sing as a warning to others."

"You know..." Mimic grabbed an ear and stroked it nervously. "Can't we just be friends? I like you...You like me? We can let your imagination run wild on Grall. I'll, ah, buy the milk and honey."

"I bet Kita's got some fascinating stories if she's the God of Evil," said Rivet.

"I do, but I'll save them for Roost. Let's figure out how we're getting into Chokecherry."

"Oi!" squealed Mimic. "Who do I get to go as? Princess Broccoli? Queen Brussel Sprout?"

As the Angel talked, her body rippled in a diamond pattern that rotated, changing her features and clothing to match the Verisom she was thinking about. Everyone stared at the elder Verisom, wearing pounds of jewelry and yellow sarong.

"What?" said Mimic, her voice regal and refined.

Jynx giggled. "You're so old and stuffy."

"Huh? I am not!"

"Yeah, you are," said Rivet. "You look just like your queen."

Mimic looked at Kita. "Please tell me the wings didn't make me old."

"No, your mind did. I called you Mimic for a reason. Think about whoever you want to be, and your body will transform."

"So..." Mimic shifted again, this time into Kita, much to

the amusement of the other Angels. "What do you think? Wow, I even sound like you."

"Yes, but you can't do this..." Flames burst from Kita, burning across her body in a raging inferno.

"There are lots of wannabes, but there's only one Momma," said Jynx smugly.

Mimic shifted back to her usual self. "You can't do it either," she said in a mocking tone.

Jynx glided over to Kita and put her hand in the flames. The fire engulfed her like Kita.

"You should have guessed Kita's kid would be as badass as she is," quipped Rivet.

"I'd just singe my fur anyway. No big loss," Mimic said with a huff.

Kita doused her flames. "So, how are we getting in to see what they have to steal?"

"Void, girl. I'll just walk in as the Queen," said Mimic. "Where do we want it delivered?"

"Doesn't the Queen of Verisom have a hundred princess entourage?" said Rivet. "Where are we getting them from? And why would the Queen of Verisom want to check out some second-tier princess' research lab?"

"Aw, come on. Now's my chance to be Her Majesty!"

"Perhaps we should be more lowkey," suggested Velositi. "We can just walk in invisibly."

"Doubt we could," said Poison. "Research facilities— especially the military ones I've toured—have thermal and other sensors. Along with biometric scanners and acoustic devices."

"Perhaps I have a solution," said Alliance. "How about we use Kita's status as ruler of the Angels to get a tour as a prospective investor. Princess Catnip can disguise herself as one of Chokecherry's board of trustees to be the tour guide."

"Is my mimic ability good enough to fool the sensors, Kita?"

"The more details you have about a person, the more realistic you'll be. We'll have to designate a target, get samples and scans. I can do that. I just need to know who. And I don't rule the Angels; Kimmy does."

"Oh no. I am the ruler of the Empire of the United States only. The flock is yours...but you do have to keep me happy."

"How about we all go?" said Jynx.

"When we get that far, we'll see," said Kita. "I like this plan, Kele. We'll need more information on the building, personnel, and its security systems."

"I can get that," said Poison. "If it's not in the Tet-Sec database, I'll ask them for it."

"Since when do the Verisom hand anything over?" said Rivet.

Poison shrugged. "I'll tell them it's for the fire codes. Those trump everything on a space station."

"You get that, and Catnip and I will decide on a target," said Kita.

"Flexi and I will stake out the building," said Venom.

"Can I go to?" said Velositi. "Sitting around watching is something I am good at."

"Sure," said Venom. "I can get you in close to scan one of our air bikes."

"I will work with Kele on what we need to get you inside," said Apocalypse.

"What do I do, Momma?" said Jynx; she sounded down.

Kita stroked her braid. "What do you want to do?"

"I want to work with you, but I'll help Mom, too."

Kita looked over at Apocalypse. "Kimmy, can Chelsea help you?"

"Sure. She could use a lesson on how business and government work."

Kita put a hand on Jynx's shoulder. "If your mom says you do well, I will take you on the collection mission—if you do exactly what I tell you. Understand?"

Jynx bobbed her head, rocking her pigtails. "Yes, Momma. I will. I promise."

"It's actions, kid," said Rivet. "Promises don't mean jack. They just get you in trouble. Anyone who promises you something is lying."

"I'm not lying," said Jynx softly.

"It's ok," said Kita. "I know you're not lying—if you were, I think your mom would want a word." She rarely invoked Apocalypse's ability to tell a lie with Jynx. It didn't seem fair to her to live under constant scrutiny. Kita had done it before and hated it, but Apocalypse wasn't Galina and never used the ability against her. Often, they worked together, one reading emotions and the other detecting lies. They made a formidable pair when negotiating.

"No," said Jynx. "I'll prove I can do it. I want to be part of the team."

"Something I'm missing?" asked Poison.

"Chelsea learned a life lesson earlier," said Apocalypse. "Getting shot hurts."

"Void, little girl!" exclaimed Mimic. "You took a bullet?"

"A bunch," said Jynx; her face was both embarrassed and proud at the same time.

"Suckers hurt," said Rivet. "Welcome to the club." She made a fist and offered it to Jynx, who looked at it confused. "Make a fist and bump yours to mine. It's how Diamocks show respect to each other."

Jynx did as instructed with a smile.

"You still want us to go shopping and train?" Sage asked Kita, motioning to Dominica.

"Yes. Once we get to the planning stages of the heist, we'll contact you. Until then, make a name for yourselves."

"I can help with that," said Alliance. "I've gotten several inquiries from other sponsors wanting to challenge the first Angel Prii."

Kita made a sour face for a moment. She'd been trying for days and gotten nothing. "Great. I don't care about the money. I want the fame."

"That might be a problem getting quality opponents," said Alliance. "The other sponsors are in this for the money. I understand we have plenty?"

"I don't care if you make the purse ten million credits. Do whatever you need to do to get noticed by the underground leagues."

"I doubt we'll have to go that high. The first bout should be a big splash, as Al'ice is new and interesting. I will work with To'va about picking a good opponent for Al'ice."

"Don't overextend yourself," said Kita. "Just because you have a VI and a computer doesn't mean you can be everywhere."

Alliance's picture appeared on the TV. "With the VI, I might just be able to."

"Ok, let's get going," said Kita. "Karen, Kele, I need to talk to you about burying these charges from Princess Mulberry and Princess Okra. And I have a forest I want saved. I'll tell you where it is later."

"And what did you do?" Venom said with a laugh.

"I hit a Verisom male a little too hard and broke his neck. His princesses are trying to bilk this for all the money the Angels have."

"If only they knew how much you actually have. They'd hire more lawyers," said Apocalypse with a smile.

"They're not getting the bloody moon," huffed Kita.

"I'm sure there's more to this story," said Poison.

"Isn't there always with Kita?" said Rivet.

"Ha, puppy dog," said Venom. "You haven't scratched the surface. Wait until we get home."

Rivet pushed away from the table. "We won't get there sitting around here. It's time we get to work. It's your turn to buy the snacks for this stakeout."

"We'll swing by the vehicle yard so Velositi can get her disguise. Hey, General, mind if I take the cruiser?"

"Go ahead," said Poison. "I'll call for a ride if I need it. I'll see you in a couple of days."

"If anyone has a problem, call me," said Kita.

"Call me first," said Alliance. "I'll call Kita."

Kita raised an eyebrow. "It's been a long time since I had an assistant."

"Not an assistant, an executive administrator."

"Well, executive administrator, let's get started."

———————✕———————

Kita sat with Alliance, Apocalypse, and Jynx in the gallery of a Prii tourney. Located on Petal Seven, Kita had never been here before, but the sponsor of the local pro, a Prii named Ki'lee, had agreed to a match—as long as it was on their home ring and Kita paid the entrance fees. Alliance had done a fabulous job of negotiating the match, keeping the fees to a minimum and the rules fair. Kita was grateful. She would have paid ten times as much to get Dominica the exposure.

The pit darkened as spotlights zoomed around, briefly illuminating the gathered crowd. The announcer introduced Dominica and her pip Cu'lu first, doing his best to hype the rookie. She was dressed in an updated fashion of the ancient Prii leaves and triangular top. She wore a short blue and green skirt high in the hips and low across her stomach. The purple sequined triangular top covered her chest, and a large hood hid her face. There was some applause at the mention of her amateur record—thirty-nine wins and zero losses. On cue, Dominica and Sage entered the pit; most of the crowd jeered while the Angels cheered. When Dominica reached her place at the arena, she swept off the large hood she was wearing to reveal her glowing horns. This caused a stir among the crowd on what it could mean.

Dominica's opponent Ki'lee and her pip Tr'va were announced to great fanfare, then the pit's lights came on. The competitors and coaches met and bumped fists, then the announcer read the rules for the match. Kita didn't hear anything out of the ordinary—no kill shots, no biting, ten-second holds, no enhancements, winning was by points or pushing the opponent out of the ring. The competitors took their sides and set their pips in the arena. Ki'lee's pip looked like a frog with a turtle shell. Dominica placed Cu'lu on the ring's sand. It made a *fsst* sound as it shook out its spikes. It looked like a hedgehog with powerful hind legs, a spiked tail, and bigger forelimbs with large claws.

"This should be interesting," said Kita. "Water versus earth."

"Which beats which?" said Jynx.

Kita shook her head. "Neither. Usually, the bouts are mud. Messy and sloppy."

"Do you want me to jinx them?"

Kita made a shushing sound and shook her head to get Jynx to be quiet. *"Don't say that out loud. We don't want people to think we can affect the outcome."*

"But I can."

"And no one will fight us if they think we cheat. Save your jinx until I tell you to. She probably won't need it until we get into the underground fights where cheating is rampant." Kita patted Jynx's thigh and looked down at Sage and Dominica. *"How you girls doing?"*

"We'll see if she listens," said Sage. *"I've given her all the advice I can until I see what this rootless can do."*

"Al'ice, how you feeling?"

"Nervous. I haven't had insects in my stomach before a match in years."

"She's no different than the rest. You have a stronger connection to the mi and have been taught how to use it. Remember your training and don't give any quarter. Take them down hard and fast."

"You seem to be good at that," chuckled Sage.

"It worked for me when I was competing in the sword ring and has worked out pretty good so far for everything else."

"Momma, when did you compete?" asked Jynx.

"When I was a teenager, I was known as the L'Ange de Yorq *of the sword tournaments in Champignon."*

"That's a Kita story I haven't heard," said Apocalypse.

"Remind me, and I'll tell you how I snuck in and won the men's tournament."

Apocalypse chuckled. *"Always have to be the best."*

"Back then, I had to prove it. Now..." Kita hugged Jynx. *"I'm just Momma."*

Jynx giggled and hugged Kita back.

"Would you say that if you weren't god?" asked Sage.

"I'd still be proving I'm better than the gods of old—but I was a mother then, too. Just this time, I have a way better kid."

"That's not a nice thing to say," said Apocalypse.

"*You never met Kylee. But maybe I'm a way better mom now. So, maybe it was me.*"

The referee called for the readies.

"Ready!" called Ki'lee.

Dominica, floating off the ground, said, "I am ready."

The lights twirled around the crowd as the music raised to a crescendo, then snapped to the arena.

"Fight!" ordered the referee when the music quit.

Cu'lu rolled into a ball and shot forward, striking Tr'va in the face. The ball of spikes rebounded off the sand and struck the pip again, repeating until Tr'va retreated into its shell. Its nose remained out, covered in scratches and drops of blood. The scoreboard jumped to fifteen points for Cu'lu.

"Never seen that before," said Kita.

"Something To'va taught Al'ice?" said Apocalypse.

"Must be. I've never seen it in the underground either."

"How do points work, Momma?" said Jynx.

"It's three points for a successful hit, two points for an ability hit, and one point for blocking an attack."

Cu'lu sprang to its feet, took two steps toward Tr'va, spun, lashing out with its claws and spiked tail, raking and smashing against Tr'va's shell, causing the defending pip to turn and slide on the sand. The scoreboard shot up again. Cu'lu jumped onto its forelimbs, whipping its tail around to hammer Tr'va, sending the pip tumbling toward the edge of the arena.

Kita glanced at the scoreboard. Only thirty seconds had passed. In her experience, tourney fights were slow and methodical. Trainers traded blows trying to wear down the opponent and score points. Kita had liked Al'ice because she was aggressive and attacked her opponent, but this was something new. Not even the underground fought like this— linking attacks, taking the fight to the enemy, and refusing to let them regroup. Tr'va hadn't launched a single attack yet—it'd been in its shell the whole time.

Cu'lu charged Tr'va striking the pip with its shoulder and pushing Tr'va to the edge of the arena. Tr'va had no choice but to come out of its shell and dig its frog-like legs into the sand. It extended its head and craned its neck to shoot liquid at Cu'lu, but the pip rolled out of the way. The liquid hit the arena sand and bubbled. Cu'lu leaped in the air, somersaulting forward and whipping its tail around, the spiked end coming down on Tr'va's head. The pip collapsed, its head and feet sprawled on the ground.

"Is it dead?" said Jynx.

Kita flipped through her lenses and concentrated her hearing. She heard a heartbeat and her scans showed breathing and blood flow. "It's stunned, but I think the match is over."

The referee was pointing at Ki'lee, who shook her head. Ki'lee's coach and sponsor were already at the referee's arm protesting.

"Come on," said Kita to the others, "let's go down and see if To'va and Al'ice need help."

"Ok," said Apocalypse, "but you're to keep your mouth shut. You let Kele, me, and To'va do the talking."

Kita shrugged and hopped the rail, leading the others to circle the large arena and land next to Dominica and Sage.

"Congratulations," said Kita as she touched Dominica's and Sage's arms.

Dominica turned with a frustrated look on her face. "If they let it stand."

"What are they saying?"

"It was unsportsmanlike, and I had an unfair advantage. I didn't give Ki'lee a chance to strike."

"But she did!" exclaimed Jynx. "She shot that stuff at you."

"Ki'lee's sponsor is saying I led with an illegal strike."

Kita fluffed her feathers in agitation. "Well, we're not without our own tourney lawyers." She turned to Sage, Alliance, and Apocalypse. "Ladies, you ready?"

"I have the rule book," said Alliance. "Scanning it, there's nothing wrong with what she did."

"Of course not," said Sage. "They're just juiced because that rootless can't do what Dominica did. It's Dominica's connection to the mi that gives her that kind of control over her pip."

"We'll get it sorted out," said Apocalypse. "You wait here and keep your mouth shut."

The three Angels walked over to the knot around the referee. Ki'lee's sponsor was a Verisom princess wearing pounds of sparkling jewelry and a brightly colored sarong. Her male Prii handler was also there. Ki'lee's side let off a wave of anger, resentment, and unhappiness when the Angels arrived.

Kita let them handle it. She turned to Dominica, "Why don't we go up to the galley and meet your new fans?"

Kita, Jynx, and Dominica glided up to the gallery, where fans were waiting for the decision and betting on the outcome. They flew around the crowd waving and getting everyone's attention. Kita picked an empty spot in the back to land.

"By the Void," a male Prii exclaimed. "She really can fly!"

The fans around them turned toward the Angels and quickly crowded them.

"Ok, everybody, step back," ordered Kita in her best command voice. "Dominica's here to sign autographs, bump fists, and answer quick questions—but nothing about the current match."

Kita's warning didn't stop the first question from being, "How'd you make your pip do that?" It was followed by, "Why do your horns glow?"

"*Ignore those,*" Kita ordered Dominica.

"Where's your male?" one of the many gathered Prii males asked. They all had their chests out, and some even banged and rattled horns with each other. It was typical male Prii behavior to attract a female.

Kita rolled her eyes but let Dominica answer. "*Answer if you want to. But don't flat out reject them. Horny men are easily manipulated.*"

"I don't belong to any male," Dominica said tersely. "I am an Angel Prii. I belong to the flock, but if the right male came along, I might bring him home to meet the rest of the girls."

"*Gag me with a chainsaw,*" groaned Kita. "*Now they're going to be everywhere.*"

"*I thought you wanted them thinking with the horn between their legs?*"

"*I do...just...ew...*"

"I wouldn't consider any of these anyway. I won't end up like my mother. But I will take their credits."

"Good. Keep playing nice. Let's move around the crowd and see if we can get them on our side."

They tried to move the crowd, but it was too dense, and the male Prii in the area seemed to be in full rut. The Angels hopped the rail and flew to another area of the galley, this one reserved for Verisom and Djinn.

"Excuse me," said Kita as she came in to land next to a Djinn. He was talking to a Verisom while his four covered wives waited to one side. "Hi!" Kita said enthusiastically to the wives. "Did you enjoy the bout?"

The four female Djinn looked at each other and backed away, trying to hide behind their male.

"You could end up like them," Kita said to Dominica.

"I'd cut off my horns."

"Why are only their eyes and tails visible?" asked Jynx.

"To keep other males from lusting after them. I don't know for sure, something about their religion. I've only ever seen one female Djinn uncovered. They look a lot like a house cat."

"They do not know Common, Human," huffed the Djinn.

"Actually, we're Angels. I was just trying to be friendly and introduce them to the star of the bout, Dominica." Kita waved to her.

"Yes, the hornhead with wings. I blame them for her poor form. That wasn't a fight. That was a mauling."

"I am not a hornhead," snarled Dominica.

"Shut your mouth," he snarled, "or I'll shut it for you." He glared at Kita. "You let your hornhead talk to civilized people that way?"

"I'm about to let her punch your muzzle in. She doesn't belong to me. She is an Angel and free to do as she wishes."

"If she doesn't punch you in the nose, I will," said Jynx.

The Djinn snarled and stuck out his hand, extending his claws. "Control your youngling, or I will teach it some manners."

Jynx burst into flame. "Try it, you shaggy throw rug, and I'll burn your fur off."

"Attendant! Attendant!" The Verisom princess cried, turning around and waving for one of the uniformed male Prii.

Kita waved her hand, pulled the drinks in the Verisom's and Djinn's glasses out, and threw them in their faces. *I hope whatever that is stains.* "Come on, girls, let's go find a better class of supporters."

"Yeah, we don't deal with racist garbage," said Jynx.

The Angels took off and ended up floating around the gallery, letting Dominica interact with the crowd.

"Angel, we're ready," called Apocalypse.

"Ok, girls, let's go get the verdict," said Kita to Dominica and Jynx. The young Angel with electric pink wings was becoming a celebrity in her own right among the Prii and Zentonians that filled most of the stands.

They glided down to the other Angels. Apocalypse turned and frowned. Sage's emotions said she was ready to kill the referee. Alliance's scales rippled, telling Kita she was annoyed.

"Didn't go well, huh?" Kita asked the other Angels.

"Idiot male," hissed Sage. *"Moron is an insult to his ancestry. He doesn't have a right to call himself Prii."*

"Sorry, Kita," said Alliance. *"I thought we had him until he met with the officials—"*

"Bunch of liars," snarled Apocalypse. *"Even when I called them on it. They'd rather disavow their own rules than say Al'ice won."*

"It's ok," said Kita giving Apocalypse a hug.

"But, how are we going to get Al'ice into the underground?"

"I'm not a grandmaster manipulator for nothing. Kele, I have video of the fight. Make it go viral. Tell the viewer it's a new fighting style that's banned in tourneys with a new champion that's better than any tourney fighter, legal or otherwise. We'll take any comer. The underground will lap it up. They're always looking for ways to increase draw. If we make a big enough splash, I bet other tourneys will buck the official line and at least offer us a friendly match." Kita sent Alliance the video. As she did, she had an idea. *"Chels, think you can hack into the scoreboard computer and put this video on loop?"* Kita passed her daughter a short clip of Cu'lu knocking Tr'va out.

"*Sure, Momma. I've been skimming their network since we arrived. How do I add credits to my card?*"

"*What have you been doing?*"

"*I hacked into their betting network and have been diverting rounding errors to my account.*"

"*Clever girl. Are you in the arena network?*"

"*I am now. Do you want me to start it now or?*"

"*Start it as they announce the winner.*"

The officials gathered behind the referee along with Ki'lee's sponsor.

Gee, I wonder how much the Verisom paid to make sure Ki'lee won.

"Trainers to the center of the pit," called the referee.

Kita nodded for Dominica to join him. The Angel floated over and stood next to the referee.

"*Smile,*" Kita instructed her. "*We didn't lose...*"

Dominica put on a smile and waved to the crowd.

The referee took both females' hands and said, "The winner by decision and forfeit is..."

"*Hit it, Chels,*" ordered Kita.

On the four-sided scoreboard above the referee, his image changed to a close-up of Cu'lu somersaulting and smashing Tr'va with its tail. The pip's eyes rolled up in its head, and it collapsed.

"Ki'lee...?" announced the referee as he looked up at the scoreboard.

The video repeated as boos and jeers rained down from most of the crowd. The Verisom and Djinn section applauded somberly.

Jynx's voice came over the PA system. "The fight was rigged. If you bet on Dominica, demand your money back."

That seemed to enrage some of the crowd further.

"*Nice,*" Kita told her daughter. "Let's go, ladies. I think we've sent the appropriate message."

THE SKY-CAR'S ENGINE WHINED AS IT LANDED ON THE STONE and concrete pad in front of the Chokecherry Industries bioengineering facility. Jynx pressed her nose against the mirrored window. Outside, male Verisom maintained the manicured landscape by eating the overgrowth. Excited, the young Angel reached for the door latch.

"Wait!" ordered Kita. "What did I tell you?"

Jynx huffed. "We're here to be served. We do nothing for ourselves. They are below us. If one speaks to me, I ignore them unless I have your permission. I only speak when spoken to by you or Mom. Do I have to do this, Momma? It seems so wrong."

Getting her to understand had taken Kita hours. It wasn't just her. Some of the other Angels weren't sure about the rules for the Vicereine either.

"I know," replied Kita. "But the idea is to project power and dominance. You didn't like how the Verisom treated us in the restaurant, right?"

"No..."

"Think of this as payback...and your momma is going to teach them how to do it right." Kita was dressed as the Vicereine, a black silk layered dress cut low on top that pushed her breasts up and dipped down her back to her butt. The front of the skirt was raised, revealing a pair of black leather thigh-high boots. A large oversized hood hid her face, and her blonde hair flowed down around her breasts. When she first came up with the design, her sister Tina had teased Kita that she could only see out her breasts. Today being an official function, Kita had carved a feather into her chest, letting the blood flow over her breasts and dress.

"Even I'm appalled," said Apocalypse.

"There's a difference between your citizens and constitutional monarchy and my father's serfs and absolute authority," replied Kita.

"You're not planning on being this way always, are you?" said Mimic. She sat across the compartment with Alliance disguised as Princess Asparagus, a leading board member for

Chokecherry. "Because not even Queen Carrot-Up-Her-Ass is this bad. She at least lets the princesses speak to her."

"It's all about control and power. And any Angel can speak to me, politely, of course. The idea is to show the other races they are not worthy."

The door opened, and a Verisom male dressed in a worker's jumpsuit stood to one side. Behind him were several Verisom princesses in lab coats over brightly colored sarongs.

"*This is the best they could do for royalty?*" chided Kita seeing the lackluster display. "*You did tell them I was royalty, right?*" she asked Alliance.

"*I did tell them the Vicereine and Empress of the Angels were coming.*"

"*I'll see whose tail I have to pull when I get out,*" said Mimic.

Kita slid around Jynx to the door and went to step out when the Verisom male grabbed her arm and pulled. Kita froze and glared at the male. "*Tell him to let go and never touch me,*" Kita instructed Mimic.

Mimic let out a long series of angry-sounding hisses, chuffs, and chatters in the female Verisom language. Male and female Verisom spoke different languages, their mouths being dissimilar enough to make them unable to replicate the sounds the other made, but they understood each other.

The male Verisom jerked away from Kita as if she'd hit him. Free of the intrusion, Kita exited the luxury sky-car. Taking a few steps, she turned, put her hands together in her oversized sleeves, and turned for Apocalypse. Her partner was in full regalia as well. Her silver and red calf-length Victorian-style leather jacket was embroidered with dragons. A silver silk shirt peeked out with a red vest. A golden dragon-head pauldron adorned her left shoulder while the heads of her tomahawks showed under her jacket. Her fur-lined hood hid her face but didn't stop her from taking Kita's arm.

It was one of the few breaks from Kita's traditional upbringing. Usually, the wife would follow behind the patriarch, but Kita wasn't about to do that to Apocalypse. She was going to make Jynx walk behind. Not to punish her daughter or disrespect her, but so Jynx could be with the other Angels and not have to suffer through her mothers' pageantry.

Jynx climbed out next. The young Angel fluffed her feathers as she floated into the air. Kita had graciously let her daughter pick her own clothes for the event. Pageantry and spectacle were not something Kita had taught her, but she approved of Jynx's choice—a black hoodie dress with a dead stuffed animal that looked like a Djinn on it. Jynx said she and Velositi had found it in a trendy Human boutique run by Zentonians. The dress' electric pink accents matched her wings. She wore some designer black and pink combat boots and black and pink striped tights. Kita had let her bring her sword, the hilt peeking above her shoulder. Like her mothers, she had her hood up. Kita doubted the scowl she wore was for show.

Kita gathered her family to one side as Alliance and Mimic exited.

On the other side of the landing pad, a Tet-Sec cruiser and skybike arrived. The cruiser's gullwing doors opened, and Poison exited wearing her Tet-Sec dress uniform. Venom hopped off the skybike wearing her dress uniform, and the bike morphed into Velositi.

Kita waited for them to join her group. She wanted as many Angels as she could justify to see the interior of the facility. It would make planning easier, and the others often had good ideas on how to compromise systems and get around security. Poison had provided blueprints of the building and all its systems. The group had studied them, but nothing beat firsthand experience.

Poison and Venom saluted Kita when they approached.

Kita returned a slight nod. Inwardly, she said, "*Hi, Ladies. Have fun chasing bad guys?*"

Poison laughed. "*More like catching up on paperwork. I swear, I leave my office for a few days, and they overflow my inbox on purpose.*"

"*Usually, I'm in the command post making sure all my cruisers are doing what they're supposed to,*" said Venom. "*But I've been doing visual inspections now that I have Velositi.*"

"*It's so much fun,*" chirped Velositi. "*But no high-speed chases yet. The petals are beautiful from the air.*"

"*Are you ready to put some Verisom princesses in their place?*" asked Kita sending all the Angels a picture of the Verisom queen on her knees.

The Angels laughed.

"*After the briefing you gave, if anyone can do it, you can,*" said Mimic.

Kita exposed a hand, briefly, motioning for Mimic to take the lead.

Mimic, assuming the persona of her disguise, Princess Asparagus, led the group toward the waiting Verisom princesses. "Chokecherry Industries is the leader in biocommunication development and deployment. We manufacture a wide range of pips to meet our customers' needs. And our target market expands by ten to thirteen percent a year. Most excitedly, we've begun expanding beyond our target demographic to other demographics and have seen thirteen percent growth in the last year in these emerging markets." Mimic stopped in front of the Verisom princesses. She looked at the four and said, "Please kneel for the Angels' majesty, The Vicereine."

The four princesses exchanged looks.

"She's not our queen," said one. "We don't kneel for her."

Mimic thumped her foot in annoyance and embarrassment. She leaned into the four and hissed, "This client is worth a carrot's truck worth of money to the company. I don't care if she wants to watch us pull each other's ears and tails. You only have to do it once. Now do it!"

The objecting princess stuck her nose in the air. "I am Verisom royalty. I kneel to no one. They bow to me."

Mimic grabbed her by the back of the head and pulled her so they were nose to nose. "You're not even in line for a warren, Cabbage. I know where you all rank. If you were more than fluff-tail princesses, you wouldn't be working here. Now get on your knees and be ready to explain your research." She thrust the other Verisom away and walked back to Kita, swinging her own tail back and forth to show she was the dominant princess.

"I apologize, Your Grace. They know not what they do. They are not used to seeing true royalty. Please, do not let their ineptitude dissuade you from seeing what we have to offer."

Kita remained motionless but said, *"Chels, help these bunnies find their knees."*

Jynx giggled. *"Sure thing, Momma."*

Exposing her hand briefly, Kita waved at the hesitating Verisom princesses as Jynx copied the gesture. Under their large feet, the stone came alive, reaching up, the rock wrapped around the waist of each princess and pulled them to their knees. Their squeaks and cries of surprise brought the nearby male Verisom running armed with gardening tools.

"Halt," ordered Mimic, as she raised her free hand as a signal for the males to stop. "They're in no danger. They're kneeling to show respect to our visitor, as you should be doing."

The males looked at Mimic, who returned a stern expression that made them drop their tools and take a knee.

Satisfied, Kita said to Jynx, *"You can release them."*

The stone receded, and the Verisom stood, their ears and noses wiggling to show their surprise, unhappiness, and submission.

"Please, follow me inside, Your Grace," said Mimic.

Kita followed Mimic inside to the cavernous, sterile lobby lined with large windows and uncomfortable furniture. A receptionist sat behind a large plastic counter that guarded the door to the lab and gestation area.

Mimic approached the receptionist and set her tablet on the counter. The tablet had been automatically hacking Chokecherry Industries networks since their arrival, searching for logins, passwords, maps, research data, and personnel lists. Anything and everything Mimic might need to complete her character. She scrolled through her tablet, then looked up at the receptionist rotating her ears to tell the other Verisom how critical the situation was.

"Rosemary."

"Yes, Princess Asparagus? I received your message. The facility is ready for the tour. I didn't expect to see you today. I thought you were gone to Verex Six."

Kita kept her face blank, but inside she was laughing Mimic. *I didn't think they'd have the tails to call us on it.* They had picked Asparagus because she was gone but didn't think any lower princesses would question her return.

Mimic smacked her foot on the polished concrete. "Does it look like I have time for small talk? I'm not about to keep the Angel's Vicereine and Empress waiting. Let us into the lab."

Rosemary's ears twitched. "I would need your keycard."

Mimic's eyes narrowed. "I have just come from a multi jump ship ride. My luggage is still on its way to Verex Six... along with my keycard. Now, open the door."

"I can't. I don't have a keycard. I can call—"

"Don't bother," snarled Mimic. "Cabbage! Come open the door." She waved to hurry the Verisom scientist over. When the Verisom wasn't moving fast enough, she bound over, grabbed her by the arm, and pulled her to the door.

"You'd think this was some Djinn visiting or something," she huffed at the pair of Verisom. "Open the door." She shoved Cabbage at the reenforced door.

From her pocket, Cabbage produced a keycard. She scanned it, pushed the handle down, and held the door open as Mimic led Kita and the other Angels through.

"Girl, they would be pissed if they ever find out who you are," said Venom to Mimic.

Mimic was so far down on the list of Verisom princesses she barely counted.

"Yeah, but it sure is fun pulling their tails."

Cabbage led Kita and the group down a hallway with large glass windows and security doors. The Verisom stopped and looked at Mimic.

The Angel glowered at the researcher. "Well, are you going to explain?"

Cabbage's ears rotated in an expression of uncertainty. "Your...Grace, on your right, is our DNA research and development lab. We use it to develop new specimens for our target demographic. We've also developed a new line of specimens for our expanded demographic."

Kita's hand appeared briefly. *"Ask her what the difference is,"* she said to Mimic.

"Explain the difference between the two lines."

"Our expanded demographic line contains our most popular specimens from the target demographic line. However, the expanded line has been modified to remove the organ our target demographic needs to control the specimen. We market the specimens as pets and companions to our expanded demographic, allowing them to have their favorite specimen they see in the tourneys at home. The expanded specimens also lack many of the abilities the target specimens have, making them useless to our target demographic."

Inwardly Kita frowned. She didn't like where this was headed.

Kita's hand shifted again. *"What's the price differential?"*

"I found the last board meeting's minutes. Give me a second to scan them."

"Researcher," said Apocalypse using her royal tone, "How much does a specimen cost?"

Cabbage's ears twitched in uncertainty as her eyes shifted to Mimic. "I don't know the exact amount, but it's a lot—"

"Shut up," snapped Mimic. "Your Highness, our pips have two price structures. For our expanded demographic, the pips are five hundred thousand credits and come with lifetime medical care. We have contracts with various manufacturers to provide licensed food, toys, and habitats. Everything a proud pip owner needs.

"Our target demographic requires a pip companion, or they experience excruciating headaches and hormone imbalances. Here at Chokecherry Industries, we pride ourselves on being able to meet their needs. For our target demographic, we offer two programs—our professional program and our companion program.

"Our companion program allows our target demographic to lease a pip of our choosing for the low quarterly payment of five thousand credits. This does not include food, habitats, or medical coverage. Companion program users sign an agreement to bring the pip to us for medical care every thirty cycles. Depending on the pip's needs, this can range from two hundred to thousands of credits. Users are required to buy licensed food and habitats for the safety and wellbeing of the pip.

"Our most popular package is the professional program. For the low sum of two hundred and fifty thousand credits, our target demographic can purchase a pip of our choosing. If the purchaser wants a specific pip, the price increases depending on the pips' abilities. Our top-of-the-line pips can cost over a million credits. We require the professional users to sign a medical contract and a tourney contract. The medical contract stipulates the user will bring the pip to us for all medical care for injuries sustained in and out of tourneys or every thirty cycles. The tourney contract gives us the right to collect fifty percent of the winnings if they compete in tourneys. If the pip dies, naturally or otherwise, we have a death stipulation that the user will bring us the pip. If death is the user's fault—by neglect or injury—a twenty-five percent penalty is added to their outstanding balance. If the user cannot care for or pay for the pip, they sign an agreement that they will return the pip to us at a significant penalty. If the pip is released without our permission, there is a finder's fee and a hundred percent penalty added to their balance. If the user dies, the pip is immediately remanded to us, and the debt passes to the next of kin."

It took all of Kita's willpower to remain calm. The fact that Dominica had signed these agreements twice and didn't own them outright after she paid the debt made her blood boil. She had spent over six hundred thousand credits to pay off Dominica's pips, and Chokecherry had never revealed these stipulations to her. Especially if the Prii needed them, like Mimic said. She'd never heard of a Prii female being in pain without a pip, but then, she'd also never seen a Prii female without a pip.

"*Angel,*" said Apocalypse, "*this...this is so wrong it's disgusting. It's indentured servitude bordering on slavery.*"

"*It's not my fault!*" Mimic exclaimed on the Angel communicator, even while she droned on verbally about the company's quarterly earnings. "*I had no idea this was going on.*"

"*No one is blaming you,*" said Kita. "*I had no idea this was going on, either. Poor Al'ice. Now I understand To'va's rage. But what can we do?*"

"*We have to do something,*" said Apocalypse.

"*If we destroy the facility, all the female Prii will suffer even more. I don't have enough credits to buy the facility. All I can say for sure is it'll end when we deactivate this universe.*"

"*That seems cold comfort. Kele, isn't there something the Aurori or Grand Panel can do?*"

"*Chokecherry Industries is a private corporation owned by a sovereign government. I didn't realize their terms were so harsh or that the Prii females needed the pips for their health. That might be the leverage we need. If we can find proof of it, I can pass it along to the Grand Ambassador and ask that she convene a medical review board. I know the Verisom and Djinn will be against it, but the other races might be more open.*"

"*Thank you,*" said Apocalypse. "*What are we going to do for Al'ice and To'va when we go home?*"

"*I'll bring their pips' DNA and make them whatever they want,*" replied Kita.

"*If we wait for the Grand Panel to act, it'll never happen,*" said Venom. "*We need to expose them and do something now.*"

"*If the information fell into Tet-Sec's lap, we could launch a raid,*" said Poison.

Venom sighed. "*Tet-Sec would take forever, and the Verisom and Djinn officers will tip these long-ears off. Kita, we have to do something.*"

Kita hid her frown. This wasn't part of her agenda. "*If we do something now, we jeopardize getting the pip we want. I'm not against the idea, but we have to be patient.*"

"*These are fellow Angels we're talking about,*" Venom reminded. "*We can't let Al'ice and To'va be held hostage by these long-eared slavers.*"

Kita ground her teeth. "*I understand your concern. I'm working on a way to free Al'ice and To'va outside of burning down Chokecherry.*"

"*What about the other Prii?*" objected Poison.

Kita rolled her eyes. When they left this universe, there would be no other Prii. "*I have a plan. When we come to steal the pip we want, we'll take footage of the other military pips, and Catnip and I can hack into their files and download their data. We'll turn it over to Tet-Sec and several news agencies. That'll put immediate pressure on Tet-Sec and the Grand Panel. Kele, can you arrange that?*"

"*I can when I have the data and footage.*"

"*Why don't we just turn them loose and let them run free on the petal?*" said Jynx.

Kita smiled inwardly at her daughter. "*We could do that.*"

"*And if someone gets hurt?*" said Poison.

"*All the more pressure on Chokecherry.*"

"*Let's wait on doing that until we see what we might be letting loose,*" said Apocalypse.

"*Can we have an ultraviolet forest full of pips when we get home?*" Jynx asked.

"*What's happening?*" said Mimic. "*How do you fit a forest in that tiny embassy?*"

"*I'll explain later,*" replied Kita. "*Continue the briefing.*" She waved her finger to signal she was ready to move forward.

"Yes, Your Grace," said Mimic. "On this other side is our nursery and gestation center. Cabbage, you want to explain to Her Grace?"

The other Verisom wiggled her ears in confusion. "Wouldn't Princess Huckleberry be better? It's her department."

Mimic's ears stood erect to show her annoyance as she leaned into the researchers. "I don't care who does it. Just do it and quit making us look bad."

Huckleberry stepped forward. She had a large black spot around her right eye and black spots on her ears. "Your... Grace," she said, starting slowly. Her ears showed her uncertainty and discomfort. "The gestation center can accommodate up to twenty-five specimens at a time, allowing us to create a lengthy waiting and delivery period for our target demographic. Our professional program users are given elevated status for their delivery. There is an option to buy priority delivery for a hundred thousand credits. Express delivery comes standard with those users who buy specimens over a million credits—"

"They actually give someone a break?" said Venom.

"If you can pay for it," replied Poison.

"—For those in our expanded plan, express delivery is standard. It takes thirty cycles for a specimen to reach maturation. After we uncork a specimen, they are taken to the nursery. There they spend thirty to sixty cycles until fully matured. Expanded specimens are taken to the activity area where they interact with other expanded specimens and staff to be socialized."

She motioned to a large open area surrounded by a waist-high barrier. Inside contained a sandbox, water, food dishes, and various enrichment items.

"We have found this decreases the number of returns by our expanded purchasers. Those specimens bred for our companion and professional programs are placed in isolation tanks until they mature."

She pointed to a wall of small glass tanks barely big enough for the pip to take a few steps and turn around. There were water and food dishes attached to the side and sandy bottoms.

"Studies have shown that bypassing the specimen's socialization period, it decreases their life span by twenty-five percent. It also makes them harder for the target demographic to connect with. The specimen is more likely to reject the target demographic, forcing them to return the specimen to us, incurring a contractual penalty, and forcing them to pay for another specimen. We then offer the returned specimen to another target demographic for full price.

"This model has shown to be highly profitable and generates a constant flow of target demographic users. Once a target demographic user enters the system, it's virtually impossible for them to get out. Target demographic users will need to purchase several during their lifetime. Chokecherry is the only supplier of specimens, and we own the patents for all of the research and development for specimens and how the target demographic connects to the specimens. We annually grow ten to thirteen percent, and the wait time for specimens increases every month."

It took all the self-control Kita had not to kill every Verisom in the facility. Chokecherry was deliberately hurting her friends for greed and turning them into slaves. Things she despised. Her instincts told her to blow the facility up and leave a crater, but her mind knew that wouldn't solve the problem, only create a greater one. The only way to do that was to get what she was after.

"It...ah..." Mimic gulped. "We here at Chokecherry have several social plans in place to ensure the target population's growth. We offer free specialized healthcare to our target demographic and introduced a hormone into their gestation cycle to produce more of the target demographic—without their knowledge, of course. This has a forty percent effective rate. We offer a bounty rate to the target demographic male population. The more of the target demographic they impregnate, the more we pay. We also pay the males to run the tourneys for the target demographic. We've sponsored laws and regulations to keep the target demographic from opening their own tourneys. Through generational social engineering programs, we have removed the target demographic from their ancestral role as dominant in the male-female relationship and made them subservient to the males—"

"*Enough,*" ordered Kita in a voice she only used as a god. Her gaze lingered over the four Chokecherry Verisom. Her mind briefly drifted over how to shove them into the pips' isolation tanks.

"Of course, Your Grace." The blood drained from Mimic's ears.

The other Verisom looked between Mimic and Kita, confused.

"*I swear, Kita, I had nothing to do with this,*" Mimic pleaded. "*I didn't know it existed. I'm just as appalled as you are.*"

"*It's not you, Catnip,*" said Apocalypse. "*But this is very shocking and sickening. Amazingly, it's gone on for so long under the Grand Panel's and Tet-Sec's noses."*

"*I'm thinking of excuses to raid the place,*" said Poison. "*But it's going to be tough. The Verisom have powerful allies on the Grand Panel and in Tet-Sec.*"

"*Let's move on to the military pips,*" ordered Kita in an icy tone.

"Yes, Your Grace," said Mimic. She looked at Cabbage. "Let's see the military pips."

"The what?"

"The..." Mimic paused and glanced at her tablet. "...special usage pips. That's what Her Grace is here to see."

Cabbage's ears twitched violently. "We're not allowed in that sector."

"You don't have to go in; just open the door."

"My keycard won't open it."

"Fine. Take me to the door. Then go get Rosemary to open the door."

Cabbage eyed Mimic suspiciously but muttered, "Your tail," under her breath. She led the Angels down the hallway to a reinforced metal door with no marking on it. There was a keycard reader and a speaker mounted on the wall next to it. Cabbage stopped next to them. "Rosemary can't open the door either. You'll have to call and see if they'll let you in."

"Get out of the way," hissed Mimic. "I'm not scared of anybody." She hopped in front of the speaker and keycard reader. She tapped on her tablet. "*Ah, Kita, this door and keycard reader aren't on the schematics or connected to the network. I can't hack it.*"

"*Try calling and see who answers.*"

Mimic stabbed the call button with a black painted claw. "Hey, whoever there, this is Board Member Asparagus. I have a VIP tour to see our special usage pips. Hurry up and answer the door." She turned to Kita. "Sorry, Your Grace, I left my keycard in my luggage, which should be on Verisom by now."

The four Verisom researchers exchanged confused glances.

"I thought you were going to Verex Six," said Cabbage.

Mimic chattered her teeth angrily. "Shut up. This isn't time for small talk. I had them send my luggage to the palace. The last thing I want is some Zentonian male rummaging through my underwear."

Kita chuckled to herself over the mad ear twitches of the Verisom. Zentonian males were known for being hyper-sexual during certain times of the year, and they found Verisom females extremely attractive. As far as Kita knew, she'd never heard of a Verisom having sex with a Zentonian, not even in the movies or porn—or even the wealthy paying for it. However, there was a wide genre of graphic novels and fiction on the subject—primarily written and drawn by Zentonian males.

The door swung open with a bang, and the oldest-looking Verisom female Kita had ever seen stepped out. Her wizened fur was patchy and gray, but her right ear had more sparkling piercings and hoops than Kita had ever seen in a Verisom— including Kita's former fiancée Cotton, who'd been third in line for the throne. Whoever this ancient Verisom princess was, she was important...probably more so than Mimic's impersonation, Asparagus. Her lab coat gave Kita a clue. On the breast pocket was the royal Verisom seal, not the Chokecherry logo the rest wore.

This should be interesting...

"Asparagus! What in the Void are doing here?" the old Verisom snarled. "And what in a spotted male's flea-infested crotch do you want? I've got things to do."

"*By the Crushing Depths,*" bemoaned Kita. "*It's my great grandmother in bunny form. I would think one would be enough for the universe.*"

"*I can see where you came from,*" said Venom.

Kita chuckled. "*We shared similar qualities and looks. If you didn't look closely, we could pass as twins.*"

"*That's just what the world needs,*" teased Apocalypse.

"I, ah..." Mimic fumbled for a response as the other Verisom princesses looked on with amusement. "...We...have a special VIP tour. The Vicereine and Empress of the Angels are here to see what you've been working on. They're interested in investing huge sums of credits in Tet businesses. Why don't you introduce yourself and tell them what you've been working on?"

The old Verisom's nose and ears twitched violently. "Have you gone dead under the ears, Asparagus?" She snapped as she reached out and pinched some fur from Mimic's cheek, yanking a tuff out and throwing it on the floor.

Kita winced inwardly. That was the ultimate Verisom sign of dominance. Whoever this old Verisom was, she was important and probably in the royal line.

"*Zhi,*" said Kita, "*can you release a few of your pets to get inside? I don't think we're getting in, and I don't want Catnip to look like she has mange.*"

"Eh, I'm used to it."

"*Sure, Kita. I'll drop a few friends on the way out, too.*"

"Explain yourself, Asparagus. Why are you not on Verex Six?" the old Verisom demanded.

"I...I..."

The old Verisom looked around Mimic at the Angels. "I don't give a male's left testicle who you are. This research lab is off-limits and...and by the Void, Asparagus! You let Tet-Sec in here?" The old Verisom reached out and ripped a fistful of Mimic's black and white fur out. "Get out, all of you! This is a royal Verisom facility. We don't need investors. I'll file a complaint with the Grand Panel and my embassy. Now get out! Before I have my males throw you out."

Kita raised an eyebrow, though the old Verisom couldn't see it. "*Jynxie, bring the Verisom to their knees. It's one thing to be asked to leave. It's another to threaten physical harm.*"

The young Angel flittered over to her mother and pulled a hand from her hoodie dress's pouch. Metal tendrils rose from the floor and wrapped around all of the Verisom, including Mimic, and pulled them down to their hands and knees.

Kita motioned with a finger to Apocalypse. She stepped forward, spread her wings, and looked down at the kneeling Verisom. "I am Empress Apocalypse, the Dragon God, partner to The Vicereine of the Angels. Your behavior and your words insult us. Your lack of respect is appalling. I would expect better from someone who wears the Verisom royal crest—"

"You ignorant winged Human, after I take your DNA, I'll have you plucked, basted, and fed to the sand fleas."

"*She thinks like Kita,*" said Poison.

"You have to have power to back up those threats?" said Apocalypse.

"Featherhead, I have more power—"

Jynx darted around her mothers, drew her sword, and glided down to the old Verisom.

Kita kept in character and didn't move, but asked, "*Jynxie, what are—*"

With a lightning-quick flick of her wrist, the sword hummed through the air and took the old Verisom's heavily ornate right ear. Jynx twirled and stabbed the ear out of the air. The old Verisom let out a howl as blue blood ran through her white fur.

Jynx recovered the ear from her sword, and with a flourish, put the sword away. She glided up to Kita and presented the appendage to Kita.

Kita's hands appeared from her sleeves, and she took the trophy from her daughter.

"*Thanks, Jynxie. This will be quite the object lesson, but I fear it may cause more problems than it solves.*"

"*I thought I was protecting you and Mom's honor.*"

"*You were, sweetie,*" said Apocalypse. "*But this now gives them a reason to be violent to us.*"

"*Don't worry, Chels,*" said Kita. "*I've been playing this game longer than this bunny has hopped. Let them up.*"

The metal tendrils receded, releasing the Verisom. The old Verisom didn't get up. The other Verisom stood to one side, their ears and noses twitching wildly as they hissed and chuffed l, but Poison and Venom moved to keep them from helping the older Verisom.

Kita and Apocalypse moved to stand in front of the old Verisom. Apocalypse knelt, took off her glove, and placed her hand over the old Verisom's wound. The blood ceased to flow as Kita handed the ear to her partner. Apocalypse placed the ear on the stump and reattached it. When she finished, she stood and nodded to Kita.

The old Verisom ran her hand over her ear and wiggled it back and forth. "What the Void are you?"

"Angels," said Apocalypse firmly. "We are the apex predator of the universe."

"I'll have your DNA, and when I'm done, an army of winged males to wipe you from the Void," the old Verisom snarled.

Kita sighed to the other Angels. *"Just like my great grandmother. She never knew when to quit. Zhi, how are your arachnid friends doing?"*

"We're in and exploring. I've dropped a few ant queens to feed us the data. Give us a few hours and will have the place mapped out, and we'll know what they're working on."

"Good. Catnip, spoof the cameras and the logs. Make it look like we were never here. Chels, help her if she needs it."

"But, Momma, what about what's behind the door?"

"What lesson have I always told you?"

"Adapt and overcome."

"The plan is adapting."

"Yes, Momma."

"Love, when I give the signal, devour the research assistants. That should slow down Chokecherry."

"I can't get big enough to eat them, but I can cook them."

Kita stepped forward within arm's reach of the wizened Verisom.

She spoke in a low, menacing tone, "You *play* as god..." Then lifted her head, revealing the lower part of her face, and roared, "...and I *am* god."

Her left arm shot forward, seized the old Verisom by the neck, and lifted her off the ground as her big feet struggled to find the carpeting. With a sweep of her right hand, Apocalypse transformed into a red and silver dragon big enough to fill the hallway's width. Kita turned the old Verisom so she could see.

The Angels scattered, giving Apocalypse room to swing her spike-lined tail and slam it into the Verisom researchers' thighs, dropping them to their knees. Apocalypse swung her long spike and armor-plated neck around to face the four. Her head dropped low, and her jaws opened revealed rows of sharp, curved teeth. A stream of flame billowed out, engulfing Cabbage, Huckleberry, and their assistants. Their screams died in the roar of fire as the smell of burnt fur and meat filled the air. Apocalypse flapped her bat-like wings to clear the air of smoke and odor.

Kita turned the Verisom to her. "What do you think of my creation?" Kita squeezed her hand, causing the old Verisom's red eyes to bulge. "You think you are a master of the power of creation...I will show you the grandmaster."

Behind Kita, the other Angels gathered.

"But the power of creation is nothing to the power of Reality."

The Verisom's eyes widened, and her mouth opened, revealing her big buck teeth. Light shot from her eyes, mouth, ears, hands, and feet. Her white fur rippled as she let out a distorted shriek. Kita dropped her to the ground, where she curled into a ball. A bright light grew in intensity and became blinding. When the light vanished, a lump under the Verisom's lab coat was all that remained.

"What did you do, Momma?" said Jynx.

Kita knelt and lifted the lab coat, revealing a white rabbit. She picked it up and stroked its soft fur. Her head snapped up, and she glared at a male Verisom peeking his head out the door. He withdrew under Kita's heavy glare.

"Should I kill him?" said Venom.

"No," replied Kita softly. "Leave him to tell the tale. No one will believe him anyway. It's time to go. We have what we need."

"I hope Zhi's bugs can hack a server," said Mimic. "None of what's beyond that door is on the servers I hacked."

"We'll get it. We have enough to start the Tet-Sec and Grand Panel ball rolling. We'll give them more when we return. I have a feeling this place will be disrupted for a while."

"What are we doing with the bunny?" said Poison.

"I'll give her to To'va as a present."

———————×———————

"SO, YOU REALLY ARE GOD," VENTURED RIVET AS THE Angels sat around the living area of the embassy planning their heist of Chokecherry. She had the new pet bunny in her lap and was stroking its back and ears. "Can you magically change Catnip into one of these?"

"Hey!" the Verisom protested as she tapped on her tablet, uploading data from Chokecherry to Kita to be interpolated and correlated.

Mimic wasn't the only source of data. A stream of ants marched across the table to Venom. The insects and arachnids she'd dropped in Chokecherry were reporting back. The ants could pass information almost as fast as the data networks through the use of pheromones. Back on Roost, Kita had helped Venom create a computer program that turned the pheromone into data they could use.

"It's not magic," said Kita. "In the universe, I came from gods could wave their hands and manipulate the equation, but that's not allowed in my universes. I used the same method to change her as Kimmy uses to change into a dragon—"

"Oh! You should have seen that Flexi," crowed Mimic. "Horns, claws, tail, teeth—and fire! She burnt those hoity-toity tail fluffers up."

"So, she could turn back, right Momma?" said Jynx.

Kita smiled over to Jynx, working out the details. "She could if she knew how. Maybe she'll figure it out."

"So, she's like me. Her mind is still in there, just with an animal brain?"

Kita nodded. "She can understand everything we say. I'm sure she's already working on trying to change back."

"That sounds like a Kita punishment," said Velositi.

"What happens when she figures it out?" asked Jynx.

"We'll see where we are when it happens. I can always put her to work under Sprokkit."

Velositi chirped laughter.

"There's a fate worse than death," chided Venom. "Ok, ladies, the ants have given me everything they found. Kita, you mind showing what I made?"

Kita opened her hand and filled the center of the room

with a holographic image of the restricted lab at Chokecherry. The image was built of billions of points of different colors as the ants and spiders detected water and other liquids, electricity flowing through wires and devices, and different surface types. Kita's computer put it together to make an image.

Venom got up and walked into the hologram. "My babies have found four large tanks, here," she pointed to four cubical voids on the map. "They couldn't get in, but they're big and are connected to these machines here. There is some kind of communications set up here that look like they go over something long and narrow—"

"A horn?" said Dominica.

Venom shrugged. "No idea."

"It could be a device to boost the signal coming from a female Prii's horns," said Sage. "They wouldn't need to if they let the females connect to the mi."

Kita noticed the glow coming from the Prii's horns had diminished some. "What about you? How's your connection?"

Sage wiggled her nose and rubbed her lower horn. "We need to go back to the forest to reconnect. There's just not enough up here for us."

Kita nodded. "You're to go before the heist. I need you both at your best."

"Who's going with us? The Yellow Fist Pack might still be looking for Angels."

"I'll figure that out when we figure out how we're getting into Chokecherry."

"The place is going to be in an uproar," said Apocalypse.

"I have an idea," said Poison.

Kita looked at the Angel. She was in her daily wear Tet-Sec uniform with her black hair in braids wound into a bun at the base of her skull. "Go ahead."

"The missing Verisom scientists haven't been reported to Tet-Sec yet—probably never will. But we can counterfeit a search warrant to gather clues for their disappearance. We go in disguised as Tet-Sec and *find* the military pips and confiscate the one we want or all. Zhi can get us a Tet-Sec truck to get away in."

"Where are we going to store it?" said Alliance.

"I've got some warehouse space," said Kita. "That sounds like an easy plan."

"How are we moving the tank?" asked Velositi. "It would look suspicious if we just picked it up."

"Steal a gravlift," said Rivet.

"Or just take me to one, and I will copy it."

"Isn't that a little undignified for you?" said Apocalypse.

"It is only for a few hours. I will require Kita to bring me something else to copy when we finish."

Venom waved a wing. "We've got a brand new skybike that's a copy of the racing bikes hidden in the garage. I don't trust anyone not to wreck it."

Velositi's eyes lit. "That sounds perfect."

"I'll bring it to the warehouse."

"I've done up the missing person paperwork," said Poison, "and will activate it in the computer—if that's the way we want to go."

"Won't that alert the rest of Tec-Sec?" asked Apocalypse.

Poison shook her head. "I will bury it like the other times we've used Tet-Sec as cover. It'll never reach the investigators. We'll take their place instead."

Apocalypse cocked her head and smiled wryly at Kita. "I should have known you'd have help on the inside."

Kita chuckled. "It helps to have friends in high places."

"Don't you take an oath or something?" asked Jynx.

"Hierarchy of oaths, kid," said Venom. "You should have seen my face when Kita waltzed into my office—"

"Then they came to mine," said Poison. "If anyone could find her friends, it would be Kita."

"I'm still looking for Anna, Nicole, and Lizzy," said Kita. "I believe Nicole and Lizzy are on Earth fighting in the colony wars. Anna won't let herself be found unless she wants to be."

Poison smiled at Jynx. "What Kita does is illegal, and we do help on heists and cover it up, but she only steals from those that can afford it. We've never stolen from a Tet facility or from ordinary citizens."

"Kita as Robin Hood?" Apocalypse said with a giggle.

"I do give some of it away to the needy." Kita motioned Dominica. "But the wealthy are stupid about their security and easy marks. Most of the time, it's the rich stealing from the rich. My preferred clients treat it as a game. Sometimes, we're hired to recover items stolen from them. They don't care about the item. It's just one-upmanship among them. I don't really care as long as they pay."

"Have you ever had anyone who won't pay?" asked Jynx.

"I have, and they regret it as we take something far more valuable."

Rivet laughed. "Yeah, I remember the night we took apart that luxury sky-car and left the parts all over the property."

Kita smirked. "Ok, Karen, let's go with that plan. Zhi, Flexie, and Velositi will secure the Tet-Sec truck we'll need. Karen, will you need any help?"

"No. I just need to visit my office."

"Kele, how goes promoting Al'ice?"

"I've gotten several inquiries from underground and legitimate tourneys. I've been monitoring the diplomatic correspondence from the Verisom. Princess Mulberry is still upset about the restaurants and that Tet-Sec is dragging their feet—thanks to Karen. They want to file an injunction against the Angels, but I have the Aurorian Diplomacy Corps digging up legal challenges that no one's seen in centuries. I know eventually this will go to trial. I want to know what the strategy for that will be?"

Kita steepled her fingers. "We'll be gone, and they won't exist. Just keep stringing them out for a few more weeks."

"You want to explain that?" said Mimic. "Because some of us aren't god, and it's a little spooky when you say we won't exist."

"Everyone here will exist. Let's just say, right now, you're only seeing a small part of Reality. When this is over, I'll take you to see a bigger part of Reality—that's with a big R."

Mimic's ears twitched in confusion, so did Rivet's quills.

"I don't get it," said Rivet. "What am I missing?"

"Reality has layers," said Apocalypse. "Right now, we're in the innermost layer. When this is over, we'll go to the next layer out. This is where the Angels exist. There's a third layer where Kita and I exist. We create and control Reality."

"So, I'm just a dumb bunny," admitted Mimic. "You're talking metaphysics?"

"Home," said Jynx.

"You'll see," said Kita. She looked at Dominica and Sage. "Kimmy, Chels, and I will escort you to the forest so you can do what you need to do. Catnip, see what you can do about getting into Chokecherry's military lab computers."

"How am I supposed to do that?"

"Converse with the bunny." Kita waved at the bunny in Rivet's lap. "And we have her lab coat with her ID badge."

"Oh, well, easy-peasy-Princess Lemon-squeezy." Her fur became a diamond black and white pattern as they flipped, and she changed into the wizened elder Verisom. She waved playfully to the bunny on Rivet's lap. "I guess I'll wander over and see what trouble I can get into."

"This doesn't look good," Kita said as she stood in front of the door to the ultraviolet forest. The OFF-LIMITS sign had a yellow X painted over it. Above the sign was painted a yellow fist. The lock on the door was missing, and Kita could smell burnt wood. "Everyone, stay here. I'll check it out."

"Kita, if they're in my forest, I will—"

Kita turned invisible as Apocalypse grabbed Sage's arm. "Let her make sure it's safe first."

Kita pulled back the door enough to let her slip inside. She walked down the short passage and stopped at the exit. It was as she feared—the forest was a smoldering skeleton of what it had been. Only bare dirt and charred stumps of the trees remained. The ultraviolet lights overhead had been destroyed—and Kita guessed the fire extinguishing system with them.

She glided over the destruction, looking for any signs of life. "Hello?" she called. "Anyone here?"

Moving toward the pond, the waterfall no longer flowed. The water was choked with dirt and ash. Kita doubted any of the fish could survive. Gliding up to the top of the waterfall, Kita searched the area that had been Sage's home. It was ash now, but she hoped to find something.

The sound of scurrying caught her attention. Kita picked up a burnt log and found a pip with armor like an armadillo curled around a hide bag. Tossing the log aside, Kita corralled the pip and lifted it up. She tucked it under her arm and stroked its back. *It's a fireproof pip. Probably the only one to survive the carnage.*

The pip relaxed in her arm, allowing Kita to pick up the bag. Undoing the drawstrings, she opened it and found thousands of seeds. *The forest lives on.*

Kita retraced her steps to the door. She pushed it open, and both Dominica's and Sage's noses twitched at the smell.

"What's burning?" demanded Sage.

Kita shook her head. "You don't want to see. Here, I recovered this little guy and these." Kita handed over the pip and bag.

"What in the mi happened to my forest?" wailed Sage.

Kita grimaced and shook her head. "It's gone. Everything is gone. I'm sorry."

Sage hugged the armored pip as she collapsed, sobbing. The other Angels gathered around her, doing their best to comfort her.

"Hey, Kita!" called Mimic.

Kita stood and took a few steps away from the other Angels. *"Yes?"*

"So, I'm in Chokecherry—and this communication suite you gave us is unreal, by the way—and you'll never believe who the old carrotface is!"

"No idea, who?"

"Princess Cranberry!"

"I don't know who that is."

"*She is only the aunt of Queen Chokecherry and fourth in line for the throne. You won't believe the way people hop for her.*"

"*I can imagine...*" Kita remembered how the Verisom acted around Princess Cotton, Kita's one-time fiancée in another universe. "*...listen, I'm in the middle of a crisis. I need you to scout that lab and get your hands on all the data, records, and security passwords you can.*"

"*What's the crisis? Can I help?*"

"*The Yellow Fist Pack burned down the ultraviolet forest. Al'ice and To'va are rightfully upset. I need you to get as much information as you can and get back to the embassy.*"

"*Ok. Void. Is my heart supposed to hurt? I've never felt bad for anyone before...but I just want to hug Al'ice and To'va.*"

"*Part of being an Angel. We play, fight, and console together. We find strength and comfort in each other...even the most hardened and emotionless of us...like me.*"

"*I've seen your emotions...I wouldn't call you emotionless. Well, I'll give them a hug and buy them a drink when I get back. What should I tell the employees where I've been? You should have seen Rosemary's face when I got out of the cab. It was priceless.*"

"*Tell them you've been in negotiations with the Vicereine and the Angels. We're offering our expertise in bioengineering and genetics, plus a large sum of cash. We want to see their data before we commit.*"

"*Ok. I, ah, got a look at what was in those tanks. They're unlike anything I've ever seen. The big one is the size of a jacksaur. It's called X5—here, I'll send you a picture.*"

Kita received an image of a gorilla with a long, large tail running from the back of its skull, down its spine, coiling around its feet. The feet had retractable curved claws like a cat, and the front hands had spikes on the knuckles. Large fangs jutted from its lower jaw.

"*That's the one we want. Get as much information on it as you can.*"

"*Right. I've seen a pair of Prii females around. I think they're the test subjects. I'll find out.*"

"*Ok. Be careful.*"

"*Hey, this is me you're talking about.*"

"*I need to go. I have to call Karen about the Yellow Fist Pack.*"

"*Oh, yeah. Get the bastards.*"

Mimic disconnected, and Kita called Poison.

"*Hey, Karen. I know you're busy, but I have an emergency.*"

"*Oh, dear. What happened? I got a funny feeling.*"

"*The Yellow Fist Pack burned down the ultraviolet forest. I need you to pull all the information you have on them.*"

"*Shit. Al'ice and To'va must be devastated. I'll grab everything I can. We have a thick file on them. They're more pirates than mercenaries. The only reason they can operate in the open on the Tet is that their leader secured a letter of marque from the Djinn king.*"

"*I thought I killed the Yellow Fist's leader.*"

"*Their leader is a Djinn name Rark GeFraw. I know where their headquarters is. What are you thinking?*"

"*Burn them to the ground.*"

"*I will put out an APB for Yellow Fist Pack members and have them brought in. That will make it easier for us. I don't think we have the firepower to destroy their headquarters. I'll check to see what other properties and assets they have.*"

"*I want GeFraw.*"

"*I'll see if we can flush him out of his headquarters. Tet-Sec suddenly targeting his people is something he can't ignore. After bringing in some of his people, I'll reach out to him and see if he's willing to talk. We might be able to ambush him coming or going.*"

"*I want to do it after we hit Chokecherry. Al'ice and To'va are going to want to get theirs.*"

"*I understand. I will figure something out. When do you want to hit Chokecherry?*"

"*As soon as we have the assets we need. Catnip is there now, getting intelligence and data. This is what we're after.*" Kita sent her a picture of X5.

"*Wow. That's quite the beastie. You girls get back to the embassy. The APB will only take me a few minutes. I'll contact Zhi and see where she and the other Angels are at. We'll meet you back at the embassy, and we'll find a window for our heist. I'm thinking the sooner, the better. Chokecherry is still off-balance, and I would think the return of one of their senior people will reduce their alert level.*"

"*Thanks, Karen. I need to go attend to Al'ice and To'va.*"

"*Give them a hug for me. See you soon.*"

Kita closed the connection and turned back to the knot of Angels. She walked over to them and touched Jynx on the wing.

"Chels," Kita said, getting the young Angel's attention. "Go into the forest and get a couple of handfuls of dirt and something to carry it in. Also, a little bit of water."

"Ok, Momma." She flittered through the door and disappeared down the access passage.

Kita sat in front of Al'ice and To'va. She reached out and touched both. "I'm sorry," she whispered. "I know your friends can't be brought back, but it's not the end. We can regrow the forest."

Sage raised her head from Apocalypse's arms. "Not in my lifetime. I should have known better than to trust you. The trees said you were a death-bringer. But you had Al'ice and... and...I didn't listen..." tears tumbled down her gray freckled cheeks. "The mi is gone. We're forever rootless. This is a fate worse than death."

"I know it seems that way...and I can't replace the pips and other animals that were lost, but it's not the end of the trees or the mi. You have their seeds. We can regrow the forest, and I promise it'll be in your lifetime."

"You said yourself we're leaving!" yelled To'va. "Where can we possibly go that these seeds can be any good!"

"I am god. Here my power is limited, but at home, my power is infinite."

Jynx flittered up, carrying a metal pot filled with soil. A ball of water floated next to her. "I hope this is enough, Momma."

Kita took the pot. "Let me have a seed," she asked of Sage.

"Take them," Sage snarled. "They're useless."

Kita opened the bag and took out a seed, and pushed it into the soil. She took the water from Jynx and watered the seed. "Al'ice, put your hand over the seed and concentrate on growing it."

Dominica wiped her tears with one hand and put her hand over the pot with the other.

"What are you doing?" hissed Sage.

"Watch and see."

Out of the soil came two cotyledon leaves. The stem grew tall, and new leaves grew.

"I—I can feel the mi," exclaimed Dominica. "I know this tree! To'va! It's a child of Toomica." She moved her hand and offered the pot to Sage.

Sage took the pot and stroked the leaves gently. "It is," she gasped. "How?" Her barbell-shaped pupils were big and bright as she whispered her plea to Kita.

Kita smiled. "My power may be limited, but I'm still god. A long time ago, there was an Angel named Eden. She could grow an entire forest in days. It's a powerful ability that you both have. When I told you I wanted you to grow me an ultraviolet forest, I wasn't kidding. This little pot of soil contains all the biome information I'll need to create you the perfect conditions to grow your forest."

The two Prii Angels hovered their hands over the plant as they did, the glow of their horns increased.

"I feel so much better," said Dominica.

"We'll outfit a room at the embassy with ultraviolet lights, and you can grow as you want. We'll take them with us when we leave."

"Can we get some more soil?" said Sage.

"As much as we can carry," said Kita. "But we need to hurry. The others are expecting us back at the embassy soon."

"Ah, what is all that?" said Venom as Kita and the other Angels entered the embassy living area carrying metal baskets full of dirt.

"What's left of the ultraviolet forest," said Kita as she led the others into an empty room to deposit their haul.

"I felt a disturbance," said Velositi. "What happened?"

"The Yellow Fist Pack burned down To'va's and Al'ice's ultraviolet forest," said Kita emerging from the room. "I found To'va's seed collection, a pip, and we brought as much soil as we could. When we get home, I'll make a biome sphere for them. Until then, To'va and Al'ice are going to turn that spare room into a garden where they can connect with the mi and recharge."

"I am so sorry," said Velositi as she glided over and gave the Prii Angels a hug. Rivet and Venom joined her. "I am sure Kita has a plan."

"I'm working on it with Karen. They're a bigger organization than I thought, and she's using Tet-Sec to round up as many as she can."

Venom let out a grunt. "They're nothing but pirates protected by the Djinn Crown."

Kita shrugged. "Nothing wrong with being a pirate. I've known a few."

"True," said Velositi. "Their mistake was crossing us."

Kita smiled. "So, did you get what we need?"

"Sure did," said Venom. "We checked out a truck, got the skybike, Velositi scanned a large gravlift, and I grabbed us some Tet-Sec work uniforms."

"Outstanding. Catnip should be—"

The elevator dinged, and Mimic and Poison exited.

"Speak of the devil," chuckled Kita.

"I thought that was you," said Venom.

"Once upon a time in my life. Hey ladies, how'd it go?"

Mimic's ears twitched frantically. "We need to go if we're going to get what we want."

"Oh?" said Kita.

"Yeah. The Queen wants all the secret research shipped back to Verisom—tonight. I told her the earliest the facility would be ready would be tomorrow. She's already sending males to dismantle the facility."

"Well," said Kita. "I guess we better get over there. We have what we need. Catnip, anything special we need to know?"

"I don't think so. This should go just like the Fermi job."

Kita nodded. The Fermi job had disguised her crew as workmen to enter a wealthy Zentonian residence to steal several pieces of artwork. Not only did they do the construction job, but they walked out with the artwork under their drop cloths.

"You go ahead of us and act like you're there to supervise the move. The rest of us will go get the truck and Tet-Sec vehicles and arrive a little later. Slow them down as much as possible. When we get there, Karen will lock the place down under Tet-Sec authority, and we'll go in and take the military pips. We'll load them up and take them to the warehouse."

"What about Al'ice and To'va?" said Karen. "Tet-Sec doesn't employee Prii females."

Kita stroked her braid as she thought. "Hide your wings and go with Catnip. You're new Prii there to help move the pips."

"What do I tell the Prii already there?" said Mimic.

"Have them teach Al'ice and To'va all they know about the pips."

"Ok. Ladies, ready to see your prize?"

"A little nervous," said Dominica.

"Just act like you belong there."

"Al'ice and I will work on the pips," said Sage. "Just keep those rootless busy."

"No problem. Let's go before it's too late."

"Ah, Kita," said Rivet. "The bunny got away."

Kita's face contorted between surprise and annoyance. "She figured it out that fast, huh? Well, it's a long hop between here and Chokecherry. Let's hope we beat her there."

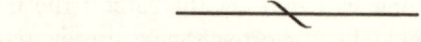

Kita, dressed in forensic investigator overalls, followed Poison into the cavernous lobby of Chokecherry.

"*Kita,*" called Venom. "*The back lot is full of trucks and Verisom males moving stuff. I don't see any tanks with pips. Should we proceed?*"

"*Yes. Order them to stop and use your cruiser and skybike to keep them from leaving. We're approaching the main counter and should have access momentarily.*"

Rosemary was seated behind the counter on a call. The two disguised Angels stopped before her, and Poison pulled out a tablet and turned it on. The Angel shoved the document at the Verisom—who ignored her.

Kita let Poison wait. She walked around the counter and went to the security door, pulling out a copy of Cranberry's keycard she'd made. She pressed the card against the reader, waiting for the light to go green. When it flashed red, Kita frowned.

"*Ladies, we have a problem,*" Kita called to all the Angels in the area. "*I think Cranberry made it back. Everyone, hold positions while Karen and I deal with her.*"

As Kita spoke to the others, Rosemary got up and approached her. Kita spun around to meet her.

"That area is off-limits to you," said the receptionist.

Kita pointed behind her. "She says otherwise."

Rosemary turned and seemed to acknowledge Poison's presence for the first time. "Tet-Sec has no authority here. This building and surrounding grounds are sovereign Verisom territory. I must ask you to leave."

"This document is a sovereignty override signed by the Grand Panel. Tet-Sec has been informed that five Verisom personnel from this facility have gone missing—including the director Princess Cranberry."

"I can assure you, officer, no personnel from this facility have gone missing. Now, please leave."

Poison stood her ground. "Then I wish to speak with Director Cranberry."

"That's not possible," rebuked Rosemary. "She's busy overseeing our move and doesn't have time to oversee wild clux chases."

"I have the authority to shut this facility down, and I will. Out of courtesy, I brought a small group to conduct my investigation so as not to impede your work, but I will call in a full Tet-Sec investigation unit if I have to."

Rosemary's ears twitched in annoyance. She went to her desk, bent over, and tapped out a message. "She will see you when she has time," said Rosemary looking up.

Poison touched a communicator on her jacket. "This is *General* McKnight. I'm at the Chokecherry Industries on Petal

One, sector seventy-two. I need a full crime scene investigation unit sent to my location immediately. Better bring a digital forensics team and scent tracking team as well. Over."

"Roger, General. Teams are being dispatched."

Kita hid her smile at Jynx answering. She and Apocalypse were outside as reinforcements and scouts—in case the Verisom tried something.

Poison looked at Rosemary. "I suggest she hurry. As soon as my team arrives, I'm shutting you down. I suggest you tell them to save their work."

Rosemary's ears stood straight up as she tapped out another message.

Kita moved back next to Poison. The pair exchanged a troubled look. Kita was worried about the Angels she'd sent earlier.

"Catnip...Al'ice...To'va...are you girls alright?" She waited, her concern growing the longer she went without an answer. Turning, she glared at Rosemary and said, "Is your lab encased in a Faraday cage?" Kita could usually penetrate such shielding, but not always.

Rosemary returned Kita's glare with a disapproving twitch of her ears. "That is confidential information."

"My team needs to know so I can communicate with them."

"May I suggest chalk and slate?"

Kita balled her fist, ready to punch the Verisom when the door opened. Cranberry stepped out guarded by four male Verisom in space armor carrying heavy repeaters. She wore her lab coat with the royal Verisom crest, and a keycard hung below.

"I see you really are just Humans," said Cranberry, her ears moving in delight. "The wings are elaborate costumes."

Kita bared her teeth as her black and pink wings exploded into view, fully open. Poison's orange, purple, and black wings opened behind Kita.

"Where are my Angels?" Kita roared.

Cranberry's ears twitched in enjoyment. "Getting

acquainted with X5. They should be lunch now. Do you have any last words I should tell them?"

"Onca uncia pardus!" yelled Poison as she waved her glowing fingers in the air to cast a spell. Behind Cranberry, her males froze—their weapons clattering to the floor. At the counter, Rosemary—trying to join her boss—went rigid and fell over.

Kita launched herself at Cranberry, landing on the Verisom's chest, driving her to the hard marble floor. Kita pulled back a flaming fist and struck Cranberry under her right eye, burning away the fur and leaving angry blisters.

Poison caught Kita's next blow. "We need her alive if we're to save the others."

Kita grabbed Cranberry by the throat and dragged the Verisom through the pip lab.

"*Kimmy! Jynxie!*" Kita yelled.

"*What is it?*" said Apocalypse sounding concerned.

"*Cranberry has Catnip and the others. Get around back and help Zhi with the males.*"

"*What do you want us to do?*"

"*I don't care if you go full dragon. They're not allowed to leave and keep them from stopping us rescuing the others.*"

"*Got it, angel. Hurry.*"

"*I'm moving.*"

Kita stopped in front of the door to the military lab. "Open it," she ordered Cranberry.

"Go fluff your tail," the elder Verisom spat.

Kita slammed Cranberry's head against the wall next to the door's keycard reader. She grabbed the keycard from Cranberry's lab coat and pressed it to the reader. The light flashed red. Kita let out a rage-filled growl.

Shaking Cranberry by the neck, Kita snarled, "Open it, and I'll kill you quickly."

"It's deadbolted," laughed Cranberry. "It can only be opened from the inside."

Kita smashed Cranberry's nose against the keycard reader's speaker. "Order them to open it."

"No. Kill me if you want. You're not saving them."

Kita lifted Cranberry in the air and spiked her to the deck, causing her to bounce. Bursting into white-hot flames, Kita pressed herself against the door, trying to melt her way through.

"You'll be here forever, Momma," said Jynx as the young Angel glided up as a ghost. She passed her mother and disappeared through the door.

Kita backed away as the door latches *clanked* and the door swung open. She dashed into the room. Two female Prii had their horns hooked up to a device and were looking at the transparent plastic tank containing X5. Mimic was on her side, bleeding profusely from bites and slashes to her abdomen, chest, legs, and head, but she wasn't out. Her one good wing was extended, trying to protect Dominica and Sage. The elder Prii Angel's horns were glowing brightly as she appeared to be fighting for control of X5. Dominica had her pip Cu'lu out and was trying to use it to distract the monster.

On the far side of the lab, a large cargo door was opened to the back of a transport truck. Several male Verisom were wheeling large pieces of computer hardware into it.

"Stop!" roared Kita as she threw Cranberry at the pair of Prii females hooked up to the machine. The Prii sidestepped the body, and one pointed at the tank.

X5 hopped forward and drove his clawed feet into Mimic. The Angel collapsed, her wings falling to the tank's floor. X5 spun, its tail splitting into five slivers. The slivers swung and slashed at Dominica. Sage broke from her attempt to control X5 and jumped in front of Dominica, her wings spread to protect the younger Prii Angel.

"No!" screamed Kita as she flashed toward the Prii controlling X5.

X5's slivers plunged into Sage's chest. The Angel's head lulled back in a gasp.

"To'va!" cried Dominica as she attacked X5's slivers with Cu'lu.

Ultraviolet blood leaked from Sage's mouth as the glow from her horns became intense. Ultraviolet light exploded from her, weaving between her and Dominica. The younger

Prii Angel shrieked as the light penetrated her, lifting her off the ground and escaping through her horns, eyes, mouth, wingtips, and hands. X5 roared, and its slivers pulled apart, cutting Sage into five parts.

Kita lowered her shoulder to slam into the Prii, but she was jerked sideways as a series of rounds from a heavy repeater slammed into her chest. She slid sideways under a table.

Dominica clutched her fists, ultraviolet light escaping between her fingers. She reached out with a hand, and light shot out and engulfed X5. The beast reared, banging its spiked fists against its chest. The young Prii Angel waved the creature to her.

"Momma!" cried Jynx as she skidded into land next to Kita.

"I'm alright, Jynxie. Just took a few rounds."

"What's happening to Al'ice?"

"I think we're seeing mi in action."

"I've lost it!" cried the Prii attached to the machine. "Shock it! Shock it!"

The other Prii spun around and slammed her fist down on a big yellow button. In the tank, large electrodes extended and crackled to life. Bolts of electricity zapped around the tank striking X5, Mimic, and Dominica.

"Stop," Kita yelled. "You'll kill them!" She stumbled to her feet, lit a fireball, and threw it at the pair.

Jynx glided into the air, raised her hands, and ripped the machine the Prii were using from the floor. In the tank, the electricity stopped. X5 lay on the ground. Dominica remained upright in the air, her horns and eyes glowing brightly.

"Come on," said Kita to Jynx. As they walked toward the tank, another burst from a repeater struck Kita. She threw her wings wide and wrapped herself around Jynx to protect her. Turning her head, she spotted the Verisom male with the repeater by the cargo door. *This is Kita. I need someone to take care of a Verisom male with a repeater. He's shooting at Jynx and me.*

A dragon roared as its head came into view through the doorway. The mecha-dragon opened its mouth and devoured the male.

"Thanks, Velositi," Kita yelled to her girlfriend. Taking

Jynx's hand, they glided over to the Prii. "Open the tank," she demanded.

The pair backed away with their hands up.

Kita turned around to Cranberry, pointing a pistol at her. "You think a couple more are going to bother me?"

"What have you done to my creation?" snarled Cranberry with a terrifying glare.

Kita's glare matched hers. "I've got two dead Angels. This time, there will be no escape for you."

A thumping came from the tank. The group turned to see X5 banging on the side with Dominica hovering behind it, all her horns glowing.

"I don't think it's your creation anymore," said Jynx.

"What did you do?" Cranberry yelled at Kita.

Kita raised a hand. "I didn't do anything. I think this involves a force beyond your control."

"Or yours, god."

Kita raised an eyebrow. "I suggest you let them out."

"Are you crazy? They'll kill us."

"Velositi? Are you still out there?" Kita called.

The mecha-dragon head slithered through the door, her chrome spikes and scales reflecting the ultraviolet light coming from the tank. There was a screech of metal, and a crunching sound as the mecha-dragon sat on the truck blocking the door.

"Kimmy, I need you. Catnip might be dead. I'm not sure."

The mecha-dragon head swung around and looked in the tank. Her head was as big as X5. The two beasts stared at each other for a long second, then turned away.

"I don't think Angels have anything to fear," said Kita to Cranberry. "But you might want to run because I'm letting them out."

"She's not going anywhere," said Jynx as she turned, drew her sword, and put it to the elder Verisom's throat.

"Impressive speed and technique, Jynxie."

Jynx smiled and bobbed her head back and forth, making her pigtails bounce.

"How do I let them out?" Kita asked Cranberry.

"They'll kill us."

"If they do, then we get a quick trip home. It's the end of the line for you."

"You're delusional."

"But I'm safe in my delusions. Are you?"

"You're not god! There is no such thing. You're just alien beings we know nothing about. Let me study you, and I'll know all your secrets. I figured out the Prii. How hard can you be?"

Kita turned and looked at Dominica, then at the other Prii. "Have you? I think you're missing something."

Apocalypse glided in, following the mecha-dragon's neck. She patted Velositi and glided over to Kita. "Ah, so, I hope you didn't have a plan for all those males."

Kita wasn't sure if the question was for her or Cranberry. She shrugged. "Just in the way is all."

"Good, because Velositi and I ate most of them. They were armed." She glared at Cranberry.

The elder Verisom waved the question away. "One male is as good as another. You didn't damage the equipment in the trucks, did you?"

"She acts like she's living through this," quipped Apocalypse. "Where's Catnip?" she asked, looking around.

"And what are you?"

"God."

Cranberry looked at Kita. "How many people believe your delusions? And if you're god, why do you need two of you?"

Kita smiled lovingly at Apocalypse. "Because the main plane of Reality is a boring place. Now, open the tank and let my Angels out. Catnip is in there, love."

"Big green button on that console over there." Cranberry pointed to a machine next to the one Jynx had destroyed.

Kita glided over, found the button, and stabbed it with a black-painted nail. The top of the tank retracted. "Al'ice!" Kita called. "Kimmy needs to come in and look at Catnip."

Dominica floated out of the tank. A stream of ultraviolet light lifted X5, Mimic, and the parts to Sage out of the tank.

"Oh no," gasped Apocalypse. "What happened?"

Kita sighed heavily. "X5 tore To'va and Catnip apart...then

something happened. I'm not sure what. I'm waiting to see what comes out."

Dominica glided down and placed X5 next to her. The other Angels she placed at Apocalypse's feet. She opened her mouth and spoke in an ethereal voice. "We are Ultraviolet, the rage of the dying light. The avenger of a destroyed planet. The soul of a people destroyed by genocide; their children enslaved. The embodiment of the mi, the blood of the universe." She reached a hand toward the Prii that had helped the Verisom. Streams of light ran from her hand and wrapped around them, and lifted them off the ground. Light burst from the Prii' mouths, horns, and eyes. "Children of the light, you have been deceived and betrayed your sisters. You help the corrupted destroyers create a creature unknown to the universe. Let you be cleansed and free."

The light receded from the Prii, and they were set back down.

"Go!" said Ultraviolet. "Go and tell the others mi has been restored, and their salvation is at hand."

"Out that way!" Kita pointed out the cargo door. "I'll tell the others to let you out." She turned to Ultraviolet. "Is Al'ice still in there?"

Ultraviolet knelt before Kita and Apocalypse. "There is no Al'ice or To'va...only Ultraviolet."

"You don't have to kneel," said Apocalypse as she knelt to check on Mimic.

"We kneel to recognize the masters of this universe. The mi is at your command."

Kita gave Cranberry a sideways glance. "Told you so. The universe knows its creators."

"So, you're the universe?" said Apocalypse. She looked confused as she ran her hand over Mimic's body, checking her injuries.

"The mi is what holds the universe together. We flow through everything—connecting it—like blood through the bodies you inhabit."

"Are you like the Force?" said Jynx.

Kita snickered. "I don't think so, Jynxie."

"Preposterous," snarled Cranberry. "There is no such thing."

Kita stroked her braid. "It is possible this universe has a consciousness. It might even be a living being. If so, Ultraviolet is its manifestation."

"How?" said Apocalypse, her hands glowing. "Chelsea, I'm going to need you."

The young Angel looked at Kita.

"I got her," said Poison coming up behind Cranberry and putting a hand on the old Verisom's shoulder. "Kita, those up front are restrained and immobile. Kimmy, an ambulance is on the way."

Jynx knelt next to her mother and, following her instructions, ran her hand over Mimic's legs, healing the bleeding injuries.

"Thanks, Karen. I don't know, love. When we go home, we'll have Ryan and Sprokkit take a look. If it is conscious, we may not be able to just shut it down. But I might need a bigger brain on this. One that's seen it." She looked at Cranberry with a wicked grin.

Ultraviolet's head snapped to Kita. "Master, I must protest."

"Stand, please," said Apocalypse, waving Ultraviolet to her feet. The Angel didn't stand but hovered off the ground. "I don't like this idea either, Kita. Just kill her and let her be right that there's no afterlife."

Kita snatched the pistol from Cranberry. With a backward glance, she tossed it in the tank. "Jynxie, how do people become Angels?"

"Friend, need, potential, and reward," she replied while healing.

"There is a fifth way—punishment. I've only done it once to the Angel Toxic—Kara Laramie. She steered my daughter Lina down a path of greed. She did accept her fate as a fallen angel and served me well—service which I rewarded. She became Countess Laramie in my empire and later the god Deer'g. She eventually found peace and happiness with the

Angel Stormy—Amanda Garing." Kita looked at Cranberry. "The question is, will you be as useful?"

"We can't take her back to Roost!" exclaimed Apocalypse. "She could destroy everything. What if she finds a way to us?"

The corner of Kita's mouth ticked up. "Knowing it can be done gets you ninety percent of the way there. Can she go the other ten percent?"

"Don't do it. She got out of the bunny. She could ruin our home, our friends, our family."

"Yes," said Kita. "She could also move our research ahead leaps and bounds."

"I'm not working for you," huffed Cranberry.

"She's not lying," said Apocalypse.

"Compromise," offered Kita. "We take her with us, as is. See if she comes around. Let her meet the other Angels and see what they can do."

"I'm gone as soon as you go to sleep."

"Luckily, Angels only sleep every couple of weeks."

"Master, if I may," said Ultraviolet.

"Call me Kita and her Kimmy. You're one of the flock."

"Are you sure Al'ice is gone?" said Jynx, looking up from Mimic.

"Yes. Our consciousness and the mi combined, and we share these bodies. I am sorry about your friend."

"Nuts."

"What do you have in mind, UV?" said Kita.

Ultraviolet opened her hand, and a stream of light surrounded Cranberry's head and went in through her mouth, ears, nose, and eyes. Cranberry lifted off the ground as the light engulfed her. There was a bright flash, and the light vanished, leaving Cranberry on the floor.

"Her consciousness is now slaved to us," said Ultraviolet. "We are her master. She will do as we command."

"She still knows what's happening to her?" asked Kita.

"Yes, but her will is ours."

"Can you do that to us?" said Jynx.

"No. Only children of this universe."

Kita wasn't so sure, but she'd have to think about it later.

"Ok, let's get everything loaded. I want all the data and the machine the Prii were using." She knelt next to Apocalypse. "How is she?" Kita had been ignoring the pain and heartache she felt but couldn't help let it escape in the question.

"I don't know. We're healing as many of the bleeding wounds as we can. I don't know about her vitals. She's not breathing, but I detect a heartbeat. Her lower region is pretty messed up."

"Ambulance is here," announced Poison.

"Get them in here," ordered Kita. "If anyone asks, we're here to help the Verisom move, and we had an accident. She stuck her finger in the tank. UV, take your people outside and get in the truck Zhi directs you to."

"Yes, Kita."

"Velositi, can you move that damaged truck out of the way so Flexi can back our truck in? Then we need to move these other specimen tanks. We can't leave them behind, either."

The paramedics rushed in, following Poison. Kita pulled Apocalypse and Jynx back to let the newcomers work.

"They know more about her than we do," said Kita. Which was partially true. They wouldn't know about the changes of being an Angel, but Apocalypse knew nothing about Verisom physiology. Kita wrapped her arms around her family for a few long moments. "Ok, let's go help the others."

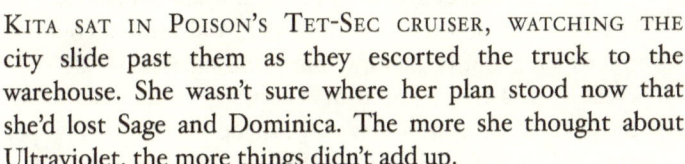

KITA SAT IN POISON'S TET-SEC CRUISER, WATCHING THE city slide past them as they escorted the truck to the warehouse. She wasn't sure where her plan stood now that she'd lost Sage and Dominica. The more she thought about Ultraviolet, the more things didn't add up.

A usual good judge of character—though she had made mistakes in the past—Kita's stomach didn't sit well with the transformed Angel. The part about Ultraviolet being the manifestation of the universe—even though she had declared it to score points with Cranberry—lacked evidence. Everything Ultraviolet had said Kita had heard from Sage and had to do with the Prii and Uvra, their homeworld. Kita believed the mi to be something, but exactly what she wasn't sure. She'd seen Dominica and Sage interact with it and how the plants and animals in the ultraviolet forest responded to it.

In her studies, Kita had heard of viruses, bacteria, and fungus communicating with other living things. It could be possible that the mi was one of these things and had formed a symbiosis with the rest of the living things on Uvra. From observing Sage, the mi seemed to amplify her connection to the pips.

But what was Ultraviolet? The mi spoke to Dominica, so it must have some kind of intelligence—maybe like Venom's ants, it was a collective subconsciousness or even a hive-mind.

That thought made Kita shiver. But how had it become sentient? Did the electricity spark something between the mi and Dominica—and X5? If it was sentient—as it appeared to be—Ultraviolet bowing before its masters was a clever ruse... What was she going to do about it? Hive-minds were dangerous and lived to expand and take over. She couldn't allow that—but it might be too late already. The two Prii from the lab had been infected and released into the greater Tet population.

And what of the Angels? She didn't think the Angels from Reality were in danger. Once they left this universe, their consciousness would shift back to the bodies in Reality, and this would be like a dream to them. Only the Angels created in this universe were in danger—Rivet, Mimic, and Alliance.

That left what to do with Ultraviolet. A hive-mind could be a powerful ally—if it could be trusted. In Reality, it would have no power as Kita could strip it of everything—she doubted she could return Dominica. She would just be left with an empty husk of an Angel. Kita didn't like that idea. Better to just kill it and leave it—and take everyone home.

Kita didn't like leaving her plans unfinished. It was unlike her to run away. Typically, she found a solution. *Maybe I should talk to Ultraviolet first. The Angels have shown to be friends of mi. But how do I keep it from wanting to take over the Tet? What if it's already started? In a matter of days, it could have everyone. Hmmm.*

Undoing her restraint, Kita turned around and reached into the backseat of the cruiser.

"Need something?" said Poison.

"Grabbing my swords. I'm going to have a talk with our newest Angel when we get to the warehouse."

"Yeah, what happened?"

"I don't know for sure...but I've got some ideas. I need to find out whose side she's on."

POISON GUIDED THE TET-SEC CRUISER THROUGH THE BAY door into Kita's warehouse. Around the cavernous space sat pallets of rare artifacts, art, and precious items—including ten pallets of comet ice and a dozen stacked with precious materials. In the center was a computer workstation used to plan heists—now obsolete thanks to the computer in her head. Rivet pulled the Tet-Sec truck in next to the cruiser, and the other Angels followed.

Kita popped the gullwing door of the cruiser and headed straight for the back of the truck.

"Problem?" said Venom, climbing out of her cruiser and seeing Kita's face.

"Everyone, stay back—away from the truck," Kita ordered. "Girls, if I don't come out, destroy the truck and everything in it."

"What have I been hauling?" said Rivet. "You girls didn't load something dangerous...did you?"

"It's Ultraviolet," said Poison. "Kita wants to make sure she's on our side."

"Is she that dangerous?" said Apocalypse after climbing out of Venom's cruiser with Jynx.

"I think she's a hive-mind and so yes, very dangerous."

Apocalypse pulled Jynx to her. "What are you going to do?"

"Ask her whose side she's on."

"I thought she was with us."

"What she told us doesn't add up."

"If she lied, why didn't I know?"

Kita shrugged. "I don't feel any emotion from her. It might be the way the hive-mind works."

"We will be ready," said Velositi as she morphed into her angelic form.

Kita went to the back of the truck and pulled open the doors. "Zhi, Flexi, help me unload this equipment. Everyone else, cover us and be ready to shoot if you see UV light."

Together the three Angels offloaded the machinery and set it aside. When they reached the first tank, the small pip creature was glowing ultraviolet. Kita closed the door quietly and looked at the other Angels.

"She's been busy," whispered Kita. "You girls back off. If this door opens and it's not me, terminate it. If you can't—Kimmy, get everyone out of this universe, back to the universe room, and have Ryan deactivate it. I'll come back through the Reality machine."

Apocalypse nodded somberly. "Velositi, you take lead. Chelsea and I will wait by the door."

Velositi's eyes dimmed as she morphed into her mecha-dragon. She pointed her head at the door and opened her mouth, revealing rows of metal teeth and two nozzles that could spew an acid-laced flame.

When Apocalypse and Jynx reached the warehouse door, Kita slowly pulled back the truck door and floated inside. The tanks nearly reached the truck's ceiling and didn't leave much room on either side to slip past. Kita undid the restraints and pushed them and the pips they contained aside. When she moved the third tank out of the way, she found Ultraviolet floating at the truck's rear with X5 and Cranberry next to her.

The Angel's expression was blank, but her horns and eyes pulsed with ultraviolet light. X5's and Cranberry's eyes also glowed.

"You don't trust me," said Ultraviolet somberly in her ethereal voice.

"No, I really don't."

"I'm not a threat."

"I don't know what you are—but I can guess."

"I told you—"

"You are not the blood of the universe. I don't know what you are, but I know you come from Uvra and have some kind of symbiotic relationship with the plants and animals there. What I don't know is what happened between you, To'va, and Al'ice—"

"X5," said Ultraviolet. "I was connected to him when it happened."

"What happened," demanded Kita.

"We...don't know. We have been part of Uvra for millennia, bonding and helping flora and fauna live together in harmony. When the Prii emerged, we bonded with them and helped them live and connect with the smaller animals to help them survive. For the help we offered, they worshipped us. Then the destroyers came and demolished the forests and those within. They enslaved and killed the Prii. If it weren't for the golden ones, we would have been eradicated. But the golden ones did not give us back our planet. They let Uvra be lost, took us to this place, and planted a small grove that was barely enough to sustain life. They thought they were saving us but, instead, locked us in a prison—until To'va found us.

"We bonded with To'va and taught her the old Prii ways. She brought us new life and revitalized the forest. You brought Al'ice—a Prii of like we have never experienced. Al'ice bonded, and To'va taught her the old ways...but Al'ice could do more. With Al'ice, we awoke...we gained sentience.

"As we were discovering our new intelligence, the fire came and destroyed the grove. We were all but extinguished. Our momentary intelligence lost, until you came and saved us. You gave To'va and Al'ice the seeds and the power to germinate them—restoring us. We took refuge in To'va and Al'ice.

"I apologize, Kita, that we could not save Catnip and To'va. The machine the destroyers has created is powerful, increasing the potency of the Prii connection beyond what To'va could achieve—"

"But you and Al'ice could?"

"Yes. Al'ice is the most powerful Prii we have ever met. To'va knew this and trained Al'ice and us to work together. I do not know what happened when the lightning struck. Al'ice, X5, and our consciousnesses combined, and we have become one. Our goal is to assimilate the destroyers and those who allied with them, regrow our forest, and to serve our savior—You."

Kita relaxed some. She was fine with most of that but unsure of the part about assimilating the Verisom—though it was a fitting punishment. "Why did you lie about being part of the universe?"

"We are part of the universe—or we will be. We have the power to flow through all biological things."

"Including Angels?"

Ultraviolet's face twitched. "We would not. We are Angel—"

"And Verisom and whatever X5 is and the other creatures in the tanks."

"We are not as our savior?"

Kita crossed her arms. "If you want to be an Angel, you have to live by my rules. I have no problem with you wanting to regrow your forest—I'll even give you the space. What I'm not sure about is you assimilating the population of the Tet and universe—at least, not while I'm here."

"You are allowed to have revenge, and I am not?"

"I said while I'm here. I have no interest in living in whatever universe you'd create. I'm beginning to tire of this one and am ready to go home."

"Then leave, and we will assimilate these creatures and show them how to live in harmony."

"You realize as soon as I leave this universe, I'm turning it off. You'll never have your chance—unless I can trust you."

"What must we do to earn your trust?"

"Give me your word that Al'ice isn't in there. I will check when we leave this universe, so be honest."

"I am sorry, Kita. I have her memories, but that is all. I will honor her pledge to help you get Grall. And we will serve you. I promise, but you must let us have our revenge. This universe needs harmony."

Kita frowned. She was going to miss Dominica. Still, Ultraviolet was interesting and reminded her of Athena, the digital Angel. She could take over computers and networks in a similar way. They even kind of thought the same.

"Ok," said Kita. "You have my trust, but I will verify. If she's in there, it'll be her that comes out, not you. But tell me, I understand how you and Al'ice are woven together. I don't get X5."

"X5 was a blank mind, and together Al'ice and I filled it. When the lightning happened, the three of us mingled, but we didn't gain anything from X5—other than the control of his body."

"Three minds and two bodies..." Kita shrugged. She'd been part of stranger. *What did I used to say...every time I return from the grave, I come back a little stranger?*

"Ok. We'll unload the tanks and get you out of here." Kita turned to slide out.

"Kita," Ultraviolet called, "did you fear us that much that you needed your swords?"

Kita rolled her jaw. *Trust requires honesty.* "I didn't know what to expect or what your motives were. I was prepared for anything."

"I noticed you never reached for them."

"I liked what you said, and I trust you."

"We trust you."

Kita squeezed her way past the tanks to the empty portion of the truck. *Did I really make a deal with a hive-mind? And do I trust her? I believe what she said is the truth...and she wants to be an Angel. I'll have to figure out some kind of protection for us. I can just imagine what sort of catfight could happen. Or worse...some type of mind control over the hive-mind.* Pushing open the door, she held her hands up. "It's me. We're good," Kita said—mostly to the mecha-dragon's open mouth.

Seeing Kita, the other Angels relaxed.

"She's not going to take over our minds?" said Venom after she turned back into an Angel from a giant scorpion.

"It doesn't sound like we're what she wants."

"What does she want?" said Poison putting her hands down.

"She wants the Verisom and allies—whoever those are—probably all of the Tet."

"I guess I should warn my friends to take a vacation," said Venom.

"I don't think she's planning her assimilation until after we leave." Kita waved to the warehouse door to recall Apocalypse and Jynx. "We need to get the rest of this unloaded."

Velositi morphed from mecha-dragon to gravlift. She floated up and fit her forks under the first tank, lifted it, and slowly backed out.

"Put it wherever you want," said Kita. She didn't plan on keeping the tanks. The creatures inside already belonged to Ultraviolet.

"Successful girl talk, angel?" said Apocalypse, coming up holding Jynx's hand.

"I think so. We both agreed we trusted the other."

"What is she, Momma?"

Kita shrugged. "I think she's a hive-mind. A single consciousness spread over many organisms."

"No Al'ice?"

Kita tussled Jynx's hair. "Sorry, kiddo. I tried, but I think UV took over."

"Rats."

"You need to wait until you're older, anyway," said Apocalypse.

Kita nodded in agreement. "Sixteen is the rule."

"It is?" said Apocalypse.

"Well, I made all the other girls wait until they were sixteen —except for Lina, but she'd been sleeping around since she was...twelve."

Apocalypse looked at Jynx. "No."

"I don't want to have sex. I just like her."

Kita sighed. "Puppy-dog crushes are ok."

"Would you have let me hold her hand?"

"Remember, Al'ice was fifteen years older than you. I think it would have been a little weird for her."

"Also illegal," said Apocalypse.

Kita held up her hands to Jynx. "The Empress has spoken. We can look for a nice young Prii girl for you."

Jynx made a disgusted face. "Ew. No. Kids are so immature."

Kita looked over at Apocalypse and traded a worried look. "*I think she needs to spend time with kids her own age.*" Apocalypse nodded.

"We're going home soon anyway," said Apocalypse. "We'll try the next universe we visit."

"Can we go to Earth?" said Jynx.

"Sure," said Kita. "I'm growing tired of the Tet."

"Cool."

"Last one, Kita," yelled Venom.

Kita turned as Velositi backed away with the last tank. "Hey, open them up and let the critters out. UV will want them...I think."

From the back of the truck, Ultraviolet glided down and hovered as X5 and Cranberry hopped down and stood next to the Angel. The other animals from the other tanks ran over and stood with X5.

"Which one is she?" whispered Venom aloud.

"All of them...I think," said Kita.

"This is going to be like Athena, isn't it?" said Apocalypse.

It was a common complaint around Roost among new Angels about how to address Athena. The Angel was entirely integrated into Roost's computers, but she also had several bodies she used for maintenance or conversing with the other Angels. The problem was, new Angels never knew whether to look at the computer, the speaker, or her body. Athena said it didn't make a difference to her. As she said, "The information all ends up in the same place." But it seemed to bother newcomers tremendously.

"You may address any of us," said Ultraviolet the Angel. "But I am an Angel, and this will be my chosen inhabitance."

"Don't want to be the Verisom?" said Rivet.

Ultraviolet scrunched her nose. "Ew," she said with absolute disgust.

Kita laughed. "She said that just like you, Jynxie."

"That is where I learned the expression," said Ultraviolet. "Did I do it wrong?"

"You got it right for a twelve-year-old," said Apocalypse. "Adults are a little more subtle."

Ultraviolet wiggled her nose a fraction. "Ew," she announced with mild indignation.

"Somewhere in the middle," said Kita.

"You're not going to eat my brain, are you?" said Venom.

Kita rolled her eyes. "Sorry—"

"No," said Ultraviolet. "I understand her fear. I felt similar when I approached the truck door, but I trusted Kita would not allow me to be injured. My fellow Angels, you have nothing to fear from us. We wish to be part of the flock and to help. We do have a mission of assimilation we plan to complete, but only after the rest of you go home."

"What are you assimilating?" said Rivet.

"The universe."

"Does this mean you're trying to score a three-way with Kita?" said Venom. "I've heard acts of power turn her on."

Kita's ears turned red.

"If she wishes," said Ultraviolet. "She can have the pick of any we assimilate."

Kita raised an eyebrow at Apocalypse.

"No. Not a fantasy of mine."

"I'll politely decline the offer," Kita said with a chuckle. "I have eyes for one girl." She leaned in and kissed Apocalypse on the cheek.

Apocalypse turned her head and grabbed Kita by the neck. "Oh, come here and give me a real kiss."

Poison's communicator dinged. She pulled it from her belt and read the message, her frown growing. "Catnip didn't make it," she announced softly.

"By the Crushing Depths," whispered Kita as she split from Apocalypse. Kita dabbed at the tears in her eyes.

The sounds of loud howling and sobbing came from behind. Kita turned to see Rivet, her head buried in her arms, sitting on the concrete floor. Kita dashed to her friend and put an arm around her. Rivet threw her head back in a loud howl that ended in a sob. Kita pulled Rivet to her and kissed the side of Rivet's head. Quickly the other Angels joined, comforting each other and Rivet.

POISON'S TET-SEC CRUISER LANDED IN FRONT OF THE Angel's embassy. Kita climbed out and turned to help her family from the back seat. The Tet-Sec truck, Velositi, and Venom's cruiser landed next to them. Kita hugged Apocalypse and Jynx protectively as the others offloaded. When everyone was ready, Kita led the others up the tree and bush-lined stone steps to where Alliance sat to one side, crying softly.

Seeming to sense the other Angels, Alliance wiped her eyes and pushed herself to her feet. She looked at Kita, and her tears began anew. Kita put her arms around the Angel.

"I'm sorry," Alliance whimpered. "They came and cut off her wings and wouldn't let me have them or the body. I'm sorry. I called everyone I could...but the Grand Ambassador was downvoted by the Grand Panel. I feel like such a failure."

Kita hugged Alliance tight. She was joined by the other Angels.

"I bet they wouldn't release her to me," said Rivet.

Kita grimaced, feeling Rivet's heartbreak.

"Are you..." Alliance whispered.

"She was my partner," Rivet said firmly. The soft, leathery skin around her eyes streaked with fresh tears.

"I'm so sorry," Alliance sobbed as she hugged Rivet. "Please forgive me."

"It's not your fault. She's still a Verisom princess...more so in death than in life." Rivet looked at Kita.

The pit in Kita's stomach grew as she knew what was coming.

"Kita, if anyone can get her body back, you can. Please?"

Kita's mind reeled as it flooded with all the information on Verisom Manor and what it would take to break in and steal a body. "Of course I will."

"Kita," said Ultraviolet. "Where's the body?"

"Verisom Manor," said Alliance.

"Let us do it. We owe the Verisom. Let us prove our loyalty to the flock. We will bring back Princess Catnip. We already have our way in." She motioned to Cranberry.

Kita stroked her braid, weighing if it was worth exposing Ultraviolet, whether she could control herself, and what happens afterward. "Only Verisom Manor and you have to keep the place running like nothing happened. The rest of Verisom and the Tet can't suspect you've taken over. Bring Catnip here, and we'll have the death ceremony for her, To'va, and Al'ice."

"This isn't Al'ice?" said Alliance looking at Ultraviolet.

"We are Ultraviolet. We are a consciousness of X5, Al'ice, and mi."

"What happened?" gasped Alliance. "How can so many be dead?"

"Angels live fast and die hard," replied Kita. "Death happens. I can't save everyone."

"We don't expect you to," said Poison. "It's better to die an Angel after an hour than to live a thousand years as a Human."

"Diamock."

"Morphicon."

"Aurorian."

"Mi."

"Every Angel knows the risk of death comes with the power we wield," said Apocalypse.

Kita turned and sat down hard on the stone steps. She buried her face in her arms and sobbed for Mimic, Aspen, and all the Angels she'd lost and refused to grieve for. Mimic had been her best friend for seven years. Kita had looked forward to having her energy, spirit, and wit around Roost. And Aspen was gone. The little Angel had been at Kita's side through the tough times of building Reality and shown Kita what to do— the grandmaster of universe building, the God of Light, teaching the newly minted God of Reality how it was done. Kita had spun the justification of her death so many ways to ease her soul, but in the end, she had sacrificed her friend for her love. Aspen would say it was a worthy cause to die for. The selfishness that inhabited Kita's heart said otherwise. And all the other Angels and her children—who had died on Earth Zero. They tore at her heart, sacrificed so she could attain her power. Now, with all that power, she was unable to bring them back. Trapped by laws that even she could not break. *It's not over. I will find a way. I always do.*

Jynx, climbing into her lap, pulled Kita's mind away from her anguish. Apocalypse put her arm around Kita's shoulders and hugged her tight. The other Angels gathered, and their waves of sympathy, love, and grief eased Kita's heart.

"Thank you," whispered Kita to the others. "Losing Angels is never easy and always dredges up the pain of the past."

"May they rest in peace," said Venom.

"Sisters forever," said Poison.

"No Angel is forgotten," whispered Kita as she hugged Jynx tight.

"No Angel really dies," said Jynx, "as long as they're remembered. You should build a memorial to them, Momma. I'd like to know them."

"That's a good idea, Jynxie. Come on, let's go inside."

"We will be back by dawn," said Ultraviolet.

"Don't rush," said Kita. "Take your time, pick your target. Stealth is all about patience and planning."

"Understood, Kita. Can we take the truck?"

"Do you need a driver?" said Rivet.

"Cranberry knows, but we will not turn down help. It is your mate. If you wish to be part of her rescue, we will not deny you."

"I'll come," said Rivet. "You might need a lookout."

"Flexi, UV, be careful," said Poison. "Call us if you need help."

"It'll be the Verisom that needs help."

Kita nodded. "Everyone else, let's go inside and order a few gallons of ice cream."

———————✕———————

"KITA," SAID POISON, HOLDING UP HER COMMUNICATOR.

Kita rolled her head—resting on Apocalypse's leg—away from the movie toward the other Angel sitting across the room. "Yeah?" she said around a bite of ice cream.

"Central just messaged me. GeFraw wants a meeting."

Kita grunted around the spoon in her mouth. *I forgot about him.* "With me?"

"No. Me. He wants to know why Tet-Sec is picking up his goons."

"Because they're assholes," quipped Venom. She and some of the other Angels were hitting some wine Alliance had ordered. The new Angels were finding out you had to drink a lot to get drunk.

"I agree," said Kita. "Tell him he has to wait until UV gets back. It was her forest."

Poison frowned as she worked on her pint of ice cream. "He says he's going to start shooting Tet-Sec officers in the street if we don't agree."

"I can think of some he can start with."

"Kita!" Poison said with a disapproving glare.

"Fine. Go meet him."

"This doesn't smell like a trap to you?"

Kita rolled her head over and nuzzled Apocalypse's stomach. "Why can't I mourn in peace?" she muttered as she kissed Apocalypse.

"Because being a leader means setting aside your feelings and doing what has to be done," replied Apocalypse.

Kita kissed her again.

Apocalypse squirmed. "That tickles. Now, come on. Get up, and let's figure out how to deal with GeFraw."

"I'll skin the damn cat. When does he want me to do it?"

"Dawn," said Poison. "Down by Petal Five's docks. Warehouse seven-nine-two."

Kita opened her hand and brought up the map of Petal Five. It wasn't a warehouse but a gravel yard where quarried stone and aggregate were offloaded and stored. Several cement towers stood nearby. "Yeah, it's a trap. They're going to kill a Tet-Sec general and parade the body around town. Probably hold it for ransom to free their goons. I guess we're going as backup."

"Probably should plan this out," said Venom, slurring her words together.

"First, we all need to sober up," said Apocalypse. "We've all been binging too much on wine and ice cream."

"UV and Flexi aren't back yet," said Alliance.

"I'll send them a message," said Kita as she flicked her spoon from her couch into the kitchenette sink. Gently she rubbed Jynx's back. The young Angel had fallen asleep on her. Opening her hand, she enlarged the map so everyone could see. "Five minutes to sober up, and then we get started."

KITA OPENED THE GULLWING OF VENOM'S HOVERING TET-Sec cruiser and rolled out into the early morning darkness. She became invisible and waited for the other Angels to join her. Velositi and Apocalypse glided up next to her while Venom set the autopilot of her cruiser to land nearby. The quarry lights were visible through the darkness, and Kita could see a lone sky-car sitting in the center of the yard.

"You think he's down there?" said Venom.

"I wouldn't be," said Apocalypse. "The chance of a battalion of Tet-Sec officers coming in is too great."

"Yeah, but they're not. It's just us. Kita, are you sure this is a good idea for Karen?"

Kita felt her trepidation and concern for Poison. "Karen can take care of herself. Our presence will make sure she has time to protect herself." Even Kita wasn't sure she believed that. This was a dangerous mission; that's why she'd left Jynx with Alliance—much to the protesting of her daughter. "Come on, let's go scout the area. I'm sure they're not alone."

"We have five minutes until Karen arrives," said Poison.

The Angels spread their wings, rolled over, and dove for the quarry. Following Kita, they circled the piles of stone, sand, and aggregate. Concrete dividers created cover for ambushers, so did the conveyor belt that ran to the cement mixer towers.

"I don't see anyone," said Apocalypse.

"I see tracks," replied Kita. "Lots of people have been climbing on those piles."

"But are they fresh?" said Velositi.

Kita wasn't sure of that, not without getting down close to inspect them. Instead, she flipped to her thermal lenses, and bright orange spots appeared around the base and tops of the piles.

"They're using some kind of cloaking devices," said Kita. "Turn to your thermal vision, and you can see them."

"Damn! That's a lot," said Venom. "They were expecting the Tet-Sec battalion."

"Let's not screw around," said Kita firmly. "Everyone, take a section and kill them as fast as you can."

"There are way more than I can handle," said Apocalypse.

"Dragon-out if you have to."

"I don't think this is a good idea. We're way outnumbered and outgunned. We should wave Karen off and figure something else out."

"GeFraw doesn't come out very often," said Venom. "This may be our only chance."

"We don't even know if he's here."

"There isn't enough time to recon," said Kita. "If you don't want to go, wait here. I'll go."

"Kita!" protested Apocalypse.

Kita's eyes narrowed. So much was said in one word. "What choice do we have?"

"You've lost three Angels. Are you in a hurry to lose more?"

"If I don't go, we lose Karen."

"We can still wave her off."

"No, we can't." Venom pointed to the center of the quarry. Karen's Tet-Sec cruiser was coming into land next to the sky-car.

"*Karen!*" Kita yelled. "*It's a trap. Get out of there.*"

Karen's cruiser touched down, but the door didn't open. Instead, the engine spoiled up, kicking up a dust cloud that obscured the cruiser. It lifted a few feet off the ground, and the nearby sky-car exploded, sending the cruiser rolling and flipping through the air before crashing hard on the driver's side.

"Karen!" screamed Venom. She dove toward the totaled cruiser.

"We've got to give her cover," ordered Kita. "Velositi, go left. I'll go right. Engage as many as you can and keep them off Zhi and Karen."

"What about me?" said Apocalypse.

"I thought—"

"Don't. I'll take the center."

Kita smiled and nodded.

The three Angels split, each diving toward their assigned areas. Apocalypse fired her beams, cutting through a trio of hidden mercenaries. Velositi morphed her arms into her cannons and rapidly blasted a barrage of plasma charges that exploded on contact. Kita drew her bow—Midnight—and attached a red ball to the arrow. Taking aim at a group of concealed mercenaries. She fired, punching the arrow through a mercenary's armor and detonating the red ball.

The mercenaries threw off their invisibility cloaks and fired at the Angels. Kita dipped and weaved through the air dodging bullets while firing red ball arrows, creating explosions that ripped apart the piles of stone and mercenaries. But it wasn't enough, fast enough. The mercenaries ran around the piles and took cover on the front sides. Even with all her effort, several rounds struck her.

"Kita!" cried Apocalypse. "They're too many! I'm bleeding all over the place."

"Go dragon," ordered Kita as she winced from a bullet hitting her thigh.

Across the quarry, Apocalypse transformed into her biggest dragon form. The massive beast was as tall as the quarry stone piles. She spread her wings and reared on her hind legs, exposing her armored belly scales. Craning her neck, she opened her mouth and enveloped the side of a pile in flame.

Nearby, Velositi did the same, morphing into her mecha-dragon. The pair attacked the mercenaries driving them toward Kita. The amount of fire aimed at her slackened, and she took the time to pick off targets of opportunity.

"Keep it up, ladies," Kita urged. "We're pushing them back." Kita looked at the wrecked cruiser. "Zhi, how is Karren?"

"We're trying to get her out now. The cruiser's frame is twisted and wrecked. The ants are chewing through it as fast as they can. I'm getting some stray shots."

"I'll try and target those not shooting at the dragons. I—"

The sound of engines overhead drew Kita's attention. Four transport gunships with yellow fists painted on the sides were circling the quarry. "Ladies! We've got company! Gunships overhead."

A gunship turned its nose on Apocalypse. A loud *brap* punctuated a stream of red tracers from twin rotary guns. The bullets tore into Apocalypse's wing and sparked off her armored side scales.

The other gunships opened fire from mounted guns hammering the dragons. Two gunships flared their engines and landed in the center of the quarry disgorging fresh troops.

The dragons responded by belching clouds of fire. Velositi climbed to the top of a large sand pile and lashed her spiked tail at the mercenaries on the front while spewing fire at those in the rear.

Apocalypse flapped her wings and took to the air—rather clumsily as her damaged wing kept her from getting the lift she needed. She circled the quarry blasting it with flame. More gunfire from a gunship turned her attention. She rolled and lunged with her open jaws, but the gunship throttled its engines, blasting the side of Apocalypse's face with exhaust.

Kita scanned the chaos looking for a particular target. GeFraw was smart not to be on the ground, but she suspected him of being narcissistic enough to want to witness the wholesale slaughter of Tet-Sec officers.

"*Kita, I'm getting chewed up. I got to go,*" said Apocalypse.

Apocalypse was already gone by the time Kita focused on where the dragon had been. The mercenaries were now focusing on Velositi. The mecha-dragon looked like it had measles from all the red dots. *How much more can she take?*

Looking at the cruiser, Venom had part of the cab peeled back. "Zhi, how much longer?"

"I've just about got her out. She's not dead but messed up pretty bad."

"I'm coming to you to help."

"Ok."

Kita turned invisible and glided down next to the crumpled cruiser. Streams of ants were everywhere chewing through the twisted metal. Venom had peeled back part of the top and was pulling on a stuck gullwing door. Kita turned visible and pushed Venom aside.

"Let me. I can burn through it faster." Kita heated her hand and pressed against the metal and plastic, cutting through the door.

From atop the gravel pile, Velositi roared and flapped her wings. The dragon took off, blowing fire at a circling gunship.

"I think our time is up," said Kita. She finished cutting through the door as bullets hit the cruiser. "Get her out," Kita ordered as she drew her swords and prepared to cut through the oncoming mercenary horde.

I've got to get rid of some of them. Kita flourished her swords and slammed the hilts together. Twirling Crypt around her, she stopped it parallel to the ground and aimed the great sword at the largest group. *I hope I've got the range.* Seeing her actions, the mercenaries scattered in all directions. Kita ground her teeth. Someone in The Dark had ratted on her. As she opened her mouth to activate Crypt, a truck's horn blasted three times in the early morning light.

"Reap!" Kita ordered.

The blue light of Crypt reached out and illuminated about three dozen mercenaries. Ghostly apparitions appeared next to their bodies before evaporating into the ether. Their bodies collapsed in the dirt, but it wasn't near enough.

The remaining mercenaries regrouped and charged. Kita broke Crypt back into Dead and Buried. Flourishing the blades as bullets struck around her, she prepared for battle.

The sound of heavy repeaters and projectiles cutting into the oncoming mercenaries from behind Kita made her look. The Tet-Sec Truck sat at the entrance to the quarry with Rivet on the trailer blasting away with a Verisom heavy repeater—wearing Diamock power armor. The trailer's doors opened, and Verisom males in heavy space armor armed with heavy repeaters jumped out and charged the mercenaries, firing as they ran.

Kita thrust Dead into the air and yelled, "Follow me!" She ran forward into the oncoming horde and slammed into the first rank.

The melee attack stunned the mercenaries around Kita. Using the confusion, she danced through them—slashing, slicing, and chopping off heads, arms, and laying open chests and guts. Those mercenaries that regained their awareness tried to shoot her. Kita's dance bobbed and weaved around and between the bursts of gunfire that often hit another mercenary.

The platoon of heavy Verisom male infantry was led by three female lancers in full power armor. They formed their males into a firing line and then leaped high into the air with their axars. They fired a volley of energy bursts, blasting the mercenary ranks apart. The three landed around Kita, forming a protective ring.

Kita backed up to one of the lancers. "UV?"

"Hello, Kita. We apologize for being late. It became necessary to assimilate members of the Verisom military. We hope you are not upset I overstepped our agreement, but when we discovered GeFraw's plan to assassinate Karen, we felt we needed to take action."

"I'm not complaining. I've never reprimanded someone for taking the initiative. Just next time, warn us. Karen's badly injured, and so are some of the other Angels."

"We are sorry. We were afraid we might give away your plan to kill him. Where are the injured? I have medical units."

"*Kimmy? Velositi? Zhi? Where are you?*" As Kita made the call, the lights around the quarry went out.

"I bet that's Velositi trying to heal herself."

"*Kita,*" replied Apocalypse. "*I'm behind a warehouse near the quarry. I'm trying to pull the bullets out so I can come back and help.*"

"*Don't worry about it. UV is here, and she brought back up. She has medical units if you need help.*"

"*Yes. That would be great. I'll send her my location.*"

"*Love you.*"

"*Love you. Where are you?*"

"*Staying out of trouble.*"

"*Uh-huh. Be safe.*"

"*UV is guarding me.*"

"*Good.*"

Kita performed a double backflip landing on a Djinn mercenary's chest. She plunged her swords into his stomach then kicked her legs up around his head. Flapping her wings, she somersaulted forward, flipping the mercenary over her head landing him face-first into the dirty concrete.

A lancer landed next to Kita. "Kita, we found Zhi and Karen. Medical teams are performing aid for Karen, and an ambulance is on the way. Zhi has reported the incident to Tet-Sec, and they are sending units. You must hurry if you want to kill GeFraw."

"Hey, I'm not doing this for me. It was your forest that furball burned to the ground. I'm just trying to do right by you."

"We thank you and the other Angels for putting your lives on the line to avenge us. We will have this furball—as you call him."

A Yellow Fist gunship flew over them, peppering the area with bullets and killing one of the Verisom lancers.

"We've got to get rid of those things," yelled Kita.

"We have a pair of corvettes coming in now."

"I think GeFraw is on one of those gunships."

"With your permission, we will find out."

"Go for it. What you do with him is up to you."

"He will suffer."

Around Kita, the lancers and armored Verisom males cleared the area of mercenaries. She cleaned and sheathed her swords, then glided back to the Tet-Sec truck. Behind it, she found Venom being comforted by Rivet. A group of female Verisom medics were working on Poison. The Angel was on a backboard. Her clothes were removed, exposing red blood on her dark chocolate skin as the medics worked to stabilize her.

Kita came up behind Rivet and Venom and put her arms around the pair. "How are you girls doing?"

"UV says she's going to live," said Venom, "but she's got internal damage and bleeding along with several vertebrae out of place. She's going to need a couple of days in the hospital."

Kita nodded, stroking the Angel's black hair. "How'd it go, Flexi?"

"UV is amazing. She had Verisom Manor in an hour, then invited me in to see Catnip. I've never seen her wearing so many sparkles. And then UV found her wings. We decided to leave the body there since the embassy doesn't have a place for her. It's incredible how much UV can do. While she was helping me, she was running Verisom Manor. That's how she found out about GeFraw. I guess he's a client of the Verisom, and he told them he was going to kill a Tet-Sec general this morning. He gave them his entire plan—and the Verisom were going to let him do it."

"I bet he's surprised now," chuckled Kita.

Above them came the wail of sirens as the first ambulance arrived with several Tet-Sec cruisers as escorts. Venom broke from the group hug to guide it in and direct the paramedics to Poison. She then directed the Tet-Sec officers to set up a perimeter and tell them friend and foe.

Above them, the battle still raged. The Verisom corvettes had deployed six fast attack boats and were pursuing the Yellow Fist Pack gunships. A fast-attack boat landed in an open area near the concrete mixer towers. Velositi and Apocalypse glided over the side. Kita hurried to meet them. Kita collided with her partner and girlfriend in a massive hug.

"You girls ok?" Kita asked, fighting back tears.

"I'm fine," said Apocalypse. "Took a while to pull all the bullets out, but the Verisom medics were very helpful." Her embroidered Victorian calf-length jacket, purple silk shirt, and two-tone pants were riddled with holes and dried blood.

"The Verisom—or rather Ultraviolet—was very accommodating," said Velositi. "After tapping into the power system, I did not need further assistance, but their boat was fun to ride in."

"How's Karen?" asked Apocalypse.

"She's going to need a few days in the hospital, but Zhi's with her now. They should be ready to take her any time."

"Good. I'm ready to go home."

"UV has everything under control, but I'm going to check. I think with Zhi's help, Tet-Sec will let UV clean up." Kita led the others back to Poison, Rivet, and Venom.

"She's ready to go," announced Venom. "I need to take control of Tet-Sec. Can someone go with Karen to the hospital? I don't want her left alone."

"I'll go," said Apocalypse.

"Thanks."

"Kita," said Ultraviolet through a Verisom medic. "I have forced GeFraw to land and have him surrounded. He's threatening Verisom with war with Djinn if we do not release him."

"I doubt that," said Venom. "He's not that valuable to the Djinn Crown."

"Your choice," said Kita. "Kill him or assimilate him."

"If you will allow us, we will assimilate the Yellow Fist Pack. They will go to detention quietly and will be useful later."

Kita bit her lip. She wasn't sure how much she should let Ultraviolet expand. The more Ultraviolet took, the greater her chance of being detected. Still, she had proven her loyalty to the flock. Kita didn't think Ultraviolet would be a threat to them...*But to the rest of the Tet?*

"Go ahead, but once this is over, you're to go dormant. I don't want you getting caught. I still need your help getting Grall and doing it your way; he doesn't suffer enough."

Ultraviolet laughed. It was the first time Kita had heard her laugh, and it was eerie.

"We understand. Grall is no one of great connection that we can't duplicate through other means. We look forward to helping you get him. We will consolidate our base and observe

Tet society to plan our future expansion once you and the other Angels leave."

"Sounds good. As much as I like having your convenience, I want to remember this universe not as a hive."

"Will you let us keep this universe?"

"I'll check with Ryan, but it shouldn't be a problem."

"I wish to keep it in our forest and visit it when we feel the need."

Sentimental? I didn't expect that out of her. "I don't have a problem with it. Kimmy has her universe."

"Thank you, Kita. You are a true friend."

"No problem. Let's get this place cleaned up so we can visit Karen."

Kita helped Apocalypse out of the Tet-Sec cruiser detailed to take them back to the Angel's embassy. Offering her arm, Kita escorted Apocalypse toward the flagstone stairs leading to the embassy, but they were lined with Verisom males in space armor carrying heavy repeaters. Shocked, Kita stopped. They looked at her and came to attention. Kita and Apocalypse walked up to the first one.

"UV, is that you?" asked Kita.

"Hello, Kita. We were unable to assimilate all the Yellow Fist Pack and thought it prudent that we should guard the embassy as the Angels are known adversaries of the Yellow Fist Pack, and they might try a retaliatory strike."

"Ok. Did you get GeFraw?"

"Yes. We assimilated him and as many of his followers as we could. Tet-Sec raided their compound before we could get there, and many of his followers escaped. We felt it prudent to guard our home."

"The Angels might have to sign some form of official treaty with the Verisom to explain away our sudden friendship."

"We will prepare the necessary documents. I have also found several civil, and criminal cases against you and Kimmy leveed by several Verisom princesses under my control. I have asked the courts and Tet-Sec to withdraw them and cancel any litigation against you and the Angels."

"I forgot about those," Kita chuckled. "Thank you. I'm sure Karen and Zhi will appreciate the help. They were doing their best to bury them for me. Talk to Kele about the treaties. She'll make sure they appear legitimate to the rest of the Tet."

"Of course. Kele and Chelsea are inside awaiting you."

"Thanks," said Kita. She escorted Apocalypse to the embassy and through the sliding glass doors.

"Mom! Momma!" exclaimed Jynx. She sheathed her sword as she flew over to greet her parents. She crashed into them, wrapping her arms around them.

"She's been nervous ever since the Verisom showed up," said Alliance coming around the desk.

The Angels greeted each other with a hug.

"They belong to UV. Did you talk to them?"

"Yes. I thought, at first, they were detaining us over the legal issues, but UV assured me it was for our protection."

"Hmmm," said Kita as she turned and walked back outside to the first Verisom. "UV?"

The Verisom male turned. "Yes, Kita?"

"Is there some way you can identify yourself for us? Chelsea was spooked by your sudden arrival. I know you're trying to stay hidden, but when you're around us, it'll let us know it's you."

The Verisom male's eyes glowed ultraviolet. "Does that help?"

"Perfect."

"We did not mean to distress Chelsea."

"I know. But she hasn't had good interactions with most Verisom since we arrived."

"We understand. We will do better."

"You're doing fine." Kita patted the arm of the Verisom and went inside.

"Ok," Kita said, looking at Jynx. "If you see anyone with ultraviolet eyes, that's UV, and you have no need to worry."

"What if she takes over us?" said Jynx looking at the floor.

"I've talked to her, and her actions have proven loyal to

the flock. I don't see any reason not to trust her. Plus, you, me, and your mom aren't part of this universe's construction—we're projections from Reality—she can't access us."

"What about when we go home?"

"I'll make sure she can't. She just wants to be a member of the flock and is doing what she thinks is best for us."

"It's a little creepy."

Kita put her arm around Jynx and sat her on the couch. "I know. But it's not all that different from living and ruling an empire. You get used to people doing things for you. Right, Kimmy?"

"Hmmm. It's even harder getting used to doing things for yourself. I have to admit it's a little spooky when you're not the one in control."

"I'm ready to go home, Momma."

Kita hugged Jynx. "You sound like you need a nap. Come on, upstairs. Sleep for a few hours, and then we'll go to the hospital to visit Karen.

"What happened to Karen?"

"She went for a wild ride, but she's ok. She just needs a few days to recover."

"Ok," Jynx finished in a yawn.

"Where is everyone else?" said Alliance as Kita stood Jynx up.

"Zhi is heading the Tet-Sec investigation into what happened. Flexi went back to Verisom Manor to be with Catnip. Velositi is with Zhi. UV is...everywhere. Let me put Jynxie to bed, and we'll tell you all about it."

When she came back downstairs, Kita entered the kitchenette and opened the fridge looking for something sweet. Alliance and Apocalypse were seated at the breakfast bar.

"She go straight to sleep?" Apocalypse asked Kita.

"Yeah. She was out before she hit the bed."

"I do have some good news," said Alliance. "I got Al'ice—UV a fight later this week. I couldn't tell them what pip we would bring, but they wanted the biggest one we had."

"Wait until they see X5," said Apocalypse looking into her coffee.

"For the mystery bout, it's going to cost us a hundred thousand."

"No problem," said Kita. "We need to hype UV up and do whatever we can to draw Grall out. I think hyping X5 as a jacksaur killer would be the quickest. His fans will pressure him to see X5 go down."

"I can hype X5 as a jacksaur killer without revealing what it is. I'll start flooding the forums and networks. So, sounds like it was another rough night."

Kita shrugged. "The price of victory can bleed you white, but tonight was..."

"We won," said Apocalypse. "That's all that matters. UV got GeFraw. Wrongs were righted. Karen will heal."

Kita patted Apocalypse's arm. "No need to justify, love. I'm sure Kele wants to hear about the romantic part of the battle —dragons and swordfights."

Alliance laughed. "I'm more into romance. Like, how did you two meet?"

Kita looked at Apocalypse and raised an eyebrow. "I was being held by her Imperial Bureau of Investigation..."

KITA AND ALLIANCE ENTERED THE DEN—THE BACKSTAGE area where trainers and pips waited for their turn in the pit— and made their way to the other Angels gathered around X5's tank. They were on Petal Ten in an arena surrounded by shipyards. It was a tough, working-class crowd of mostly Human, Prii, and Zentonians.

"What took so long?" Apocalypse asked the arriving Angels. "It's almost UV's turn."

"Idiots don't know what a Great Ape is—even after I showed them a picture."

"X5 isn't really a great ape, is he?"

"I don't know. I never tested his DNA. I'm guessing that's where Cranberry got some of it?" She looked at Ultraviolet. All the Angels were wearing hoods and cloaks to mask their identities and create an aura of mystery. Kita knew astute observers would pick up on wing color—but most people were blind: one Angel looked like another.

"Yes. She bought the DNA from a Human laboratory and combined it with a forked tail cat." Ultraviolet's eyes and horns were glowing under her hood, along with her wings.

"Anyway, I had to pay an extra hundred grand to get us in. They didn't like fighting an unregulated pip."

"We will get revenge," said Ultraviolet. "We will smash their icetoga."

"That's not how you game the system," said Kita. She pointed to the display showing the current bout in progress. "See those numbers by the pip names? Those are the odds, and they update in real-time. The higher the number, the higher the chance that pip will lose...but also the bigger the payout if it wins. Smart trainers know how to manipulate that to get more bets and a high payout. Take some early blows, pretend you're vulnerable, then smack the other pip around for a bit, take some more damage, then come back for the grand finale. It's all about pageantry and drama. The more there is, the higher and more frequent the bets and the bigger payout for us."

Ultraviolet bowed her head. "We understand. We will make sure the bout is dramatic when we go for the kill."

"Don't make it too dramatic. An icetoga can be dangerous. It spits water and can freeze it. You don't want to get caught in a blizzard attack. It'll freeze you solid."

"They will be surprised how strong X5 is. Mi has increased his strength and constitution. What Cranberry tried and failed to replicate with her machine."

"Was that what she was trying to do?"

"Yes, but she did not understand the mi or its effects. We do."

"Final bout!" the den master yelled.

"Let's go. Velositi, can you move X5 to the pit gate? Then come up and join us."

"Yes. I will do that." Velositi morphed into the gravlift

under X5's tank. She picked him up and moved him over to the large metal portcullis that led into the pit.

Kita and the other Angels floated up the stairs to the trainer's platform that overlooked the pit's fighting arena. The sound of sloshing in the arena caused Kita alarm. Water from ports around the arena was being pumped into the usually sandy arena.

"Bastards," snarled Kita. Cheating in underground events was rampant, anything to give the home team an advantage. When they were done, two inches of water filled the Pit's arena.

"Jynxie," called Kita.

"Yeah, Momma?" said the young Angel as she floated next to Kita.

"Help me clear the arena. Throw it in their den."

Mother and daughter floated over the edge of the pit. Extending their hands, the water rose in two thick columns. They guided it over the pit and the opposing trainer's platform and emptied it on the stairs that led to their den. They pumped the remaining water out to a chorus of boos from the crowd.

Kita floated down in front of the referee. "They try to cheat again, and I'll have your head," she snarled at the male Prii. She glided back to the trainer's platform and the other Angels just as the lights dimmed and the spotlight shone on the announcer.

Kita and the other Angels stood motionless as he rambled on about the previous fights and how great the home pips were. When he got to Ultraviolet, the spotlight didn't know who to focus on. Ultraviolet stepped forward and dropped her cloak, revealing her glowing horns and spread wings.

"Tonight's challenger...straight from Petal Four...with a record of thirty-nine wins and one loss...her fighting form has taken the training world by storm...the glowing Prii Angel you can't miss in a dark room...Ultraviolet!"

I should have paid that moron. No mention of being the jacksaur killer.

Ultraviolet rose into the air and raised her hands to the crowd.

"Tonight, our hometown favorite, Bliz, will face off against Ultraviolet and her pip, a rare never seen before great ape, X5!"

The portcullises on opposite sides of the arena were raised, and the two pips charged in. X5 pounded the sand with his fists, then his chest, letting out a loud series of *pops* followed by a deafening roar that caused the crowd to *ooh*, *haa*, and cheer.

Bliz stomped in. The icetoga was taller than X5 and covered in long white hair. It stood erect with long arms and legs. It opened its mouth and blew out an icy breath that sparkled in the light. It answered X5 with a long, eerie howl.

"*It looks like the yeti,*" said Venom.

"*The network says icetogas lived on the remote frozen mountains of Ulva,*" said Jynx. "*In the wild, they're small, but in captivity, regular feeding and selective breeding have made them giants.*"

"*How do you know that?*" said Rivet.

Jynx made a fist and placed her other hand over it, then bowed. "*I am one with Google-Fu.*"

"*Huh?*"

"*She's got a computer in her head and is really good at searching the networks for information,*" explained Poison. "*I don't recommend playing trivia games with her.*"

"*Even if you shut off the network, it's not fair,*" added Venom. "*She and Kita just download it to their heads beforehand. The only person who's competition for them is Athena.*"

"*Who's that?*" asked Rivet.

"*Another Angel. You'll meet her when we go home. Looks like they're ready to start.*"

The house lights came up, and the two pips waited at their ends. X5 was stomping back and forth, swatting the sand with his hands and lashing his tail. Bliz grunted and howled, blowing ice crystals in the air.

The lights flashed, and the announcer yelled, "Fight!"

X5 charged Bliz, coming straight at the pip. Bliz raised his hands and spit a flood of water across the sandy arena. X5 ignored the puddles as Bliz threw back its arms and blew an artic wind across the water, freezing it solid. X5 stepped on the frozen ground and slipped, and went sprawling across the ice. Jumping toward the stricken pip, Bliz landed next to X5, raised his fists, and brought them down on X5's chest with a *crack* that echoed in the room. The crowd roared with applause and yelled for more. On the scoreboard, X5's odds went from ten to a hundred.

Kita hoped Ultraviolet had a plan. Cracked ribs weren't a great way to start and would hamper any future attacks. *Maybe I should have been clearer about what kind of drama I expected—like trading a few blows—not permanent damage.* Still, she was confident and placed a bet on the new odds. If Ultraviolet wanted to up the drama, Kita was willing to take the ride.

X5 swept his tail around, hitting Bliz's feet. The maneuver appeared to be an attempt to knock Bliz down, but the icetoga stuck to the ice and didn't budge. Instead, it reached down and grabbed X5 by the tail, spun, and threw him into the concrete sidewall—face first.

"*Ah, is there a problem?*" Apocalypse asked Kita as the scoreboard changed again from one hundred to two hundred and fifty to seven.

"*I'm hoping UV is just taking my instructions to the extreme.*" Kita placed another bet, determined to get the money back she spent getting X5 into the fight.

X5 slapped the ground as he pushed himself to his feet and knuckles. Blood trickled down the ape's face from its nose.

"*At least she hasn't given up,*" said Venom.

"*Is it common for the odds to go that high?*" asked Poison.

"*Not that I've ever seen,*" replied Kita. She debated whether to coach Ultraviolet. Breaking the Angel's concentration wouldn't help her, and Kita didn't want her upset. But she knew that being frustrated with pressure mounting on you to perform was a recipe for disaster. She decided to wait and see what happened next. *Maybe UV has a plan. She is ancient, after all.*

X5 banged on his chest, seeming to taunt his opponent. Bliz blew ice crystals in its hand, forming a snowball. It heaved the snowball, hitting X5 in the face causing the audience to laugh. Slapping the ground, X5 twirled, his tail humming through the air. Bliz let out a loud howl and leaped over X5's tail, and landed next to the ape striking him several times with its fist, hitting X5 in the face and chest, appearing to knock the wind out of the ape. Bliz stood X5 up and delivered a heavy uppercut that put X5 on his back.

The scoreboard shot up. *Is he even going to get up? Guess I'll place one more bet. What the Crushing Depths...it's only money.* Kita focused on Ultraviolet, trying to read her emotions, but like always, she didn't feel anything. Clasping her hands in her cloak out of sight so she could fidget with her nail, Kita waited to see what Ultraviolet had in store.

X5 staggered to his feet, rocking back and forth. He shook his head and roared, showing off his mouth of sharp teeth, the lower ones so large they jutted out above his upper lip. Bliz howled in return, blowing ice crystals across the pit.

"Look—" Kita's warning died on her lips as the ice crystals swirled around X5.

The ape reared, but before he could charge, the crystals solidified into a block of ice encasing X5.

The scoreboard odds for X5 jumped to a thousand to one. Now, a bet on Bliz netted nothing. The referee raised his arm for the countdown.

"Bloody moons," Kita snarled as she drew Dead.

"Kita!" hissed Apocalypse. "Don't kill her!"

Kita spun and said, "It's not for her. I'm going after Grall— then we're going home." She pushed her way through the other Angels.

"*Momma!*" called Jynx.

Kita paused. "*What?*"

"*UV's reached her limit break.*"

"*Her what?*"

"*Watch, Momma.*"

Kita turned and walked back to the edge of the pit. X5 was still encased in ice, and the referee was on four of his countdown. If Ultraviolet had something planned, she needed to do it in a hurry.

A loud *crack* reverberated through the pit as the ice around the base of X5's tail broke. The ice-encrusted extremity rose into the air, then smashed against the sandy ground, shattering the ice around the tail's base.

The referee paused his count at two while Bliz danced around the pit's perimeter, playing to the crowd. Bliz's trainer and sponsor yelled in protest to the referee. The referee raised his arm for one.

X5's thick tail split into five slender slivers. Each sliver curled back around and hammered on the ice encasing the rest of X5. The ice cracked as X5 flexed. Twisting his head, the ice broke. His eyes glowing ultraviolet, he let out an angry roar as he flexed his arms and body, shattering the ice. Slapping the sand, he charged the distracted Bliz, slamming into the yeti's back and driving him into the concrete wall. Bliz slid to the sand, dazed. X5 grabbed Bliz's head and slammed it into the side of the pit repeatedly.

Taking Bliz by the head, X5 twirled, throwing the yeti across the pit. Bliz landed with a dull *thunk* against the far concrete wall. X5 charged before Bliz had time to recover. Swinging on his fists, X5 leaped at Bliz, driving the claws on his hind feet into the yeti's side. Blue blood squirted over Bliz's long, white hair. Standing on Bliz, X5 smashed his fists into the yeti's back with a muffled *crack*.

Bliz let out a mournful yowl as X5 dragged the yeti to the center of the pit. Standing Bliz up, X5 lifted himself up on two of his tail slivers. Two others stabbed Bliz in the shoulders, holding the yeti up. X5 stabbed his rear claws into Bliz's chest and slashed down, spilling open the yeti's chest and abdomen. Rocking back, X5 balled his fist and launched upward, hitting Bliz with a massive uppercut sending Bliz's head and spine soaring across the pit into the arena next to the referee. X5 withdrew his slivers and reformed his tail, allowing the rest of Bliz to collapse to the sand—blue blood streaming away. X5 backed away, pounded his chest in a loud series of *pops* before letting out a loud yell.

"Well," said Kita, "that was surprising and entertaining."

The rest of the crowd didn't think so. A chorus of boos rained down on X5 and Ultraviolet. The Angel didn't seem to care. She put on her cloak, covered her head, and rejoined the other Angels.

"Good job," said Venom.

"I've never seen Kita worried before," said Poison with a smile.

"The grandmaster manipulator has met her match."

Kita raised an eyebrow. "Some things are out of my control. I wish I'd had the presence of mind to bet at the peak."

"I did, Momma. Fifty million credits."

Kita bit her lip. Collecting that from the house would be challenging. "Well done, Jynxie. What are you going to do with all your money?"

"I want a pony."

"I had a horse growing up. His name was Major."

"What color was he?"

"Chestnut with a dark mane."

"What happened to him?"

"He died when I was fourteen. I was gone so much after that I just rode whoever was in the stable. We'll talk about getting you a pony...maybe on our next visit to Earth."

Jynx's smile beamed.

"Kita," said Alliance, "The announcer is here. Anything you want to say?"

Kita turned from her daughter and went to the edge of the pit where a camera drone and announcer waited with Ultraviolet.

"Congratulations on your first spectacular win, Angels," said the announcer. "You definitely took the bout to the edge. What do you have to say for your spectacular comeback?"

Kita and Ultraviolet exchanged glances. "*UV? Anything?*"

Ultraviolet stepped up to the announcer. "The outcome was never in question, only how much money you would lose."

"Ah, thanks," said the announcer. "An Angel of few words. Anything from the sponsor?" He and the drone turned to Kita.

"We are the queens of the ring. X5 will demolish Grall's jacksaur, and I'm willing to wager a hundred million credits with him over the winner." Kita took her credit chip from beside her breast and displayed the amount on it. "As you can see, I'm good for it."

"That is extraordinary," raved the announcer. "You saw it here first! Angel Kita extends a personal wager of a hundred million credits to Grall that her X5 can beat the king of the ring, the fearsome jacksaur!"

Kita and Ultraviolet turned away from the camera and joined Alliance.

"That's not something he can turn down," said Alliance.

"Not after what UV did tonight."

"A small fraction of X5's power," Ultraviolet commented dourly.

"With the jacksaur, there will be no need for pageantry. Kill it, and I will take care of Grall."

KITA AND THE ANGELS FOLLOWED A VERISOM MALE BUTLER with glowing eyes through Verisom Manor to where Mimic and Sage lay in repose. A memorial to Dominica stood between them.

"*I thought the Winter Palace was decadent,*" muttered Apocalypse, recalling the Angels' trip to the Soviet palace. "*But this place is absurd.*"

Kita chuckled. This Verisom Manor was different than the one she knew. However, it still had the same gaudy interior of precious metals and stones, marble quarried from a deadly planet, and a maze layout.

The butler led them past a line of Verisom princesses, waiting to see their deceased sister and the other guests of honor. He opened a door for the Angels and waved them inside.

Rivet waited by the head of the casket, receiving blessings and best wishes from the visitors. Flowers and palm fronds decorated the caskets and memorial. Several Prii stood next to Sage and Dominica. Kita didn't know who they were, but they looked to be prominent members of the Prii people. Seeing the

Angels, Rivet stopped the line and hurried out to greet the Angels with hugs and tears.

"How are you?" said Apocalypse to Rivet.

"I'm doing ok. It's awesome seeing all these people come out to pay their respects. I know she would never have gotten their respect while alive, but at least she's getting it now."

"And you," said Venom. "Her partner deserves it, too."

Rivet bowed her head. "Yes, it is nice they're acknowledging us. I know UV is behind it, but it's nice their attitude has shifted—even those not assimilated respect and honor me. I'm not just some dirty goat-cur."

"Anyone calls you that, and I'll shove a stinger through their spine."

Rivet's quills rippled in amusement. "No one in the last week, anyway. Even the few Diamocks I've run into respect the uniform." The disgraced Diamock soldier wore Kita's black formal military uniform. Kita had given it to her when Rivet revealed she had nothing to wear. There was little formal female Diamock civilian attire. As a surprise to go with the uniform, Kita, as the captain of the Diamock ship Mauler, gave Rivet a spot in her crew. It was symbolic—the ship and crew having died orbiting the lost planet A'a—but it didn't seem to matter to Rivet. She was part of a crew and could claim a ship, and that lifted her spirits.

"Good," said Kita with a small smile. "I'd hate to turn UV loose on the Diamocks...so soon."

A Verisom princess with glowing eyes stepped out of line and joined the Angels.

"UV?" said Jynx.

"Hello, all. We are coming. We couldn't decide what to wear."

The other Angels laughed.

"I would have sent you Velositi," said Kita.

"Oh, yes. I do love picking out clothes. I find it exhilarating how pieces of fabric can change how you look."

"Follow us." The princess waved Velositi to come with her.

"How are you girls doing?" said Rivet to the others. She'd been gone since the bout on Petal Ten.

"Cleaning up the Yellow Fist Pack," said Poison. She and Venom had been all over rounding up the various squads and ships. Ultraviolet made the job easier as most of the mercenaries went quietly.

"Family time, training," said Kita, "and waiting for Grall to get back to us."

"I've stepped up the pressure on him," said Alliance. "I've pushed on all the social and sporting sites getting as many commentators and supporters as I can to openly call him out. I'm beginning to think he's either a coward or something has happened to the jacksaur." She smiled as her scales rippled in amusement.

"I'm sorry I won't be there," said Rivet.

Kita shook her head. "You have more important things to do. I wouldn't take accompanying Catnip to Verisom away from you. Having UV with you takes a worry off my mind."

"I'm sure it'll be exciting when she gets there, but she said assimilating the capital will only take a day or two. Then I can pick out a place to bury Catnip. I've heard they have wonderful beaches. I'm sure I'll find a nice place where she'll have a great view of the ocean and sand."

"We will come and visit before we leave," promised Kita.

Rivet's quills rippled to show her unease. "I am excited to move on to the next chapter of my life—now that I have a ship and crew, I feel complete again."

"Don't be in such a hurry. Cherish every moment you have with her."

"I am. I'm grateful for you, UV, and all the Angels. This would have been much tougher without you—devastating, actually. I know they would have never let me see her again—as much as my heart hurts, that would have broken it beyond repair."

Kita knew love was a foreign concept to the Diamock... and, to some extent, the same for the Verisom. That Mimic and Rivet had found it in each other was inspiring, but she had always wondered how long the attachment would last. That Rivet was already ready to move on was saddening but not surprising. Kita knew her friends and Rivet would never forget

Mimic. The years they had together were special and unique. Kita would do as Jynx suggested and create an Angel memorial —so others could know and she could remember her friends. So much history had passed.

"Come on," Kita said to Jynx and Apocalypse. "Let's go say our goodbyes."

Kita tugged on Jynx's arm, but the young Angel refused to move.

Leaning into Jynx, Kita whispered, "What's wrong?"

Apocalypse seemed to sense a problem and leaned down next to her daughter. "Chelsea, what's the matter?"

Jynx looked at Apocalypse with big tears in her eyes. "Mom, do I have to?"

"I...what's the matter? Momma and I will be there with you."

"I've never seen a dead body up close before. Every time I close my eyes, I see me. Why can't you bring her back? Or Leaf? Or To'va and Al'ice?"

"Jynxie," whispered Kita, "it's natural to be scared of death. It's something that happens to all of us at some point...even me...and facing our own mortality is scary. Every culture has an explanation of what happens after death—most of them are wrong. I can tell you two things about death: at the last second, your consciousness stretches into infinity, and the second is that it's very peaceful. A peace you'll never know until you die. You have no cares or worries; you just exist in an infinite calm. I know that doesn't sound like much, but I promise you it's the best thing.

"I'm sorry I can't bring them back. Your Mom and I don't have the power. It's a rule we set down to protect the universes and us. If we had the power, others would find a way to gain it, and that will cause more problems than it will solve. I know it seems like a quick fix to ease your, Flexi, and everyone else's heart, but I know from experience it will cause more pain than the loss of a friend. This is wisdom I have learned through experience. I know the loss of the other Angels hurts, but it will fade in time, leaving fond memories. That is how our departed friends live on, through us and our memories of them. I promise I will build the Angel memorial so you can see Al'ice whenever you want."

"It just seems wrong, Momma. To have all the power and not be able to save our friends."

Apocalypse hugged Jynx. "Sweetheart, I know it's hard to understand, but with the power your Momma and I have comes responsibility. We chose to let life and death happen by fate in the universes. If this had happened on Roost and Reality, your momma and I would have fixed it. I know they were your friends, and I'm sorry they're gone. But it's part of growing up. You lose loved ones, and you gain new ones. Al'ice is gone, and it's important to remember her, but who knows who you'll meet in the next universe. Maybe, like Momma, you'll meet the love of your life."

Jynx sniffed. "It took Momma eight hundred and thirty-two tries before she found you."

Kita and Apocalypse laughed.

"Momma is persistent."

"Lonely. And now I have a wonderful family. I'd do it all over again." Kita hugged Jynx and Apocalypse. As they'd been talking, the other Angels had gone and paid their respects to Mimic, Saga, and Dominica. "Come on," urged Kita. "It's our turn. Let's say goodbye."

KITA AND THE ANGELS—FACES, AND IDENTITIES HIDDEN BY hoods and cloaks—escorted X5 from the truck through the darkened passageway that led to their den. X5 was in his tank carried by Velositi. As they glided forward, Kita held Apocalypse's hand.

A shadowy Djinn figure stepped out of a side passage as the Angels approached. He was impeccably dressed in a pinstriped suit, his mane slicked back smelling of oils, even his claws were painted black. Under his right arm was a satchel case.

Kita stopped, hovering above him.

"Warrior KelHarg would like to extend an offer," the Djinn said in a low growl.

Kita's lip curled at Grall using such an honorific or taking a commander's name. This was the first she'd heard of it. He was no warrior, just a slimeball. "What does he want?" she growled.

"Warrior KelHarg is willing to settle the outcome of tonight's bout, now. He offers you fifty million credits to lose. And he will say you paid him what you owe and wipe the slate clean."

"*Kita,*" screeched Ultraviolet. "*We will not lose.*"

Kita ignored the Angel's protest. "Fifty million payable now, and X5 will go down after two minutes."

"*Kita!*" exclaimed Apocalypse.

"*We will not!*" yelled Ultraviolet.

"Twenty-five million now, twenty-five million when the beast goes down."

"Forget it," snarled Kita. "It's all...or nothing." Kita wasn't about to be suckered. She knew if they only paid her half now, she'd never see the other half after the fight. Grall was predictable.

When the suave Djinn hesitated, Kita spread her wings and motioned the others forward. "Come on, girls. Let's go kill a jacksaur."

The other Angels closed ranks and glided around the Djinn.

"Alright," he announced. "Fifty million upfront, and Warrior KelHarg gets to keep X5's head."

Kita stopped and turned to face the Djinn. She pulled her credit chit from between her breasts and held it up. "Payable now."

"*Kita! We will not go down. No matter what you command,*" cried Ultraviolet.

The Djinn opened his case and pulled out a credit chit. He set the amount and offered it to Kita. She put her credit chit to his, and a light lit when the credits were transferred. Kita checked to make sure.

"Tell your master he has a deal. X5 will go down after two minutes, and you may keep the beast."

"Warrior KelHarg also sends a message. If you drain the pond, he'll mount all of your wings to his wall."

Kita raised an eyebrow. Turning, Kita glided down the passageway, the other Angels following with stoic faces.

Ultraviolet remained behind. *"Kita—"*

"Enough," barked Kita. *"I expect the jacksaur to be dead in under two minutes. Grall and his trainer now have a false sense of security. He thinks he can buy me; his hubris will be his downfall. Come."*

Ultraviolet glided forward to join the others. *"You are not going to let him take X5's head?"*

"Never. Ladies, be prepared to fight our way out. This will get ugly."

KITA FROWNED OVER THE POND. AT THE EDGES, IT WAS FOUR feet deep, and the water was murky and dirty. Water plants, lily pads, and large logs added to the effect. The center of the pit appeared shallower, but it could be deceiving. The water was a clearer, lighter color, and no obstacles could be seen. Grall had gone all out for his favorite pet. *Can X5 even fight in this?*

Unlike the tourney on Petal Ten, which had been a converted warehouse and fabrication plant, this tourney pit had been specifically built for underground bouts. Luxury boxes encircled most of the pit, with a large one reserved for Grall. Most of the patrons were wealthy Djinn and Verisom princesses. A few Humans and Zentonians were in attendance. Over the pit was a large display so everyone could see the action. However, Kita noticed many of the princesses carried viewing glasses. *Can't miss a second of the bone-crushing, blood-spewing action.*

"Jynxie," Kita called to her daughter.

The young Angel floated away from Apocalypse to be next to Kita. *"Yeah, Momma?"*

Kita brushed Ultraviolet's wing to get her attention.

"I want you to watch the bout next to UV. If something happens— like they cheat or X5 gets in trouble—I want you to manipulate X5's luck. Think you can do it?" This was a new request of Jynx. Previously Kita had only had her manipulate her own luck to

protect her or an object like her coin. Manipulating another being's luck would require her to concentrate on X5.

"*I can try, Momma. I've never done it for someone else before.*"

"*I know. But now is a good time and reason to try.*"

"*We will be able to handle this,*" said Ultraviolet.

"*I don't doubt it,*" said Kita, "*But I'm covering every probability. I want Grall, and he's stacking the deck in his favor—so am I. He will find out I have much better cards, including you, Chels, X5, and the Angels. We have one shot at this. It's not you I don't trust. It's me. I won't be eaten again.*"

"*I didn't know it bothered you so much, Momma.*"

"*Only when I think about it. Which is rare, but at the moment, it's sitting just below the surface like a nightmare.*"

Jynx gave Kita a hug. "*Don't worry, Momma. We'll take care of it. Right, UV?*"

"*Yes. Knowing this plagues your mind gives us even more of a reason to win. We will win and free your mind, Kita. If we had known sooner, we would have understood and not been so resistant.*"

"*It's not your fault—it's mine. I don't like to share my weaknesses or fears.*"

"*It's what friends are for, correct?*" said Ultraviolet.

"*Yes, but even with friends, I don't like to share my fears.*"

"*We fear death. Being so close to it has made us realize the need to protect and help those who have helped us. We may someday be helpless again and need assistance. Having friends helps ensure we will never die.*"

"*I fear Momma leaving again and being mad at me.*"

"*Jynxie,*" Kita said warmly as she gave her daughter a hug. "*I'm sorry I pulled back from you. I promise I won't do it again. If something does separate us, I will find you, I promise. But I know you're smart, resourceful, and resilient. I have every faith that you can take care of yourself. But no matter how much you venture off by yourself, I will always be there if you need me. And I only get mad because I worry about you.*" Kita gave Ultraviolet a hug. "*I do my best to protect all my friends. I'll give you a sanctuary where you can live forever.*"

"*Thank you. We know our goal of assimilating this universe is dangerous, but we must prove that we are worthy of being an Angel.*"

Out over the center of the pond appeared a Human walking on the water. Kita looked at the ceiling and saw a holograph generator and a net. *They must have trouble getting the jacksaur back in his hole.* His long braided facial hair, bald head, beady eyes, and short, squat stature reminded Kita of a dwarf. He seemed to be an odd choice for the announcer of the venue until he opened his mouth and his words came out like a fatherly storyteller.

"Tonight! ...Tonight, my friends...Tonight is the night of the big...Big...BIG fight! Tonight! We have two epic pips ready to do battle! Tonight! The newcomer—coming in on a colossal kill of the storied beast of the frozen north, the bringer of the blizzard, Bliz—I give you: X5!"

Below the Angels, the portcullis opened, and X5 waded through the water letting his tail reach over the crowd as he moved to the center of the pit. He beat his chest, releasing a series of pops followed by an angry yowl.

"But...do you hear that..." The dwarf put his hand to his ear. "...Coming ...Coming down the pipe? A beastie so big and brutal...teeth as big as your fist...claws that'll cut you in half...A beastie that has no equal..."

The home side pip entrance was shaped like a sewer pipe that extended a few feet into the pit. The portcullis shook as something under the water banged against it. The crowd went wild.

"Hear that? He's here...and ready to do battle. I give you: King Jack!"

The portcullis went up, and there was a ripple in the water as King Jack swam forward, then exploded out of the water, snapping its alligator-like jaws. It rocked back on its armor-plated tail and let out a deep-throated growl. It swung its thick, muscular arms back and forth, the claws on the ends kicking up water.

X5 roared back, slapping his tail against the water. The pips eyed each other before King Jack splashed into the water and disappeared. X5 turned, scanning the water, swishing his tail back and forth, searching.

King Jack erupted from the water on X5's left side. The

jacksaur snapped his jaws closed on X5's shoulder and upper arm. X5 raised his left arm and spun, lifting King Jack out of the water and slamming him down in the shallow water of the ring's center. The maneuver exposed King Jack's underbelly but didn't dislodge him. X5 swung his tail around and slammed it several times on King Jack's exposed belly and throat.

The throat shot caused King Jack to release. He rolled into the water and swam for the deeper part of the pit. X5, bleeding with deep gouges in his left arm, grunted and yelled loudly, slapping the water, trying to bring King Jack out.

King Jack pounced from the water behind X5. The great ape leaped sideways—his tail dividing into five slivers—toward the walls of the pit. The slivers slammed into the concrete and lifted X5 above the water, almost even with the spectators.

Across from Kita, in the largest viewing suite, sat Grall and his guests. From the looks on their faces and the free-flowing of alcohol, they seemed to be enjoying themselves. The timer in her head indicated they still had another minute until X5 was supposed to go down.

Using his large tail, King Jack propelled himself out of the water at X5. The great ape caught King Jack's massive jaws in his hands and pulled on his snout and lower jaw, forcing King Jack's jaws open. X5 slashed at King Jack's exposed underbelly with his hind feet. It was armored, but not as much as the rest of him. X5's claws opened deep gashes, spilling blue blood into the pond. King Jack lashed his tail, trying to force X5 to let go. Instead, X5 withdrew one of the slivers from the wall and stabbed King Jack several times. Bringing the sliver up, X5 aimed the sharp appendage down King Jack's throat.

Grall frowned and made a motion with his hand.

"Jynxie!" cried Kita. *"It's happening now!"*

"What? I don't see it."

"I don't know. Do whatever you can for X5."

The world erupted in flame, smoke, and pressure. Kita was thrown out of the trainer's platform into the pit. She landed in the shallow water of the pit's center. As she pushed herself to her knees in the murky water, King Jack broke free of X5 and splashed into the water's depths.

"Ew! Yuck," yelled Jynx as she surfaced next to the far wall of the pit.

"Jynxie!" yelled Kita. "Draw your sword. We're now King Jack's opponents."

The young Angel drew her katana. "The water's heated. I can't freeze it. Where's Mom and the others?"

"I don't know. Let's worry about saving ourselves first." Kita glanced up at Grall, sitting with a smile on his face and his fingers steepled.

Jynx thrust out of the water and swooped toward Kita. King Jack burst from the water underneath her, grabbing a leg in his massive jaws.

"Momma!" screamed Jynx.

"Stab him!" Kita pointed Dead at the jacksaur and blasted him with a lance of flame, searing through the thick armor plates.

Jynx flipped her sword in her hand and stabbed King Jack's snout, leaving deep cuts, but the jacksaur refused to let go. The weight of King Jack was pulling Jynx back into the water.

Kita flourished her swords and put them away. She looked at Grall and shook her head. Raising her arm, she pointed it at King Jack, opened her hand, and a gravity sphere appeared around the jacksaur's body, leaving his head and part of his tail exposed. Kita clenched her fist, and the gravity sphere collapsed, taking most of King Jack and some water.

Jynx yanked open the severed jacksaur's jaws and dropped the head into the water. Her legs were covered in puncture wounds and bleeding profusely. But she didn't complain or say a word as she glided next to Kita.

They drifted up to be even with Grall. Kita swept off her hood and changed her face to her Human version. "I've come to claim what is mine."

Grall's jaw dropped. "You're...You're dead!" he roared. "I watched you get eaten! Release the net."

From the ceiling, a steel cable net fell on Kita and Jynx.

Kita threw her head back and let out a long, bone-chilling, maniacal laugh. Flames erupted at her feet and climbed up her legs, and engulfed her. As a raging inferno, she melted through the net, then raised her arms and shot flame through the arena. Drips of flame fell off her into the water, burning across the surface. Her flame crawled up the walls and over the ceiling, engulfing the entire room forcing the spectators to flee for the exits.

Jynx moved next to Kita and touched her mother's arm, and let the flame spread over her. Together, they faced Grall's suite. Jynx raised her hand, flinging pieces of furniture at the door Grall's guests were trying to escape through.

Kita shot flame at his guests, engulfing them. When the last one fell, Kita turned to Grall. The Djinn was holding a small pistol.

"And what's that supposed to do?" Kita said in an eerie voice.

Jynx opened her hand and shot a flame at the pistol and Grall's hand. He fired the weapon, but the bullet hung in the air. Unable to take Jynx's heat, he dropped the pistol. Kita knocked the bullet to the ground.

"Fools like you believe you can buy power, and when that doesn't work, you think a gun gives it to you. Knowledge is power, you fool. And you are about to get an education in pain."

"THE OTHERS WERE FINE," SAID KITA WITH A SMILE. "WE took Grall to Verisom—which has quite the insect population —and had a wonderful two-week vacation before going home and letting Ultraviolet run—" a spatter of gunfire kicked up sand around Kita's head "—free...Something I said?"

"Shut up!" snarled Turnip, standing next to the armored Djinn guard holding a mini-repeater. "None of your babbling is telling me where the Axiom is! Obviously, the pepinal doesn't work on winged Humans! Mai'la!"

"Yes?" said the Aurorian standing next to the enraged Verisom.

"If she won't talk by chemicals, make her talk the old-fashioned way."

"I, ah...What do you want me to do?"

"Cut her, slice her! Make her bleed. See if a little pain will loosen her tongue."

Mai'la held up her hand, showing her golden fingernails tipped in green. "I don't think my nails can do that."

"Moron!" yelled Turnip. "Draga!"

The guard, who had been standing next to her, turned. "Yes, Your Highness?"

"Give Mai'la your combat knife. She can earn her keep."

The Djinn pulled a foot-long blade from his belt. Flipping it to offer Mai'la the hilt, he smiled, showing off his sharp teeth.

Mai'la took the blade and waved it around clumsily. "Turnip, are you sure—"

"Do it! I don't care if you have to spill all her blood. Get her to talk. I want the Axiom!"

Mai'la looked at Kita worriedly.

Kita raised an eyebrow, trying to reassure the Aurorian. *Not like this will be the first time I've been cut up. Somehow, I doubt Turnip is as sadistic as Demetri...or as patient.*

Mai'la jumped down into the sand of Kita's prison. It was impressive that she was able to keep her heels out of the sand

and walk on her toes in her platform stiletto heels. She knelt in front of Kita, using her body to block Turnip's view.

"I'm sorry," whispered Mai'la, now holding the knife like a professional. "I don't know what to do."

Kita offered her cheek. "Go ahead and cut me. It won't be the first time."

"What's taking so long?" snarled Turnip.

"Just not sure where to start," replied Mia'la.

"Take her ear!" yelled Turnip. "She seems to like taking Verisom ears!"

So, she was listening. Kita didn't like that idea. She'd only lost her ears once, and they took a while to grow back, and it hurt —lots. *Of course, that could just be that I'd lost a lot of other body parts first.*

"How much time do you need?" whispered Mai'la as she placed the knife on top of Kita's right ear.

Kita checked the computer. The damaged files were repaired, and so was the operating system. The files from this Earth were being coalesced into her main memory. She didn't need much. Her progress wheel was at thirty-three percent.

"Five minutes," replied Kita. "And then I can get us out of here."

"I can't carve you up for five minutes!"

"I have another short story that tells what happened to the Axiom. Slice my ear enough to bleed, and I'll start talking."

"Are—are you sure?"

"It's a little blood. Weren't you listening? I've had worse."

"I was. You never said how you survived it."

Kita smiled. "Angels are fast regenerators. The pain of injury is real, but it doesn't last long."

Mai'la pressed the blade where Kita's ear joined her skull. "I'm sorry," she whispered as she winced.

The sting of the blade into Kita's ear hurt, and her cry in pain was real. "Ok, ok, ok. I'll talk. I'll tell you what happened to the Axiom, what it does, and where it goes."

"What do you mean *where it goes?*" yelled Turnip.

Mai'la twisted out of the way so Kita could see Turnip. Kita turned her head, allowing Turnip to see the blood flowing down her face.

"When it gets used by a chosen person, it disappears."

"Who is a chosen person?"

"A chosen person is evil. Frich'itit just scratched the surface of the Axiom's true power. A person of great evil is granted the power to destroy or rule the world. You have the power to create, control, and dominate the most fearsome warriors in the universe. You become invincible—mortal weapons can't stop you. Armies bow to your will; navies are yours to command. Planets cower at your feet, and you can control the stars. The chosen person becomes a god."

"I am a chosen person," yelled Turnip. "I will dominate the galaxy—"

"Why not the universe?" suggested Kita.

"Yes! I will have the universe. I will be a god among the stars! The Axiom's power will be mine! And you will give it to me! For your cooperation, I will let you serve me."

How generous. "Maybe you'd better hear how the Axiom works, so you know what to do when we find it."

"Yes. Tell me!"

"It's simple, really..."

KITA WAITED BEHIND THE LARGE BLUE CURTAIN BACKSTAGE for her daughter's name to be called. She fidgeted with her dixie cup—nervous and excited. It'd been nine months since she'd been called to serve. She'd written a few weeks ago that she wouldn't be home for Jynx's graduation. The Navy was sending her straight to her ship.

But fate had intervened, and she was given three days of leave. *Did Jynxie have anything to do with it?* Jynx could control luck, and her power had grown over the last two years. No longer could she just manipulate coins and cards, but real-life events.

"Now presenting Chelsea Lynne Logine-Roosevelt. She has earned her primary degree with honors."

The audience applauded, and Kita could hear her partner, Apocalypse, cheering. Kita used that as her cue. She walked around the curtain to stand at the end of the stage. She cheered as Jynx was handed her diploma and shook the hand of the principal and school board members.

"Ladies and gentlemen, we have a special guest tonight. Please welcome Seaman First Class Katrina Logine-Roosevelt, fresh from Norse Point Naval Training Station. Seaman First Class Logine-Roosevelt will be serving aboard *RSS Hood*."

Jynx turned around, looking in the crowd.

"Chelsea! Jynxie!" Kita called to the center of the stage.

Jynx found her mother and ran to her, the graduation gown flowing behind her, exposing the pink and black dress underneath. Her daughter crashed into Kita's arms. "Momma! Oh, Momma!" she said around tears and happy sobs.

Kita hugged her tight. "Hey, Jynxie. I'm so proud of you. Congratulations!"

"Oh, Momma! I tried, and I tried. I didn't think it would work. I can't believe you're home! I missed you so much, Momma. I can't believe you made it."

Before Kita could answer, she felt another set of arms

around her. Hugging Jynxie and knocking her cap off, Kita looked over her daughter at her partner. "Hey, love. Did you miss me?" She leaned in to get a kiss.

"It's been the longest nine months of my life," Apocalypse said when they came up for air.

"Ladies and gentlemen, the Logine-Roosevelt family," the announcer said to the cheering and applauding crowd.

Kita turned her family to face the audience. She stood at attention and saluted.

The announcer continued, "Here's to a short war. May Seaman Logine-Roosevelt and the rest of our troops come home safely. We thank her and all of them for their service."

Hearing the announcer was finished, Kita escorted Apocalypse and Jynx off the stage to seats on the floor.

KITA STEPPED OUT OF THE COTTAGE DOOR AND SET HER seabag on the stoop. The small yard of green grass and flowers she and her family had planted when they first moved in three years ago were in bloom. She was surprised how much she missed the picturesque yard, the stone wall that went around it, and the tree that grew in the corner. Apocalypse had planted some more flowers in what she called her *Kita Memorial Garden*.

Kita was happy she'd gotten to see the home she shared with Apocalypse and Jynx one more time before she shipped out again. She didn't know how long she'd be at sea. News reports and Command said the war would be short—if it started. Kita had volunteered for the Navy instead of waiting to be drafted. That way, she got her choice of assignments, and it meant Apocalypse, as Jynx's mother, couldn't be drafted.

Apocalypse slipping her hands around Kita made her lean her head back and find Apocalypse's.

"Hey, love," Kita said quietly.

"I'm sorry you have to go. I wish they'd let you stay longer."

"I wasn't supposed to have any time, but I guess *Hood* needed some emergency repairs. I blame our daughter."

Apocalypse chuckled. "She's becoming good at manipulating luck, and with her abilities and sword."

"A couple more years, and she'll be able to go it alone."

Apocalypse squeezed Kita. "I'm not ready for that. She's still my little potato with wings."

Kita laughed. "They always grow up, no matter how hard you try. I just hope she's as good an adult as she's been a kid."

"What are we going to do when she leaves?"

Kita turned to face Apocalypse. "We've got a few years yet. Let's enjoy them. I was thinking for one of our next adventures, we should see the far future."

"That would be neat. None of the universes have extended much beyond Twenty-six hundred Common Era."

"Yeah. I want to make sure the universes are stable for the long term."

Apocalypse kissed Kita. "Enough thinking about that. Me."

Kita chuckled and kissed her partner. Letting the kiss grow deeper, Kita's hands explored Apocalypse's sides before settling for two handfuls of her butt.

"Momma?" whispered Jynx from the door.

Kita tried to split from Apocalypse, but her partner latched onto her lower lip, sucking on it and sending a chill up Kita's spine. "Meow..." Kita sighed as all the baby hairs on the nape of her neck stood up. Shaking her head to not only enjoy the sensation Apocalypse had given her but also to focus, she said, "What is it, Jynxie?"

Jynx came to her slowly and hugged her. "I don't want you to go."

"I'm sorry, Chels. But it's only for a few weeks. We'll cruise the north Atlantic, most likely guarding convoys between the home islands and the colonies. The Prussians don't have much of a navy—a few big ships—but those are expected to stay close to Europe. Don't worry. I'll be fine."

"I do worry!" the teenager stomped her foot. "I have a bad feeling."

"What kind of bad feeling, sweetheart?" said Apocalypse.

"I...I don't like the numbers the computer's spitting out or the ones coming up. They're all wrong."

Kita wrapped her arms around her daughter. "Jynxie, I know it can look bad, but we don't know how those numbers are to be used. There are lots of things to happen between now and then. I'll be fine."

"You won't be fine, Momma. I know what I see. Don't go," she said, her eyes filling with tears.

"Chels," Kita said in a firm voice, "I have to go. I don't have a choice. I've made my commitment, and I will do my duty for honor and country."

"You don't believe in honor!"

"I do believe in fulfilling an oath I've made. Just as others have made an oath to me, I have made an oath to the Republic of Scotland. As I expect them to fulfill their oaths to me, I will fulfill my oath to our country."

Jynx turned and fled inside.

Kita looked at Apocalypse and shrugged. "I know it's hard, but she needs to understand."

"I know. She's never had to make or accept an oath. I don't think she understands the commitment. But I worry...I don't know the numbers in the random generator like she does, but what if she's right?"

"The *RSS Hood* is the biggest and strongest ship in the fleet. I'll be fine. We're cruising out to protect the convoy traffic. Nothing is going to happen to us."

"But what if something does?" cried Jynx from the doorway.

"Then I'll see you back on Roost."

"No, Momma! I don't want to bury you. I've buried too many friends already. Take this." Jynx held out her hand, revealing Kita's Axiom.

"Jynxie, you know—"

"Momma! Take it! Please! I know what I saw. I'd rather be an Angel than bury you."

Kita looked at Apocalypse.

"Maybe you should, angel. It is a war and...and I don't want to have to bury you either."

Kita sighed and took the pendant from her daughter.

Taking her dixie cup off and handing it to Apocalypse, Kita put the Axiom around her neck and tucked it under her shirt. In a few minutes, she'd feel its power coursing through her. She'd no longer be Human but an Angel without wings.

A navy-blue bus pulled up next to their gate and honked.

"There's my ride," said Kita as she gave Apocalypse and Jynx a hug. "Chels, be good for your mom and practice your drills. I expect you to be better than me by the time I get back."

Jynx frowned. "I'll never be as good as you, Momma. But I'll practice."

"If you do, I'll unlock some more of your abilities."

"Really?"

"You graduated school—early. I think if you can show me you've mastered what I've given you, it's time for the advanced course."

"Will you train me to be an assassin?"

"Not yet. Don't rush. You'll get there."

"Ok, Momma."

Kita kissed Apocalypse. "Bye, love. I'll be home as soon as I can."

The bus honked again.

"Time to go." Kita stole another kiss from her partner and daughter, then grabbed her seabag and ran to the bus.

Kita tapped her letter on the mailroom counter to get the clerk's attention. "Hey, Stevens, got one for you."

Stevens was a lanky, freckle-faced kid from the Iowa colony and had never seen the ocean before joining the Navy. He looked up from a magazine with a pinup girl on the cover. "Damn, Roosevelt. Are you going to write a letter every day?"

"Every day until we get back to port."

"He must be some guy."

Kita smiled. "No, she is some girl."

"Your sister?" he asked as he came to the window.

Kita laughed. "Nope."

"Ah, friend?"

"She was my girlfriend for a while."

Stevens' freckles turned red. "Ah, come on, Roosevelt. Don't tell me the most gorgeous girl on the ship goes for the same team. You're going to break every guy's heart."

"And what's the betting pool up to?"

Stevens' cheeks and ears turned bright red. "I, ah..."

Kita laughed playfully. "Every girl on this ship knows about the pool. So, what am I up to?"

"Ah, fifty bucks."

"Split it with ya."

Stevens' jaw dropped. "What? Really?"

Kita smiled evilly. "No, but who's number two?"

"Ah...Jenkins in Turret Y."

"What's the take if I end up with her?"

"What?" Stevens blinked as his face became shades of perplexed.

"How much to do I get if I sleep with her?"

"I...I don't think that's allowed."

"You boys always think it's about you."

"Well...I...we..."

Kita winked at him. "I don't care. You're allowed to daydream all you want with your hand."

Stevens turned so red he had to turn away.

I think I just blew his mind. "What? You think us girls don't know what you do in the shower? You're allowed, I don't mind. I daydream about my girl, too. How much for the stamp?" Kita said, trying to save Stevens from himself.

"Ah, twenty pence."

"Take it out of my pay."

"You keep it up, and you won't have any pay left."

"It'll be worth it when I get home. You guys think I'm gorgeous; you haven't seen her."

Stevens looked at the ground as he asked, "How...how do you girls do it...without...you know..."

"A penis involved?" Kita said it just loud enough to make him blush. "Fingers, fists, tongues, boobs, necks, collarbones, clits, both sets of lips, g-spots, and good old pussy to pussy grinding. You miss out being a man. You only get off one way. Girls have lots, and we can go and go and go...remember that for your girl. She'll love you for it, and a girl that's satisfied is willing to repay in kind."

Stevens looked bewildered.

"Someday, when I have time, maybe I'll teach you."

"You will?" Stevens looked like he couldn't believe the words came out of his mouth. "I mean, I don't even know most of what you said."

Kita smiled warmly. "We'll start with anatomy. How can you please a girl if you don't know your way around her?"

"I, ah, thought—"

The general quarters' klaxon sounded.

"Oops, gotta go," said Kita. "We'll talk about it later." She left her letter on the counter and hurried aft toward Turret X and Damage Control Two.

"Make a hole!" a senior chief petty officer yelled going the other way.

Kita pressed herself against the wall and let him and the group he was leading pass through. She joined the rush of bodies as they hurried to their stations around the ship. Kita ducked through several hatches, nodding to the sailors waiting for everyone to get to their places so they could dog them down.

Kita turned left into Damage Control Two and found it full of people. "Roosevelt here, Chief," she called to Chief Petty Officer Masterson in charge of her section. He grunted something. Kita took that as an order to get herself ready.

She went to her locker and pulled out her leathers, breathing apparatus, welding mask, helmet, and floatation device. She donned everything in a specific order, all meant to protect her from fire, smoke, and drowning. As a Hull Technician, her job was to patch any holes or leaks that sprung in the ship.

Finished with her gear, she went to her welder, loaded the stinger with a stick, attached the ground clamp to the test bar, and yelled, "Sparking!" to warn everyone else she was testing her welder.

She struck the stick against the test plate, releasing a bright flash and bit of metal. The test plate was full of dots of metal from HTs testing their equipment. When the ship went in for a complete overhaul, the plate would be ground smooth again.

With her welder working, Kita went to the patch hatch. She opened it and checked to make sure she had all the various size metal patches she might need. Finished counting, she yelled, "Hull up!"

"Make sure your shit's together, Roosevelt!" yelled Chief Masterson.

"What's out there, Chief?" ask Kita.

"Scuttlebutt from the glass eyes is the *Bismarck* and *Prinz Eugen* are trying to punch through the straight."

Kita's eyes went wide. No Prussian warships were supposed to be this far west. Everyone said they'd be in the North Sea and eastern Atlantic protecting Europe. Only swift raiders would be attacking the convoy routes. *Hood* had been guarding the Denmark Straight for a few days now, protecting the convoys coming from the colonies.

"What are the Krauts doing out here, Chief?"

"Damned if I know. Everyone, make sure your shit's together and squared away. We get to dropping lead on these motherfuckers; we'll be damn sure to get some back. Our job is to make sure the ship stays afloat. There's no way they're sinking this battleship as long as we're still breathing. Got it?"

"Yes, Chief!" everyone in Damage Control Two answered.

Kita stood by her locker, waiting and watching the damage control board behind Lieutenant Boise. Right now, it was all green, but if they got into a slugfest with *Bismarck*, it could light up like a Winterfest Tree. She was concerned with a certain set of lights that signified a hull breach. She could weld anything, and if the ship took internal damage, she could fix that, too. But the hull was the most important because it kept the ship floating.

The compartment shook as Turret X fired.

"Shit. This is for real," somebody muttered.

"Everyone, quiet," ordered Chief Masterson. "Boys, make sure your balls are screwed on tight. Shit's about to get real." He paused for a second. "My apologies, ladies."

"We're ready, Chief," replied Kita. "I've got my tits strapped down tight."

Chief Masterson laughed. "That's good, Roosevelt."

"Girls are like boys, Chief. If you don't strap it down, shit flaps all over the place."

"Shit," said another sailor, "my balls have crawled up to my belly button."

"Being scared is good," said Chief Masterson. "Heightens your senses, keeps you sharp...just don't let it freeze you, or I'll put my boot up your ass."

Turret X roared again, and the ship shuddered. A few seconds later, the ship shook again.

"Was that the five inchers?" said someone.

Alarms and lights appeared on the damage control board.

"We took a shell forward," said Lieutenant Boise.

"Not us," said Chief Masterson. "You people look sharp. Shit's officially gotten real."

Kita gulped, trying to think of what Damage Control One near Turret A was doing. She hoped she wouldn't have to find out. *Ugh, I hate waiting for something to happen. I'd rather be on the bridge like in the past.*

A series of loud *booms* came from the fore and aft part of the ship, shaking the compartment violently, throwing everyone to the floor and Lieutenant Boise out of his chair.

"What in tarnation was that?" exclaimed Brady, a sailor from the Colony of Mississippi.

The deck pitched aft ten degrees and listed to starboard almost twenty. The lights and alarms for the ship's aft sounded, but the indicators for the ship's fore were dead.

"What the hell happened?" said Lieutenant Boise looking for his chair, but it had slid against the far wall out of reach. Ignoring the chair, he looked at the board. "What's wrong with the board? Chief, send someone forward to find out what's wrong with the ship."

"I don't think that's a wise course of action, sir."

"Why the hell not, Chief? I need to know what's happening."

"Well...sir...from the angle of the floor, I'd say we're missing the fore part of the ship."

"Nothing can do that kind of damage to *Hood*, Chief. The ship is fine. Just a malfunction."

"Sir. With all due respect, this *ship* just became our tomb."

"The floor's getting steeper," squealed Brady.

Kita blinked hard as she felt her eyes moisten. *Jynx was right.* Kita reached into her shirt and touched her Axiom. *I promised her I'd come back...but I can't leave them here...*She backed into the patch hatch and opened the doors to hide her from view. Kneeling, she clutched the Axiom. *I need something only an Angel can do...*

Kita's Axiom glowed with ultraviolet light. It pulsed rapidly, and then there was a flash. Biting her lip against the pain, Kita's wings grew from her back, forcing their way through her dungaree top and pushing her other gear aside. The skin on her wings felt like it was boiling as buds formed and broke, releasing her pink and black feathers. When her wings finished growing, the pain subsided.

Taking a deep breath, Kita stood, and the lights went out.

"Shit," grumbled Chief Masterson. "Somebody, light a torch."

Kita set her wings ablaze, lighting the compartment in an eerie firelight.

"What the fuck is burning?" yelled Chief Masterson. "Get the extinguisher!"

"Sorry, Chief," said Kita. "It's the only light I can produce."

Everyone in the compartment turned as Kita stepped out from behind the locker door.

"What in the Jiminy," gasped Brady.

Kita smiled shyly. "I, ah, well...I'm not a guardian angel. I'm a fallen angel, but I promise I'll get everyone out."

"Roosevelt?" Chief Masterson reluctantly.

"Yes, Chief," she said formally as she stood at attention.

"Will somebody get the damn fire out?" yelled Lieutenant

Boise, his attention still on getting the damaged board working.

"I do believe that holy flame is coming from our heavenly angel, sir," said Chief Masterson. "I'm not about to spray her with fire foam."

"I'd prefer you didn't," replied Kita. "We need to go before the stern sinks. Everyone, grab torches and run through the decks and find as many survivors as you can. I'll go to the engine room. The rest of you take the other decks. Whatever you do, don't open the fore bulkheads and let water in."

"How are you going to save us?" said Brady. "You can't just snap your fingers?"

"By the rules of god, I'm not allowed. But I have some other tricks. Don't worry. No one is going to the Crushing Depths if I have anything to say about it. Anyone not going to look for others, grab the life rafts and get as far forward and to the highest deck you can."

"Hold on," said Lieutenant Boise. "No one's going anywhere. I don't know what's wrong with the ship, and no one's abandoning ship until I say so."

Chief Masterson cleared his throat. "Well...sir...going down with the ship is your prerogative, but God's messenger is standing in front of us telling us to abandon ship. I'm in mind to think you're outranked...sir."

"Were you listening, Chief? She said she was a fallen angel —the Devil's kin."

Kita chuckled. Once upon a time, she'd even assumed the role of the Devil, then later the God of Evil, but things changed. Now, the fallen ran Heaven.

"There have been some changes in Heaven, but I do not work for the Devil. My wings are black and pink. I do God's work to protect the innocent and deliver their retribution. On occasion, I save the innocent."

"I don't care what color her wings are if she's going to save us," said Brady.

Chief Masterson cleared his throat. "If God sees fit to save an old sailor like me, I'll be damned if I'm going to question the messenger. Boys, grab your torches and go get the others. Everybody else, grab the rafts and preservers and get upstairs."

"Wait a second, Chief," yelled Lieutenant Boise. "No one is going—"

The Lieutenant was cut off by a meaty *thwack*. Chief Masterson shook out his fist from cold-cocking the officer. "I'll carry his ass out."

If it were me, I would leave him. "Ok, I'm going to the engine room. I'll meet everyone on the highest deck we can reach. Chief, carry the LT as far as you can. I'll take him when I come back."

"A little thing like you isn't going to be able to carry his lard ass."

Kita chuckled. "With wings comes the strength of God."

"My mess. I'll clean it up."

Kita shrugged and opened the hatch to the rest of the ship. She expected it to be quiet, but the sound of metal groaning made her skin crawl. Kita turned aft and hurried through the passageway, stopping to bang on any doors she came to. If they opened, she directed the sailors where to go.

Kita's flames cast the ship in a spooky light. Shadows made her see ghosts in the dancing firelight. Normally, darkness didn't bother her, but there was no electromagnetic energy for her eyes to detect inside the ship due to the power being out. Reaching the engine room, she found the door dogged tight. Using her fist, she banged and yelled for someone to open the door.

When no one answered, she found a steam pipe. *No steam going through it now.* Finding a seam, she pulled and twisted until the pipe broke. Using her new knocker, she banged on the door. Each *clang* echoed through the dying ship like Death's bell.

Kita brought her pipe up to strike again when the wheel spun, and the latches pulled back. The door opened to a trio of sailors in greasy overalls.

"Where's your gear?" demanded the first sailor shoving a torch in Kita's face. "We've got water coming in!"

"Who is it?" said the second sailor behind him.

"It's the gorgeous turd herder from DC Two."

Kita sighed. *You weld one shitter, and you're branded for life.* "I'm here to get you out."

"What's on fire?"

"I am," replied Kita. "Now come on. Get everybody. We're getting out of here."

"What happened to the ship?" said the first sailor.

"I think we got blown in half. That's why we're listing so bad."

"Blown in half!" cried the second sailor. "We got to get out of here."

"That's what I'm telling you," said Kita. "Grab everybody in the engine room and follow me."

"Sanders, Gardner, go grab the others. Tell them to drop what they're doing and get their asses up here. Take my torch."

"Right, Chief." Gardner took the torch, and the two sailors disappeared into the darkness.

"Going to explain why you've got six feet of flame lighting your ass?" said the engine room chief.

"Let's just say God smiles on her favorites." Kita stretched her wings as far as she could in the narrow corridor.

The engine room chief reached under his shirt, pulled out a circle with an X in the middle, and kissed it. "For all the angels in Heaven, I thank you, Lord, for blessing me with your grace. As your servant, I promise to love and honor thee." He put the symbol back in his shirt. "What messenger of God are you?"

"You mean besides the gorgeous turd herder?"

He blushed. "Yeah, sorry about that."

"My name is Kita. I'm an Angel, and I'm here to save as many as I can."

"We haven't had any casualties, but the torpedo storage near boiler two and three took a direct hit. We've got water pouring in through the hole flooding the compartments."

Out of the darkness, a group of fifty sailors appeared, all wearing overalls stripped to the waist—most were soaked.

"Is that everyone?" asked Kita.

"Yeah. Even Joe got his fat ass up here."

"Shut up, Tommy." There was some pushing and shoving.

"At ease," yelled the engine room chief. "We've been graced by God. The Angel Kita is going to show us the way out."

"Everyone, follow the flames—that's me. We're headed forward to the upper decks. When we get there, I'll tell you how we're getting out."

Kita led everyone back the way she came. She checked a few more doors to make sure the compartments were empty. Satisfied she had everyone, she stopped by Damage Control Two, but it was empty. She continued going forward until she reached the stairwell. It was narrow, which meant she had to contort her wings, but Kita didn't hesitate to grab the chains and pull herself up a few stairs at a time. As Kita climbed, the groaning of the ship reached a new octave.

"We need to move," she yelled behind her. "Get up here as fast as you can."

When she reached the upper deck, she found the bulkhead door open. *Good, the others have made it.* "Everyone out the door and head forward until you find the rest of the sailors."

As the sailors hustled by her, Kita took a count. *Forty-eight out of nearly thirteen hundred. I hope the others found more.* When the last sailor passed her, Kita followed him forward until the line stopped moving. *We must be at the seaward bulkhead.*

Kita phased forward, bypassing the line of sailors via the fifth dimension. As she glided forward, the world was black and white. She found Chief Masterson and more sailors crowded around a bulkhead door with water streaming through the seal. *How far down are we?* She hoped it wasn't far, but she could go to the bottom if need be. It was everyone else she had to get out now. Kita phased back into the normal dimension next to Chief Masterson and Lieutenant Boise.

"Chief, do we have everyone?"

"As many as we could find. Did you get to the engine room?"

"Yes, Chief. I got forty-eight."

"I think we gathered a couple hundred."

Kita nodded. *How am I going to get so many out? Guess we'll see how far my heat shield can stretch.* "Ok, we're sinking fast, so we need to act fast. What I'm about to do won't hurt you, but everyone has to get inside because I'm going to open this bulkhead, and the sea is going to try and rush in." *Hopefully, I can plug it*.

"Ok, you sailors heard Angel Kita. Everyone, pack it in like your sardines. Assholes to peckers. Ladies, sorry about that. Everyone, keep your hands to yourselves. I don't need a goddamn SHARP complaint."

The sailors crowded around the bulkhead as Kita extended her heat shield.

"Holy shit!" exclaimed a few sailors as the shimmering orange edge of the shield passed over them.

"Holy light!" someone corrected.

Kita pushed as far as she could, but a few dozen sailors were left out. "Everyone, squeeze!" yelled Kita.

As the sailors pushed together, Kita grabbed the bulkhead wheel and tested it. The door stuck fast from the water pressure.

"Everyone's in!" came a yell from down the passageway.

Kita accessed the computer in her head and slid the slider on her strength to a hundred. Gripping the wheel, she pulled with all her might. As she strained, Chief Masterson, Lieutenant Boise, and some other sailors grabbed hold and pulled.

Slowly, the wheel turned. As soon as the latches released, the door flung open, and seawater pounded in, steaming off the superheated bionanites of Kita's heat shield and pooling around her feet. Kita pushed her shield through the door, plugging the hole and creating a ten-foot space on the other side.

"Ok, one at a time through the door. I'm going to expand the far side as more people fill the space and collapse this side. Chief, can you make sure people stay tight on the other side? And get a count?"

"No problem. Ok, you heard the Angel, step lively and stay together."

In single file, the sailors went through the door. Kita did her best to try and watch both sides at once, keeping her heat shield balanced. In her head, she shifted more power from her strength into her shield to make sure it didn't collapse. Opening a pouch on her belt, she took out four energy balls—chocolate-covered treats that packed five thousand calories each—Chelsea had made and given her. Enough energy to make sure she didn't falter.

"Chief," Kita called through the door.

"Yes, Angel?"

"I have to step through and move forward to keep the shield balanced."

Chief turned to those on his side, "Make a hole! The Angel needs to come through."

Kita stepped through the door—it had a high lip and low header, requiring her to twist her wings to get through. "Keep sending people through," she ordered as she moved forward.

Kita nodded to the sailors as she passed them. Many blessed themselves, and a hand touched her arm. Kita looked at the sailor and was surprised to see it was Stevens. He looked upset, and tears ran down his cheeks.

"Roosevelt, is it really you?" he said, his voice breaking up.

"Hey, Stevens," said Kita trying to sound upbeat and reassuring.

"Angel of the Lord, please, please, I don't want to die here. Please forgive my sins. I'm sorry. I—I'll live a—"

"Stevens," said Kita, "all of you, listen to me. Nothing you did or didn't do got you here. It's pure luck, that's it. But luck has nothing to do with me saving you. I'm going to get you out and to the surface. Then, I will hunt down *Bismarck* and send him to the bottom as vengeance for *Hood*. Unlike them, you're all getting a second chance at life. I hope you use it wisely. You can thank me by doing what I tell you, and we'll all get out of here alive."

Kita gave Stevens a hug. "Don't worry. It'll all be over soon. You have nothing to fear as long as I'm here. Ok?" *We all need hope...even me.*

"Thanks. I knew there was something special about you."

Kita laughed. "Just an Angel making her way through life."

"Have you met God?"

"Who do you think I've been writing to?"

"God lives in Scotland?"

"And we have a fifteen-year-old daughter who just graduated high school."

"What's God doing in Scotland?" said another sailor. "What footie does he root for?"

"Not he," said Stevens, "she..."

"I gotta go," replied Kita with a smile. "But, yeah, God is Kimmy, and she is my partner."

"Is that true?" said another sailor as Kita walked away.

"Of course it is. An Angel wouldn't lie," said Stevens. "And I know Roosevelt...she sends a letter every day to...God."

"Wow. Talk about love," said a female sailor.

Kita rolled her eyes and shook her head as she kept her heat shield moving.

"Hey, Angel!" Someone yelled from up ahead while waving his arm.

Kita hurried forward and discovered the edge of the ship. The metal was twisted, gnarled, and torn. Stepping to the edge, Kita stared into the abyss. *It's like my soul is looking back at me.* Kita tore her eyes away from the deep and looked up at the wavering morning light filtering down through the water. The top deck above them was gone—leaving them on an exposed ledge—she could see what was left of the stacks and the superstructure. *Twenty feet or so, not so—*

The reverberation shook what was left of the ship. The pitch angled aft, tilting the deck under Kita's boots even farther. *Gotta hurry. This thing is about to go under.*

"Angel Kita!" a sailor called.

Kita turned to face her. "What?"

"The back says we're out of space."

"Ok. Everybody, listen up. Fill in all available room. Get as close as you can." Kita glided above the sailors and flew down the line, wary of hitting her head on lights and other things hanging from above. As she went, she repeated her instructions. When she got to the door, she yelled for Chief Masterson. "Chief! How many more do we have?"

"About eighty, Angel."

"We got to get them through as fast as you can. This tin can could go under at any moment."

"Alright, you scallywags, everyone through the door like you got a purpose. This ship is going down, and we're not leaving anyone behind. You, on the other side, make room. I don't care if you've got to sit in each other's laps."

The sailors shifted and pushed, making room for those coming through the door. Kita floated above them, pushing people together.

A terrible groan echoed through the ship as the deck tilted. Kita phased to the front and looked up. The rear smokestack was slipping under the water. *It won't be long now.*

"Chief!" Kita screamed. "We got to go. The ship is going under!"

"Then go! Leave the rest of us."

"I'm not leaving anybody! Get your asses through that door!"

A shudder ran through the ship as it tilted back, raising the front momentarily.

"Go!" yelled Chief Masterson.

"Not without you!" Kita extended her left arm and encapsulated the area and sailors behind the door in a gravity sphere.

The ship slipped beneath the waves. Already straining her abilities, Kita lifted her heat shield, pulling it forward as the ship slid beneath them. Flapping her wings and directing the gravity wells in her feathers, she headed for the surface—using the hint of light as a guide.

Beads of sweat glistened on her forehead as her mind, body, and computer struggled to keep her heat shield from crumpling while her arm remained out and her hand open to keep the gravity sphere from collapsing. Focusing all her energy into propulsion, Kita pulled the sailors to the surface. As she went, she reshaped her heat shield into a round sphere.

As her heat shield breached the surface, the oil slick left by the ship ignited. *Well, at least the rescue party won't have trouble finding us.* Kita pulled the sailors through the fire to open ocean.

"Chief! Deploy the rafts and get everyone aboard."

The sailors hurried and pulled the inflation ripcords on the rafts filling the bottom of the heat shield with yellow. Kita flattened and elongated her shield as the rafts took up most of the available space. Once the rafts were inflated, the sailors climbed in.

"Everybody in the rafts!" yelled Chief Masterson. "The Atlantic is mighty cold; you don't want to go swimming."

Once the sailors were loaded, Kita dropped her heat shield, and the rafts fell into the water.

"Shit! It's cold," someone remarked.

"Better than Davy Jones's locker," another replied.

"Sorry," said Kita. "I need a few minutes to recharge. Then I'll go find *Chancellor of Wales.*" She dug more energy balls from her belt.

"They can take it," said Chief Masterson. "You've done more than enough. We've got flares and a beacon." He looked across the raft. "Hey, LT, get that rescue beacon barking."

Exhausted, Kita drifted upward and scanned the horizon using the enhanced zoom in her eyes. "Chief! I see the *Chancellor of Wales.* She's north by northeast." Kita grew a red ball—a thermobaric bomb—in her hand and threw it straight up. Giving it two seconds, she snapped her fingers, igniting the ball in a fiery explosion. *I hope they don't miss that.* Watching the ship, it slowly changed course, and the cloud of smoke grew.

Kita drifted down to the rafts. "They're steaming for us, Chief."

"Thank you, Kita. You are the most blessed Angel in Heaven."

"Just doing my duty to my country and my shipmates."

"I'm glad God is on our side," said a sailor. "There's no way the Krauts are going to win."

"Fate is fickle," replied Kita. "God has no control over that, but if you fight hard and smart, the Prussians don't stand a chance."

"You're going to fight for us, right?" said another sailor.

"I'm going to call the other Angels and send *Bismarck* to the bottom, but it's up to God if she wants to stay and fight."

"Why wouldn't God stay and fight?"

Kita chuckled. "She has a fifteen-year-old daughter she's taking care of."

"There's a child of God?" exclaimed Chief Masterson.

"God's a woman?" replied Lieutenant Boise.

"Yes, and yes," replied Kita. "She's my kid, too."

"We're humbled by your sacrifice to be here," said Chief Masterson. "We thank you mightily for it. You didn't have to."

"Scotland is our adopted home, and we're willing to sacrifice to defend it, just like the rest of you. Now, I must go if I'm to catch *Bismarck*. Tell the Admiralty the Angels are chasing him, and any ships they send to help would be welcome. I'll radio the fleet when I find *Bismarck*."

"Will do, Kita. Thank you for bestowing your blessing upon us. This day will never be forgotten."

"Don't remember me, Chief. Remember all those who lost their lives today. They are the true heroes." Kita spread her wings, and with a mighty flap, she rose into the air.

"Chancellor of Wales, *this is Seaman First Class Roosevelt of the* Hood. *Did you see our flare?*"

"*Aye, we've set our course in that direction. How many survivors are there?*"

"*I have over two hundred, most from the stern of the ship. Do you know what direction* Bismarck *headed?*"

"Bismarck *and* Prinz Eugen *steamed south by southeast. They've left the engagement area.*"

"*Thanks, I'm in pursuit. The survivors will explain.*" Kita cut the radio and called on a different frequency. "*Jynxie? Kimmy? Can you hear me?*"

"*Momma! Are you ok?*" said Jynx sounding happy, but concerned.

"*Angel, what happened?*" replied Apocalypse, unable to keep the worry from her voice.

"*The* Hood *was sunk. I saved a few hundred sailors, but I had to reveal what we are.*"

"*Are you telling me you're stuck out in the middle of the Atlantic? What did you tell them?*"

"*The truth, I'm an Angel of God...you being God.*"

"*Kita! We came here to be lowkey and not draw attention to ourselves.*"

"*I know, but I didn't have a choice. Playing into their beliefs was the fastest way to save them. I was hoping you'd come help me sink* Bismarck, *and then we could go back to our little home.*"

"*There is no way we can stay here. They'll be all over us! We'll come help sink the ship, but after that, we're going back to Roost. I'm not about to play the God they believe in.*"

"*Mom, what about my friends?*" whined Jynx.

"*I'm sorry, honey. You'll have to make new friends in the next universe.*"

Kita received a pouting cat image. She was sure Apocalypse got it, too.

"*Sorry, Jynxie,*" said Kita. She didn't receive a reply. "*I'm going to catch* Bismarck; *I'll send you my location, and we can meet up.*"

"*Ok, angel. We'll see you soon. Chels, go get your Axiom.*"

Kita disconnected from her unhappy family and headed south by southeast.

------------×------------

THE SMOKE FROM *BISMARCK'S* STACKS LEFT A TRAIL MILES long for Kita to follow. Using her advanced vision, she could see the ship on the horizon. She kept her distance...not only waiting for the others to arrive but also stewing over her decision to save the sailors.

She didn't regret the decision—they were on her side, and though not loyal to her personally, she owed them as duty and honor dictated. What caused her insides to ache was what it had done to her family. They were supposed to be giving Jynx a chance to grow and have a normal childhood while Kita and Apocalypse got to live a worry-free existence enjoying each other and raising Jynx in a stable environment.

Kita had spent time analyzing what had and had not worked for raising her other kids. Kylee was her biggest failure, and Kita blamed that on constantly being gone and not being a stable presence in the girl's life. She'd also given Kylee way too much freedom and unfettered access to her abilities without proper guidance or training.

She considered the twins, Spike and Quill, her greatest success. She and Sarin and spent lots of time with them teaching and training. They also spent four years living as a family aboard *Emperor's Wrath*. Kita had played the role of homemaker while Sarin went to work in the ship's mental health department. Kita remembered the time fondly—the girls were happy, and she and Sarin had a happy relationship for the most part. Kita's brittle bones at the time had prevented a lot of the physical intimacy Sarin desired, but they'd made it work.

Scotland was supposed to be that for Kita and Apocalypse, and for the most part, it had been. The war had disrupted them, but Kita had only planned to serve and go home so they could continue and Jynx could continue to mature. It wasn't that they didn't use their Axioms, they did so Kita could continue training Jynx, but it was only for short times when they went away on secluded getaways.

And now, I've ruined it. But I couldn't let them die. Maybe in my past, I would have, and it's not like they're going to survive once we shut the universe down. Maybe I'll let it run for a few centuries and give those I saved a chance to live. It's not going to hurt anything, but Kimmy's right, we can't stay. But the other Angels are still here. I'm sure they'd be happy to live out their lives instead of having their time here abruptly ended.

Kita brushed a tear from her eye. She was happy and enjoyed their little family life. It was a shame it had to end so soon.

"*Hey, angel, where are you?*" called Apocalypse.

Since spotting *Bismarck* and *Prinz Eugen,* Kita kept broadcasting her position to Scottish forces and the other Angels.

"*Hi, love. I'm about ten miles to the west of* Bismarck. *Where are you?*"

"*Coming in from the north. We bumped into the attack fleet Force H sent to sink* Bismarck. *We're aboard* Rodney. *The fleet is getting ready to engage.* Ark Royal *has launched its planes, and we're about to join them."*

Kita let out a sigh of relief. She wasn't sure how she was going to sink *Bismarck* by herself. With Apocalypse and Jynx, it would have been hard enough, but Bismarck wouldn't stand a chance against the Scottish Navy.

"Then I'll meet you over Bismarck. *How's Chels?"*

"Sulking. She thinks we're pulling her away from her friends on purpose."

Kita sighed. She wished she could do more. *"Jynxie, I'm sorry. I didn't mean to ruin your life. I promise we'll go somewhere where you can make new friends."*

"Why can't we stay here?" the teenager shouted at both parents. *"I want to be with my friends. Can't we just sink the stupid ship and go back? Just tell them I'm not the daughter of God."*

"Jynxie," said Kita softly. *"It'll never be like it was, and it'll be worse than when you were little. The best thing is just to go back to Roost. I know starting over will be hard, but there are more friends out there."*

"Yeah? How long has it taken you?" Jynx screamed.

"I'm sorry, Chelsea. But we don't have a choice."

"It's always about you! It's never about what I want."

"Chelsea, that's enough," said Apocalypse. *"It's time to go. We can talk about it more at home."*

Kita sighed as she hurried to catch her quarry. The plume of smoke became larger, and *Bismarck* grew on the horizon. From above, Kita heard the scream of dive bombers. A squadron was racing down from twenty thousand feet aimed at the fleeing battleship. Anti-aircraft guns around the ship opened up, firing at the planes coming in at seventy-degree dive angles. The water on either side of the ship erupted as the bombs missed their target. *Bismarck* shook as a bomb struck its A Turret. The initial explosion was followed by two more as the dive bombers found their mark.

Behind the last dive, bomber came an animalistic roar. Through the smoke and fire came a giant silver and red dragon. *The Dragon God lives.* The massive beast thumped down on the B Turret, reared back on its hind legs, and blew a lance of flame across the bridge and forecastle. Using her massive claws, Apocalypse tore at the heavily armed superstructure.

Following Apocalypse came Jynx. The teenager flew alongside the ship using her ability to create magnetic fields to rip the secondary armament from their mounts and flung them into the ocean. An enterprising group of sailors turned their AA gun on her, but the stream of bullets stopped in the air, then turned back and destroyed the gun.

The whistle of heavy shells screamed through the air before fountains of water sprayed over *Bismarck's* deck. The rain of shells increased until Kita thought she could walk from *Bismarck* back to the Scottish Navy.

Kita was happy for so much firepower. She didn't possess any armor-piercing weapons. And her gravity sphere couldn't make a hole big enough to sink the ship. Her heat, as powerful as it was, would take a long time to melt through the twelve inches of plate armor surrounding the hull's main belt. The best she could do by herself would be to fight her way inside and blow up a powder magazine or boiler.

By the time Kita reached *Bismarck,* the ship was aflame and listing badly. To its starboard side, Scottish destroyers were coming to finish the job with torpedoes. But the beast wasn't dead. The D Turret swung out and fired at its tormentors. The action only brought more attention as torpedo planes skimmed low over the water and sent their payloads streaking toward the exposed hull. The torpedoes exploded in large showers of water, tearing giant holes in the hull. *Bismarck* shuddered and went dead as thousands of gallons of seawater poured into the stricken king of the ocean.

Watching the destruction of the vessel, a wave of inferiority swept over Kita. Once upon a time, she'd possessed the power to tear a starship a thousand times the size of *Bismarck* to pieces with just her mind. Now, she lacked the power to destroy a simple seafaring battleship. It was a bit of introspection that humbled her. *What am I going to do to fix it? Can I do anything about it?*

The mighty ship groaned as it rolled over. Prussian sailors jumped into the water, most without life preservers and trying to cling to any debris they could find. Kita glided down and helped those she could to find something to grab. She herded them together in hopes that someone would be by to pick them up.

"What are you doing, Momma?" said Jynx as her daughter glided down next to Kita as she carried a Prussian sailor over to a floating barrel.

"The code of the sea, Jynxie. The battle's over. Now we help the survivors."

"They didn't do that for you."

"True, but that's what makes our side better than theirs. And maybe your momma is just feeling generous." Kita floated over to Jynx and hugged her. "Thank you, Jynxie. I'm glad you listened to your intuition—or whatever it was. You spared me a horrific death."

"I wish I hadn't. I'd still get to be with my friends."

Kita sighed as her shoulder slumped. "I understand what you're going through, and I'm sorry. I know you didn't mean that the way you said it. But like your mom and I told you, with our power comes responsibility, to us, to you, and to the universes. I'm sorry, but I know someday you'll understand and, in the future, if you find friends that you think will work on Roost, we'll talk. I know Roost isn't just my home; it's your home, too."

"What's going on?" said Apocalypse as she flew down into Kita's arms and gave her a kiss.

"Nothing," said Kita. "Just trying to make it up to Jynx."

"Well, she doesn't have to sulk over it. Admiral Fisher told us what happened and what you did. Saving so many is worth a little disruption on our part. Chelsea will find new friends, and we will find a new universe to live in."

"It's not fair, Mom!" Jynx yelled.

"Life isn't fair. Best you learn that. There will be others. Now, come on. Let's go say goodbye."

Kita leaned into Apocalypse. "So, I was going to have Ryan run this universe for a few extra centuries to give those I saved a chance at life."

Apocalypse raised an eyebrow. "That seems generous, especially for you. I have no problem with it."

"Does that mean I get to stay?" cried Jynx.

"No," said Apocalypse. "Now that these people know what we are, it's not safe for us. You're coming back to Roost."

"Why do you have to be so mean? Why do I have to suffer?"

"Because you're a teenager. Now, come on."

"So, there is one little problem," said Kita, interrupting her story as her computer finished coalescing the data from the current Earth—flooding her mind with memories.

"What?" screamed Turnip. "Your story made no sense."

"Well, if you were paying attention, the Axiom chose me. There is only one chosen person for the Axiom—me. And now my computer is fixed, allowing me to finally be free of your inane babbling and ranting. I swear, it's evil like you that gives evil like me a bad name."

Kita pushed up with the gravity wells in her wings, lifting herself out of the sand. She raised her arm and encased Mai'la in a gravity sphere, then raised her arm in the air. Kita turned around, opened her wings, and shook her feathers, blasting Turnip and Draga with sand.

Satisfied she was as clean as she was going to get, Kita soared over Turnip and set Mai'la down on the walkway behind her. "How you doing, partner?" Kita called to Mai'la over her shoulder.

"Katrina! You do remember!"

"I do, but it's Kita. Only my parents called me Katrina—and that's when I was in trouble." Kita swung around to face Turnip. "And you—my deranged easter bunny—are under arrest. You'll just have to go quietly; I don't have my cuffs."

"Kill her!" screamed Turnip.

"You know it's a major felony to kill a cop, right?" replied Kita.

Draga raised his repeater and fired. Kita spread her wings to shield Mai'la and held up a hand to stop the bullets while the other guards ran toward them. Kita waved her arm and sent the bullets back at Draga and the other goons, striking their armor with *pings* and sparks. *These little peashooters aren't going to stop them.*

Kita drew Dead and Buried from her back and flourished them, setting the blades alight. *I wonder how Turnip's Djinn is doing looking for these.* "Mai'la, take care of Turnip. I'll take down the kitty cats."

Backflipping, Kita landed with both feet on Draga's chest, kicking him over the rail to fall down between the vats where he landed hard on the concrete floor. The other three guards charged up the main walkway. Kita performed a series of handsprings and twists to dodge the bullets. She landed in the splits in front of them and swept her blades across their legs, severing the middle guard's and damaging the outer guards' armor.

Kita rolled backward and kicked her feet up, catching the two outer guards under their chins, sending them crashing onto their backs. Windmilling her legs to stand, Kita leaped into the air and landed between the pair of fallen Djinn, driving Dead and Buried into their throats.

By the Crushing Depths! A pair of armored arms wrapped around Kita's chest lifted her into the air and spiked her into the metal walkway railing. A fiery pain shot up her right side from three dislocated ribs. A fuzzy hand grabbed her head, its claws raking across her scalp, leaving bloody trails down the side of her head. Kita's head whipped back and slammed into the metal rail several times, making her discombobulated.

"What's it take to smash your skull, Human?" roared Draga.

"Many have tried to find the limit, but no one's succeeded."

"Worthless cop!" Draga's thumb pushed into Kita's eye, his claw popping out the organ.

"By the Crushing Depths..." Kita hissed at the pain. The injury wasn't going to blind her, but it did ruin the perfect aesthetics of her face. *That's going to be fun to put back later.*

Kita grabbed Draga's wrist and squeezed, crumpling his armor and crushing the bones. The Djinn roared in pain as Kita forced his hand away from her face. She spun up from the rail and punched Draga in the jaw with a loud *pop* as it dislocated.

Kita grabbed him by his mane and slammed his muzzle into the walkway, grating until she heard the satisfying crack of his nose. Extending the barb from the heel of her left hand, she jabbed it into his neck and injected him with a powerful sedative to knock him out.

"When you wake up, you'll be in the San Francisco City Jail."

"Don't move!" yelled Turnip.

Kita turned her head toward the Verisom. She had Mai'la by the throat, her short claws digging into the Aurorian's neck.

Kita held up her hands and stood up. "Come on, Turnip. You kill her, and it's over for you. You're looking at life in Alcatraz. Let her go, we'll forget about it, and you can plead your case to the judge. Artifact smugglers don't do hard time. You'll go to a nice minimum-security prison upstate for five years and another five on parole. This doesn't have to end badly for anybody. But you kill her, and the entire San Francisco Police Department will be after you. Think about it. Don't be stupid. We can all walk away from this."

"You fool! I will destroy you!" Turnip's eyes glowed green as the tips of her fingers hardened into claws. Next to her buck teeth, long vampiric fangs grew.

Now, where did you get Anna's Axiom? She must be close by. Kita hadn't seen the Angel since entering Universe 888. Cardinal liked to keep to herself, and Kita had trouble keeping track of her.

Turnip slashed Mai'la's throat. Golden blood spilled down the Aurorian's chest, staining her dress. With a flick of her wrist, Turnip tossed Mai'la aside.

"Now, I'll slash your throat, and both Axioms will be mine."

"You want to go a few rounds as an Angel, I'm game. Just know I'm mama bird, and you will never have wings." Kita grew a fireball and flung it at Turnip, knowing fire was a weakness of Cardinal and the Verisom.

Turnip exploded into a hundred bats and flew around the warehouse. *I guess she figured out how to do that.* Kita stood her ground, waiting for the creatures to gather. She wanted Turnip in one piece so she could beat the life out of her.

The bats swarmed behind Kita and reformed into Turnip. The vampire Verisom struck at Kita's back with her claws. Kita phased behind Turnip and punched her in the back of the head. Catching Turnip's ears, Kita spun and pulled, throwing the Verisom into the grating of the walkway.

Turnip kicked her big rabbit-like feet into Kita's chest, launching her across the walkway into the railing, bending the metal. Kita's dislocated ribs screamed at her. Turnip flashed to Kita, a swipe of her claws leaving large gashes in Kita's cheek and severing Kita's dangling eye.

Great. Now I have to find that. Kita kicked up between Turnip's legs, smashing the Verisom's tail and sending her over Kita's head into a vat of white liquid below. Kita stood up and looked down at the thrashing Verisom. *I wonder if there's a Verisom Harley Quinn.*

Turnip grabbed the edge of the vat and launched herself out and over Kita, landing on the walkway, drips of white liquid falling from her fur and leaking through the walkway's grating.

Kita extended her heat shield as Turnip fluffed her fur and shook, spraying the liquid everywhere.

"Come on," egged Kita. "I'm barely getting started."

Turnip flashed at Kita, grabbing the fallen angel by the throat and lifting her up. "Worthless Human! You will suffer for eternity for what you've done."

Kita stretched an arm up to the fire suppression system sprinkler that ran overhead. Flinging a fireball at it, she activated the heat sensor and showered the pair with water. The white liquid still on Turnip's fur reacted with the water and ignited, burning off her fur, charring and blistering her skin.

Turnip squatted on her giant feet, howling in agonizing pain. She clawed at her mangy fur and melting skin.

Kita leaned against the walkway railing and crossed her arms. "You done whining? You'd think I'd done something horrible to you."

Turnip screamed something in Female Varisomese and launched herself at Kita again. Sidestepping, Kita spun with a flare of her wings, catching Turnip by the back of the neck. She slammed Turnip's mouth into the walkway rail, shattering her teeth and fangs. Kita grabbed Turnip's mangy ears and swung the vampire Verisom over her head, slamming Turnip into the walkway grating again, leaving a Verisom-sized dent and dozens of cuts in Turnip's fragile skin. Hundreds of Turnip's burn blisters burst, making her scream.

Kita held Turnip up by her ears and glared into her green eyes. She reached into Turnip's tie-dye sarong and pulled out the brilliant red feather-shaped Axiom that belonged to the Angel Cardinal. With a yank, Kita pulled the pendant free, and its power left Turnip.

"Anna would be ashamed of how you've used her power. But where her Axiom is, she is not far. I would leave you for her, but I'm not done with you yet."

Dragging Turnip over to the vat filled with white liquid, now boiling and burning from the water raining down in it, Kita dangled the Verisom over the rail.

"Anything else you want to say?"

Turnip's big red eyes burned with hate. "To the Void with you, Human."

"I *am* god, and I do plan on returning home." Kita tossed Turnip backward.

"Noooooooo!" the Verisom landed on her back with a big splash. She thrashed until she sank from sight.

Kita glided across the walkway to Mai'la's lifeless body. She checked for vitals anyway, ignoring the massive amount of blood spilled. Not finding any signs of life, Kita called it in.

"*Dispatch, this is Inspector Katrina Roosevelt. I have an officer down. Send immediate backup to Eight-Five-Three-Seven Arbol Court. Requesting an ambulance and med-evac. Over.*"

"*Katrina, this is Flexi. What happened?*"

"*Turnip killed Mai'la.*"

"*Oh no. Are you alright? Don't worry. I'm coming.*"

Kita shook her head. "*Don't bother, Flexi. I'm going home. I'll see you there.*"

"*I'm sorry, Kita. You don't want to...*"

"*No,*" Kita said, tears forming in her eyes. "*I don't want to deal with the fallout of Turnip, and I don't want to attend another funeral. I want to go home.*"

"*I understand. I'll take care of everything.*"

"Thanks, Flexi."

Kita took in Mai'la's face one last time, running her fingers over the Aurorian's eyelids to close them. After placing Cardinal's Axiom in Mai'la's hand, Kita closed her remaining eye, and her consciousness became a pinprick of light. She rode the light back to her computer. Away from Universe 888 and back to the safety of home.

KITA APPEARED IN THE UNIVERSE ROOM NEXT TO THE current iteration. The trip back to her computer had reconstituted her body, but not her mind.

"Oh, hey, Kita," said Ryan. He was in charge of the universe room and the brains behind their increasing and continuing stability. "I didn't expect to see you back so soon. Something to report?"

Sprokkit stomped over to them. The large Morphicon was a gifted scientist and worked tirelessly on improving the universe computer. "I have not noticed anything that would require Kita to leave early."

"Maybe Momma-K missed us," said Stunner. She was one of Velositi and Kita's girls. Unlike her sisters, she found science more stimulating than the battlefield.

Kita didn't know what to say. Instead, she sat down hard, curled her legs up, and put her head down to cry into her arms.

"Mom, I'll be right there," said Athena, the AI that ran Roost and another of Kita's daughters.

"What's wrong?" said Sarah, Ryan's wife, peeking out from behind a workstation. She often helped in the universe room but wasn't an Angel. She preferred to remain Human, though she did have the basic Angel nanite package.

An Angel with silver and gray skin glided in on silver and aqua blue wings. She landed next to Kita and put her arms around the crying Angel. "Mom, what's wrong?" said Athena.

Ultraviolet came in next. She knelt in front of Kita without touching the ground. "We felt a disturbance. Kita, what is the matter?" She reached out and stroked Kita's hair.

"I hate being the good guy," Kita sobbed into arms. "I lose so many."

"Oh, Mom," Athena hugged Kita.

"We're not having very good luck, are we?" said Ryan.

"It's ok," sobbed Kita, "but then I have to think about all of them, and I lose Mai'la on top of it." Kita looked up at Athena. "What am I doing wrong?"

"Maybe Jynx is messing with the random number generator," said Sprokkit. "She wasn't happy about being sent away to school."

"My sister isn't the vindictive type," said Stunner.

"I did get a note from Kimmy," said Ryan.

Apocalypse had taken Jynx back to universe 832, so their daughter could attend West Point. Kita and Apocalypse agreed Jynx needed to learn some professional discipline and leadership skills.

"What'd it say?" said Kita, wiping the tears from her eyes.

"Ah, Chelsea is about to finish her first year, and Kimmy returned to her role as Empress of the Empire of the United States. She's doing well and enjoying life in the White House. She wishes everyone well and sends her love. Ah, do you really want me to kiss you like she says I'm supposed to?"

Kita chuckled. "That's ok. I was so close. I thought I had another Angel."

Athena hugged Kita tenderly. "Oh, Mom. I'm sorry. I know how much you care for all of us."

"We are sorry," said Ultraviolet. "Another member would have been great. You have suffered another great loss. Perhaps what you need is to see life."

Kita nodded. "That would be nice. It seems all I've seen is death lately...or, at least, that's all I remember."

Ultraviolet and Athena helped Kita to her feet.

"Come," said Ultraviolet. "You have not seen the ultraviolet forest since its planting. Everyone is welcome."

"Sounds like a great idea," said Ryan.

The group followed Ultraviolet through Roost, passing the giant terrariums full of trees, water, and flowers, and into the underwater section. Kita had based this area on her brief time in the underwater theme park Angelica on the ocean moon GX-30CB. The tunnels passed through deepwater areas and shallow reefs, hosting an assortment of fish from different worlds.

Ultraviolet turned down a large hallway that led into a meadow of purple-green grass. Trees barely as tall as Kita grew throughout the enormous metal cavern. A series of ponds connected by streams cut through the meadow. Glowing flowers sprang through the grass and grew on the trees. Different pips stuck their heads up to see the visitors.

Out of the young forest came X-5 and the elderly Princess Cranberry, carrying Universe 876. They bowed and greeted the group.

Kita chuckled about Cranberry. *You* did *make it to Heaven. But I bet you would have preferred being the bunny.* "It's beautiful, UV. I know it's not To'va's, but I hope it helps."

"We have so much more, thanks to you. We understand these last universes have not been as we all had hoped, but that does not mean hope is lost. We will create another universe, and hope springs eternal. Only fate knows what friends we will find there."

Did you enjoy EARTHS?
Tell the world what you think!

Leave a review on
Amazon or Goodreads

SPECIAL THANKS TO THE FOLLOWING PATREONS!

KITA'S PARTNERS
Anna Haig
Ian Tainsh
ParadoxicMouse

KITA'S LOVERS
Monica and Shirlee RichardsonMiller
Skye Miller

ANGELS
Adam Dunsmuir
Joshua Le Tourneau
Kat
Natalie Nicholls
Noble Seven
Vivenne Sullivan
Xrebelion
Aj Bobb

KITA'S CREW
5m7kabedfr76
Sarah Ilbrink

KITA'S FRIENDS
K.V. Wilson
Mark Gardner

ABOUT THE AUTHOR

L. Fergus is an Amazon Bestselling author with Birthright, Razor's Pass, and Rebirth. All titles were #1 new releases in LGBT Science Fiction. Before Amazon, L. was a Wattpad Featured Author and #1 writer of science fiction. The Fallen Angel Saga has more than four hundred thousand reads. The books Birthright, BykeChic, and Rebirth have won over twenty awards, including Best Overall.

L. lives with four dogs: Rust, Moxy, Stormy, and Valor, and five cats: Nova, Jupiter, Crater, Pluto, and Forest Fire.

If you want the most up to date stories consider becoming a patreon at:
  www.patreon.com/FallenAngelKita

Join L. Fergus' mailing list at FallenAngelKita.com for news about upcoming book releases. Follow L. on Facebook at Facebook.com/FallenAngelKita, Twitter @FallenAngelKita and contact L. at:
  L@FallenAngelKita.com.